Praise for *D*

"exceptional

– *San Francisco Book Review*

"*Destiny Springs* jumps right in where *Reckoning Waves* left off... mimicking real-life themes of family, romantic relationships, friendship, and justice."

– *Los Angeles Book Review*

"A man once happily in love is tragically sent on a cross-country chase for safety and revenge. The story is exciting, but what I loved most was being close to the intensity of his grief and anger as those who love him and those who don't come closer and closer to him and to each other."

– Sandra Scofield, *The Last Draft: A Novelist's Guide to Revision*

"The narrator of Elliott Foster's *Destiny Springs* pauses at times to describe how Corey Fischer, aka Corey Flanagan, a visual artist and the protagonist, attempts in his paintings to portray the emotional and psychological complexity of the people he is painting. Even the antagonist, Cecilia, who, in the hands of another writer, might be nothing but a villain, elicits the reader's sympathy..."

– Brian Duren, author of *Ivory Black* and the award-winning novel *Whiteout*

"Buckle your emotional seat belt as once again author Elliot Foster takes you on a powerful and gripping page turning thriller of love, loss, vengeance, murder & redemption. The human spirit of each character is truly put to the test as secrets are revealed and past mistakes demand their reckoning."

– Nicole Dupre Sobchack, actress, writer and co-founder of Wraptastic Productions

"*Destiny Springs* is a masterfully written, fast-paced and thought-provoking exploration of how sometimes everything we think we know is false."

–Terrance Newby, author of *Dangerfield's Promise*

DESTINY SPRINGS

ELLIOTT FOSTER

CALUMET
EDITIONS
Minneapolis, Minnesota

FIRST EDITION January 2024

10 9 8 7 6 5 4 3 2 1

ISBN: 978-1-962834-05-6

Cover and book design: Gary Lindberg

For Marco

Art and love are the same thing:
It's the process of seeing yourself
In things that are not you.

–Chuck Klosterman

Also by Elliott Foster

Whispering Pines (Wise Ink Publishing)

Retrieving Isaac & Jason

Panic River

Reckoning Waves

DESTINY SPRINGS

ELLIOTT FOSTER

**CALUMET
EDITIONS**
Minneapolis, Minnesota

Part 1: California

Chapter 1

Cecelia Jackson slammed both fists against the steering wheel of her idling car. She mistakenly thought she had Corey boxed in but then saw him riding shotgun in a truck that pulled out of the driveway and sped away. She could recognize Corey anywhere, even if he had changed his last name from Fischer to Flanagan. She had been hunting him for the past six months, beginning shortly after his escape from justice in a southern Minnesota courtroom. If only Cecelia had confronted him there in Freeborn County after he exited the courthouse a free man. If only she had brought her gun to Minnesota like Bennett's ghost suggested. If only she had killed Corey when she first had the chance.

If only, if only, she now heard Bennett say. *"If only" ain't gonna get us justice, darlin'. Instead, you gotta be thinking, "Now what?"*

Cecelia looked to her right at the framed photograph of her dead husband duct-taped to the dash. In the picture, he wore a green camouflage-colored baseball cap and a matching long-sleeve shirt. A cheeky grin surrounded at the top by his adorable dimples, his bottom lip extended outward and clenching a pinch of chaw. It was her favorite photo of Bennett, taken at the annual Pine Bluff Sportsmen's Dinner after winning the award for *Best Shot.*

"You're right. *Now what* I'm going to do is follow that truck."

Cecelia threw the car into drive and made a series of back-and-forth moves until she fully turned three-sixty and saw the white pick-up waiting for the traffic light at the end of the street to flash green. While turning around, she scraped the side of an SUV, denting the panel above its front wheel. There wasn't time to stop and leave a note. Instead, she gunned the engine and careened toward the truck.

"I'm not gonna lose him now after we came all this way, babe. Count on it."

It's okay. Even if he escapes again, we know where his car is. He'll have to come back for it sometime.

"True. But I'm tired. I want to get him tonight and then go home to Julia."

Cecelia had left Arkansas three days earlier after dropping off her daughter with Grandma, saying that she was heading for a ten-day camping trip in the Smoky Mountains with friends. It was to be an off-the-grid girls' trip. And part of that story was true— the *off-the-grid* part. Cecelia promised her mother she'd be back to pick up Julia after that. To keep her vow, though, she needed to find and kill Corey soon, leaving time for the long drive home.

She followed the Toyota Tacoma when it turned left onto Crenshaw and then a right as it joined Pacific Coast Highway headed north. Cecelia could see Corey's head through the rear window of the pick-up. The mere sight of him quickened her heartbeat. For the past several days, she continually refined her fantasy, brainstorming for the most painful way to kill him. Her dreamy plans began with a desire to shoot him in the groin—in a remote location where no one could help. Then, she'd watch and laugh as her husband's killer bled to death while begging for mercy. But how could she find such a sweet spot here in the dense metropolis of LA? Her fantasy morphed as she sat in her car, focused on the back of Corey's head. Her whole body tensed as she pictured jumping into the back of the pick-up and throwing open the rear window, pulling the trigger of her handgun as Corey's skull exploded, just like she'd seen in those TV crime shows.

Once the fantasy faded, questions flooded her mind. Who was the man driving the truck? Where were they going on a Friday night? What if her car ran out of gas and she had to abandon the pursuit? She glanced down to see that there was still half a tank and exhaled in relief. This was the second time today she had trailed Corey on the streets of Hermosa Beach, following him from a distance. Tonight, she kept more space between her car and the vehicle in which Corey was riding. Her accidental bump against the rear end of his Mini on the freeway earlier today had been a rare, careless mistake. She chastised herself for that all the way back from LAX.

This months-long pursuit had otherwise been a meticulously planned scheme, accomplished mostly on her own but with occasional help from the voice of Bennett's ghost as well as from a real-life man, Ron Hillstrom—her lawyer in her husband's wrongful death case. Hillstrom proved helpful beyond the necessities of the lawsuit, always giving Cecelia whatever she wanted if she asked sweetly with her pretty southern drawl. He wanted to fuck her. She could see it in his eyes and hear it in his patronizing tone. She played along—the vulnerable widow in need of a strong, intelligent man. Who knows, she might let him when this was all over. There wasn't anyone else to satisfy her needs now, so why not? In the meantime, Hillstrom ferreted out the information she asked for, and that led her to this moment, including that Corey Fischer and Corey Flanagan were one and the same person and that he lived somewhere in California.

Her own research revealed more. After numerous sleepless nights at her computer, she stumbled upon Corey's photograph on the Southern California Emerging Artists website. Her heartbeat began to race the moment she saw the photo of Corey holding a gold medal and standing alongside his award-winning art. The text underneath confirmed his identity and location: *Corey Flanagan, Hermosa Beach.* Cecelia then narrowed her search to the beach communities south of LAX. As she read on the City of Hermosa Beach website, *Surfer-artist Corey Flanagan paints landscapes of the South Bay–a view of Palos Verdes from the vantage point of the Redondo and Hermosa Beach piers and all along the Strand in between.* After that, the online trail ran cold. So, she set off from Arkansas to track him down.

She walked the Strand between the Redondo and Manhattan Beach piers for an entire day. Rollerbladers and bicyclists and runners and elderly walking clubs passed her by. She scrutinized aces from behind her polaroid lenses. Cecelia had transformed herself into a human facial detection program—Corey's image burned into her memory from staring at him for three straight days in the Freeborn County courtroom last year. She had even snapped a photo of him with her phone after sneaking the device into the public gallery despite the warning sign at the door—*No Phones or Other Electronic Devices Allowed.*

She got no further with the random search effort and finally called Hillstrom for help. He reminded her that she was due to be in Minneapolis this week to sit for her deposition in the wrongful death case. *Oh, Ron*, she remembered saying to him in her extra sultry voice. *We're just gonna have to reschedule. I've got plans with girlfriends, and they can't be changed.* Hillstrom began a soft protest, but Cecelia interrupted. *Besides, if we can postpone it for a week or two, I'll be able to spend more time with you preparing our case. For an entire week, I'll be completely yours.* Hillstrom relented and said that sounded fine. Cecelia then asked him for a little favor. *Could you please find me the address for Corey's workplace, darlin'?* She kicked herself for not taking greater advantage of her unscrupulous lawyer in this search. Hillstrom gave her Corey's work address in Redondo Beach within minutes.

She immediately drove to Riviera Village and parked her car a block away from *Framed By The Beach*, then waited. Corey eventually emerged from the shop and hopped into a black Mini-Cooper before driving away. She followed him for the next ninety minutes through a series of stops, including the detour to LAX and back with another remembered face—Billy Preston—who Corey dropped off at the airport. After that, Corey led her to a nondescript apartment building in Torrance a few hours ago. That is where she had double-parked to box him in, only to watch as Corey escaped her trap once more. Now, she turned west on Pier Avenue in Hermosa Beach, several seconds after the white truck ahead of her did the same. She followed behind as the pick-up parked at a metered spot one block shy of the ocean. She pulled into an open space three car lengths ahead and watched in the side mirror as Corey stepped out and approached a meter. She quickly scanned the horizon to get her bearings. Ahead of her in the distance lay the Pacific Ocean, and a pier jutted out into it. In between sat a large concrete plaza, less than a quarter full of people and bordered on two sides by buildings housing a variety of cafes, bars and shops. The paucity of people out and about on a Friday evening surprised her. She spied a poster on a nearby lamppost advertising a festival in neighboring Manhattan Beach. Good. There'd be fewer potential witnesses if this were where she ended Corey's life.

Cecelia turned her gaze to the action behind her as reflected in the mirror and watched as Corey and the other man began walking toward the plaza. She ducked down in her seat as they approached the back of her car, then remembered the photograph of Bennett taped to the dash. What if Corey caught sight of it through the window? She reached into the backseat without looking, grabbed her jacket and covered the picture just as Corey and his companion came even with the Malibu. Her side window was cracked open, and she heard snippets of the conversation as they passed by.

"I'll love the surprise no matter what, Miguel. Just like I love you."

Miguel. He must be Corey's latest prey. Bile rose in her throat. This was the first time she had heard Corey's voice. Despite staring at him for all those hours in the courtroom, she never once heard him speak. The coward refused to take the stand in his own defense, instead letting Larry Preston sign a fraudulent affidavit and take the blame. The timber of the voice flowing in through her cracked window was lower than she'd expected—almost masculine sounding—and definitely lower than Bennett's.

As soon as the pair walked several yards ahead, she exited her car, gently shut the door, then approached the meter. She squinted to read the minuscule directions; it only accepted cards, not coins. She fumbled with her purse to fish out a pre-loaded debit card while glancing up to keep track of where Corey and Miguel were headed. She struggled with the unfamiliar instructions and ended up buying four hours' worth of parking, though she only meant to purchase one. Once the display on the meter read, *Thank You for Visiting Hermosa Beach*, she looked up and noticed that Corey had sat down atop a metal bench on the plaza facing the sea while Miguel walked away from him toward the far end of the square. Corey was alone. The nearest bar sat at least a hundred yards away, and an Aerosmith song blared through its open doors. Ha, *Janie ain't the only one who's got a gun*, she thought. A few people walked along the Strand beyond the bench, but this was her chance. She moved away from the meter and back toward her car. She opened the passenger side door, then grabbed her handbag from the floor and flung it over her shoulder. She pulled down the visor and quickly checked herself in the mirror. A paisley-patterned scarf still covered the top of her head. The rouge, lipstick and mascara that she had painted on herself earlier in the day still lay perfectly fixed upon her face. She looked good. She looked ready. She would blend into the crowd. Before shutting the car door, Cecelia pulled on a pair of oversized sunglasses, then leaned down and planted a quick kiss atop the camouflage-colored urn buckled into the passenger seat. She didn't bother to wipe away the red lip-shaped evidence like she used to do from Bennett's face.

"Wish me luck, honey. This night's for you."

She crossed the street and entered the plaza. Most people walked in pairs right past her and didn't look up. She strode purposefully toward the ocean as a damp onshore breeze tugged at her. She could feel the moisture pulling down on her make-up but resisted the urge to rub her increasingly dewy face. Instead, she focused on Corey. There he sat—on a bench and craning his neck to watch the breaking waves—as if he hadn't a care in the world. That would change soon enough. Corey Flanagan, the homosexual

manslayer who always caught a break, once again flaunted his fla-
grant lifestyle as he waited for his latest lover and probable victim
to join him.

She kept her gaze upon the back of Corey's sandy-haired
head with an occasional glance toward Miguel, who stood in line
at SeaSpresso off to her left. Cecelia approached the bench. Adrenaline accelerated her pulse. Anticipation quickened her step. She
closed the distance between herself and the man who assaulted
and then shot her husband. Bennett had died from a combination
of causes. Gore had gushed from the bullet wound to his chest,
draining him. At the same time, he choked on blood-filled vomit.
All the while, Corey disappeared like a serpent and evaded capture for four agonizing years. With those events racing through
her mind, Cecelia pulled the handbag a bit tighter to her side. She
felt the sharp outline of the gun through the soft leather.

Corey was cornered for real this time. The ocean upon which
he longingly gazed hemmed him into his destiny. He wasn't going anywhere. And, he surely had no sense of impending danger.
Instead, he seemed to be ignorantly waiting for Miguel to bring
him something to eat or drink, likely one of those fufu coffee bev-
erages all the gays on TV shows adored. Cecelia shook her head
at the instant irony, feeling the bittersweet mixture of vengeance
and loss. There Corey sat on the bench staring out toward the sea,
as clueless about his coming fate as Bennett was four years ago.
Neither man could see the violence coming.

"Hey, watch where you're going!"

She nearly ran into a couple walking perpendicular to her
across the plaza. She apologized, then looked back toward the
bench to ensure Corey hadn't heard the exchange. Thankfully, he
continued staring toward the sea. Still, she should be more careful.
The last thing she wanted was to draw Corey's attention too early or
to encounter witnesses who might later describe her to the police.
If she had to speak again anywhere near him, perhaps she'd adopt
one of those beach girl accents like she heard on TV. The bench atop
which Corey sat lay at the far end of the plaza where the sidewalk

met the sand and few people lingered. It might just be far enough away from the crowd that Cecelia could kill him, then escape unnoticed down a side street adjacent to the beach and backtrack to her car. She was now within fifty yards of the bench. Glee filled her heart as she stood on the verge of vengeance.

She tugged the bag tight to her side, casually slipped her hand inside the purse, and felt the Smith & Wesson Shield nine-millimeter, orienting herself by blindly gripping the polymer stock, then fingering the trigger and frame. The smoothness of the lightweight handgun calmed her. Deftly, she lowered her hand to ensure that the magazine was secure. Then she felt the suppressor lying inside the bag beside the gun. She would need mere seconds to affix the silencer to the firearm once she withdrew them from her handbag. *Good call with the silencer babe,* she could hear Bennett say. Cecelia removed her hand from the purse, carefully wiped a bead of sweat from her brow and resumed walking.

Forty yards separated her from the bench. Within minutes, Corey would be dead.

Thirty yards. Twenty. Ten, then five. She stopped and reached back into her purse with her right hand. Her shaky left hand reflexively reached into the air with her fingers curled forward as if she were about to grab Corey by the hair and yank his head backward so that he could see Cecelia's face as she fired a bullet into his chest, her updated fantasy for killing him. She had played various versions of this scene in her mind—hunting him as if he were prey, cornering Corey so he had no escape from her justice and inflicting as much fear in him as Bennett surely felt at the other end of Corey's gun. She wanted Corey to pay but also wanted him to acknowledge his executioner. And she wanted him to suffer. It would be easy to kill him right now, from behind and into the back of his head. All she had to do was remove the handgun and affix the suppressor, then stand exactly where she was planted right now and pull the trigger. Corey would never know what hit him. But that wasn't the plan. There wouldn't be enough agony in that.

"Here you go, a decaf cortado made especially for you, love."

Cecelia turned immediately to her left and away from both the bench and Miguel's unexpected voice. Her eyes had been so fixed upon Corey that she hadn't seen Miguel's approach.

"Goddamn you, faggot," she muttered under her breath.

She walked a few feet toward a towering palm tree that rose from a small patch of dirt surrounded by concrete at the edge of the pier. She leaned against the trunk and pretended to look down at her phone but never took her eyes off the bench from behind her sunglasses. She saw Miguel sit down and hand Corey a paper cup. The smiles on both men's faces made her want to retch. Nothing about the scene before her was natural. Yet here Corey was—smiling with delight and giving his fairy companion a disgusting kiss on the mouth. The kiss kept going for an uncomfortably long time. Bennett had never kissed her like that, with lips parted softy and a hand cupped tenderly under the chin. What in the hell is that?

Patience, Cecelia. Breathe. She could hear Bennett's voice preparing her for what lay ahead. *It'll happen. You'll get that little bitch. Just wait.*

She stood back from the tree and moved behind it upon seeing Corey and Miguel rise from the bench, then began walking toward the pier. She scanned the horizon, noting how surprisingly empty the pier had become—too late for fishermen with darkness descending and too early for tourists still finishing their restaurant meals or lovestruck locals hoping to capture the half-moon's rise. She watched and followed at a distance as Corey and Miguel casually made their way toward the far end of the pier—the tip dead-ending at the sea. This is where it would happen, on the rapidly depopulating pier. A mild light-headedness flooded her brain as she watched the two men walk in the opposite direction from everyone else as if navigating their way upstream against the current to spawn. She smiled, and her heartbeat quickened. All she had to do was keep following them to the end and then blow Corey's brains out.

* * *

Corey and Miguel reached the end of the pier. They stood, side by side, gazing out to sea. The deck upon which they stood swayed slightly as waves crashed against the support pylons below. Once again, temptation tugged Cecelia forward. Corey was an easy target with his back to her and no one to save him other than Miguel. She'd kill him, too, if necessary. Still, she willed herself a scrap of patience and stood next to a fisherman's outpost roughly twenty yards away. She wanted to shoot Corey in the front just as he had done to Bennett.

She watched as Miguel set his paper cup atop the ledge of the pier, then reached into his pocket, pulled out a small jewelry box and knelt on the concrete platform—all without attracting Corey's attention. Corey blindly reached out to grasp Miguel's hand, only to find empty space. His body spun back toward Miguel, and he dropped his own paper cup as his hands sprang upward to cover his mouth. Now, Corey faced her, but he was focused on Miguel. Perfect. She watched as Miguel took one of Corey's hands into his own, spoke words she was too far away to hear, and then opened the small box from his other hand, lifting it up toward Corey.

"It's a fucking ring," she muttered. This was a proposal—between two men. It might be legal in California like every other vice, but that didn't make it right. Cecelia's left thumb began to rub the combined engagement and wedding ring on her own hand, pushing it in a complete rotation while contemplating its inadequate weight. *It's the best I could afford*, Bennett's distant voice echoed into her ear. "Oh yeah?" She whispered. "But didn't you spend a fortune outfitting a fancy bedroom in the sleeper compartment of your truck? Was it more important to be cozy at overnight truck stops than putting a fine rock on your fiancé's hand? Asshole."

Cecelia shook the thoughts from her mind as her thumb ceased its fiddling. She stretched out both hands as if summoning the strength to complete her mission. In the rapidly descending darkness, she removed the scarf from her head and the sunglasses from her face, pushing both inside her handbag and then reaching deeper inside to remove the gun and the suppressor. At this point, no disguise was needed. She wanted Corey to recognize her. She wanted him to look her in the eyes. And she wanted him to panic and beg for mercy.

With Corey now facing her direction but with his eyes still fixed upon Miguel, Cecelia secured the silencer to the gun, raised it into the air with both hands and walked toward the end of the pier. The firearm shook in her trembling hands as Corey suddenly looked up, and recognition exploded across his face. She gripped the gun tightly with both damp hands as her entire body shook with rage. She pulled the trigger as Miguel rose from his knee to look in the direction Corey was pointing. A bullet raced in between the two men. Cecelia had tripped on the uneven platform, the bullet leaving her gun at the same moment she began to fall. She broke the fall with her hand as the gun smashed onto the platform.

"No!" Miguel yelled.

Cecelia rose quickly with the gun still firmly in her hand, but her purse dropped to the platform. She noticed that the silencer had become bent from the fall, so she unscrewed it and threw it over the edge of the pier. She then focused on Corey, who remained standing next to Miguel, seemingly in shock. She spun her head around like an owl to see if anyone was coming, but no one was nearby. She advanced, both men seemingly frozen and trapped at the end of the pier with their only viable exit blocked. Ten yards shy of reaching them, she once more lifted the firearm with quivering hands, quickened her pace and pulled the trigger. It, too, missed the men's heads, though not by much. She couldn't believe it. Had the barrel of the gun been damaged, too? She stopped to examine it. Despite the fading daylight, she could make out that the Smith & Wesson was intact.

She looked up to see Miguel grab Corey's arm. "Come on!" He hopped atop the ledge and pulled Corey with him. "It's our only choice," Miguel yelled. "Jump."

With Miguel's left hand in Corey's right, they leaped into the air as she ran after them and fired once more, the shot ringing out into the dark sea air. Corey and Miguel disappeared from her sight. She didn't know if she had hit Corey or not. She ran toward the ledge and looked down into the sea. There was no sign of anything other than dark water.

"Shit."

Cecelia turned around upon hearing a commotion in the distance. Two lifeguards ran toward her atop the dimly lit pier. She looked down and noticed something shiny lying on the platform of the pier—a cell phone. She reached down to grab it, then ran toward her handbag a few feet away and slipped both the phone and her gun inside. She pulled a baseball cap out of the bag and pulled it atop her head tight, the peak resting just above her eyes. She ran back to the edge of the pier and leaned over the railing, screaming Corey's name. She then turned toward a pair of approaching lifeguards and said, "Help! My boyfriend's been shot. He and the mugger fell into the sea!"

The guards' mouths fell agape. After looking down into the empty ocean, they turned and ran back toward the open end of the pier. Cecelia followed them at a jogging pace toward the beach, her handbag slapping against her side. As she neared the shore, she heard approaching sirens and saw alarmed onlookers streaming out of the plaza toward the base of the pier. Her heart raced like a rookie NASCAR driver as she saw the lifeguards now standing on the beach—pointing and talking with wild gestures. She stopped to catch her breath and inhaled a foul scent before realizing its source. Her body reeked of sweat. She recognized that odor as the same one pouring from her body on the night she learned that Bennett had been raped and killed.

Damn. Now what?

Corey and Miguel were somewhere in the water beneath the pier—dead or alive—and she needed to know which. She could hear Bennett asking the same question from up the street. *Did you shoot him or not?* His shrill voice implored her from his seat in the car. *Remember what I taught you about hunting? You gotta finish the kill. Now, go put that son of a bitch out of our misery.* Cecelia stood still for a moment, her hand resting atop the guardrail of the pier for support. She couldn't go after them in the water because she didn't know how to swim. Besides, how would she maneuver in the cold ocean fully dressed while trying to hold a slippery gun? She saw the two lifeguards enter the water carrying inflated life-preservers, their figures lit from behind by the flashing lights of emergency vehicles winding their way across the plaza. A gawking crowd swelled at the water's edge. She needed to do something, fast.

Cecelia walked amongst the people near where the lifeguards entered the water, craning her neck like the others, trying to see the unfolding drama underneath the pier. Corey had been in the water now for nearly fifteen minutes. She heard sirens followed by skidding tires as two ambulances abruptly stopped. EMTs jumped out, took stretchers from the back and ran down the beach toward the water. A fire truck arrived behind them. Cecelia moved deeper into the crowd to avoid standing out. Her heart bumped up against her sternum, almost painful. All this furor had been set in motion by the sound of her gun and then the lies she told the lifeguards. A battle of competing voices raged inside of her—Bennett goading her onward and Julia begging her to come home. Cecelia remained paralyzed in the middle, wanting both. She needed to confirm Corey's fate. So, she stood amid the throng watching. Noisy speculation from the crowd drowned out her thoughts.

"Someone got shot!"

"The gunman's on the loose!"

"No, he's in the water."

"It's probably gang related. We should get out of here!"

"The police are here, but what if we get caught in the crossfire?"

Suddenly, both lifeguards emerged from the ocean, dragging inert bodies. EMTs descended upon the spot where the guards set the two men on the sand. The gawkers ahead of her blocked Cecelia's view. Rumors continued to flow back throughout the crowd.

"They're either unconscious or dead."

"No sign of a gun."

"There's an awful lot of blood."

Several police officers pushed their way through the crowd, yelling at onlookers to move aside. After seeing their uniforms and holstered guns, Cecelia knew that she needed a different plan. If Corey was indeed dead, she could hear about it on the news. But if he somehow emerged and awoke unscathed, wouldn't he immediately identify Cecelia as the shooter?

She pulled the cap's peak further down her eyes, politely saying, "Excuse me," in a forced California accent as she made her way out of the crowd and toward the plaza. With guidance from Bennett, she crafted a new scheme while walking toward the car and glancing back at the plaza. She saw the EMTs load Corey onto a gurney and into one of the ambulances. She reached her car and revved the engine, then followed that ambulance as it snaked away, sirens blaring, through evening traffic.

Chapter 2

Corey's head felt heavy against the pillow, and his eyelids resisted his attempt to open them. Machines and lights buzzed all around, and a tube stuck out from his arm. For a moment, he thought he was back in the psych ward, but this time his wrists weren't cuffed to the bed. He didn't know how long he'd been unconscious. The clock on the wall showed a quarter past ten, and darkness through the hallway window told him it was late at night. He strained to recall the day's events. There had been a quick morning swim at Hermosa followed by a mid-day shift at the store, then driving Billy to LAX. The anniversary dinner at Miguel's apartment. Espresso at the beach, followed by Miguel's surprise proposal atop the pier. And then, Cecelia Jackson firing bullets at both Corey and Miguel until they had no choice but to leap into the sea.

His head throbbed, and so did his ribs. He noticed dried blood caked to both arms, but a quick self-inspection revealed no wounds. The T-shirt and fancy button-up he sported earlier this evening was nowhere in sight. He heard a collection of noises beyond the door to his room—a bevy of voices, footsteps. He wet his lips with his tongue and tasted brine. That tang triggered an instant recall of his most recent conscious memory—fighting the oceanward riptide beneath the pier and struggling to grip a metal pylon encased with barnacles. To his right, Miguel's head had rested against the same pylon, his lover's mouth open barely above the rhythmic rise and fall of the tide. A sharp-edged shell must have cut Miguel's forehead, for Corey recalled seeing blood running down the middle of Miguel's sweet face. Despite feeling initial relief in knowing they had found their way to the post under the pier, Corey cringed at the recalled shock of being thrust into the dark waves. He remembered gazing skyward, silently praying that Cecelia Jackson wasn't leaning over the edge of the pier with her gun aimed at him. He couldn't see anyone.

He also remembered Miguel saying, *I'm going to throw up*, just before he did. Vomit exploded from Miguel's mouth, splattering the dark pylon in chunks of pink and white. There were streaks of red, too. Corey recalled his shock at the sight of ruby-colored mucus hanging from Miguel's bottom lip. That blood didn't come from the surface wound on his head. All Corey could do was implore him to hang on. He recalled striving to keep both himself and Miguel calm by talking about inane things, like suggesting they come back out here in the daylight so Corey could finally teach Miguel how to surf. He leaned in and spoke into the side of Miguel's head, uttering words in between his own shallow breaths. The cold ocean water generated chills across Corey's skin as heat fled his body through his soaking-wet clothes. Miguel's damp, black hair brushed against Corey's lips, providing a modicum of comfort even though Miguel's failure to respond gave Corey a growing unease. It was then that a powerful swell hit them both from behind, knocking Corey's head into the pylon and sweeping him away from Miguel toward the shore. The last thing Corey remembered was swallowing gulps of seawater before someone grabbed him by the arm.

A woman wearing green scrubs walked into the room and directly to Corey's bedside. She had a lovely brown face. That's when he also noticed a uniformed police officer sitting on a chair in the corner, staring at him.

"Hello, Corey. I'm Asha. I'm an RN. You're in Torrance Memorial Hospital. Do you know why you're here?"

"Sort of. From my aching head and ribs, as well as this blood under my fingernails, I assume I was injured after jumping off the pier?"

"I see. Yes, you probably have a concussion. The x-rays aren't back yet, but you likely also have broken ribs. You were holding your side and moaning when you first arrived. As for the dried blood under your nails, it probably came from the man across the hall, the other man who was pulled from the ocean with you."

"Miguel! Is he all right?" Corey struggled to sit up in the bed.

The nurse glanced back at the officer before returning her gaze to Corey. "He's being treated by a different team and receiving the best possible care. Do you know his full name? He had no identification when he arrived."

Corey quickly recited Miguel's name and address, noticing that the police officer scribbled on a notepad. "He's also my boyfriend. And it's important you tell his doctors that Miguel has HIV."

The nurse excused herself and left the room. The police officer moved closer to Corey's bed.

"Hi, Corey. I'm Officer Suarez. Can you tell me what happened?"

"We jumped off the pier because a woman shot at us."

"You're saying that neither you nor your friend had a gun?"

"No! She fired the gun at us. That's why we jumped."

The nurse returned and whispered something into the officer's ear before he turned and walked hurriedly out of the room.

"What's going on?" Corey's voice was loud and high-pitched.

The nurse placed her hand on his shoulder. "I think they're just trying to sort out what happened. But that isn't our concern right now. We need to take care of the injuries you sustained in the fall and then by almost drowning."

"I'm fine. I just need to see Miguel. Was he hurt worse than me?"

"Corey, it's best that you remain calm. But yes, your boyfriend has serious injuries, and the doctors are assessing next steps. Now, before we look at your x-rays, is there anything more you can tell me about Miguel? Perhaps a family member we can call for medical history?"

"Yes, he has a sister in Texas. Hand me my phone, and I'll get the number for you."

"I'm sorry, there wasn't any phone with your belongings when you arrived—only your wallet in a zippered pants pocket."

Corey closed his eyes. His head throbbed worse now than a few minutes ago. "Maria Diaz. She lives in Houston. I think she's on Studemont Street. And she works at the Hyatt Regency downtown."

"Thank you, Corey. I know you're worried about your boyfriend. Let me give you something for your headache while we await your scans. Then I'll go see if there's an update on Miguel. All right?"

He opened his eyes and stared at the nurse. What other choice did he have but to answer, "Yes." He watched as Asha left his room, then returned a minute later with a small paper cup holding two red and white capsules and another larger cup topped by a lid with a straw.

"Here, swallow these and wash them down with a small sip."

He took the cups and the pills from the nurse.

"That's good, Corey. Now, I need you to lay back and stay calm. Press this button if you need anything." He looked in the direction she was pointing. "I'll be back soon with an update on Miguel."

Corey watched as the nurse walked away and out of sight. Somewhere out there, beyond this room, Miguel was presumably lying on a different hospital bed. A pit formed in Corey's gut as he remembered the look on the faces of both the nurse and the police officer. The pit grew as Corey once more recalled the rough shape Miguel seemed to be in when Corey last saw him under the pier. Surely Miguel would be all right? He only had that scrape on his forehead and nausea from the cold and rollicking waves. But there had been blood in Miguel's vomit. Corey looked up as a different nurse popped in, then back out of his room.

"Oops, sorry."

He tilted his head back against the pillow and once more closed his eyes. He instinctively whispered aloud the Our Father, the words quietly emerging from his barely parted lips. "...Forever and ever, amen." He stared at the ceiling. He hadn't uttered that prayer in nearly six years, since the day of his father's funeral, but the words flowed through his mind and lips with ease, for it was a prayer he'd recited hundreds of times as a kid. *Why am I making that petition now? Will it do any good? Do I really believe in the power of prayer?* He shook his head back and forth, unsure of the answer. His mother would say yes, so he figured it couldn't hurt. Corey closed his eyes and repeated the prayer once more.

Asha still had not returned to his room. *Does that mean Miguel's condition is stable or that she's figuring out how to tell me something worse?* His mind again traveled back through the key events leading up to where he was now, more slowly this time and with him straining to recall the details. He remembered arriving at Miguel's apartment and knocking on the door, which opened quickly to reveal his lover naked and standing inside. Corey recalled that Miguel had whispered, *Happy One Year Anniversary*, before pulling Corey inside, then shutting and locking the door. Corey had set the packages held in his arms aside and swallowed Miguel up into a tight embrace. Their ensuing deep kiss lasted a long time, lips pressed together hard with open mouths, stirring inside Corey the same feelings from that first date at the taco place exactly one year ago, minus the awkward burrito breath.

Corey wondered now what he had done to deserve such unexpected happiness with this unconventional man. Miguel was like no one Corey had ever met—kind and generous with his feelings, not to mention cute and smart. Miguel routinely made Corey feel as though he were the most important person in the world, and flashbacks to their love-making sparked a shudder in Corey now as he exhaled and dropped his shoulders more fully into the hospital bed, remembering the random places where they had sex, always ending with orgasms deeper than Corey had known before.

He then recalled their exchange of anniversary gifts last night. Miguel had presented Corey with a Tag Heuer diving watch. He searched his wrist for it now, but the silver band with its blue face was missing. Hopefully, it was with his belongings here in the hospital and not sitting on the bottom of the sea. In turn, Corey presented Miguel with two paintings. The first was a playful reminder of their first date—a caricature-like depiction of Corey and Miguel wrapped inside a burrito with the taco stand's iconic gray donkey braying, *It was love at first bite!* The second painting, in a representative style, was a portrait of Miguel's late mother. Though Corey hadn't met Mrs. Diaz before her death the previous December, he had used the photograph affixed to her funeral program and filled in details of her personality taken from the many stories Miguel had shared over the past year. It was always clear how much warmth filled Miguel's face with each spoken remembrance. Corey then remembered how a buzzer in the kitchen interrupted their conversation, summoning them to dinner. Corey smiled now as he remembered the finely decorated kitchen table, set in a semi-formal style with traditional plates, water glasses and flatware—all of it inherited from Miguel's late mother. In the center of the table sat a ceramic baking dish Miguel had pulled from the oven, yet another prized Diaz family possession. Inside the dish, as Miguel described it, was *Pollo en Escabeche Oriental*, a Yucatan-style chicken and onion stew, though Miguel had concocted this batch with seitan in place of chicken to accommodate Corey's vegetarian diet.

After dinner, they washed and dried the dishes as their playful conversation continued. What Corey wouldn't give to be back there now and wishing they had never gone to the pier. But Miguel had been insistent as they continued the after-dinner cleanup. That was when Corey dropped the heirloom baking dish after it slipped from his hands and crashed to the tiled kitchen floor. The pit festering inside his stomach now matched the one that rose in him last night as he anticipated a harsh reaction to his clumsiness. Instead, Miguel gently cleaned and bandaged the gash on Corey's hand and uttered unforgettable words. *It's only a platter and not my mother. Besides, now I have a beautiful painting of Mom that you created. I'd rather have that than some old plate.*

Suddenly, a pulsating siren rang throughout the ER. Corey's stomach sank alongside his hopes. He gingerly rose from his bed, placing his feet unsteadily onto the cold tile floor. He grabbed the portable stand supporting the IV connected to his arm and moved toward the hallway to investigate the commotion. He instantly recognized Miguel's face on a bed being wheeled toward him. Miguel's eyes were closed. A deep red circle stained the white sheet spread atop his body. It looked like every available hospital worker was either adjacent to Miguel's moving bed or following quickly behind.

"Miguel!" Corey's screamed. Asha rushed toward him, and he yelled at her, "Tell me what's going on!"

The sirens continued to wail as Asha reached for Corey and placed a hand firmly on each of his arms. "Go back to your bed!"

Corey raised the volume of his voice to match hers. "Is he going to die?"

"They're taking Miguel into emergency surgery upstairs. That's all I know. Now, please. Back to bed."

"No, I need to be with him!" Corey struggled to remove himself from Asha's grip. "Miguel! I love you," he screamed toward the moving bed passing in front of him. Asha held Corey tight. "Let me go. I need to be with him. I never answered his proposal last night!"

He tore himself loose from Asha's grip, regained his footing and ran toward the moving bed, grabbing ahold of the railing and causing the gurney to stop rolling and a pair of orderlies to trip and fall.

"Yes, Miguel. I'll marry you. Yes!"

Miguel's eyes remained closed. There was no reaction. The red circle on the bed sheets looked bigger than before. Corey felt hands grab him from behind and drag him away from the gurney. He could only watch and wail as the rest of the staff whisked Miguel down the hall and out of sight.

* * *

Corey awoke in the same hospital bed as before, but this time, his recognition was slowed. The last thing he remembered was a pair of men in blue scrubs holding him down while the nurse injected something into his IV. He noticed her now hovering over him.

"Corey?"

He nodded.

"How are you feeling?"

"Cloudy. My ribs hurt."

"How about your head?"

He lifted his hand to his forehead, feeling the hardened scab where he had hit the pier. He was surprised that his arms weren't cuffed to the bed after remembering the mayhem he had caused. It was then he noticed that the police officer had returned to his spot on the chair, which now sat closer to Corey's bed.

"My headache seems to be gone."

"I'm glad. I want to let you know that Miguel is still in surgery. We have our top doctors working on him. They are truly the best in LA, so he's in excellent hands. We'll get you an update on his condition as soon as possible."

Corey shuddered and clenched his arms close to his body under the thin white sheet.

"Are you cold?"

"Mmmm hmmm." He didn't dare open his mouth for fear that everyone nearby might hear his chattering teeth.

"I'll get you a blanket. Hold on." Asha walked over to a cabinet and withdrew a quilted cover. She returned to the bed and laid the blanket atop Corey's body, covering him completely below the neck and taking care to thread the IV line under the blanket along the railing so it wouldn't get torn from his arm.

"Better?"

"Yes, thank you."

"The room temperature is set to 72, so I think it's plenty warm. You're likely cold from being in the frigid ocean and maybe still suffering from a bit of shock."

"Shock?"

"Yes, from the cold water and the fall when you apparently banged your head on something. And the trauma of seeing your partner in distress likely triggered you once more. The human body is an amazing, protective ecosystem, often pulling blood from its extremities back toward the heart when it senses danger. As a result, shivering follows. You'll be warm again soon."

The ice-cold immersion had indeed stunned Corey more than the impact of crashing feet-first through the sharp ocean surface. His mind reached back across thirty years and fifteen hundred miles, remembering a similar sensation during his first polar plunge into the frigid Mississippi River flowing past his hometown. Corey was only twelve years old then, but his recollection of that impulsive jump sent goosebumps exploding across his body each time he pulled the memory forward. Today, both the remembrance and the shivering arrived without conscious thought. Corey was chilled to the depths of his being.

"Thank you, nurse."

"Call me Asha."

"Okay. Asha. And I'm sorry about causing such trouble. It's been..."

"It's okay, Corey. You've been through an ordeal. Your reactions are normal. I promise—things will get better. Your x-rays came back, and the radiologist will explain the results. But as a preview, the fractures are mild and didn't puncture your lungs. The contusion to your head will heal quickly, too. You just need to rest here awhile and let us monitor your progress, okay?"

"Okay."

"Can I get you something to eat or drink?"

"Just water, thanks. I'm not hungry."

"All right. Do you feel well enough to answer a few more questions from Officer Suarez?"

The officer smiled at Corey, wearing a friendlier face than an hour ago. "Sure."

He endeavored to answer the officer's first open-ended question—*start from the beginning and tell me what happened.* The details were difficult to remember, but he explained how emergency sirens announced their harried approach at the beach and how lights from the ambulances lit up the canyon-like alley of store-fronts where Pier Avenue meets the shore, the strobe of red and blue whirling around him. He also mentioned the people. He nei-ther recognized nor remembered any faces. Instead, he recalled a feeling of claustrophobia from the swelling gaggle of gawkers at the beach.

"Thanks, Corey. But if you can, start even earlier—before you arrived at the pier."

He strained to tell the story of his evening with Miguel, start-ing with their anniversary dinner and then everything that hap-pened next. His pauses led to prompts from the officer. *Were you followed from Miguel's apartment? Did you see anyone while wait-ing for your after-dinner coffee? Did you notice anything suspicious when you walked onto the pier?* Corey answered no to these ques-tions and to several more posed in a similar vein. To the next line of questioning, Corey hesitantly answered yes. *Do you know of anyone who might want to hurt you or Miguel? Have you received any prior threats? Did you recognize your alleged assailant?* Corey knew that it was Cecelia Jackson who assaulted them and who wrought this unspeakable harm. He knew it as surely as the sun set in the west. But how could he explain who Cecelia was and why she had a motive to kill?

Corey resisted his innate reflex to lie or deflect, choosing in-stead to tell the harsh and humiliating truth. With as few words as possible, he told the officer that he recognized the shooter atop the pier—Cecelia was the widow of the man that Corey had killed. The previously kind smile evaporated from the officer's brown face. He then embarked on a series of rapid, sharp questions, writing furiously into a handheld notepad as Corey answered. He suppressed his own feelings of shame and spared no incrim-inating details. Even as the officer's questions turned toward a critical testing of Corey's suspicious tale and toward probing whether this story about an apparent madwoman was real, Corey remained firm. He soon sensed—or hoped—that his forthright-ness was paying off and that Officer Suarez believed him.

Do you know where this woman lives? Did you see which direction she went? Do you have any idea where she might be now? To these last questions, Corey answered with a consistent *no*.

The nurse interrupted. "Officer, may we continue a bit later? Do you have what you need for now?"

Suarez nodded and closed his notebook. He thanked Corey and wished him well before telling him that detectives would be following up soon with more questions. Then, he left. The nurse returned to Corey's side.

"Are you sure I can't get you something to eat?"

Corey heard but ignored her question. His verbal retelling of the surreal evening had returned him to a state of near shock. Did all of what he described actually happen? Where was Cecelia now? What if she followed the ambulance here and came in to finish him off? She would have to do that, wouldn't she? It was a no-brainer for a lunatic with nothing to lose.

"Corey?"

"Did you hear what I told the officer?"

"Yes. And again, I am so sorry for all you've been through."

"Am I safe here? What if that woman tries to attack us again?"

"Yes, you're safe, Corey. There's an officer guarding the entrance 24/7."

His eyes darted around the makeshift room. He noticed every time someone passed outside the door. How could one single security guard possibly prevent a crafty predator like Cecelia from sneaking her way into the ER?

"Corey, did you hear me? You're safe. I promise."

The gravity of his situation felt like a weight resting atop his shoulders. He barely muttered "yes" through fear-filled eyes.

"Hon, is there someone you'd like to call?"

Corey turned to look at Asha. He tried to focus on what she had said.

"A family member? Or a friend, perhaps?"

He hesitantly nodded his head. Asha exited the room, returning seconds later with a white cordless phone in her hand.

"Tell me the number. I'll dial it for you."

Corey stared at the nurse. His mind was irresolute. "I don't know who I should call—my best friend or my mom."

Asha lowered the phone to her side and leaned over the bed. "Either one sounds right to me, hon. Who would you rather talk to right now? Whose voice do you want to hear?"

Corey began to answer but halted. He wavered between two choices. He continued to stare at the nurse. "What would you do, Asha? Who would you call?"

She took her free hand and lay it gently atop Corey's chest. "I think either one will bring you comfort, Corey. But if you really want me to choose, I will."

He slowly nodded his head.

"Okay, then. Tell me the number. Let's call your mom."

Chapter 3

Charlie Moore parked the car near an all-night diner, then completed the last five blocks on foot. Darkness engulfed Pine Bluff as midnight approached, and most folks were indoors for the evening—their houses buttoned up with drawn shades and light from television sets illuminating the back sides of curtains in nearly every house. He spied a group of teenagers crowded around a front porch and swore under his breath, then took a two-block detour before returning to his route along Front Street toward the home he had staked out on GPS. He slowed his approach when he reached a point three houses away. From here, he noticed total darkness in the Jackson home. According to the intel from Rebecca, Cecelia had left several days ago and didn't bother to leave a single light turned on. Not that she need worry about a break-in. Crime rates here were low—mostly petty theft, like stealing a kid's unchained bike from the front yard. The house likely had no alarm system, so he'd be able to break in through a backyard door or window undetected. Charlie could breach a locked point of entry quieter than a field mouse. He'd done it a hundred times without being caught.

He pulled the cell phone from his pocket and glanced at the screen. He'd missed a call from Rebecca. Well, not exactly missed; rather, ignored. He was already a day late on his promise to search Cecelia's house, but there was that girl at the bar two nights ago in Little Rock, and, well, his priorities took a detour. He would finish the job tonight and give Rebecca what she needed by sunrise—

something useful for her defense of the wrongful death suit—preferably something scandalous. At a minimum, he hoped to find information that might unnerve or incriminate the lead plaintiff, Cecelia Jackson. Charlie loved this type of assignment. He cared little about who got hurt or whether justice prevailed. Instead, he relished the challenge of uncovering what people endeavored to hide, to bring their deepest secrets into the light of day. And, of course, the money. Charlie excelled in private investigations and deserved every penny he earned.

He left the sidewalk two houses shy of his target, avoiding a streetlamp thirty feet ahead. He snuck behind a blue rambler, then crossed the lawn and unfenced border, stepping onto the Jackson property for the first time. Something stirred in the bushes. A tiger-striped cat stared at him, its head barely protruding from the holly. Charlie neither flinched nor gasped. Not much startled him anymore. He had extricated himself from innumerable jams and surprises in the past, contriving viable excuses on the spot or resorting to violence as a last resort. He kicked mulch from the flowerbed toward the cat, and it ran off. As he approached the rear of the house, Charlie took a 360 scan of his surroundings. Every home within sight sat quiet, with random faint voices emerging from TV characters or one-sided phone calls. No one appeared to be outside in any of the nearby backyards or perched at a window to possibly spot him at the Jackson's doorstep. Everyone in this part of Pine Bluff was exactly where Charlie Moore needed them to be—locked inside their homes and minding their own business. With hands wrapped in leather gloves, he tried turning the door handle. Locked. It took him less than two minutes to find the spare key, hidden under a garden gnome surrounded by variegated hostas along the backside of the house. He smiled at Cecelia's dull imagination. By the time he finished, no one would know he had been inside.

He unlocked the rear entry and walked inside, closing the door quietly behind him. Light from streetlamps crept into the house ahead of him, so Charlie didn't yet need to engage his headlamp. He moved among the rooms quickly. The kitchen, dining room and living areas were impeccably neat, adorned with modest furnishings and a plethora of wall art in non-matching frames. Three bedrooms and a bath completed the rambler's main floor design. The daughter's room was predictably feminine and appropriate for a pre-teen—a four-poster bed with pastel-colored blankets and pillows and a small TV on a stand across the room. Charlie moved on. There wouldn't be anything of value to Rebecca in there.

He moved to the master bedroom. His initial thought—*unimpressed*. A tan blanket covered the queen-sized platform bed with mismatched gray throw pillows set in front of two others adorned in white cotton. Clearly, no one had slept here in days. The bed was tightly made. A layer of dust covered the nightstands as well as a dresser across the room. He inspected each drawer, finding nothing but shirts and undergarments for both a woman and a man. Charlie paused to remember the timeline Rebecca had provided. Four years since the husband had been killed, and the wife still hadn't discarded his underwear? He found a small box of non-descript jewelry hidden beneath a pile of bras in the middle drawer, its contents not worth locking up. And if there had been something worthy of stealing inside, Charlie would easily resist temptation. Though he'd already committed a felony by breaking and entering the home, he drew the line at theft, not because he was above making a quick buck at someone else's expense, but rather because he aimed to never leave a trace. To him, the perfect search was one where no one could tell he'd ever been there.

He moved to the closet and discovered more clothes—again, for both husband and wife—along with shoes, a box of china and a bag containing three vibrators as well as a vial labeled *Sexual Lubricant for Her and Him*. He wondered if the dildos were for both her *and* him as well. These days, you never could tell. At the rear of the closet hung an ivory-colored wedding dress wrapped in thin, clear plastic. He removed the dress from its hook to view it fully. It was far more elegant than he would have guessed, based upon the lower-middle income neighborhood in which he stood. *This fine dress must've come from a relative with a higher station in life,* he figured.

He returned the dress to its hook and shut the door, then walked to the window and pulled back the curtain barely an inch. The scene outside remained quiet—no cars and no one walking their dog or smoking a last puff on the porch before bed. As he moved to leave the room, Charlie paused to look at a framed photograph on the wall. He recognized the images of Bennett and Cecelia Jackson from pictures Rebecca had sent to his phone. Standing between them was a young girl, perhaps eight or so years of age—most likely Julia. The three of them were leaning back against the hood of a blue car with a small camper trailing behind.

He left the master bedroom and hoped for a bigger prize behind door number three. He tried turning the door handle but found it locked. He felt above the doorjamb for the expected key. Nothing. No matter. He reached into his pocket and removed a ring of small tools. He flipped through them until he found the item he wanted, slipped it into the keyhole and opened the door. This last bedroom appeared to be all-purpose—a place to sew, craft and pay bills. Only three items hung on the wall—a latch hook creation portraying the Golden Gate Bridge, a black and white photo of a man standing next to a big rig, and a painting. From across the dark room, Charlie couldn't tell what the painting depicted, so he moved in close. He pulled a small flashlight from his pocket and shined it directly upon the canvas. He saw a muddy river banked by towering green bluffs and a sunset in the distance. Along the shore lay a narrow sandy beach and behind it a grove of large trees. It reminded Charlie of the Upper Midwest. In the lower right-hand corner was the artist's signature—Corey Flanagan. Sticking out from the back was a price tag with the name of a gallery in Minneapolis. Charlie took two steps back and snapped a photo of the painting with his camera. He recognized the artist's name as being connected to Rebecca's case and was also struck by how out of place the painting was with the rest of the home's decor. He would share this discovery with Rebecca and let her decide its significance.

He then moved toward what used to be a closet, but which now was missing its doors. A tall, narrow table sat inside the alcove with a corkboard above it nailed to the wall. Three piles of papers rested atop the table, each stacked perfectly neat. Atop the leftmost pile was a court document captioned *Cecelia Jackson, Administrator for the Estate of Bennett Lee Jackson vs. Estate of Larry Allen Preston, His Heirs and Assigns.* Charlie bent the top one-third of the pile and thumbed through the pages, confirming that pleadings from the Jacksons' wrongful death suit filled the stack. He left that entire pile alone. Rebecca surely had this material already. The second pile was shorter and full of handwritten notes on yellow legal pads. He read the topmost one, quickly gleaning that Cecelia had been asked to write about her life with Bennett—when and where they met, details from their wedding, how they named their daughter Julia after Bennett's maternal grandmother and who could attest to the depth of Bennett's excellence as both a father and a spouse. The script on the cursive writing was feminine—presumably Cecelia's.

The second page caught Charlie's interest, but not as an investigator. This one surprisingly caused an uneasy feeling to rise inside his heart. On the page, Cecelia had written about the couple's plans and dreams for the future—building a new home in rural Pine Bluff, Bennett attending night school to finish his college degree and finally getting their passports so they could visit Paris on their twentieth anniversary and kiss beneath the Eiffel Tower. He scanned several more pages in this middle stack but ultimately photographed none of them. These looked to be documents supporting Cecelia's case against the Prestons. The assignment was to find something Rebecca didn't already have, something incriminating against either of the Jacksons that could be used as leverage in Rebecca's hard-nosed negotiations.

When he turned his attention to the final pile, Charlie discovered it was filled with more than just paper. There were a few important documents on top—a life insurance policy, bank statements and the Jacksons' Certificate of Marriage—but further down, he found an item that piqued his interest—a leather-bound journal tied shut with suede laces. Small colored tabs stuck out from several pages. He opened it and read from the first tabbed page. The handwriting was the same as that from the yellow legal pads, although this script was more jagged. He read from that first page about the day when an Arkansas State Trooper appeared on the Jackson's doorstep, informing Cecelia that Bennett had been murdered in the back of his truck. For an instant, the pit inside his heart spread throughout his abdomen, and an image of Charlie's mother appeared in his mind. *So strange*, he thought to himself— *feeling guilt at reading Cecelia Jackson's intimate journal just like when I secretly read Mom's diary years ago*. His entire way of earning money involved peering into the private lives of others, yet for some reason, reading Cecelia's words now caused him angst.

A second tab revealed Cecelia's feelings a week later when the medical examiner's report revealed that Bennett had either been raped or engaged willingly as a recipient of rough sex. *Either could have happened*, Charlie read in the journal. *Does the truth really matter? No, because Bennett was taken advantage of and his assaulter must pay*. Charlie heard a noise outside the house. He set the journal down and walked to the window, this one overlooking the backyard. A raccoon ambled away from a tipped-over garbage pail. He checked the time on his watch. It was now past midnight. He needed to finish up here by twelve-thirty if he wanted to make the drive back to Little Rock ahead of bar time. That gal from last night had promised him one more round.

He returned the journal to the table. He'd come back to it, time permitting. Instead, he focused on a shoe box that sat underneath the table on the floor. He opened it and furrowed his brow at the lone, strange content—a white prescription bottle labeled with Bennett Jackson's name. The drug was Truvada. Charlie grabbed the cell phone from his coat pocket and typed that name into his search app. He clicked on the first entry and read the result. *TRUVADA for PrEP (pre-exposure prophylaxis) is a once-daily prescription medicine for adults and adolescents at risk for HIV who weigh at least 77 pounds.* He snapped a photo of the white bottle, then returned it to the box on the table and closed the lid.

Charlie next looked at the corkboard and surveyed its content using his flashlight. The first item he noticed was a clipping from the *Fayetteville Observer*, dated November 30, 2013, and headlined: *Local Man Found Dead in Minnesota.* He didn't bother to read it. He already knew what it would say. A second clipping from the same paper, dated November 15, 2016, also caught his attention: *Arrest Finally Made in Unsolved Killing of Bennett Jackson.* This one, too, he neither read nor photographed. A third, older clipping from the *Observer* dated July 8, 2011, was affixed to the board in the upper right corner. This one was shorter, the paper more yellowed.

Sting Operation Nets Four at County Rest Stop

By Melissa Tuttle-Jones

Undercover detectives operating on tips from witnesses, waited in the bushes with binoculars at the Wayside Rest Stop off State Highway 65 on Monday afternoon. Neighbors and passersby had complained about cars and trucks parked for long periods of time at the rest stop throughout May and June. The complaints alleged that the drivers, all men, would exit their vehicles when a second car or truck entered the lot and parked alongside the first. Witnesses contend that after some visible back-and-forth communication between rolled-down windows, one of the men would then enter the other car for a short period of time. In some instances, both men exited their respective vehicles and entered the public restroom.

On Monday, according to police, detectives noticed a Dodge Caravan enter the rest stop and park adjacent to a red Ford Ranger. As previous observers had reported, the drivers each rolled down a window and engaged in unspecified conversation. Moments later, both drivers stepped out of their vehicles and entered the restroom marked "Men." Detectives waited a few minutes before descending on the restroom, where they discovered two individuals in close proximity and their pants rolled down to their ankles. The yet-to-be-identified suspects were issued citations for indecent exposure. These two suspects were then taken into custody and arrested for lewd behavior. Their vehicles were then towed to the county impound lot.

Later that same day, detectives observed similar behavior from the drivers, both male, of a late-model GMC Yukon and a blue Chevy Malibu. The Yukon reportedly had two child booster seats in the second row, but no other passengers were inside at the time. The driver of the SUV entered the passenger side seat of the Malibu, where detectives witnessed the men engaged in oral sex. Those suspects were also taken into custody, and their vehicles impounded.

This is a developing story.

Two additional news articles were pinned to the poster board, but they were photocopies rather than actual items cut from a newspaper. Surprisingly to Charlie, both had to do with Corey Flanagan. The first was from the *Barron News Shield*, purportedly Wisconsin's and the nation's first newspaper. The article was headlined, *Twin Cities' Couple Involved in Local Shooting; No Charges Filed*. Charlie read enough to glean that the story involved two men hunting at a cabin during Deer Season in 2013, where one ended up shooting the other before fleeing the scene. The two men were apparently involved in a romantic relationship and the injured man pressed no charges. A second photo-copied item must have been downloaded from the internet for it listed no source. It was an obituary for Francis Aloyious Fischer, age 63, of Pepin, Wisconsin. Two items from that obituary were circled in red ink—the words *passed away suddenly at his cabin in Barron County* and *survived by his wife, Virginia.* Charlie snapped photos of all the pinned items. He then took pictures of several index cards affixed to the poster board as well, containing handwritten names, addresses and other information.

Margaret Preston 236 Pine, Pepin Wis (wife of "alleged" killer Larry)

Billy Preston 1440 12th Street, Huntington Beach CA (Larry's son/knows the truth)

Corey Fischer/Flanagan Somewhere in CA (rapist/killer)

Nick Parker 2448 Central Avenue, Mpls MN (Corey's first victim/former lover)

Carol Zaeske 1100 Portland Ave #12, Mpls MN (Corey's friend/co-conspirator)

Ginny Fischer [current location unknown] (Corey's mother)

Fischer Cabin 18403 County Rd V, Barron WI (first shooting, owned by Frank's wife)

Damn, Charlie thought, this woman had either done her homework or hired a private investigator of her own. And her attention focused mostly on connections to Corey Flanagan, more so than against the targets of her lawsuit—the Prestons. "Creepy," he said under his breath. "Cecelia Jackson, what are you up to?" He pondered whether her absence from Pine Bluff had anything to do with tracking down more information about Corey. Rebecca would be interested in this. He scoured the poster board for anything else of interest, anything that looked out of place. Nothing. As he turned the light from his phone away from the board and toward the other items on the desk, he happened to scan the beam across the floor. Something caught the corner of his eye. He reached down to the floor and grabbed a photograph with a single push-pull pin stuck through a tiny hole at the top. It must have been attached to the board but fallen off at some point. He didn't recall jostling the desk in any way, thus reassured that he had not caused the separation. He brought the photo closer to his face. It had a layer of dust, which he gently blew away.

In the photograph, two women stood in front of a rustic brown house surrounded by a dense grove of towering pines. The picture looked as if it had been taken with a telephoto lens at a substantial distance. Given the setting and the size of the dwelling in relation to the women, Charlie wondered if perhaps the structure was a cottage. He didn't recognize either of the women, seemingly engaged in conversation and oblivious to the fact that someone was snapping their photo. The older of the two women appeared to be in her late fifties or early sixties, while the younger one looked not much past twenty-one. Both women were pretty with blondish hair worn long, the younger woman's tied into a ponytail. He wondered about the photo's significance, and about who took the picture, and why. On the backside, someone had scribbled the words *Fischer Cabin, Barron County*. He snapped a photo of both the picture and the backside, then returned it to its place on the floor.

Charlie turned his head toward the bedroom door after faintly hearing a siren in the distance. He left the room and walked toward the front window. Though he saw no flashing lights outside, the siren was getting louder. Had a neighbor noticed his light shining inside the house and called the police? He wasn't about to wait and find out. He figured that he had already gathered enough material to justify his outrageous fee. He raced toward the back door, exited the house after turning the lock behind him, then slipped off the property and began walking briskly down the street. Upon spying the flashing lights cresting the hill on the street ahead of him, he ducked behind a hedge of arbor vitae to watch a squad car pass by. Sure enough, the squad car stopped directly in front of the Jacksons' home, and two patrolmen walked purposely toward the house. They pounded on the front door while announcing their presence. Within moments, they kicked the door in and entered the house with guns drawn.

Chapter 4

Corey watched as the nurse hung up the phone.

"Your mom is on her way, hon. She'll be here within half an hour."

Corey nodded despite knowing this news already. He had heard both sides of the brief conversation as Asha stood next to him by the bed. He heard his mother's gasp and her utterances of shock upon hearing the barest of details from the nurse who obviously knew how to deliver difficult news. He then heard his mother's rapid series of questions aimed at Asha like bullets from an automatic weapon. And he had listened to Asha affirm that Corey would be fine—physically. Everything else would be explained after Ginny arrived at the hospital.

"Okay, then. Would you like me to turn on the television?"

Corey shook his head, no. Words escaped him, but he would need to find some before his mother showed up.

"All right. Try and rest. I'll be at the nurse's station. Ring your call button if you need anything."

Corey watched as Asha left the room. She had left the door open, allowing the barely muted buzz of the ER to stream inside. Perhaps her use of the word "physically" when describing Corey's well-being to Ginny had been deliberate. By now, Asha and the attending doctors had likely accessed his medical records on My-Chart and seen his mental health history once he told them that his name used to be Fischer. Corey's earlier *déjà vu* returned. It was as if he were back in Minnesota and lying in the psych ward. He wouldn't be surprised if they stationed an orderly inside his room or even cuffed his hands to the bed rails like before. He turned his head toward the wall to avoid watching the staff and random patients walk past his room. He wished that there was a window to look outside but then remembered the lateness of the hour and that everything around him was dark. He felt tightness in his face and the inclination toward a self-pitying cry, but no tears welled up behind his eyes. *Shouldn't I be lonely and afraid and sad enough to induce a gusher? Aren't I affected by all that happened and by what might yet befall Miguel? Don't I care whether he lives or dies?* Corey scoured his mind and emotions, trying to make sense of his feelings—yet another similarity to the morning he awoke chained to a hospital bed all those years ago.

As he stared toward the wall, noticing the blandness of the décor and the stark, utilitarian furnishings in the room, his mind raced forward to the most recent time he was inside a hospital seven months ago. He had gone with his mother for a final visit to see Larry Preston the day after murder charges against Corey had been dismissed and one day after Larry had sacrificed his own reputation by falsely confessing on his deathbed to having killed the man whom Corey had shot. *Had karma now come to collect from Corey what was due? Was this indeed his penance for another act of weakness—letting someone else pick up the pieces of his broken life?*

Thoughts of Larry segued into thoughts about Larry's son. It was only scant hours ago that Corey gave Billy a ride to LAX. He remembered listening as Billy previewed his weeklong trip to Minnesota. The highlight, of course, would be time spent with Rebecca. Their long-distance relationship meant packing their infrequent visits with shared adventures and plenty of sex. It was refreshing to see Billy in love again for the first time in twenty years. Since his divorce from Amanda, Billy had enjoyed a raging single life that lacked one ingredient—true love. That changed last year when Billy met Rebecca. The mere thought brought a weak smile to Corey's face. During their weekly Sunday brunches at the museum in Long Beach, Billy had no longer regaled Corey with stories of awkward first dates or mind-bending sexual positions. Instead, Billy's near-constant discussion of his bond with Rebecca led Corey to believe that Billy's twenty-year bachelorhood might be coming to an end. Maybe Billy still had a spark of romantic possibility hidden behind his macho facade. And maybe—just maybe—Rebecca had won Billy's carefully guarded heart and would be the one with whom he finally shared a love affair to last him the rest of his life.

But Corey also recalled that serious business had summoned Billy to Minnesota this week as well. He would be sitting for a deposition on Monday morning in the wrongful death case against Larry Preston's estate. Billy was the designated witness for the defense, and he would likely be grilled about his father's finances as well as the assets Larry creatively shed in the weeks before he died. During that car ride to LAX earlier today, Corey listened intently as Billy recapped the status of the case. Liability was a given; once Larry confessed to having committed the killing, there was no question but that his estate owed compensation to Bennett Jackson's surviving wife and child. Rather, the issue at stake was how much.

Corey's good mood earlier this morning while driving had melted away like an ice cube under the California sun. He apologized to Billy yet again but was quickly shushed. Though Corey had expressed regret and guilt about the situation multiple times, Billy always offered absolution. "The civil case will proceed as it must," Billy had said. "What's done is done. What will come will inevitably come."

Voices in the hallway distracted Corey from his thoughts. An older woman with an accent spoke rapidly at the nurse's station. He could see the woman just beyond the threshold of his door. She was surrounded by two men in blue scrubs and two younger women on either side of her, each of them with a hand on the old woman's shoulders. Then, he heard weeping and watched as the men in blue scrubs stood silent while the two young women enveloped the older one in a tight embrace. And though Corey felt like a voyeur to the old woman's distress, he listened to the voices elevated above the woman's sobs.

"He's going to be all right, Mrs. Rangel," said the first man.

"*Tu hijo va a estar bien*," said the other man.

"She knows," replied one of the younger women while turning her head toward the doctors. "Mama's just a bit overwhelmed with relief that she won't lose her only son."

At that moment, the older woman raised her head and cried out through her tears. "*Gracias al Senor y a los doctores.*"

Corey discerned that the old woman understood the good news along with the gravity of what was almost stolen from her. He once again wished he could get up and close the door without drawing attention to himself, especially after the old woman turned toward him and suspended her sobs. Their eye contact lasted for several seconds, and hers felt to Corey like a magnet. He couldn't look away. A weak smile arrived on her lips as she nodded her head in his direction before lifting her hands together as if in prayer and gesturing them toward Corey. Then, she turned back toward those standing with her, and the conversation resumed in muted voices with words Corey could no longer hear because he pulled a pillow over his head. Would this woman's good fortune and silent offer of blessing extend across the room to Corey as well? And then, even farther down the hall to Miguel?

He lifted the pillow just enough to see the back of the woman's head, her hair a mix of coal and silver. Though he could no longer see her face, he remembered the details. Her cheeks were flush and plump with an absence of makeup. Her eyes were dark brown and her nose slightly too big for her face. Her expressions were a jumbled combination of worry, anxiety, gratitude and relief. He wondered if he'd be able to paint the woman's face from memory whenever he next sat in front of his easel—the wetness of her cheeks, the deep thoughts welled up behind her eyes, and the near absence of wrinkles despite her likely being well past seventy years old. Her entire visage exuded peace and strength, sending a feeling of calm through the air and across the room toward Corey during the mere seconds that they had been locked in each other's sight.

I'm happy she received good news, he thought to himself. Though he didn't know her, he felt an inexplicable connection in their shared moment, their common experience of anticipated loss. *Maybe I have a thing with older women*, he wondered. *We often seem to gravitate toward one another—the younger gay man and mentoring, nosy old women.* The encounter made him think of his favorite older woman, not counting his mom. His frame shop client, Mrs. Graner, had been in to see Corey during his short shift at the store earlier today. She had been waiting inside the shop when he arrived. Corey was the only employee Mrs. Graner would permit to handle her framing needs. *You are late, no?* he remembered her saying this afternoon. *You may have a beautiful eye for framing, Corey, but punctuality in business is tres nécessaire.* He had offered her an apologetic grin. The old lady's harmless chiding through a strong French accent made even the most pointed criticisms seem mild. He said that he had her artwork ready in back, then ran into the storage room before emerging moments later with a brown paper-wrapped frame smaller than a hardcover book. *Ah, merci mon Corey*, she had said. *I cannot wait to mount it.* He asked if she had time for tea, expecting the answer to be a resounding yes. Mrs. Graner routinely insisted upon the two of them catching up on local gossip from the Riviera Village over cups of jasmine. Corey looked forward to their chats. Mrs. Graner was unlike any other person he had met since moving to California, more like a favorite great aunt with whom he shared laughter, light banter, and random personal stories of life and love.

Malheureusement non, was her surprising reply. I'm off to the Los Verdes Country Club. It's my monthly luncheon with the Rolling Hills Ladies of Art Club, and I'm already running late. Those older women can be insufferable about tardiness, you know. She then winked as Corey laughed. *Yes. So I've heard*, he replied, though Corey remembered feeling sad that his friend wouldn't stay for even a ten-minute chat. She then affirmed that they would see each other next week at the Long Beach Museum of Art for the Emerging Artists' Auction, and Corey agreed. *And you will finally get to meet Miguel too*, he added, a promise he now wasn't certain he'd be able to keep. But Corey remembered Mrs. Graner's sweet and pointed reply. *He is quite the bel homme, that Miguel. Make sure to keep him happy, Corey. Finding such a merveilleux Latin lover at your age will not happen twice. Au revoir. I'll see you next week.*

* * *

Corey was awake and staring at the ceiling when a familiar face entered his room.

"Mom..."

She walked to his bedside as he started to get up.

"No, lie back down." She dropped her purse into a chair, then leaned in to embrace him. They held on to one another tight, but neither shed a tear.

"I'm sorry you had to come all this way so late at night, Mom."

Ginny pulled back from the embrace and looked at Corey, offering a tepid smile but no verbal reply. Instead, she continued holding his arms with hers, then leaned in once more and gently kissed his head beneath his bandaged wound. Asha entered the room, and the two women exchanged greetings. Ginny thanked the nurse for the care given to Corey. Asha recapped his medical condition—a mild concussion, scraped forehead, four cracked ribs, exhaustion and shock.

"Are you ready for the detectives to come in now?" Asha gently prodded.

"Detectives?" Ginny asked.

"Yes. They have more questions for Corey."

"Yes, it's fine," Corey answered. "Is it all right if my mother listens in? I'd prefer to only tell this story once."

"I'll check. Be right back." Asha disappeared into the hall. The detectives arrived moments later and were fine with Ginny's presence. In fact, they began with a few questions to her—who she was and what, if anything, she knew about the incident, as well as the alleged assailant, Cecelia Jackson.

"Why are you asking me about her?" Ginny turned her stare from the detectives toward Corey. He let the officers answer. Her jaw dropped as soon as she heard it.

"Cecelia Jackson? Of course, I know that name. She's the wife of Bennett Jackson, the man who died accidentally after an altercation with my son and a family friend. You think she shot at Corey and Miguel?"

"That's what we're trying to uncover, ma'am. What, if anything, do you know about her?"

"I only met her once, though we didn't exchange words. I can still hear her screaming voice from the courtroom, though—words that I'll never forget."

"And, for the record, where do you currently reside?"

Ginny provided her address and phone number. "I only moved here a few weeks ago to attend nursing school in Santa Monica and also to be closer to my son."

She then listened as Corey replied to the detectives' questions and revealed the shocking details from this long and violent night.

* * *

Asha returned to Corey's room as soon as the detectives departed.

"How are you feeling?"

"My headache returned, but I'm sure it's from stress more than the bump on my head."

"Understandable. You'll be susceptible to PTSD in the coming weeks, Corey. You've been through a traumatic ordeal. The doctor's recommending psychological therapy. Have you done counseling before?"

Corey looked first at his mother, then swallowed hard before replying to the nurse with raised eyebrows. "Um, yeah. I've seen a few shrinks in my day."

"We can provide you with names of therapists affiliated with the hospital, or you can see whomever you choose."

"Thanks."

"The doctor has also prescribed painkillers—Oxycotin—and strongly suggests that you not return to work or do anything strenuous for at least a week."

"I'll pass on the oxy. Addictive substances aren't exactly my friend. Tell the doc thanks anyway."

Asha nodded her head. "All right then. Good self-awareness. I'm sure you'll be fine with ibuprofen. I'll bring you back a slip for prescription strength. You can pick it up from the hospital pharmacy before you leave."

"Does that mean I'm free to go? Can I see Miguel now?"

"The doctor would like you to stay another hour. Give us time to wrap up your paperwork and do a final round of diagnostic tests. I'll also go check on Miguel and be back as soon as I can."

Once they were alone in the room, Ginny walked closer to Corey's bed. He anticipated any number of probing questions about what he had told the detectives, but he hoped that she would talk about anything else. He wanted to stop obsessing about Cecelia if possible. And true to most of those moments from Corey's childhood when he needed nothing more than a comforting and empathetic presence, Ginny seemed to read his mind. Rather than asking about the horrifying scene after Miguel's proposal of marriage, she spoke about that beautiful moment itself.

"I guess it's safe to tell you now that I knew the proposal was coming."

"Oh?"

"Yes. I didn't know exactly where or when it would happen, but I knew Miguel intended to ask."

"How did you know that, Mom?"

"Miguel invited me to lunch last week and asked me not to tell you. I felt it was a justifiable deceit, especially once your sweet boyfriend began to speak."

Tears now filled Corey's eyes, then trickled down his face and onto the pillow. "Tell me."

"We met last Wednesday at A Votre Sante in Brentwood. Miguel picked me up during his lunch break. It's a beautiful spot to eat—distinctly French, or at least how I envision a Parisian café might look. Anyway, we each ordered food and then engaged in small talk. He asked about my new apartment and told me more about his work at the firm. It was nice getting to know him, Corey. I find Miguel both charming and kind. During our brief time together, I saw and heard a man who had been raised right by his mother—he opened doors and was exceedingly polite. At times, I felt like I was talking with an old friend.

"As soon as the waiter brought our entrees, Miguel set his silverware aside, took a long sip of his lemonade, and said he had something important to ask me. *Of course*, I replied. *Go ahead.* This is what he said. *Mrs. Fischer, I want you to know that I love your son. We've known each other for less than a year, but he is the love of my life. I want to have a lasting relationship with Corey, Mrs. Fischer. And as part of that, I want to have a good relationship with you.*

Corey wiped his eyes with his shirt sleeve and suppressed the urge to sob.

"That's when he reached his hand across the table, setting it gently atop my own. His gesture surprised me. We don't typically do that sort of thing with strangers back in the Midwest."

Corey's near-sob emerged as a cackle instead. Ginny's story of Miguel's touchy-feely nature resonated, and he thought about Miguel's frequent soft caresses. What Corey wouldn't give to feel Miguel's hands touching his own right now.

"Then, he finished. *Mrs. Fischer, I'd like your blessing in what I'm about to propose to Corey at his favorite spot along the coast. I plan to ask him to marry me, and it would mean the world to me to have your support.*"

Corey smiled through his tears. "What did you say, Mom?"

"I answered Miguel without hesitation. *Yes, you have my blessing. I would very much like for you to become my second son.*"

Ginny leaned in and once again embraced Corey. They ex-changed *I love yous* and shed tears on each other's clothes. Into Corey's shoulder, she whispered, "he even showed me the ring."

Corey pulled away. "The ring! Oh my God, I don't know what happened to it. It's either still in Miguel's pocket or back on the pier or..." He didn't have the courage to finish the thought.

"Don't worry, honey. I'll ask the nurse when she comes in if they have it."

"But what if it's not with his stuff? That ring belonged to Miguel's father!"

"Then I'll ask the detectives to search the pier. Please don't get upset until we can ask a few questions, Corey. We'll find it, I promise."

His eyes darted between his mother, his own hands, and the door. If only he'd have answered Miguel's proposal right away, that ring would be on Corey's finger right now. But he didn't. And it wasn't.

Ginny stepped back and took a rosary from her purse.

"Let's pray together, Corey, like when you were a boy. Let's pray for Miguel."

He nodded, then watched as his mother wrapped a familiar silver rosary around their joined hands.

"Hail Mary, full of grace. The Lord is with thee. Blessed art thou among women and blessed is the fruit of thy womb, Jesus." She repeated that mantra two more times before concluding the rote portion of her plea. "Holy Mary, mother of God, pray for us sinners, now and at the hour of our death. Amen."

Corey was surprised at the calming effect of that ritualistic prayer. It mesmerized him as a kid and stole his attention away from the chaos now as an adult. Ginny kept holding onto the rosa-ry encircling their joined hands, then petitioned her God for more out loud—the same God to whom she had prayed every day of her life since she was a little girl. She prayed for instant bless-ings upon both Corey and Miguel. She prayed that the doctors at Torrance Memorial might have clear vision and an abundance of skill. She prayed for forgiveness upon whoever had set this tragic event into motion. And she prayed that God would save Miguel—granting him and Corey many more years of health and happiness. "Amen."

Asha entered the recovery room as Ginny finished her prayer. Corey watched as Asha approached the bottom end of the bed and placed both her hands on the footboard. He looked up at the nurse's ashen face while still holding onto the rosary and to his mother's hands.

"Corey. Mrs. Fischer. I'm afraid I have sad news. I'm sorry to tell you that Miguel has passed away."

* * *

An hour later, Corey and Ginny were preparing to leave the ER. Asha had brought him a brand-new pair of jeans and a UCLA sweatshirt, along with a T-shirt, boxers and socks to wear underneath. The shirts were baggy on Corey's thin frame, but he welcomed not having to get back into his old clothes even if, by now, they were dry. A priest had come and gone, offering Corey and Ginny a modicum of peace and promising that he'd follow up with them at home the next day.

Asha came to see them one last time. A police officer trailed behind her. She offered them the opportunity to see Miguel's body—a chance to say goodbye. Ginny looked to Corey for an answer. He accepted with trepidation, then remembered to ask about the ring. Asha told him that Miguel arrived at the hospital with nothing other than the clothes he was wearing, a tube of lip balm and a ring of keys in his front pocket. She promised to give those two things to Corey before he left the hospital. They followed the nurse down the hall with a police officer in tow. Asha explained that they would view Miguel's body in a private room before it was transferred to the basement morgue. His body had been moved to this special space so that authorities might continue their investigation, including an autopsy once the medical examiner arrived. Asha also explained that they could view but not touch the body—no holding of Miguel's hand, no placement of a kiss upon his head. The opportunity to see him was an unusual courtesy at this point, she explained. There was an active investigation into Miguel's death, and the body, which formerly held such a deep well of kindness, was now evidence in that impending probe. Corey listened to the nurse with most of his attention yet watched the police officer in his peripheral vision. Was the officer accompanying them to ensure proper handling of the evidence, or was Corey being observed as a potential suspect in the crime because they thought his tale about Cecelia had been nothing more than a lie?

Once inside the room with Miguel's body, Corey forgot about the officer. He forgot about everything other than the fact that the man he loved lay on a table ahead of him, a white sheet pulled to the base of his throat. The peaceful, sleepy visage of Miguel's face belied the truth beneath that starched bedsheet. Corey took three steps toward the gurney. Asha motioned with her outstretched arm that Corey had come close enough. He must now do his semi-private grieving and say farewell from there. Ginny and the officer stayed in place somewhere behind him. As he stood mere feet from the love of his life, Corey let his shoulders drop with heavy defeat. His bulky, borrowed sweatshirt soon began moving up and down against the skin of his chest, lifted and dropped in synch with his heaving shoulders and shaking head. Though he couldn't touch Miguel's cheek or kiss his still full and pinkish brown lips, Corey knew that Miguel's body was still warm, that a small fraction of life still coursed through the man covered by that sheet. And though Corey accepted for the moment that Miguel was dead, he couldn't help but feel his lover's presence and imagine his spirit slowly lifting itself from the shackles of a bullet-torn body, taking all the warmth that was Miguel with it to wherever souls fly next.

Once the viewing ended, Corey and Ginny walked to the hospital's waiting room. Beyond them lay the exit, but the prospect of walking through the glass doors was anathema to him. Leaving here without Miguel or his body felt too final. He wasn't yet ready to move on. Ginny stood by her son with a hand against his lower back. It wasn't clear what to do next. Should he go home? No, the police said it wasn't safe if the alleged killer was still at large. Should they find a late-night diner for cups of coffee and a bite to eat? No, Corey wasn't hungry. He couldn't foresee ever eating again. Instead, he let his mother lead him by the hand as they exited the hospital.

Chapter 5

"Billy!"

Rebecca's voice flew above the crowd as Billy exited the arrivals door at MSP International. Amidst the sea of mostly white faces, he spotted a lone Asian one—the face of the woman he loved. Hair, black as night, fell softly over her olive-toned skin, brushing the top of her navy, pinstriped jacket. He figured she had come directly from work, though it was now a quarter past ten at night. Still, a smile shone like a crescent moon across her tired face.

"Hey," he said before dropping his carry-on bag to the floor and sweeping her up into a tight embrace. Rebecca's skin against his cheek and her perfume's familiarity calmed him. Into her ear, he whispered, "God, I've missed you."

He released his grip on her torso enough for them to lock eyes and come together in a soft kiss. To some standing at the baggage carousel, the couple's locked lips probably lasted an awkwardly long time. For Billy and Rebecca, it wasn't nearly long enough. She withdrew first, then pulled away and brought her arm out from behind her back.

"Here. These are for you."

He hadn't previously noticed the petite bouquet.

"Flowers? As the man, shouldn't I be bringing them to you?"

"Just accept them, tough guy, and save your alpha male instincts for later."

They kissed again.

"So, how was the flight?"

"Pretty smooth. And I had a whole row to myself."

"Nice."

"There was one odd thing."

"Oh?"

"Yeah. The guy sitting across from me also had his side of the row to himself. I did a double take, then stared at him for the longest time as he gazed out the window on take-off."

"Why's that?"

"I could have sworn it was my father. At that point, all I could see was the back of the man's head, but he had Dad's same distinctive bald spot with his hair cropped short and wisps of white that needed to be shaved from the backside of his wrinkled, pink neck."

"So... was it Larry's twin or an apparition?"

"I wasn't sure at first. But once the man turned his head around and caught me staring, he gave a friendly wave, and I could see it wasn't Larry. The man's face was less chubby than Dad's, but the sparkle in his smile was the same."

"I'd say you had a nice moment, Billy. Who knows, maybe Larry placed that guy across from you as a way of saying *I've got your back* from the beyond."

"Yeah, maybe. It's ironic, of course—thinking I've seen my father while I'm on a trip back here specifically related to him."

"Yes, the lawsuit."

"It's certainly weighed heavy on my mind the past few days—anticipating my deposition, then also imagining how my family will come up with money for a settlement. And all of it's because Dad took the fall for Corey. So, yeah, he's been on my mind lately, and now I see his image on the face of strangers. Am I nuts?"

"No. You're human. Cut yourself some slack."

"You're right, and I'm sorry to get so heavy this early in the trip. You sure you still want me here for the week?" He cast her a playful look and reached out to hold her hand as she steered the car toward the exit.

She gripped his hand firmly with hers. "Not a doubt in my mind. And you can talk about your father any time you'd like. He was special to me, too, you know. I owe my professional success to his mentorship back when I was a clueless law student."

"Fair enough. We'll save the lawsuit talk for another day. Tonight, my focus is being here with you." He squeezed her hand before letting go.

"Are you sure I won't be a distraction for you this week? Because you can certainly sleep in the guest room if you need time and space to think about the case. I wouldn't want me or my new red teddy to keep you from a good night's sleep."

"Your red teddy won't be distracting, darlin, because it won't stay on your body for long."

They exited the parking ramp and were soon heading toward Rebecca's house near Minnehaha Falls. Billy reached over and began rubbing her shoulders and neck. He could see the tension in her jaw, barely hidden behind her near-constant smile.

"Long day?"

"Hmmm, yeah. You could say that." She looked to be recapping the day's work in her mind. "But the best part of it just arrived."

Billy gave her an affirming squeeze.

"Hungry?" she asked.

"Starved. You?"

Rebecca shot him a knowing glance and a grimaced face.

"You haven't eaten yet today, have you?"

She shrugged her shoulders and raised her eyebrows but offered no confession. It was a frequent topic when they spoke— Rebecca's habit of letting the pressures of her caseload supplant not simply the idea of eating healthily but oftentimes eating anything at all. Billy's concern for her nourishment was half-hearted. She was more than capable of self-care. And her slender physique aroused him, especially once her clothes dropped to the floor. Billy enjoyed a carnal lust at the idea of Rebecca wanting his taller, thicker frame to dominate her petite yet strong one.

"We can stop and grab burgers at the Nook—they're open til eleven. Or we can reheat something frozen at home."

"The latter."

"Okay, Let's work up a good appetite first."

* * *

Billy lay in bed, the light summer covers half draped across his bare skin. He watched as Rebecca rolled off the mattress and slipped into a nearly see-through black robe—a gift from Billy on her last visit to California.

"Damn, babe. Mmmm."

She turned back toward the bed. A smile filled her olive-skinned face. "What?"

"That was amazing, that's what."

"You think so? Better than Black's Beach?"

Now, both Billy and Rebecca wore broad smiles.

"Well, that was something special, too," he said. "I'd never been naked in public until your last visit."

"I'm sure someone saw us, but I didn't even care."

"You mean the hang gliders? Those guys were three hundred feet in the air and probably focused on not falling to their death. Besides, it's an official nudist beach, so no one would be surprised to find us naked."

"And fucking up against the cliffs? I'm pretty sure that isn't legal."

"You're the lawyer."

Rebecca threw a decorative pillow at him. "Don't pin that on me. I still can't believe we made love on the beach. Not that I'm complaining."

"Well, technically, we were back up against the cliffs, behind some scrub brush, not on the beach. Although, I did end up with plenty of sand up my ass."

"You're the one who wanted me on top."

Billy rubbed his hand through his thick blonde hair and laughed. "Maybe we should recreate that scene out in your backyard. It's dark, and grass is a hell of a lot softer than sand against my tush."

She laughed and nodded her head. "If you're up for it, sure. But first, we need food. I've got a take & bake pizza in the fridge—meat lovers, your favorite. Once the oven preheats, it'll only take a sec."

"Thanks, love. Need help?"

"I'm good. You rest." Her eyes moved down toward his waist, then she cast a nod of her head toward a bulge under the blanket. "Besides, my galley kitchen isn't big enough for the *three* of us."

He laughed. "Okay."

As he waited for Rebecca to return, Billy scrolled on his phone. First, he checked for a text or missed call from Corey. He remembered that it was Corey and Miguel's one-year anniversary and wondered what surprise Miguel had in store. Surely, those two were celebrating in the same way Billy had spent his late evening here with Rebecca. But the only notifications on his phone included a text from his sister and a voicemail from a competitor trying for the umpteenth time to convince Billy to sell his business and cash out. Neither one required a response tonight. He turned his attention to Twitter—skimming the day's news and reading various analysts explain the past week in the life of his beloved Dodgers.

He set his phone on the nightstand once Rebecca re-entered the bedroom carrying a tray with the promised food. He sat up in bed with the covers tight to his waist and pushed the pillows up against the headboard for support.

"This looks awesome, babe. Thank you."

She leaned in for a kiss. "You're welcome." She handed him a glass of red wine and set the pizza atop the blanket, then lifted her own glass into the air. "Cheers to us."

"To us."

They each took a celebratory swallow. Rebecca set her glass on the nightstand before climbing into bed.

"This tastes really good."

"Thanks. All I did was bake it. So, what do you want to do tomorrow? Farmer's Market? Bike ride around the lakes? Movie?"

"All of the above, as long as we end up back here," he said, patting the bed.

Did someone miss me?"

"Just a little."

"I hope I'm worth the long wait."

"Oh, you are. And I'm glad we have a whole week ahead of us. I'm gonna try to forget about work and simply focus on you." She smiled and sank her teeth into a slice of pizza. Billy hesitated. He enjoyed the playfulness of their interactions, but a serious feeling unexpectedly rose from his gut, reaching his mouth before he could think about whether to talk or stay mute. "Truth?"

"Please."

"This is the best sex I've had in my entire life. With you, it's powerful—unlike anyone else I've ever been with. I don't know how else to explain. It just is."

She leaned over and kissed him softly on the lips. "Same. I've never been intimate with another man the way I have with you. You touch me—everywhere."

He smiled. He took a large bite of pizza, and Rebecca returned to her plate as well. As he chewed his food, Billy's eyes focused mindlessly on the wall as thoughts raced through his head. After swallowing, he cleared his throat and looked back at Rebecca with a forced smile.

"You said *man*."

"I'm sorry, what?"

He uttered a shallow laugh. "After I said that our lovemaking is better than with *anyone else*, you said it was better than with any *man*. Maybe you're reserving judgment for a future same-sex encounter?" He laughed once more and teasingly prodded her torso with his elbow.

Rebecca smiled and paused. Then she mimicked his light laugh. "Well, if you really want to know—yeah, I've been intimate with a woman. It's been a few years, but I wasn't trying to be cagey. Sex with you has been better than with *anyone else*."

He could feel his face react to this new knowledge.

"Oh boy, maybe I shouldn't have mentioned that."

Billy shook his head and turned to face her. "What? No, you're being honest, and it sounds like that was long before we met. It's not for me to judge."

"But you're worried, aren't you?"

His eyes remained locked with hers. "Well, yeah."

"Billy, I'm not a lesbian, obviously. I'm not certain whether I'm bi-sexual or if that was just something I needed for a brief period of my life."

"That's not what worries me."

"It's not? Then what is?"

"Something we haven't talked about—something I've assumed but have been afraid to ask."

"And that is?"

"Are we exclusive? I want to be, but I realize we've only been at this for a little over six months and long-distance at that. I guess I don't want to seem obsessive or jump the gun. And, with what you've shared, maybe you need more than just me?"

Rebecca smiled, then reached out her hand and caressed his cheek. The tension in Billy's face dissipated. "You're right. You're being obsessive."

He opened his eyes wide with contorted eyebrows. "What?"

"You're obsessed with me, clearly." She rubbed his back and continued to smile. "And the feeling's mutual." The tension in Billy's face fell away. "I want you and only you, ya dumbass. Now finish your pizza and go brush your teeth. We're heading outside in five minutes."

* * *

Billy awoke in the middle of the night and turned his head toward Rebecca, who slept soundly by his side. They had each fallen asleep fast after a tender goodnight kiss, a few blades of grass stuck to crevices of their skin and the taste of Malbec still faint on their lips. Billy rubbed his temples. How much wine had they consumed? A bare hint of dawn peeked through the blinds in the dark bedroom. He checked his phone—three thirty in the morning here in Minneapolis or half past one back home. He sat up against the pillows and looked at the home screen of his phone for notifications. No new texts or missed calls. The Dodgers lost a close one in extra innings, 6–5.

He looked over at Rebecca as she murmured something indecipherable in her sleep and turned her head toward him with her eyes still closed. Her naturally long eyelashes trembled ever so slightly with each intake and release of slumbered breath. He turned his phone screen toward the wall so that the light wouldn't shine upon her face. He continued scrolling. Twitter was the only social media outlet on his device, and he perused a variety of unimportant news items before closing the app. He returned to his text messages. Still nothing from Corey. Billy tapped his best friend's name and began to write one himself.

Hey, lover boy, you there?

He watched the screen and waited for the familiar dancing dots to appear, indicating that a reply was imminent. Nothing. He set the phone down on his chest and looked around the room once his eyes readjusted to the dark. The space was no bigger than his own bedroom back in Huntington Beach, but certainly was more charming. Rebecca's entire Craftsman home exuded an aura of well-built, handcrafted workmanship. Most everything about the space seemed just right—certainly for a single person and likely for two as well. Her taste in decorating was also pleasing—minimalist, with soothing colors and quaint touches appropriate for a 1930s-era home. What a contrast to his clichéd bachelor pad.

He felt his phone buzz and lifted it from his chest. His health and fitness app reminded him that he fell four thousand steps short of his daily goal. "Yeah," he muttered aloud, "but I made up for that and more after two rounds of sex." Once again, he checked for a reply from Corey. Nothing. Why hadn't he responded? "Typical," Billy complained softly. How many times had he been there for Corey when he was needed? Why did it always seem that help in times of crisis only ran in one direction for much of their friendship? He began typing a longer message. Perhaps by getting his thoughts down on the screen, he might more easily fall back asleep, whether Corey answered him or not.

Can't wait to hear about your big night! Mine was great too. Realized I missed R more than I thought. But she threw me a zinger I didn't expect. REALLY need your perspective, man. I'm in new territory you've already traveled. Where in the hell R U? Don't tell me that gay burrito print got you a one-way ticket to Fuscksville with Miguel! Anyway, call me tomorrow as soon as you can. Sorry to be vague. Here's the short harsh truth: I love her, C. Deeper than I knew! But I'm scared and she's got some "past" I'm not sure how to handle. I don't want to mess it up, but it's really gnawing at me. Not that either U or I are relationship experts LOL, but I know you can help. Your LTR lasted 4x longer than mine. Besides, how am I supposed to figure things out with R when most of the choices I've made about women in the past thirty years have been universally wrong?

Chapter 6

Hours earlier, Cecelia had followed the pair of ambulances at a distance all the way from Hermosa Beach. This was by far the easiest part of her long quest to track Corey, she figured. The lights and sirens from the ambulances could be seen and heard from a half-mile away. And, thankfully, the ambulances both headed toward the same hospital. She had found a parking spot in the front row of the lot and backed her car into it so that she had an unobstructed view of the emergency room's front door. It was the best she could do at the time.

She took a deep breath and thought hard about what to do next. She turned off the engine and pushed herself against the seat to stretch. She intertwined her fingers and brought her hands together as if in prayer but then turned them inside out as the sound of cracking knuckles filled the inside of the car. It felt good to release all the tension that had been building since the pier. Cecelia didn't know whether Corey was alive or dead. Either was a decent possibility. Perhaps she got him with her last bullet, or maybe he hit his head against the pier during his fall into the ocean and drowned. She much preferred the former. He deserved to die by Cecelia's hand and not by some fluke occurrence with an absence of pain. She reached for a bottle of water in the cup holder and took an extra-long sip. The lukewarm contents quenched perhaps the deepest thirst she could remember.

She set the empty bottle down and then reached inside her purse. She pulled out the cell phone she had found atop the pier.

It clearly belonged to either Corey or Miguel. As she lifted the device, the screen transformed from pitch darkness into something light. Behind the date and the time and an image of a padlock, she saw what looked like a work of art. Bingo. Most likely, the phone was Corey's unless his lover was an artsy-fartsy type, too. The passcode asked for six numbers. She entered a pair of easy combinations. 123456. 987654. Not surprisingly, neither of those first two attempts unlocked the phone.

"Damn."

She threw the device back into her purse. She'd try again later. Who knows how long she might be out here? Cracking the code on that phone just might help pass the time if this current stakeout went deep into the night. She looked over at Bennett's urn still strapped into the front passenger seat. "Sorry, babe. I can't tell you whether we got him or not."

She caressed the top of the ossuary and gave it a tap before bringing her hands back to her lap. She looked straight ahead through the windshield and watched people walk into and out of the ER. Only one other ambulance arrived in the ensuing hour. It seemed to be a relatively quiet night. She saw a security guard walking through the parking lot an hour into her stakeout. But he was glued to his phone, seemingly in conversation with someone through his earbuds. He passed by the Malibu without so much as noticing Cecelia sitting inside. Perhaps having Bennett along was indeed her lucky charm—his spirit protecting her against detection by the police. Or maybe the Malibu had some version of an invisibility cloak, shrouding Cecelia from the eyes of the law. She shook her head and exhaled. No, the Malibu was not magically concealed. After all, wasn't Bennett apprehended in this very car at the rest stop off Route 65 outside of Pine Bluff?

She looked out the driver's side window, away from her husband's urn. She ran her fingers through her auburn hair and slowly rubbed her neck. Something pulled her gaze back toward the urn. Who else had sat in that seat, the one occupied by Bennett's ashes right now? She never asked him for a name or an explanation, and she never read a copy of the police report that accompanied his arrest. She didn't have the courage to challenge her husband then and wasn't about to confront him now.

Her nose began to twitch. She had been sensitive to unfamiliar odors from a young age. There wasn't anything noisome in the car now as she sat in the hospital parking lot, but in her mind, she remembered those distinctive smells from years ago. Before racing to the police station to post bail for Bennett, Cecelia had to retrieve his car from the impound lot. Her best friend, Trish, had given Cecelia a lift to the edge of town, where she paid the exorbitant recovery fee to retrieve their car. Now, her twitching nose could still detect the scents from back then—aromas that aroused feelings in her groin just as they apparently affected Bennett the same way, too. There was the scent of male sweat—musky, leathery and strong. This one was similar to, yet distinct from, that of her own man; the masculine smell assaulting her nostrils in that impound lot belonged to someone else.

But there was another odor wafting toward her nose back then, an aroma she had often inhaled through her own nose and tasted on her tongue. It was a uniquely pungent yet enticing combination of aspirin and bleach that Bennett had shot all over her face the first time they had sex. How could she ever forget that smell? And why did the family car reek of it when she retrieved the Malibu from the impound lot? She couldn't answer the question back then and refused to try and answer it now. The past was the past, and she'd tried to expel from her mind the thoughts of whatever or whomever Bennett had done. And even though he had taken the car to be detailed and scrubbed the very next morning, she could still sense that pungent aroma every time she stepped into that car since. Cecelia shook her head and rolled down the window to let in a breeze of fresh air.

* * *

After two hours of waiting, she noticed a car round the corner into the lot rather fast and pulled quickly into a parking spot before the driver—a woman—jumped out. Despite the lateness and darkness of the hour, the parking lot was well-lit. Cecelia watched as the woman ran toward her and then as the woman's purse got temporarily caught on the Malibu's side mirror. Cecelia had seen that face before and recognized it within seconds. She first saw Ginny Fischer in a Minnesota courtroom. Ginny had made it obvious that she was Corey's mother, what with her fawning over him at the defense table during breaks in the proceedings and reaching out for his hand or offering hugs at seemingly every opportunity. She had also seen Ginny's face during the investigation into finding Corey's whereabouts. She found Ginny's photo in two places—the online picture directory for St. Bridget's Parish in Pepin and the mortuary website in a collage of photos accompanying the obituary for Corey's father, Frank. Ginny's sudden presence here meant that Corey, or at least his body, was still inside. And the fact that Ginny rushed like a spawning trout upstream meant that Corey was most likely still alive. The woman probably wouldn't race into the hospital just to look at a corpse.

"Look, Bennett. It's the mother. The bad news is, we didn't already kill him. The good news is, now we know that he's inside with mommy."

* * *

Another two hours went by without another sign of either Corey or his mom. Cecelia's stomach growled, and her heavy eyelids cried out for sleep. Suddenly, her hopes ascended. She sat up in her car seat upon seeing Corey and Ginny emerge from the emergency room doors. Ginny seemed to be practically carrying her son, supporting his torso with her arms and guiding him back toward Ginny's car. Cecelia reached into her purse and withdrew her gun. Here, in the remote and near-empty parking lot, justice would be served at last. She didn't care about the bright overhead street lamps. No one was there to witness the kill, and she'd already confirmed there were no security cameras in the lot. All she had to do was jump out of her car as they passed by, shoot Corey in the heart and the groin, then escape undetected and begin the long trek back toward Julia and start their brand-new life.

Suddenly, a uniformed officer emerged from the ER and ran toward Cecelia's car. She ducked down in her seat right before he passed. Then she raised her head and turned to peer through the rear window. The officer reached Ginny and Corey and accompanied the pair all the way to Ginny's car. Cecelia didn't have the nerve to confront a presumably armed lawman, too.

"Shit. This queen is one lucky son of a bitch, Bennett."

Patience, patience, she heard Bennett say. *He can't hide forever, darlin'. Just follow him until the time is right. We'll get him. We'll get him! Now, follow the mother. She'll lead us to our next chance to kill the son.*

Cecelia turned back toward the front. She splashed some water from a new bottle onto her face and used her shirt sleeve to wipe the droplets from her skin. She started the Malibu, then waited for Ginny's car to move out from its spot, and then the sheriff's car, too. The unexpected presence of the sheriff's vehicle made the pursuit both easier and more fraught with risk. She followed the two cars at a distance as they drove away from the hospital and then north onto the 405. The cars ultimately led Cecelia to a missing piece of her puzzle—either Corey's or Ginny's residence in Santa Monica—most likely the latter. As Ginny steered her car into the underground garage, the gate closed quickly behind, and the sheriff's vehicle pulled to the curb and idled outside the complex.

Cecelia frantically searched for an inconspicuous place to park. Not seeing one, she pulled in front of a fire hydrant down the street. No one would be checking this time of night, and the sheriff's car seemed to be hovering at the building's entrance, so he likely wouldn't venture up the street on foot. She gazed at the nondescript three-story building and knew that Corey and Ginny were somewhere inside. Yet she didn't know which apartment, and the complex had at least a dozen units. She desperately wanted to exit her car and walk to the locked front gate. She pictured herself perusing a list of last names adjacent to a column of labeled squares, searching for Flanagan or Fischer. She would press any button other than that one, or alternatively, all of them, hoping someone might absentmindedly buzz her in. Then, she would walk inconspicuously through the building, straining to hear Corey's distinctive voice through one of the doors. But she discarded the idea. She had already pressed her luck on the pier and then by stalking him at the hospital. Why risk detection by the sheriff hovering like a hawk just outside the main door?

Cecelia waited for an hour, but the sheriff's vehicle didn't move. It was now three o'clock in the morning. Hunger tempted her to make a run for late-night fast food, but vengeance kept her in place. She opened another water bottle and sipped on it until it was drained. Then, she used a plastic garbage bag to relieve her bladder. By four o'clock Saturday morning, she figured neither Ginny nor Corey would be coming outside for at least the next several hours. And her furtive plan to gain entry via an ignorant neighbor wouldn't work this late at night. So, she started the Malibu's engine and drove back toward her motel in Inglewood.

She stopped at an all-night McDonald's drive-thru after exiting the 405 and ordered the largest meal on the menu. While waiting for her food, she turned the car radio to a twenty-four-hour news station and heard a voice say, *"One man has been killed and another injured."* She quickly turned up the volume. *"The incident happened at the Hermosa Beach Pier late Friday evening. The police are still searching for the shooter, and the public is asked to contact the Hermosa Beach Police Department with any information that might help apprehend those responsible."*

One man has been killed. Obviously, that had to be Miguel. It made sense now why he wasn't with Corey and Ginny as they exited the hospital hours ago. Cecelia's bullet had missed its intended mark and struck down a man she cared nothing about. Prior to today, she didn't know he existed. Prior to tonight, she didn't even know his name. Miguel—clearly a spic and probably illegal at that. Who besides Corey would even care that he was gone? And as for Corey's feelings, she felt vindication, not shame. Fuck him. If Corey indeed cared about Miguel, then it was a bonus that Miguel had been shot down. Corey needed to suffer, just as Cecelia and Julia had suffered. He would finally know the kind of pain that they did.

She brought the food back with her to the motel, then showered, packed and ate. She planned to check out of the motel for good after a couple hours of sleep. Then, she would return to Santa Monica. There was little to no chance Corey was going anywhere in the wee hours of the night. A new day held far more promise. Perhaps the sheriff would deem the location safe and depart. Regardless, Corey had to emerge at some point. And she would be there ready to follow him, to find the place to finish the task she had attempted the night before, a task that she had been planning for seven long months.

Chapter 7

Soon after she moved to California, Ginny selected four of Corey's paintings to hang in her apartment, arranging the artwork in a four-block pattern—the earliest on the upper left and the most recent at the lower right. Each piece was a gift from Corey at key milestones across the years. In addition to their commonality as gifts, the four paintings also revealed a progression in Corey's craft, starting with the first one produced when he was thirteen. Each time these gifts were bestowed, she asked him whether the piece had subtle meaning. Yet his answer to that question at age forty-five was the same one he provided as a boy, words he learned from that influential first instructor. *The meaning of any artwork is in the eye of the beholder. The artist's message will become clear once the piece is studied long enough.*

Now, after returning from Torrance Memorial in the middle of the night, Ginny ushered Corey up three flights of stairs and into her sublet apartment, then closed and locked the door. The air inside smelled stale, and he watched her open the kitchen window. She helped Corey remove his shoes and sweatshirt and directed him toward the living room recliner.

"Here, sit for a minute. I'll run you a warm bath. Can I get you anything to eat?"

"No, but tea would be nice."

"Take a look at the far wall. You might recognize some of the artwork."

Corey sunk into the upholstered chair and stared straight ahead. It was the first time he'd been to his mother's apartment since he helped move her in. He looked at his artwork hanging in a collage pattern on the opposite wall. He knew what his mother was doing—trying to distract him from his pain and loss. He recalled it was a tactic she often used when Corey was a boy—forcing Corey to look at something positive amidst the surrounding darkness. Back then, the darkness was Corey's abusive father. Today's darkness seemed many times worse.

In the upper left-hand corner, he recognized his portrayal of a man seated in a red leather booth inside a diner. There were menus on the table, a cash register on the front counter and a pass-through food window off to one side. A *Slippery Sam's Cafe* sign hung on the wall behind. In front of the man was a bowl with colorless contents. Only Corey knew it was filled with soup. A row of windows appeared to the man's left, a jukebox on his right and tables full of patrons filled the cafe behind the man's back. Bold colors defined the man's head—hair dark as coal and ruddy skin redder than pink in hue. His cheek rested comfortably upon folded hands supported by a pair of elbows placed at the table's rim. The first artwork's point of view was painted from directly ahead of the man as if the artist were sitting directly across the same table. But the man's gaze was to his right, seemingly oblivious to the artist in his presence. Instead, his eyes locked upon a woman standing at a table full of customers with only her backside visible in the painting. She held a pen in her only detectable hand and wore dull, salmon-colored clothing with a white waistband and matching bandeau. Anyone who knew Corey—including his mom—would recognize the man in the painting as Frank. Corey had presented this painting to Ginny as a gift when she turned thirty-two.

On the upper right hung a painting Corey created in college. Ginny had unwrapped this one in 1992, a Christmas gift presented after dinner and before heading to St. Bridget's for midnight mass. Ginny had told him more than once that this was her favorite among all of Corey's work, crafted in a surrealist style with muted colors that Ginny said she had never encountered before that solemn night. The piece intrigued viewers with its bizarre portrayal of a familiar scene—a little brown cabin surrounded by a coniferous forest with smoke rising from its chimney and frost blanketing the ground. It was, of course, the Fischer family cabin, the one Ginny inherited when Frank passed and sold three years later. Neither she nor Corey had any affinity for the place when Frank was alive, and neither of them wanted to visit there again after he died.

Deep within the depicted forest stood a hunter adorned in orange vestments half-hidden behind a fat, fallen pine and wearing an exaggerated look on his face. A dark round hole to the left of the collapsed conifer suggested where the once-tall pine was yanked from the spot it had likely rested for decades. The man's head extended beyond the dead log's bottom, his hands hugging a large, exposed root and his eyes open wide and fixed upon a deer stand within the canopy of a nearby oak. Atop that roost stood an immature buck with short, fuzzy stubs protruding from the crown of his brown head. The sheer lunacy of a deer in the trees and a hunter on the ground made Ginny laugh back then. Corey remembered her asking him about the menacing look covering the deer's face and about why the barrel of a shotgun extended out from its nimble arms. The buck stood firmly on its two hind legs, the front ones freakishly holding the rifle aimed at the hunter's peeking head. Corey provided no clue as to its intended message. *The meaning of any artwork is in the eye of the beholder. The artist's message will become clear once the piece is studied long enough.*

The piece on the lower left depicted a landscape and had been a gift to Ginny before Corey moved to California almost four years ago. At the center of the work, a series of bluffs towered above a wide river valley, their wooded hillsides covered in browns, greens and white. A lone man sat in a canoe halfway across the broad river. Ginny surely recognized the setting—the unmistakable vista from the lower end of Lake Pepin, looking across the Mississippi toward the bluffs of Minnesota. The images were cast in faint yet identifiable detail, consistent with Corey's impressionist phase. Light blues with spots of white filled the sky, varying shades of gray fell upon the river below and a mixture of browns with flashes of red and white birds completed the landscape in between. Corey remembered that he had created several pieces near this same setting in 2014, during the year he lived with his mother in Pepin between the end of his relationship with Nick and the beginning of his life in LA. Two of those other pieces from this phase flashed through his mind now in particular—the boy in the treetops staring across the lake toward St. Bridget's and the image of Jeff Olson in a boat with his granddaughter during a storm, a real-life scene Corey had witnessed while standing next to Ginny at a wayside rest.

The final piece hanging on the lower right was something Corey hand-delivered to Ginny on the day she moved in three weeks ago—a gift celebrating her decision to move west. In contrast to the other pieces, for this one, Corey had revealed a tantalizing hint of the artists' intent. *Life demands growth,* he told her. *We should honor our progress as human beings, no matter how long it takes.* In the center of the work stood a man facing the ocean, his arms spread wide like Christ at Golgotha. A brilliant, setting sun shone in the distance, obscuring whether the man was naked or simply wearing a flesh-colored cloth around his waist. Behind the man stood three figures several yards away. A dark-skinned man stood on one end with a blonde-haired one on the other. In between, locked arm in arm with them, was a woman—shorter and clearly older than her companions, with the back of her head painted gray turning white. Ginny could surely identify the three people in the painting. As for the man at the focal point of the piece, she should know his identity, too. The man stood on the edge of the sea with its uneven, rocky coast. Directly in front of him was a round opening in the rugged shoreline filled with blue water and faint light streaming in from a secondary, submerged opening in the porous rock.

Corey heard Ginny enter the living room and set a steaming cup of tea on the end table next to Corey's chair. His eyes were still fixed on the paintings, but he detected a whiff of chamomile.

"Do you like how I've arranged your paintings?"

"They're your paintings now, Mom. I gave them to you."

"Of course. I only meant that you painted them. They're all beautiful, Corey, even more so hanging together than when I received them one by one."

"Thank you."

"But now that they're together, I've noticed a few things."

"Oh?" He turned to face her, then lifted the cup of tea from the table between them and took a short sip.

"Yes. Each piece is distinctly different in style, setting and skill level. Yet they have similarities as well. Each canvas is about the same size, and each piece clearly has its own innate meaning or source of inspiration."

"True."

"Once they were hung, I also noticed that each painting contains a dark hole near its focal point." Ginny rose from her chair and walked closer to the array of art, a cup of tea firmly in her grasp. With her free hand, Ginny reached out to the first painting of the diner and placed her left index finger directly onto the canvas, feeling the contours of the perfectly round black bowl, circling that aspect of the artwork with her finger, and feeling the emptiness of that colorless pit. "Here."

Corey looked at the spot she pointed at.

"Now, look at these." She turned to the other three paintings, one by one, and did the same. She ran her finger over the crater where the pine tree uprooted, over the rounded cave hidden beneath the towering river bluffs, and then across the cavity in the rocks at the edge of the sea where the man in the fourth painting appeared ready to dive into its chilly depths. She took a step back. Both of them beheld the four paintings once more, with Corey summoning to his conscious mind the concealed meanings within the uncanny dark holes.

"Virtually identical," Ginny said as she turned to face Corey, who remained sitting in his chair and facing the wall.

"Perhaps," he said softly, "but one of them is different."

She turned to look again at each painting. "Oh, my goodness. The last one—the chasm in the rock in front of the man."

He rose and walked over to join her by the wall.

"This one is the most recent. I'm guessing that you painted it sometime this summer, a summer that was probably the happiest stretch of time for you that I can remember. The hole in this ocean cliff is the only one not painted black. Instead, it looks as if there's light inside the depression along the rocks shining through an unseen point of entry and mixing with the dark seawater to create a warmer hue. It looks a lot more hopeful than pitch black like the others. If I had to guess, I'd say the color is midnight blue?"

* * *

After saying goodnight to his mother and toweling off following a hot bath, Corey settled into the guest bedroom and shut the door. The twin bed had large, soft pillows and far too many blankets for a warm summer night. He crawled under the covers wearing the borrowed boxers he'd received at the hospital. He would ask Ginny to take him shopping for clothes sometime on Saturday afternoon if the police continued to advise him not to go home to retrieve his own. He turned off the bedside lamp and took several deep breaths.

Soon after falling asleep, Corey dreamt. A police officer stepped forward to the edge of his hospital bed. He felt a chill run across his body at the sound of the officer's deep voice. *We're going to need you to come down to the station, Mr. Fischer.* Then, Corey was whisked away in a squad car and found himself inside a windowless room, a room he had seen before while being interrogated back in Wisconsin in the wake of crashing his car into a ditch after swerving to avoid hitting a deer. There was nothing to look at in the room aside from Corey's own reflection in the two-way mirror. He was offered black coffee but instead asked for tea.

The generic labeled tea bag they brought him held a bitter mix of leaves that tasted as though they'd been imprisoned in their wrapping since long before Corey was born.

When an officer eventually did enter the room, it turned out to be the same stern detective as before—Barron County Sheriff Todd Coles. Coles wasted no time in getting to the point. *So, you and this Mr. Diaz were lovers? How did you meet? Did you often get upset with him? Tell me about that big fight you had, the one where he almost dumped you last year? Are you a jealous type of person, Corey? Did Miguel ever cheat on you, or you on him?*

Coles was relentless, even denying Corey's plea for a restroom break or to call a lawyer. *Why were you walking on the pier? What proof do you have of being followed? Tell me more about this alleged woman. How come no one else remembers seeing her? If she was after you, as you contend, why was it Miguel who died instead of you?* The rapid-fire badgering continued. *We know about your record of prior assaults. Tell me again why you shot your lover, Nick? And how did you escape prosecution for that crime? Then you shot Bennett later that same night after sexually assaulting him at a truck stop? But you got Larry Preston to step forward and claim responsibility? And now you allege that the widow of the man you killed is the one who shot Miguel, though as far as we know, the two of them never met? Who in their right mind would believe this, Corey? Who could believe anything you have to say?*

He awoke breathless, the bed damp with sweat. His mind raced in multiple directions as he struggled to determine what was real, what was nightmare, and which was actually worse. The truth of his reality came flooding back to his mind. The pier, the proposal, the woman with the gun. Miguel pulling Corey over the ledge and dropping thirty feet into the sea. Finding each other in the dark, cold water, then clinging to the crustacean-laden pylon. The blood, the rescue, the emergency vehicles, the hospital. Weeping in his mother's arms upon hearing the news of Miguel's death. Yes, all of this had happened exactly as he remembered it, and precisely as he recounted the story to every person who asked, including his mother and the empathetic detectives at the hospital, but not the callous, accusatory one conjured up inside Corey's dream. He considered his surroundings and felt a deep thirst. The room was small. The bed atop which he lay was a trundle, mostly serving as a place for Ginny to sit and watch TV. There was an alarm clock on the nightstand that read three o'clock, but no water bottle as he'd hoped.

Corey heard a noise in the hall and tensed up. It sounded faintly like someone turning a doorknob ever so gently and attempting to remain undetected. His heartbeat accelerated. Had the sheriff left them alone? If Cecelia had been able to find him once, couldn't she find him again? She must have made her way into the apartment and come to finish the job she started last night. He scanned the room for a weapon, something he could use to blunt the impending assault. Underneath the nightstand, he noticed a basket full of yarn and partially knit creations. A ball of powder blue string lay pierced with a pair of needles. Corey crept from the bed with soft yet fleet steps. He grabbed the knitting needles and then proceeded toward the edge of his closed bedroom door. He bent his ear toward the crack in the frame, straining to hear what his assailant was doing so he could act quickly to save his mother and himself. Footsteps approached along the carpeted hall. He took two shallow breaths, twisted the knob and pulled the door open before rushing into the dark hall. Someone was several feet in front of him, though he couldn't see who it was. The moonlight shining through the shears and doorway of the room from which he had escaped fell upon Corey's backside, casting a six-foot-tall shadow toward the person in the hall.

"Corey!"

He held the needles high above his head, ready to strike. But his mother's familiar voice, despite its suddenly piercing shriek, forced him to halt the attempted stabbing mid-air.

"What on Earth?"

His hand fell to his side and the needles to the carpeted floor. He took in and then released a giant breath, the first one he had inhaled since emerging from the bedroom.

"Mom, you scared me."

"I scared you? I was only going to the bathroom. And then suddenly, you burst through the door and nearly stabbed me. What..." Ginny didn't complete the thought. Instead, she paused before saying more. "Here." She re-tightened the belt on her robe and reached out with one arm to embrace and redirect her son.

"No, Mom. I'm fine." Corey abruptly turned toward the guestroom, walked inside and slammed the door. He offered neither an apology nor an explanation. He said nothing to his mother at all. Once inside the guest bedroom, he remembered having dropped the knitting needles to the floor but wasn't about to grab them now. He would wait until Ginny returned to her room. Instead, Corey collapsed on top of the bed face down, buried his face into the pillow and released a hoarse, muted scream. A few moments later, he turned toward the window opposite the bed. Moonlight streamed into the room. He felt more exhausted than he could ever remember, yet sleep wasn't likely after the violence from last night, the terrible nightmare that recently woke him and then almost stabbing his own mother in the hall. Agitation, fear and post-traumatic stress raged throughout his veins, his heartbeat elevated from the influx of so much adrenaline over the past few hours, and his mind a constant hamster on a wheel—going over and over again what had gone wrong, not only tonight but across all the years of his life.

At that moment, Corey thought of his best friend, Billy—the only one besides Miguel or Ginny who had the magic ability to calm him in times like this. The alarm clock on the nightstand read 3:10 a.m. That meant it was just after five o'clock in Minneapolis, still too early to call. Without his cell phone, he couldn't send a text. And even if he could, how would he possibly reduce everything he wanted to say into less than a screen full of words? Instead, he rested his head once again on the pillow, his throat still parched. He swallowed two gulps of spit. In two more hours, if he were still awake, he would call Billy on Ginny's phone and fill him in then.

Chapter 8

After sleeping late and enjoying a quick coffee on the back patio, Billy and Rebecca drove east to Saint Paul. It was a beautiful late Saturday morning, the midwestern skies half-filled with cumulus clouds and a breeze moving the white masses eastward at a slow pace. Humidity seeped into the air; not much by Minnesota standards, but certainly less dry than what Billy had grown accustomed to out west. They arrived, parked, and entered the sprawling market. Rebecca dictated a shopping list as they walked—tomatoes, basil, salad fixings, garlic and onions. She had promised Billy a home-cooked Neapolitan meal. He laughed now remembering his own earlier reply. "Pizza yesterday and pasta tonight? For a Korean-born gal, you sure like to *cucinare Italiano*!" Not that he was complaining. Billy's fervor for eating good Italian cooking was as deep as Rebecca's desire to prepare it. Besides, he was no more Etruscan than her. His family had descended from Scots and Swedes.

Rebecca bumped into a client halfway down the first aisle and offered introductions. "Billy, this is Mike. Mike, Billy." The client shook Billy's hand and then requested a moment to talk shop with Rebecca, to step away and help him solve an urgent business matter. Rebecca asked Billy if he wouldn't mind going on ahead. He approved with a shrug of his shoulders and a brief kiss in response to her imploring stare, then continued along the produce aisle alone. First, he picked up a semi-ripened tomato. Rebecca had urged him to choose slightly red ones, with a hint of green still visible through the skin. He selected several more, paid cash and received the paper bag while thanking the vendor, who smiled wide. He walked on to the next set of produce stands in the middle of the farmers' market. For Billy, the long rows of stalls bounded by a light rail stop, the Saints' baseball stadium and a pair of old warehouses converted to condos were like a fairy tale from his youth, triggering a series of simple, happy memories from his Midwestern childhood attending farmers' markets with his mom. After purchasing a cucumber, lettuce greens and sweet onions for the salad, he circled back to the spot where he had left Rebecca ten minutes earlier. She was still engaged with her client—speaking toward Mike with wild arm motions. Though he was too far away to hear the conversation, Billy smiled at the familiar passion in Rebecca's non-verbal gestures.

He continued walking toward the bread truck and joined the long line. He jumped with fright the moment Rebecca grabbed him without warning from behind and whispered into his ear. "Is that a cucumber you're holding or are you just happy to see me?"

He turned around, kissed her on the lips and said, "Take me home, and you'll find out."

She laughed. "Sorry about that interruption, but thank you for getting our stuff. My client sure is an interesting guy—a self-made millionaire, though you'd hardly know it. Mike drives a beat-up old car—a 2003 Lexus, I think—and says that his favorite grocery store is Sam's Club, due to the discounts, of course. He'll open his wallet wide for family and close friends, however. He apparently loves taking people out for fine dining and craft beer—people other than his lawyer, that is. Every time he and I have lunch, he pleads comparative poverty. *You're buying, Rebecca. You damn lawyers have more money than God*, he always says. Not that he isn't right."

Billy shook his head and laughed. "How'd he make his money?"

"Get this. He buys and sells vinyl. Up there in his sweet penthouse condo." Rebecca pointed skyward and to Billy's left. "He apparently had the foresight that most others didn't. All those years while you and I dumped our albums and bought CDs, this guy purchased every piece of mint-condition vinyl he could find. Now he sells them online all over the world, and he's making a fortune. That's what we were discussing—his increasingly global reach. Mike wants me to help him establish a shell company in the Caymans to avoid paying U.S. income tax on his international sales."

"Sounds smart."

"It is. So is he. Rich, handsome and smart—not a bad combination."

"Now, if you can only convince him to buy his lawyer a decent lunch."

Rebecca smiled. "Not to worry. I intend to bill him double for that ten-minute chat. You know, weekend legal rates and all. Plus a surcharge for on-the-spot advice."

Billy laughed. "Sounds like you two are a perfect pair—the savvy, rich client and his bloodsucking lawyer."

They reached the front of the bread line and purchased a baguette. Afterward, they ordered lattes and found a place to sit and watch the crowd from a bench in Mears Park.

"Speaking of legal matters, we need to talk about the lawsuit against your father's estate."

"Yeah. I was waiting for you to bring that up. Not that I can afford your Saturday rates, but it needs to be discussed."

"You already know I'm doing this one *pro bono*. Your family is getting the best damn legal advice in Minnesota for free."

"Nothing in life is free, darling."

Rebecca uttered a nervous laugh. "Anyway, here's where we're at. Your deposition is set for Monday morning. By the way, the Jacksons' lawyer expressed his appreciation for you coming here rather than all of us going to LA."

"Well, I had other reasons to visit Minneapolis." He winked. "So, any chance that my goodwill might convince them to settle low?

"Don't count on it."

Billy nodded his head with a contorted half-frown. "So, what's he going to ask me?"

"We'll go over all of that tomorrow during our prep session. I asked my colleague Joe Palka to act the part of opposing counsel when we role-play the depo. Joe's a tough questioner. If you can handle him, you'll have no problems with Cecelia's cupcake lawyer on Monday."

"Great."

"Anyway, high-level, in addition to your deposition, they have ones scheduled for your mom, the manager at Pepin State Bank and your sister. On their side, my main target is Cecelia. I don't plan on deposing her daughter, even though she's a co-plaintiff. I don't see any sense in that."

"Hmmm. Will Cecelia be present to listen in at my deposition? I know hers is scheduled for the following day."

"Apparently not. I got a call from her lawyer late Friday while you were in flight. He asked if we could postpone Cecelia's deposition for two weeks. I pressed him for a reason, but he was evasive. He mentioned receiving a cryptic voice message that she needed to reschedule. It was only after I threatened to cancel your depo and move it to California that he confided he hadn't been able to reach his client all week. He even apparently tried tracking her down through her mother, who said that Cecelia had left her daughter with the grandma and took off with some friends, saying she'd be back in a week or so."

"That's odd. Do you believe him?"

"Who knows? Ron Hillstrom isn't the sharpest or most ethical lawyer in town, but this case is worth half a million dollars, and he nets thirty percent. Why be evasive now on the cusp of his big payday?"

Billy had heard this steep number a week earlier after reading the plaintiffs' expert disclosure. Larry Preston's estate was barely worth that much, including the value of the home in which Billy's mother still lived.

"I can guess what you're thinking," Rebecca said. "It's a lot of money. But remember, that's at the high end. We've got plenty of evidence yet to evaluate before we get to a realistic number."

"I know, I know. But, if Cecelia stands to collect a substantial sum of money, why flee and avoid her deposition, assuming Hillstrom's playing it straight?"

"Your guess is as good as mine. He did seem genuinely surprised at having to cancel her deposition. And the story about him calling Cecelia's mother sounded legit."

"Fine by me. The longer she drags this out, the more time we'll have to find the money. I do my best to keep Mom out of those worries, but it's on her mind—my siblings' too."

"I know, Billy. The demand is high, but trust me—I'll do everything I can to minimize the pain."

"I do trust you and am confident you're doing everything in your legal powers to help."

"Yes, and possibly some illegal ones, too."

Billy raised his eyebrows and cocked his head.

"I initially wasn't going to tell you about that. I wanted to shield you from having knowledge about a questionable tactic I'm using in this case."

"And that is?"

"I hired a private eye. He's, um, searching a particular house down in Arkansas this weekend." Rebecca then told Billy about Charlie Moore and what she hoped to gain. He listened quietly, suppressing the desire to say and ask more while they were in public.

When she finished talking about the Pine Bluff reconnaissance mission, Rebecca set her paper coffee cup down on the bench and reached out to hold Billy's free hand with both of hers. "I'm sorry you all have to go through this, especially in light of the fact that Larry played absolutely no role in Bennett Jackson's death."

"You mean other than confessing to the killing?"

"Well, there is that. But you know what I mean."

"I know. Corey's the one who should be paying the literal price if anyone."

"Yeah, I guess. But he didn't murder Bennett. It was an accident. Well, if we believe him, that is. You do believe him, don't you?"

"Of course, but that's not the point. He killed a man, and it was Corey's unforced errors that set the whole damn scene in motion. We wouldn't be having this conversation if he had acted like a rational person in the first place."

Rebecca continued holding Billy's hand and gave it a tight squeeze. He knew she was limited in what she could say. After all, Rebecca had been Corey's criminal defense lawyer and learned things from him back then that she probably couldn't share with Billy, or anyone, now. Yes, the Prestons were aware of the potential conflict of interest and had waived it so Rebecca could represent them. But her duty of confidentiality to Corey remained.

* * *

On Saturday morning, while Billy and Rebecca were at the market, Corey awoke in a strange bed. He could hear his mother fussing in the kitchen down the hall, but she might as well have been miles away. In the moment, Corey felt as if he were totally and utterly alone. His heart yearned for Miguel. Yet he knew the cold and bitter truth—he would never again hear that voice or feel that smooth, brown skin. And he would never be able to tell Miguel yes—yes, of course Corey would marry him. That failure—his inability to answer until it was too late for Miguel to hear—would likely remain the single biggest regret in Corey's life. He replayed in his mind once again the happier events from the night before—the home-cooked dinner, espressos by the beach and the moment Miguel asked Corey a question that some only hear once in their lives, if they hear it proposed at all.

A soft knock on the bedroom door interrupted his thoughts.

"Corey, are you awake?"

"Yeah, Mom. Just getting up."

She opened the door a few inches and pushed her head inside. "I made some food. Are you hungry?"

He wasn't. But then he remembered how she showed up for him last night in his most desperate hour, like she had been there for him almost every time he needed her in his life.

"Sure, I'll be right out."

While appreciating his mother's care and generosity, Corey yearned to be in his own place. Ginny's apartment, though sufficient and safe, wasn't truly hers. She had sublet the flat from her friend Elizabeth, who in turn had leased it for the past twenty-five years. In effect, then, Corey was borrowing space in a twice-borrowed apartment. He was as far from something permanent as an astronaut circling the moon. He put on the same borrowed clothes from last night and headed toward the kitchen. Ginny had made fresh-baked banana bread and a mixed-fruit salad. She also made them each a cup of English Breakfast tea. Corey sat down, sipped his tea and ate some fruit. They exchanged few words. Following the silent breakfast, he showered and then asked to borrow her car. His Mini was still in Hermosa. Corey needed to go for a drive—by himself. He promised Ginny that he wouldn't go to his apartment without first calling the police to confirm it was safe. In return, he reminded her to lock the door and not answer it for strangers. He knew he was being overcautious. There was no chance Cecelia knew where Ginny lived. And in a city of five million people, it would be nearly impossible for her to find out. But better to be safe than sorry.

He set out on Montana Avenue and made his way north on 26th toward San Vicente. From there, he turned left and drove toward the sea. It felt like a soothing route on which to begin his unplanned journey, those massive Kaffirboom Coral trees majestically and symmetrically lining San Vicente's median every few feet, all the way to the ocean. At the end of that stretch, he turned the car down the steep winding lanes into the Palisades, returning to the oceanfront where Entrada meets Highway 1. Here, he was forced to decide. He could drive north past Topanga into Malibu and on toward Point Dume, an endless stretch of scenic highway squeezed into the narrow gap between the Santa Monica Mountains and the Pacific. Alternatively, he could drive south, back into the heart of the LA basin and toward all the awful events that had opened a gigantic hole in his heart the night before, the events away from which he desired to take flight. Yet, he knew there was no escape, regardless of which direction he might turn. What happened could not be undone. This was a loss he would bear forever. This was a pain he would feel in his soul for as long as Miguel's memory lived on. This was the new reality Corey must live with for the rest of his natural life.

He turned left toward the city. He needed more than merely an escape; he needed a modicum of peace. And he needed something that reminded him of Miguel. There was nothing like that in Ginny's apartment, and he was forbidden by the police from going home. The only other place holding memories was his cell phone, which was lost last night. He suddenly thought of the one place he might feel closer to Miguel. He felt his front pocket to double-check for the keys to Miguel's apartment. They were among the few items that the hospital staff had found in Miguel's pocket—personal effects they handed to Corey once Miguel died, with Maria's permission. He steered his mother's car onto PCH before merging onto the 10 freeway and then connecting to the 405 South. The drive toward Miguel's apartment in Torrance would take no longer than twenty minutes. He calculated the chance of Cecelia knowing where Miguel lived to be small. If she were still in the area and looking for Corey, she would be staking out his apartment or perhaps the frame shop where he worked. She couldn't possibly know where Miguel resided, could she?

Cecelia Jackson. At the thought of her, Corey pounded the steering wheel with his open palm. How did he not see it coming—that she would pursue him and inflict the same fate Corey had exacted upon her? Hadn't Billy warned him a month or more ago that Cecelia and her lawyer were posing questions about Corey's whereabouts as part of the wrongful death suit?

Billy. Corey's thoughts segued to his best friend. In every single crisis to this point in Corey's life, the first person to whom he turned had been Billy. This time around, Corey had taken his time. He felt no desire to share last night's tragic story with anyone, not even directly with his mom. It was the nurse who had provided

Ginny with initial details of the violence on the pier. The rest Ginny learned by listening as he gave the detectives a chronological account. And, of course, she was there with him to hear the news of Miguel's death in real time from Asha. But now he felt compelled to share what happened with Billy. He decided he would call him from Miguel's apartment this afternoon.

* * *

He pushed the key into the lock and let himself into the apartment. The mid-morning sunshine illuminated the main room, so he didn't turn on any lights. He closed the door behind him, leaned against it and exhaled. He shook his head back and forth and pursed his lips, thinking back to yesterday evening when he had arrived at this same spot for their anniversary dinner. One the one hand, it was less than twenty-four hours ago. And yet, it was now also an expired lifetime in between. He walked into the apartment, not exactly sure why he was here. Something had drawn him to this place, perhaps to feel closer to his beloved or maybe for the guarantee of silence. He looked around the rooms with a different lens today, noticing things he had taken for granted or ignored on previous visits. A silver-framed photo of Miguel and his sister on the living room bookshelf. The stained spot of carpet beneath the bedroom window where last winter's storm damage remained unrepaired. The near-constant hum of traffic filtering in from Crenshaw Boulevard through single-pane windows in the second bedroom.

His thoughts traveled to the now pointless question of whether he would have been happy moving into this apartment with Miguel. They had only talked briefly about the idea of cohabitating. But if they had become engaged, a decision on where to live would have been the next obvious choice. Corey's backyard cottage in Hermosa was too small; it barely fit Corey's meager belongings and substantial collection of artwork and supplies. Indeed, the discussion on future joint housing would have focused on only two choices—Corey moving in with Miguel, or the two of them finding someplace brand new. But *had they become engaged* was past tense and conditional. Where the two of them might make a future home no longer mattered. It would never come to pass. He walked into the kitchen and opened the refrigerator door. For the first time since Miguel's proposal on the pier the night before, Corey smiled. On the top shelf of the fridge sat the covered plastic storage container holding leftovers from their anniversary meal. He remembered the delicious taste of Miguel's cooking, and his gut felt instantly warm. Those thoughts didn't make him cry, though. Instead, they brought him joy—a memory he could embrace forever. He closed the door and turned to survey the rest of the kitchen. It dawned on him that Maria would eventually come here to sort through and dispose of Miguel's things. But that wouldn't happen for some time. For now, she was in Houston making arrangements from afar.

That thought gave Corey purpose. He set about to clean the apartment—washing the kitchen counters, scrubbing the neglected bathroom fixtures, and vacuuming the carpeted floors. When Maria did arrive here in the coming weeks, she would find an immaculate space. When he deemed the effort complete, he walked over to the sofa and collapsed. He lay there for a few minutes before sitting up. Certainly, he would come here again when Maria arrived in town. But today may be the only time he would ever be in the apartment alone. He breathed deeply, detecting the faint scent he attributed to Miguel. He felt a sudden need to capture and keep it. He walked into the bedroom and stepped inside the walk-in closet. This space smelled exactly like Miguel. His clothes, his deodorant, his cologne—everything that Corey's olfactory sensors associated with Miguel was present in this closet. It triggered a thought. Corey needed that scent near him. He also needed a few pairs of clothes to carry him over until the cops would let him back into his apartment or Ginny took him shopping. He reached up and pulled down a duffel bag from the shelf and carefully packed it with two pairs of jeans and a few shirts. Thank God that Corey and Miguel were roughly the same size. After packing the items into the duffel, Corey spied the familiar portrait unwrapped and leaning against the bedroom wall, one of the gifts he gave to Miguel last night. It was the depiction of Miguel's mother. Maria would surely want to take the painting home with her to Texas once Miguel's apartment was emptied of his possessions and the physical evidence of his short life finally erased or dispersed. And Corey would be happy for her to have it.

Chapter 9

Rebecca finished chopping garlic and added it to the pot on the stove. The tomato-based sauce would simmer for the afternoon before she paired it with fresh-made pasta from an Italian deli near the farmer's market in Saint Paul. Rebecca and Billy had arrived home a few hours earlier, having stopped for a salad and champagne lunch on the way back to Minneapolis. Billy stood at the threshold to the kitchen, watching as Rebecca stirred the contents of the pot and stared down inside as if the concoction held deep secrets.

"You still scheming about how to arrange that Cayman shell company for Mike? Perhaps a trip down there with your male suitor might help the cause?"

Rebecca looked up at him and smiled. "I wish. No, I'm still thinking about my conversation yesterday with Cecelia's lawyer. I don't know. Something he said felt strange."

"How so?"

"Well, in addition to postponing the depo for Cecelia, he told me that his client wants to depose Corey as well, so he needed Corey's home and work addresses."

"Corey? What for?"

"Good question. To me, it makes no sense. If Corey corroborated the story from Larry's affidavit, it adds nothing to their case. At best, Corey would reinforce the lie that Larry caused Bennett's death and confirm that Bennett was the aggressor, forcing Larry to act in self-defense. If we go to trial, a jury might find Corey sympathetic and reduce or deny any award to the plaintiffs."

"So then, why take his testimony?"

"I asked Hillstrom that same question. He said something about Cecelia wanting more from this case than money. She wants justice. She wants the truth. Her lawyer basically admitted that she's the one pushing for Corey's deposition, not him. I mean, the lawyer knows that his case is already rock solid—a confession on the record that your father caused Bennett's death."

"But if Corey tells the truth, that upends her case against my father's estate, right? Who knows, maybe she thinks Corey has deeper pockets than we do?" Billy shrugged his shoulders.

"I don't think so. Hillstrom was candid. He basically told me this was Cecelia's request and that he tried to dissuade her because Corey was judgment-proof. So, they generally understand his finances. And they know he lives in California but need an address where they can serve him notice."

They walked outside to the patio with a decanter of chianti and sat down. Billy poured them each a glass of wine. The cell phone in his pocket buzzed. It buzzed again every three seconds until he reached down and withdrew the phone.

"Huh. It's Miguel. Mind if I take it?"

"No, not at all. In fact, I need to call the private investigator and get an update on what he found in Pine Bluff."

* * *

Corey felt rested after his brief nap on Miguel's sofa. He had hardly slept last night, either before or after the nightmare. Both his body and mind were spent. He checked his watch—almost three o'clock in the afternoon. It was time to get back to Santa Monica. He would call Ginny before he left Torrance so she wouldn't worry. But he had a more difficult call to place first. He would rather have that conversation with Billy from here, in private, rather than where Ginny would be forced to hear the awful saga once more. He reached for the cordless phone sitting atop the end table and dialed Billy's cell phone. After a half-dozen rings, Billy answered.

"Miguel! How's it going? I can't wait to hear about last night."

For a moment, Corey felt disoriented and didn't respond.

"Miguel? You there?"

At the second mention of Miguel's name, things suddenly made sense. But the reference to *last night*? What did Billy know about last night?

"Miguel?"

"It's me, Billy. Corey. I'm at Miguel's apartment."

"Hey, man. Good to hear your voice. I left you a message and sent at least three texts. I'm guessing you've been too busy to respond?"

Billy's playful demeanor couldn't be more different from Corey's muted replies.

"Listen, Billy. I've got some really bad news."

* * *

While Corey told Billy what happened in slow and gruesome detail, Rebecca listened quietly on her cell phone to a report from Charlie Moore. They each sat in an Adirondack chair on the back patio with cell phones stuck to their ears. Billy stared at Rebecca as he listened to Corey in disbelief. Rebecca stared back, listening to Charlie's tale of Bennett's homosexual past. Rebecca seemed to be conveying to Billy with her eyes the same message he wanted to tell her—*oh my God, you are not going to believe this*.

Her call with Charlie ended first. Billy continued listening on his phone while maintaining eye contact with Rebecca. She mouthed a question. *Is that really Miguel?*

Billy slowly shook his head, no.

Is it Corey? she mouthed next.

Billy shook his head, yes.

She graduated to a whisper. "I need to speak with him. It's important. It's about Cecelia."

The mention of Cecelia's name caught Billy by surprise. Corey had just finished saying her name.

"Corey, can you hold on a second? Rebecca's here and has something to say." He moved the phone to his chest to shield his whispered conversation with Rebecca from Corey. With the briefest of details, he told her about the shooting on the pier and the fact that Miguel was dead.

"Oh my God. But Corey's still in danger. I just learned things from the private investigator that make me sick. Here," she said while motioning toward Billy's chest. "Put him on speaker."

Billy pulled the phone away from his body, hit the speakerphone button and set it down on the table between his chair and Rebecca's.

"Corey?" Rebecca's voice was harried.

"I'm here."

"Where are you?"

"At Miguel's apartment. Why?"

"Okay, listen up. I need you to get out of there."

"Rebecca? What's going on?"

"I am so sorry for your loss. Billy told me what happened. I can't fucking believe it."

Corey's heart pumped hard and fast inside his chest.

"How sure are you that it was Cecelia who shot at you and Miguel?"

"One thousand percent. I'm not sure if the police believe me, but there's no doubt."

Rebecca then told him how she had hired a private investigator to clandestinely find dirt on Cecelia for use against her in the case.

"Corey, are you there?"

"Yes. Keep going."

"Okay. I need to tell you some things that will be upsetting. I know that sounds impossible, given what you've been through already, but I'm quite serious. Cecelia has been stalking you, researching every possible angle—where you live and where your friends and family live. She even has a piece of your artwork hanging on her wall."

"What the hell? Why? Which one?"

"I don't know. The private eye is sending me the photos right now. Cecelia also knows the location of the Fischer family cabin up in Barron County."

"How..." Corey's voice trailed off. He didn't even know what questions were relevant anymore.

"Unfortunately, there's more. It appears that she's been gone for some time. The investigator says there's no sign that anyone's been home for days."

"Your guy was inside her house? How?"

"Yes. The *how* isn't important. What matters is what he discovered. Cecelia Jackson is obsessed with you, Corey. And she is clearly intent on exacting revenge."

The words coming from Rebecca's voice strained belief. And yet, Corey knew they were true. He had seen the look in Cecelia's eyes on the pier. He heard the crack of the gunshot aimed at his head. He felt the weight of her error as he remembered the image of Miguel's body last night.

"Is your mom with you?"

"No, she's at her apartment in Santa Monica. Why?" His hands began to tremble. He gripped the phone tighter.

"Damn." Rebecca's voice faded away. Corey could picture her face in his mind. He had experienced this same interaction several times when she defended him in the criminal case last year. Her voice would trail off as the wheels of thought in her mind accelerated. She was processing, calculating and planning what to do or say next.

"Rebecca," Corey shouted. "Tell me what to do!"

"Okay, let's both take a breath. According to the private eye, Cecelia did not have your mom's address posted to her cork board, so it's likely she doesn't know where Ginny lives." Rebecca paused, then continued. "But that doesn't mean she hasn't discovered it since. From what the investigator described, this woman is meticulous and cunning. And she's intent on doing you harm as well as anyone else who gets in her way."

They were quiet for several awkward seconds. Finally, Rebecca said, "Listen. Here's what I want you to do. Call your mom as soon as you hang up with me and tell her to keep the door locked and have her prepare to leave. Then, drive to her place, both of you get in a cab and go directly to LAX."

"LAX? Why?"

"You're coming here, both of you. Billy's going to call the airlines now and get you two on the next flight to Minneapolis." Rebecca cast a hard nod in Billy's direction. "You need to get as far away from LA as possible and be with people who can protect you, who love you. Cecelia won't think to look for you here, and it'll give the police time to apprehend her."

He heard Rebecca whisper something to Billy and then Billy's voice in the background saying, "Got it."

"Corey, I'm going to hang up with you now and call the Hermosa Beach Police. What's the name of the detective working your case?" He couldn't remember. "That's fine. I'll figure it out and tell him everything I've learned and about your plans to leave town. After that, I'm going to call Cecelia's fucking lawyer."

"Okay."

"Call us once you get to the airport, and of course, any time before that if you have questions. And for God's sake, be careful. There's no telling what this woman might do or where she might be."

They ended the call. Corey bolted up from the sofa and did a quick visual scan of the room. He left the vacuum where it stood, still plugged into the wall. He walked to the front door and then looked behind him to make sure he hadn't forgotten anything vital. He made a conscious decision not to take out the trash in the interest of time but did think of one thing he wanted. He walked into the kitchen, opened the refrigerator door, and grabbed the leftovers from last night's meal, the flavorful final dish Miguel cooked for Corey or for anyone ever again.

* * *

Cecelia sat in her car, parked outside Ginny's apartment. Thankfully, the sheriff's car had disappeared sometime since she left at 4:00 a.m. She'd been watching the building for a couple of hours now, and there had been no sign of Corey or his mom. One or both had to come out eventually, right? They may or may not have enough food to get by for a few days, but at some point, Corey would need to get clothes or a toothbrush. And he'd eventually need to go out to satisfy his insatiable sexual hunger, she figured. A predator like Corey couldn't go long without seducing yet another man.

She saw a Yellow Cab pull up to the building's front door and wait. No one came out. After several minutes, she pulled Corey's cell phone out of her purse and looked randomly back and forth between the device and the taxicab. She also retrieved a page of notes that held key information from her months-long investigation into the life of Corey Flanagan, information she thought might lead her to him. She entered three different combinations of numbers into the phone, wary of eclipsing the limit of ten failed passcode attempts and thereby locking the phone for good. She had already wasted two tries last night. She noticed a piece of white tape on the backside of the device, with an address written on top—4100 18th Street Hermosa Beach. She had seen other people affix their home addresses onto their devices back in Arkansas as a means of recovery in case the device was lost. She entered the six digits from the tape—410018. No dice. Next, she entered 040474, Corey's birthdate, and then tried his mother's—102653. Both attempts failed to open the device. She decided to give it a rest and think harder before making the final five tries without the phone locking for good.

* * *

Corey exited the freeway at Cloverdale and made his way via side streets to Ginny's apartment, well above the posted speed limits. He nearly ran into the back of a pickup truck stopped at the light on Olympic Boulevard because his eyes were moving rapidly between windows and the rear and side view mirrors. Scanning the streets for potential danger felt pointless. He had no idea what kind of vehicle Cecelia might be in and whether she was alone at the wheel or in the passenger seat while an accomplice drove.

As he neared Ginny's apartment, he purposefully parked two blocks away and walked along the alleyways, avoiding a direct approach from the front. Through a hedge of bushes, he saw a Yellow Cab parked in front of the building. He whispered a silent prayer of gratitude that his mother had followed the short, shocking directions he'd given her during a brief call twenty minutes earlier from Miguel's apartment. He met her at the building's back door, and they entered the lobby. Inside, he confirmed his mother's lifetime record of being both attentive and thorough—she'd packed a bag for herself, precisely as he'd requested. After looking out the front window and seeing nothing of alarm, Ginny and Corey walked briskly out the main door of the building and dropped into the backseat of the cab. The taxi drove away from the side of the street and moved without incident toward the freeway and then on toward LAX.

* * *

Cecelia Jackson watched helplessly as Corey and Ginny emerged from the apartment building and rushed into the backseat of the waiting cab. She cursed herself for not suspecting that the Yellow Cab had been their planned getaway. With the sheriff's car long gone, Cecelia could've moved in closer but didn't. She wouldn't make that mistake again. She started the Malibu, gunned the engine, and pulled away from the curb before completing an illegal U-turn in the middle of the street. She caught up to the cab as it entered the 10 Freeway East.

* * *

Ginny and Corey exited the cab beneath the Delta sign at Terminal 2 after Ginny handed fifty bucks to the driver and told him to keep the change. Cecelia's Malibu approached belatedly after getting caught behind a car rental shuttle bus that merged in between her and the cab at Terminal 1. She stopped at the curb where Corey and Ginny had alighted several seconds before, only to see them through the clear glass doors as Ginny flashed her phone to a security guard who allowed both mother and son to pass behind well-guarded lines filled with travelers. Cecelia grabbed her phone and typed information furiously into a search engine. At this late hour, there were only a few remaining flights departing from Terminal 2. All of them were on Delta, and only three destinations were left—Atlanta, Salt Lake City and the Twin Cities of Minneapolis and Saint Paul.

* * *

At Ginny's urging, Corey sat by the window while she took the one on the aisle. There was no one seated in between. Corey looked out the window as the plane took off over the ocean before eventually turning east. It was then that Corey's stomach fell. He remembered what he had unwittingly left behind. The leftovers from the previous night's anniversary dinner must still be in their plastic covering in the back seat of his mother's car parked on a random Santa Monica street. It was a meal that would now spoil and never be eaten. The hot weather and elapse of time would inflict their punishment, leaving behind little more than a rotten smell. But that was beyond his control now. *At least I was able to savor Miguel's fine cooking when it was fresh*, he reflected. *That was satisfying enough.*

He felt his mother's eyes staring at him, but he didn't look back to see if that was true. Ginny, of course, couldn't read minds, but she certainly knew how to read her only son. He imagined her pitying him there in his airplane seat, thinking about these past twenty-four hours. His life had been ripped apart, and the man Corey should have married was now lying in a morgue. From the corner of his eye, he saw Ginny reach for her purse resting on the empty middle seat. He subtly looked to his right and saw her pull out her phone, open the photos application and scroll rather fast. He recognized the ones she finally stopped at—photos taken on the night Ginny arrived in California. After a tiring day of unpacking boxes at the new apartment, Ginny had treated Corey and Miguel to dinner. He remembered how happy they all were on that night a few weeks ago. Ginny interrupted Corey's daydream with a gentle nudge to his arm. She handed him her phone, urging him to take it. He did. Then, he stared at the photo she had pulled up on the screen—a picture of Corey and Miguel outside the restaurant, standing beneath a pair of palm trees, looking alive and happy and free.

* * *

After watching Corey escape into LAX, Cecelia drove to a nearby Fatburger and ate for the first time that day. She needed to fuel her body and figure out what to do next, to somehow confirm her suspicion that Corey and his mom were headed to Minnesota. After ordering food, she opted to eat inside and take advantage of the free Wi-Fi. She checked her own device and accounts first but saw nothing immediately important. Next, she took Corey's cell phone from her purse and once again opened the home screen. She only had five chances left to crack the passcode but figured what the hell. She needed a lucky break, and this was about her only avenue left. Besides, what was the point of saving her final attempts until later? She needed the information right now. She gazed at her investigatory notes once more and decided to try something new. She typed the abbreviated address of Corey's best friend, Billy, where she had first spotted Corey on Friday afternoon. 144012. No good. She looked again at her notes. She remembered making a brand-new handwritten entry last night after learning where Miguel lived. She tried the digits associated with that—1974482. Nada.

She had three chances left. After that, she'd either have to charm a clerk at Best Buy to unlock the phone for her or give up altogether. She tried the first six digits associated with the phone number of Corey's former lover, Nick—612729. "Damn," she muttered under her breath. "That was a stupid guess." Two chances remained. She looked again at her newest notes and entered the numbers and letters from Miguel's license plate—633487. The screen simply vibrated and wouldn't let her in. She set the phone down and bit into her burger. She ate the rest of it while studying every note on the unfolded page in front of her. The answer had to be in here somewhere, she thought. "Think, Cecelia, think!"

One item on the page caught her attention, for it was wildly different from all the rest. It was the rural route number for the Fischer family cabin in Wisconsin, the site of Corey's first attempted murder back when he tried to kill his partner, Nick. *Criminals always return to the scene of the crime*, she recalled. *Maybe Corey's secret number was a chilling and sadistic joke about that day, the same day when Corey killed Bennett.* She doubted it would work, but it was the only idea she had left. She entered 184033 and suppressed an emerging scream when she saw the phone light up. She touched the Google Mail app and looked at the emails popping up on the screen. The third one down was from Corey's Delta Airlines account, confirming he was booked on a flight from LAX to MSP.

Now she knew for certain where he was headed, though her glee was tempered by the fact that she didn't know where he might go after arriving in Minneapolis. No matter. She'd have plenty of time to think about solving that riddle. She punched in Minneapolis to the Maps app on her own device. Nineteen hundred miles. She figured she could cover that ground in a little more than two days if she got a head start tonight. It was far less risky than booking a flight and showing her ID at security. She ate the last of her fries and refilled her soda at the self-serve station, then returned to her car, started the engine and began her long journey north and east.

Part 2: Midwest

Chapter 10

Corey walked into the Mall of America at eleven o'clock on Sunday morning, the very minute the doors opened to the public. Ginny, Billy and Rebecca followed behind. Corey suggested that he come to the mall alone so that the others could enjoy a quiet day at Rebecca's. But they wouldn't hear of it. Each of them insisted that they had things to shop for, too, though Corey knew the truth—all three were worried about him being on his own so soon. He acquiesced and let the trio follow him like the parents of a toddler as Corey shopped for clothes and a new phone.

Contrary to his hope that the foursome might split up to shop alone or in pairs once inside, he was followed into every store. He tolerated their fawning praise at each pair of pants or shirt he selected, knowing they were trying to be kind even though it bugged him to have them hovering. At the electronics store, tensions boiled over. Rebecca suggested he upgrade to the latest model. Billy insisted he get the extended warranty. Ginny questioned him as to how the helpful store clerk would be able to transfer the data from Corey's lost phone to a new one. And each of them had different advice about which color phone he should buy.

"Enough," he finally snapped. "I can handle this. I'll meet you at the mall entrance in an hour." He then turned to the clerk to complete the necessary steps, not wanting to look upon the shocked faces of his loved ones.

"Will you be trading in an old phone today?"

He explained that the old one was lost. Then, after confirming his mother was out of earshot, Corey repeated her question about how to retrieve information from his old device.

"No worries. If you stored everything in the Cloud, we'll download the data onto your new phone. But anything new since the latest Cloud upload can't be retrieved, sorry. The good news, though, is that if you find that old phone and it's still functioning, you can use it just like an iPad. If you're connected to Wi-Fi, you can still access all your apps." Corey nodded his head. "Now, I just need you to enter a secure passcode, and then I can finish up."

The clerk handed the phone to Corey. He thought for a moment, then punched in the same code he used to have. It was the one sequence of numbers he could never forget, representing the address of the Fischer family cabin in Wisconsin. He finished at the store and walked back into the mall. He found an empty bench and sat down. Fifteen minutes remained before the agreed-upon time to meet. He wished he'd told them to meet in two hours instead. He looked at his new device and confirmed again that all the old apps showed up on the screen, but he wasn't in the mood to explore them right now. Instead, he leaned against the back of the bench and watched the bustling crowd of shoppers pass by. He didn't see anyone he knew, which was no surprise. He'd left Minnesota without warning four years ago and hardly looked back. Other than that fateful trip last year, he had not stepped foot in Minnesota after moving away, and he only kept in touch with one person from his old Midwestern life—Carol.

He thought about her now. Wouldn't seeing her be a relief? Carol had always been a bright spot in his otherwise heavy life. If he couldn't get time alone, maybe seeing Carol was the next best thing. He felt bad wanting to escape from Billy, Rebecca and his mom. Really, they were only trying to help. Ever since arriving here last night, they provided repeated expressions of sympathy, with each of them often asking what he needed and inquiring how he was holding up. Yet, Corey perceived their expressions of love like a late-season snowfall—quietly heavy and relentless, blanketing the ground with soothing layers while simultaneously suffocating an expectant spring. He needed to get away from them, if only for a few hours. He reopened the new phone and sent Carol a long text message, giving her the briefest of updates and asking if they could meet and talk about anything other than his woes. He then texted his boss and his landlord, letting them know he would be out of town for at least another week. Then, he closed the phone screen and headed toward the meeting spot.

* * *

Later that day, Corey pulled on the heavy metal door and inhaled the warehouse's familiar aromas—rusted metals, damp stones and timbers soaked in creosote. Those smells brought him instant comfort and a flood of memories from the eight years he worked and breathed here. Once inside, he entered another set of hefty doors and climbed the wooden stairs, with these scents assaulting him like the pheromones of a long-lost lover. He wore an unexpected yet genuine smile, grateful that Carol had suggested meeting here. His feelings and emotions from the past three days were all of one theme—morose, lost, frightened, empty and sad. Since the moment he learned of Miguel's death, he struggled to muster happy thoughts. It was as if Corey were buried deep at Calvary, his capacity for a moment of happiness only rising on this, the third day, in the presence of Carol's sunny disposition.

He exited the broad stairwell on the third floor and then walked toward the fourth door on the left. How many times had he made this same mindless trek? The answer was more than he could count, and every single one of them a small journey, a temporary escape from the rest of his long-ago, tumultuous life. Today's visit was different from all those near-daily sessions when Corey had come here to think, to exhale and mostly to create art. Today was more akin to the time spent here nine months ago—to see the studio of its now-solo occupant, his longtime friend and almost lover, Carol. They texted and called one another every month or so since their reunion last year, and Corey felt warm at the prospect of seeing Carol once more.

"Hey there!" She practically leapt through the doorway and into the hall, throwing her arms around his upper body and squeezing him tight. The unexpected assault left him breathless. "I saw you through the window, exiting the Uber." She released him from the bear hug but kept hold of his shoulders and looked him in the eye. A faint smile adorned his face. Carol's initially wide smile soon faded to match his subdued one.

"Corey, I'm so sorry for your loss. But I'm glad you came."

"Thanks, Carol. Seeing you is exactly what I needed. You're a welcome refuge."

"Come on, let's go inside."

He entered the studio as Carol pulled the hulking door shut behind them.

"Tea? Something stronger?"

He turned to face her and caught that inimitable glint in her eye before she winked. Corey recalled his last visit here in 2018—while awaiting trial and staying with Nick—when he and Carol sat on the studio's sofa and shared cups of tea and a relaxing joint.

"Tea would be lovely," he said. He watched as Carol walked toward the combination utility room and kitchen. He took a seat on the studio's well-worn sofa. She returned less than a minute later and handed him a cup of tea.

"Here you go." She then pulled a white bag from behind her back and waved it gently in the air. "Maybe you'd like one of these, too?"

"Oh my God. Are those Bogart's? I haven't had their dough-nuts since before I moved to California."

"I recall you were fond of them."

"What, because one or the other of us stopped there on the way to work at the museum practically every day?"

"Mmmm, sounds about right. I got your favorite—Brown Butter Glazed." She reached in and pulled out a soft, sugary doughnut and handed it to Corey on a napkin. He immediately took a large bite. A barely discernible "thank you" emerged from his pastry-filled mouth.

"You're welcome."

He swallowed the bite of dough and sipped his tea, which tempered the sweetness of the doughnut. "Seriously, thank you. Not just for the pastry itself, but for anticipating my needs."

"Of course. As they say, what are friends for?"

"No, I mean it. You knew I needed a happy distraction and found one. I appreciate that."

She smiled in return before grabbing a doughnut for herself, sitting down, and taking a bite. Carol sipped her tea while Corey savored his treat.

"So, let's talk about art or whatever you want. Heck, now that you're back in Minnesota, we should do what everyone here does 365 days of the year—talk about the weather."

Corey laughed, then said, "Let's stick with art."

"Tell me everything. Last time we talked, you were still fixated on landscapes?"

"Um, yes and no. I think I finally mastered the painting of Malaga Cove. It took forty attempts, but I stopped trying two months ago. That last effort seemed to capture the sunlight and sea spray against the earth-toned colors of the cliffs. Or, at least, as well as I can."

"Nice. Did you submit that one into any shows or competitions?"

"I did, at Miguel's urging, of course. He thinks that every one of them is a masterpiece."

"That's sweet, Corey. I really wish I could have met him. I'm so sorry for your loss."

He nodded his head and accepted the sympathy but wanted to talk about something else.

"Yeah, he was always supportive, but I never think my work is good enough."

"You don't give yourself proper credit. Why do we do that to ourselves?"

"I don't know. I used to think it was because we were around such masterful works of art all day at the museum. I mean, how could anything we create measure up?"

"And now?"

"I guess I view it differently. Could be a new self-confidence or maybe just my perfectionism shining through. You know that feeling. If we give it one more try at the pottery wheel or on the canvas, that will be the *pièce de résistance*, the one for which we win a Silver Lion at the Venice Bienalle."

Carol's smile communicated recognition. "You're talented, Corey. Believe it. So, what's next, another landscape?"

"Probably not. I've lost motivation for that. In fact, I seem to have lost inspiration for my next phase of art altogether, even before Friday night."

"That's natural. No need to push yourself, but also don't let it throw you off your path. Painting is your passion. You're good at it."

"I guess. I've thought about returning to portraits or something with more detail than landscapes. You know, like capturing the wrinkles of someone's face or the slight upward turn of lips at the edge of a smile. I want to create something more personal than panoramic landscapes."

"Not to be a downer, but you had a portrait phase already, remember? I suppose you could do it again, maybe in a different genre? Perhaps realism rather than the abstract ones you mastered years ago?"

"Hmmm. That's an option. But I need to get inspired before starting out."

"Or maybe you should return to the basics—discover hidden passions that have been suppressed all along."

Corey set his chin into the open palm of his left hand, his fingers pointed toward the ceiling and clutching his cheek. He looked down at the cooling cup of tea, then up at Carol. Maybe she was onto something. She did know him better than most. Or at least she knew his artistic mind better than the rest. "Definitely food for thought."

"Hey, do you remember the artist Chuck Close?"

"Of course, he's world-renowned. What, are you going to tell me that his work reminds you of mine?"

"No, but his story does, in a way. I mean, the guy knew he wanted to be a painter from a young age. He also overcame multiple disabilities as well as the early death of his father."

That last reference initiated a tiny tremor in Corey's gut. He realized that throughout the entire ordeal of the past three days, he hadn't spared any thought for Frank. He had dwelled upon other losses of the past few years—Larry, Miguel's mom and a co-worker at the frame shop—but not once about the man who conceived him, the same man whose early death triggered a spiraling series of events and choices both good and bad.

"And?"

"And Chuck Close found ways to reinvent himself as an artist in the wake of personal tragedy, at times when he needed to jumpstart his inspiration."

"To be fair, in this hypothetical comparison, Close was paralyzed from the neck down following a seizure, if I recall. He literally had to strap a paintbrush to his wrist. My loss is emotional. There's nothing physically impairing my ability to create."

"That's not the comparison I was talking about. Although," Carol said, staring off toward her shelves of art books, "that paralysis did happen to him at about the same age you are now." She shook her head subtly and looked again toward Corey. "But I'm talking about what happened earlier in his life."

"Remind me."

"Let me look it up to get my story straight." She stood and walked over to the bookshelf, perusing its objects briefly before grabbing a thick, hardcover book and walking back to the sofa. She sat down and thumbed through the volume, then halted at a particular page and smiled. "Here. *Although Close was known for his skillful brushwork, he hit a plateau early in his career. So, he chose to make painting hard for himself, to force an artistic breakthrough by throwing away his tools.*"

"I don't remember that. You must've had a better art history teacher than I did."

"It's not history, Corey. The guy's still alive. This is from an interview he did in 2009."

"So, how did he paint if he had no brushes?"

"Well, first, he turned to photography and experimented by building images in grayscale from a griddled photo. Later, he would apply oil-based paint. In essence, he created paintings that appeared to be photographs. And the everyday nature of his subject matter worked to secure the paintings as super-realism."

"Okay, that rings a bell. He would place grids on both the photo and the canvas, right? And then he created paintings cell by cell, copying to the canvas what he saw in each grid of the photograph?"

"Exactly. And, again, he did this by abandoning traditional tools, opting instead for airbrushes, rags, razor blades and an eraser mounted atop a power drill."

"That's right." Corey motioned toward the large book in Carol's lap. "Let me see."

She handed it to him. He perused the pages filled with both words and snapshots of Chuck Close's more famous works. "It says here that his first paintings in this style were all derived from a single black and white photo of a female nude, which he copied onto the canvas and painted in color."

"Yes, that's true." Carol's voice indicated that she had more to say but didn't. He moved his eyes up from the book toward her with an inquisitive look, noticing a familiar expression on her face that he had seen many times before but not in nearly five years—a look of germinating ideas like when they were brainstorming how to display museum exhibits back when they worked together at the Minneapolis Institute of Art. The conversation moved on, and teacups were refilled.

Carol walked Corey around the studio, showing him her latest pieces, both finished and those still in process. The time passed with Corey's mind lost in a comforting conversation. He noticed how Carol often touched him in ways that Miguel did, mostly on the arm and when she was either excited to show him something new or to laugh at a shared memory. This afternoon reminded him how much he missed spending time with her. He had yet to find someone in California to fill that same space in his life. There was Billy, of course, and Miguel. But they were men and played different roles in his life, both in comparison to each other and in contrast to Carol.

"Corey, I need to ask for two favors."

"Of course. You name it."

"First, I need you to come back here tomorrow. Are you free?" The tone in her voice suggested mystery.

"Sure, I guess. What do you have in mind?"

"I've got an idea on how to re-inspire your art."

"Sounds good to me. What's the second favor?'

"I'd like you to call Nick."

Corey responded with his eyes in a look that mirrored the voice in his head—*hell no.*

"Trust me on this. He knows what happened to Miguel. I called him right after you texted me. He'd really like to talk to you but is hesitant to reach out."

"Carol, I'm not sure about that. I don't need any more expressions of sympathy, and especially not from him."

"I don't think that's the point I'm trying to make here, Corey. Surely you remember who Nick is? He's not exactly a master of thoughtfulness and empathy."

"You're right about that," he laughed. "Then what would be the point of calling him?"

"Like I said, I'm asking for a favor here. It's not about Nick helping you but about you doing something for him. Believe me, you'll be glad you did."

Chapter 11

At dinner time on Sunday, Cecelia pulled into a truck stop on the edge of Salt Lake City. She had stopped outside Sacramento to replace her Arkansas license plate with a stolen one from a shopping mall parking lot. After the nine-hour journey from northern California, she desperately wanted to drive on, to reach Minneapolis as soon as possible. But once again, fatigue and hunger stopped her. She had eaten nothing but a bag of peanuts and two sticks of beef jerky all day. Needing fuel for herself and her car, she pulled into the huge asphalt-covered lot. She also needed a shower. Her plan upon leaving LA included sleeping in her car. She wanted to avoid unnecessary interaction with people—people who might recognize her. The car was comfortable enough with the stolen pillow and blanket from the motel back in Inglewood, but she would need a shower at a truck stop like this one to freshen up. It was Bennett who gave her the idea. For years, he had told her stories about the benefits of gritty truck stops and the colorful characters he met there. *It's nice having a single place to shit, shave and shop for a meal but also to meet like-minded truckers.*

The irony of now stopping at a truck stop on her own didn't elude her, but the practicality of its offerings urged her on. In addition to evading detection, her motive for avoiding motels involved thrift. She'd brought plenty of cash with her from Arkansas, but that was for an expected one-week trip. Now, who knows how many more days she would need to track down Corey? And then what? Would she drive straight home? The one and only witness to Miguel's killing had been Corey. If she finished him off in the next few days without creating new witnesses, the remainder of her original plan might still work. She'd make sure that the unregistered gun in her purse disappeared for good. And her alibi couldn't be cracked. Cecelia's girlfriends were still at the remote mountain cabin in Tennessee. And they would vouch that she was with them for the entire week, precisely as the three of them had promised.

After showering and eating a hot beef sandwich with mashed potatoes and gravy, she returned to her car. It felt good to be in fresh clothes and fueled up for the next stretch of the drive once she slept for a few hours. Though fatigued, sleep evaded her. She had more investigatory work to do. She reached for Corey's phone once again, noticing that she had three solid bars of Wi-Fi from the truck stop. She typed in the passcode and perused the device for clues as to where he might be going next. She found a helpful email—an e-receipt from the Mall of America Apple Store detailing the cost of Corey's new phone. She turned the device's screen toward the passenger seat. "Look, Bennett, he's still in Minneapolis. Remember how you told me about that giant mall one time?" Other than that, she found nothing useful—no other relevant emails, calendar entries or notes jotted down into the device. She clicked on Venmo to see if Corey had any activity there. He didn't. For a moment, she fantasized about gifting herself some money but remembered that she had planned to leave no electronic footprints.

Out of boredom or curiosity, she opened the photos app. The very first picture was one of Corey and Miguel atop the pier from Friday night. *How strange*, she thought, *I shot and killed someone I didn't even know.* A faint pain rose in her throat. She closed the photos app and returned to text messages again, hoping to find a distraction from those uncomfortable feelings stirred by the photo. Corey's most recent texting conversation had been with someone named Carol, probably the same one Cecelia uncovered in the investigation. Prior to that, there was a long, boring one from Billy to which Corey had not replied. The next one down was from Miguel. Cecelia quickly noticed that Miguel and Corey's final chat wasn't one of words; instead, it was an exchange of naked selfies, both the entirety of their bodies and close-ups of their cocks. She pushed the phone's off button hard and threw it onto the passenger seat next to the urn. A long-suppressed memory of a similar discovery on Bennett's phone took hold in her mind. The pain in her throat sunk down to her stomach, and her head began to throb. *What in the hell was in that hot beef, she thought.* She opened her car door and emptied her stomach. Then wiped her mouth clean, pulled the door shut and lay her head back against the seat to rest.

* * *

Corey fished around his pants pocket for the spare key Rebecca had lent him. He struggled with the aging lock for a moment before putting his shoulder into the heavy wooden door and pushing himself inside. The Minneapolis weather had turned partly cloudy during the hours that Corey had been inside Carol's studio, reminding him how fickle a Minnesota summer could be. He closed the door behind him and removed his jacket and shoes. He stepped into the living room, then walked over and pulled the blinds all the way to the top. He was determined to let as much sunshine pour into the dimly lit space as possible. Then he plopped down into the soft leather sofa. The time with Carol had been gratifying, but he cherished the chance now to sit in silence, secretly hoping that Billy and Ginny were in their respective rooms and would leave him alone for a while. Simone sauntered into the room. Corey patted the sofa cushion next to him, but the cat stopped and sat directly before him instead. A stare-off lasted for several moments before Simone tired of the temporary amusement. She began bathing herself, dropped to the rug and stretched her back and front paws in opposite directions, reaching for the lone ray of sunshine streaming into the house. Corey found himself mimicking the damn cat, stretching his own tired feet atop the coffee table, then reaching his arms into that same beam of fading sunlight and stealing it from the indifferent cat.

He took note of the decor. Boy, he thought, did Rebecca ever need help. He stereotyped his former lawyer as a busy professional on the rise—not rich enough to hire a high-end designer and no time or talent of her own to develop a consistent, elegant style. The black leather sofa was bookended by a pair of chestnut leather chairs. *There are other fabrics*, Corey chastised her in his head. *And what about the use of a pattern—any pattern—rather than solid colors?* What's more, the furniture, wall decorations and accessories were modernist in style. While they exuded a semi-consistent contemporary chic, this was a 1930s craftsman home. He wondered why the image Rebecca projected externally conflicted so acutely with what lay hidden inside. Corey had convinced himself long ago that the degree to which a person's outward portrayal to the world differs from what lies in their core spoke volumes to an inner conflict. It had been true in Corey's own life for decades until he moved west. His immaculate high-end condo with Nick had concealed their untidy relationship. Corey's confidence in leading tour groups through the museum and speaking *sans* notes about art belied his deep insecurities as the creator of his own work. And the fit, muscular physique Corey had crafted after years of running long-distance and eating a near-perfect diet masked mental vulnerabilities so grave that he twice tried to end his own life.

The sound of someone clomping up the basement stairs irritated him slightly; he wanted to stay alone. He assumed that his mom and Billy were in their respective rooms. So, who was downstairs? Perhaps Ginny was checking on Corey, as she had done practically on the hour ever since Miguel died? Whomever it was had reached the top step, the crossroads between the basement, the home's rear door and the kitchen. After hearing glass jars clanking down atop the granite counters, Corey rose from the sofa to investigate. He guessed that Ginny might be about to cook something. The thought made him hungry. The doughnut with Carol had been the day's only food, its empty calories digested hours earlier and leaving his stomach wanting. He was surprised to see Billy in the kitchen instead.

"Hey, what are you doing?"

Billy spun around. "Jesus, man. You scared me. I didn't know you were home."

"Maybe those pods in your ears prevented you from hearing me come through the door?"

"What?"

Corey motioned with each pointer finger toward his own ears and cast Billy a mocking look.

"Oh yeah. Hi there. When did you get home?"

"A few minutes ago. I thought everyone was gone or asleep."

"Rebecca ran to the office and should be home in a couple hours. Listen, I'm sorry about all of us hounding you earlier. You better now, man?"

Corey shook his head, yes. "What are you doing?"

"I want to surprise Rebecca with a home-cooked meal."

"Surprise? I'd say *shock* is more likely, followed by retching and a difficult night's sleep."

Billy threw a kitchen towel at Corey. "Very funny. Get in here and help me then, for Rebecca's sake. You can be my assistant."

Corey laughed while folding the towel, which he had caught mid-air. "All right. What's on the menu?"

Billy showed Corey the recipe in the notes app on his phone. It was a Preston family favorite—rouladen with warm German potato salad and braised asparagus. Corey washed his hands and began slicing red potatoes. As they worked in the kitchen, they alternated between discussing cooking tasks and a general catch-up on their respective afternoons—Billy preparing for his deposition at Rebecca's office and Corey at the studio with Carol. They spoke more quietly than normal, Billy having alerted him that Ginny was napping in the guest room on the other side of the kitchen wall.

"I think Rebecca will be plenty impressed with your culinary skills, man. I sure am. You've never made anything this good for me back home."

"Sorry, but Rebecca earned it. She gives a much better blow-job than I assume you ever could."

Corey laughed. "Is that what it takes to be fed this well at your house? Damn, then I guess it'll continue to be ramen or mac and cheese for me. Unless, of course, you're switching teams?"

He turned away from his potato peeling, expecting to see Billy's inimitable impish grin. But all he saw was a serious face. Billy continued preparing the main course at the counter opposite Corey and didn't laugh at that last joke. He sliced the topside cut of beef thin and began to lay strips of bacon atop the flattened meat before adding gherkins and rolling the creation into its oblong shape fastened together with toothpicks.

"That was a joke, by the way."

"I heard it."

An unusual silence followed. This wasn't like Billy at all. Corey watched him fumble to complete the beef concoction, then brusquely threw the full glass dish into the oven and slammed the door shut. Corey wondered what he had said wrong. Perhaps his joke had gone too far?

"Billy? What's going on?"

"Nothing. What do you mean?"

"I don't know. I thought we were in the middle of our normal back-and-forth jabs. Then you went quiet on me. I was only kidding about you switching teams. You know, finally coming over to the dark side?" Corey tried once more to keep things light.

"I know." At first, Billy faced the wall away from Corey and said no more. But then he turned around and leaned against the counter, staring at the oven's glass door. With the vegetable peeler in one hand and a half-stripped potato in the other, Corey leaned against the opposite counter. He stared at Billy, waiting for eventual eye contact. After an uncomfortable half-minute, Billy's look met his. Billy lifted his palms and mouthed the question, "What?" Then, he stopped and looked momentarily into the backyard through the kitchen window before returning his stare toward Corey. "Let me ask you something." Corey waited for the question, unnerved by Billy's unusual change in demeanor. "All these years since coming out, have you exclusively been with men?"

It was not the question Corey expected. "Um, are you asking if I've had sex with women?"

Billy shrugged his shoulders as a grimace crossed his face, his eyebrows raised up, and his head nodded yes.

"That would be a no. The thought never crossed my mind."

"Well, you did have that thing with Carol. Something sexual went on between you two, right?"

Corey uttered a nervous laugh. "Um, that was like twenty years ago. Before I met Nick and before I knew for certain what I liked." He shook his head as if ridding his mind of cobwebs. "Why are you asking me this now? I mean, for God's sake, three days ago, I was on the verge of marrying a *guy* who I love with all my heart."

Billy's shoulders fell, and he exhaled. A tension that had been building across the galley kitchen dissipated like steam being released from a suddenly opened tea kettle. "I'm sorry, man. I wasn't asking about you. That was insensitive on my part, especially now. I guess I was asking in general. Once someone realizes their true sexual preference, do they ever switch back the other way? Or, I don't know, dabble?"

"Dabble?"

Corey's repetition of that awkward word generated a smile on Billy's face. But the look on Corey's remained contorted. He had no clue what motivated this strange series of questions from his best friend.

"Yeah, do people go back and forth—experiment with being gay even though they're solidly straight? And if they do, does that mean they're unsure of who they really are?"

Corey beheld the man standing before him, a guy he had known since his earliest life memories. He knew Billy and his life story better than anyone else in the world, and the same was true for Billy about him, too. He set the potato and the peeler on the counter, then crossed his arms around his chest

and again waited for Billy's eyes to meet his. "Bill, are you trying to tell me something?"

The look on Billy's face turned toward surprise in less than a
second, then just as quickly to apoplexy. "Oh God, no. I'm not worried about being attracted to guys. You know me—I'm as straight
as they come." He laughed. "I can see why you're wondering,
though, based on what I asked. But no, I'm not gay." A broad smile
emerged on Billy's face. He switched to a deep, mocking voice.
"Not that there's anything wrong with that."

Corey laughed at their oft-used reference to the 90s sitcom
Seinfeld, both at the long-term shared humor and because his
friend seemed to have returned from whatever strange detour
he'd been on.

"Thank God. I'm glad to have the real Billy back."

Chapter 12

On Monday morning, Corey exited the Uber and walked into Stanley's Cafe. The iconic Minneapolis diner had been a staple of Nick and Corey's brunch routine for years when they were together, back in the days when Corey drank. Today, he wondered if Nick was being his typical insensitive self by suggesting this as the place to meet, with its innumerable beer taps and colorful array of liquor. But he quickly cast the thought aside. Corey had learned in recovery long ago to assume positive intent and that others' behaviors didn't control or excuse his own. Nick was seated at a table in the corner and gave an exaggerated wave of both arms as Corey scanned the rest of the room, noticing the paucity of patrons on this mid-week morning at eight o'clock.

"Hey, thanks for meeting me here. You look good." Nick rose from his chair as Corey sat down in his. He wasn't about to give Nick the chance to walk around the table and offer an awkward hug.

"Thanks. You, too."

"I took the liberty of ordering us both coffees."

"Thanks, Nick. And it looks like you remembered how I take it—one pink packet and a splash of cream."

"Oh, I clearly remember how you take it." Nick grinned proudly at the innuendo. Corey laughed weakly, mostly at Nick's unfailing ability to say the most juvenile thing possible. He wondered, too, if Nick was being unexpectedly kind by not ordering his old usual—a breakfast margarita. Or perhaps the bank had clamped down on executives showing up at work with booze on their breath. A waiter came to the table, and they ordered food. Corey's stomach growled at the prospect of once again tasting Stanley's famous blueberry waffles. After the waiter left, a conversation began, with Nick offering seemingly sincere condolences for Corey's terrible loss. Corey shared little of the actual details from last Friday night and even less about Miguel or their life together prior to that. He hesitated to speak Miguel's name in front of Nick; doing so seemed like a betrayal. He did give more detail about Cecelia, though, both what Corey witnessed on the pier and everything that the private investigator had uncovered in Arkansas. He ended his story and then purposefully moved on to something else.

"So, Carol tells me things have been kind of rough for you as well? She didn't provide details but simply said you might appreciate hearing from me."

"Yeah, I do. It's good to see you, Corey. Despite everything that happened between us, I've always considered you my best friend."

Corey took a sip of his coffee, bringing the cup to his lips and letting it linger there longer than normal as he blew on the hot liquid before taking a drink.

"Anyway, the thing is—Evan left me."

Corey set his cup on the table. "I'm sorry to hear that." He instantly wondered whether Evan had returned to the wife he had abandoned in favor of Nick. "What happened?"

"I guess you could say he decided to take a break. So, I'm in a month-to-month rental while he thinks things over at our house." Corey remained silent and took another drink of his coffee while his imploring eyes urged Nick to say more. "Well," Nick continued, "it seems that Evan got upset when he caught me with another guy."

Ah, Corey thought to himself as the voice of Captain Obvious sprang up in his mind. "So, you two didn't have an open relationship? I thought that's what you always wanted."

"Oh, we did," Nick replied before lifting the coffee cup to his lips to take a sip, not offering more details.

Corey cocked his head. "Then, what exactly was the problem?"

Nick glanced out the window, then turned back toward Corey as a cheeky grin formed across his face. "I, uh, guess I forgot to get Evan's buy-in about our relationship being open."

Corey shook his head with a knowing smile. "Yeah, that might be where things went wrong."

They both laughed, and the conversation moved on to less serious topics—Nick's work at the bank, Corey's latest series of paintings and a recap of how each of their respective parents was faring in their golden years. It was once again Nick who ventured toward something heavy.

"So, how long will you be in Minneapolis?"

"I don't know. I guess until the authorities in LA tell us it's safe to go home."

"LA is *home*, huh? That didn't take long."

"Yeah, I suppose it sounds strange, given that I lived here or in Wisconsin for the first forty years of my life."

"No, not really. I get it. That's where you belong, Corey. Maybe Billy was right all along that you should have moved west ages ago."

Corey pursed his lips with a bare smile of satisfaction.

"What else do you have planned while you're here?"

"Not much. I'm headed to the studio after this to work on some art with Carol. Otherwise, just hanging at Rebecca's house with Mom, I guess, and Billy too—at least until this weekend when he flies home."

"Any plans to visit Wisconsin?"

"No. I got enough of that last year before all the chaos ensued."

"What about your new sister?"

Corey had forgotten that Nick knew about Samantha, about how Corey accidentally discovered her that tragic day when he took a self-absorbed detour to Barron County on his way to Pepin.

"I haven't given her any thought, to be honest—at least not in the past few weeks."

"Maybe you should. I mean, you've got time to kill." Nick paused upon seeing Corey grimace. "Sorry, poor choice of words. You know what I meant. If you sit around Rebecca's house, all you'll do is mope."

Corey began to speak but stopped when Nick raised his palm.

"Hear me out. I'm not trying to diminish your grief. It's obviously raw. But I know you, Corey. You're a dweller. You obsess on things. And sitting around wallowing in it while trapped in a strange house will only increase your misery. Why not funnel those feelings into something meaningful?"

Corey folded his hands, then rested his chin atop them. Part of him hated that Nick had made a good point. This man sitting across from him could be cruel and crass and callously self-centered, but sometimes Nick showed flashes of wisdom, too. And Nick clearly knew what made Corey tick as well as or perhaps better than anyone else.

"Hey, here's an idea—I'll drive you there."

"What?"

"Well, someone has to take you, right? I mean, I doubt any rental agency is eager to loan you a car. Aren't you on the *no drive* list after what happened last year?"

"Ha, ha. I do have insurance, though me driving into Barron County is probably a nonstarter. That sheriff made it clear I was never to cause trouble in his jurisdiction again."

"Then I'll take you. I could use a day off from work, and a ride in the country might give me space to clear my head."

"I don't think so, Nick."

"Come on, Corey. It's only a ride. I'll take you there, and you can have your talk with Samantha while I drive around and look at hunting land. My parents sold theirs up north. My brothers and I want to find a new place for ourselves."

Corey tried to picture being with Nick in a car again for that much time. Could it work? Would it end in disaster? Was

Corey out of his mind for contemplating such an insanely un-
thinkable idea?

Nick kept prodding. "I'll buy the coffee and pay for the gas.
You'd be doing me a favor. What do you say?"

"Actually, the idea had crossed my mind. I'll think about it
and text you later."

After they finished eating, Corey pulled out his new phone
and ordered an Uber.

"Whoa, look at you!" said Nick, touching the phone with his
forefinger. "A new phone without paint spots and duct tape holding it together."

"Shut up, you. I got it on Sunday to replace the one I lost in
the shooting. You'll find this odd, but I didn't have a cell phone for
the first three years after moving to LA."

"Oh, I know. Remember how difficult it was for me to track
you down last year?"

A stream of uncomfortable memories raced through Corey's
head. "Yeah, I recall."

"Hey, can I see it?"

Corey slid the phone across the table.

Nick fawned over the enhanced camera and big screen. "Say,
do you have Snapchat? Looks like you don't. I'm going to download it for you."

"What? No, I don't use much social media."

"Trust me, Corey. You're going to need this one."

"Fine." He reluctantly recited the mobile's ID as Nick's thumbs
worked busily on the device.

"It's great for sending photos and messages that you don't
want lingering on your phone. Once you send or receive something, it disappears after being viewed or read. It's brilliant."

"Why would I care about that?" Corey looked on as Nick accessed the App Store and installed Snapchat on the phone.

"I don't mean to be harsh, but you're single again, Corey.
Someday, you may date and swap nudes with a guy. You don't
want those sitting around for someone to discover by accident."

"I assume you're speaking from personal experience?" Corey looked at Nick, shook his head and rolled his eyes.

"Yeah," Nick laughed. "Evan may have stumbled upon a few things I wish he hadn't."

Laughing, Corey said, "You are a piece of work, but thanks for the humorous distraction."

Nick handed the device back to Corey as they prepared to leave. "There, now it's on your phone, and I connected you to your very first Snapchat friend—me. Oh, and you should really clear out your notifications. You've got alerts from both your health app and Venmo."

"Why bother? I never use either one."

They walked outside, ready to part ways. "Thanks, Nick. I appreciate the conversation."

"Ditto. Tell me you'll think hard about going to see Samantha this week?"

Corey bit his lip. "Yeah, I'll consider it."

"Good. And thanks for listening to my relationship woes."

Corey laughed and reached out to meet Nick's outstretched hand. "Sorry, I know it's not funny. Good luck fixing things with Evan."

"Thanks." Nick continued to grip Corey's hand as if he'd never let go.

"I think this is my ride coming up the street. It was nice seeing you, Nick. Friends?"

Nick gave Corey's hand a tighter squeeze. "Sure. With Benefits?" He winked.

Corey shook his head side to side and laughed once again. "Just friends."

Nick laughed in return, then finally let go of Corey's hand. "Okay. I'd like that."

* * *

A few miles upriver, Billy sat alone in a conference room incessantly tapping his foot. He awaited the arrival of a court reporter as well as Cecelia Jackson's lawyer, Ron Hillstrom, while Rebecca was still in her office down the hall. The day before and then again early this morning, Rebecca prepared him. She told him not to be afraid of what opposing counsel might ask but also to be careful not to perjure himself by perpetuating his father's lie. She predicted that Hillstrom would ask no questions about who killed Bennett. The lawyer had a vested interest in maintaining the falsehood of Larry's guilt. Eventually, both attorneys and the court reporter entered the room, and the deposition began.

"Before we begin with the deposition of Mr. Preston, I want to state for the record my objection to your ongoing refusal to produce Mrs. Jackson for hers."

"I told you, Ms. Sayres—my client is on vacation and out of reach. You can depose her once she's back home."

"That's bullshit, counselor, and you know it."

"No, it's not, and no, I don't. I told you on Saturday that she's somewhere in Tennessee. You can't prove otherwise."

"Yes, I can. Corey Flanagan saw your client in California the night she shot and killed his partner, Miguel."

Hillstrom turned to the court reporter. "Turn that damn thing off." She recorded his words verbatim, then stopped typing. "Listen, Rebecca, if you're going to keep badgering me on this ridiculous falsehood, I'm going to call the judge and ask for sanctions. This is a properly noticed deposition, and I'm entitled to proceed. If you have any legitimate evidence to support your defamatory accusations, then produce it. Otherwise, the hearsay of Corey Flanagan—a well-known liar—simply isn't enough."

Rebecca turned and whispered into Billy's ear. "I wanted to see what he'd say when confronted. I honestly don't think he knows anything. Are you okay to proceed?"

Billy shook off his shock at the sharp interchange and nodded yes.

Rebecca looked up at Hillstrom. "Fine, go ahead."

"The court reporter will resume her recording. Now, please state your full name and address for the record."

The court reporter sat to Billy's left, recording every spoken word. Rebecca sat to his right, and Hillstrom stood directly across the table.

"For goodness sakes, sit down, Ron. You are distracting my client."

He kept pacing on his side of the table. "Nothing in the civil code requires me to be seated."

He ambled between ends of the room and began to question Billy sharply.

"Are these accurate copies of the bank records from your father's law business?"

Billy took his time to review each page, exactly as Rebecca had coached him. The family, upon her advice, had designated Billy as the person most knowledgeable about both his father's business and personal estate. As a matter of law, then, Billy was the witness who could authenticate records and answer questions for the defense.

"They are, yes."

"And is this your father's signature upon the quit claim deed filed two days after he signed the affidavit taking responsibility for Bennett Jackson's death?"

"It is."

"Let's talk about those couple of days. I understand your father was being treated at the Mayo Clinic and was admitted for several nights at St. Mary's Hospital. Is that correct?"

"Yes." Billy's answers were crisp and short, exactly as Rebecca had instructed. She glanced over and gave him a barely perceptible, approving nod.

"And during that time, you were staying in the area and spending time with your father in the hospital?"

"Yes."

"But you also made an overnight trip to Pepin, as I understand it. What was the purpose of that visit?"

Rebecca raised her pointer finger along with her voice. "Objection. Attorney-client privilege."

"Nice try, counselor. Even if Larry Preston was his son's lawyer, which I doubt, that privilege only extends to communications. And, then, there's the crime-fraud exception. I'm entitled to explore it."

"Tread carefully, Stinger. I'm giving you very little latitude."

Hillstrom started to reply but stopped. Rebecca had invoked Ron Hillstrom's law school nickname instead of his formal one. It was the same tactic she used to trigger him during their oral advocacy course back at Marquette. He turned his penetrating glare to the witness instead.

"Answer the question."

Billy looked at Rebecca for approval before turning back to Hillstrom. "I drove to my father's law office in downtown Pepin to retrieve something. Well, three things."

"And those were?"

"A handgun wrapped in a canvas bag which was sitting inside the office safe, Corey's medical records and a legal form from Dad's files."

"Was it this document?" Hillstrom showed Billy a State of Wisconsin Quit Claim Deed, a short, standardized legal form whose blanks were filled in with the names of Billy's parents and the legal description for their home in Pepin. "We'll mark this as exhibit A."

"Yes, that was the form, although when I retrieved it, the blanks were yet to be filled in."

"But you helped your father fill in those blanks while he rested in the hospital, correct? When you returned to Rochester the next morning?"

"That's correct."

"And what was your father's state of mind that day when he filled out this form?"

"Objection. Mr. Preston is not a doctor."

"I can still ask the question. This witness is, after all, the person designated by Larry Preston's estate as most knowledgeable about everything to do with this case. I'm entitled to ask him essentially anything in that capacity." Hillstrom waited for Rebecca's reply, but she simply motioned with her hand for him to proceed. He turned his head toward Billy. "Mr. Preston?"

"My father was as sharp that day as he was his entire life. He knew exactly what he was doing. As you know, he signed another important legal document that same morning, an affidavit submitted in court for the case involving Mr. Jackson's death. And in that affidavit, witnessed by my father's doctor as well as a notary and the district attorney, he was deemed to be of perfectly sound mind."

Rebecca cleared her throat and cast Billy a look of disapproval. He had seemingly ignored all her advice in one single answer. He sounded defensive, didn't pause before answering Hillstrom's incendiary question and volunteered more information than the question required. A simple *yes* would have sufficed, but he reacted with emotion, succumbing to the opposing lawyer's trap.

"I happen to agree with you, Mr. Preston. By signing the quit claim deed on his deathbed, thereby transferring ownership of the home away from himself and out of his eventual estate, your father knew exactly what he was doing to my client."

Rebecca objected to Hillstrom's statement, reminding him that this was a deposition and that he should save his spurious arguments for trial. He moved on. By the time they broke for lunch, sweat stained both armpits of Billy's dress shirt. Between Rebecca's glances and the frequent clearing of her throat, he knew that he had messed up.

When the deposition resumed at one o'clock, Hillstrom's questioning took a different turn, away from inquiries about Larry Preston and the estate's finances. Instead, he zeroed in on Corey. Though Rebecca objected on the basis that Billy was a designated witness for the estate of Larry Preston and did not in any way speak for Corey Flanagan, Hillstrom pointed out that Corey had recently been added as a defendant to the lawsuit. As a fact witness, Billy could be asked anything at all about the parties' possible collusion and discoverable assets. On that first part, Billy's answers followed Rebecca's pre-planned script. He himself had no knowledge of anything discussed between Larry and Corey. Billy wasn't present for any conversations between those two men relevant to this case.

"Fine. Let's focus on Corey's resources to the extent you know them. I understand that his father, Frank Fischer, died a few years back and that he sold life insurance for a living. Any idea how much money Corey inherited when his father died?"

"Actually, I do. At least, according to what Corey told me. Nothing. Not a damn thing."

"Oh, Mr. Preston, come on now. Did you forget that you are under oath?"

"Objection. Badgering. Get to the point, Stinger." Rebecca winked at Hillstrom.

"Your client is being untruthful, Ms. Sayres. I'm reminding him of his obligation to tell the truth. We know from Corey's criminal trial that he owned a gun, a gun that he inherited from his father."

"Oh, that." Billy's face grew red. He felt the need to explain his essentially truthful reply—that other than those mocking guns and the cabin, Frank Fischer had cut his only son completely out of the will. "You see..."

Rebecca stopped him. "Wait for counsel to ask you a question."

Hillstrom pounced. "Did you want to clarify your earlier answer, Mr. Preston? Perhaps this time tell us the whole truth and nothing but the truth?"

"Yes. What I meant was, Corey inherited little from his father—only a few hunting rifles and the rustic family cabin up north."

"That would be the property in Barron, Wisconsin?"

"Yes."

"From what I've seen in the county records, the place is more than a *rustic cabin*, as you say. A two-bedroom home with outbuildings set atop forty acres of prime hunting and farming land has got to be worth some money."

Billy began to reply, but Rebecca interrupted. "Don't respond until an actual question has been posed."

"Let me ask you, Mr. Preston. That little game your father played with the family home in Pepin—quit claiming it to your mother to keep it out of his estate and thus out of reach for my client—did your father help Corey do the same thing?"

Billy looked confused. "I'm not sure what you mean."

"Sure you do, Mr. Preston. Let's not pretend here. Did your father help Corey quit claim the Barron County property to his mother?"

"Not that I'm aware of. Corey wanted nothing to do with that cabin after his father's death and especially after what happened there during that fateful last visit with Nick."

"Yes, we know all about those events from the criminal trial. But if Corey inherited that property from his father—property that the county values at over two hundred grand—why is it now titled in his mother's name?"

"I don't think it is. As far as I know, Corey rejected that bequest and told his mother to sell the place and keep the money."

"So, it would surprise you that the current owner of the property, according to county records, is an LLC owned by Mrs. Frank Fischer?"

"I guess. I don't really know or care."

"Well, I do, Mr. Preston, as does my client. And once we do a full title search, I'll bet we'll find your father's dirty fingerprints all over the documents whose purpose was to hide Corey's assets like your father tried to hide his own."

"Is there a question anywhere in sight, Stinger? Again, save your wild theories for the judge. If you've got nothing further for my client, then I think we're done here."

The deposition continued, with Hillstrom asking more questions about Corey's finances, whereabouts and wealth. When the inquiries ended, Rebecca renewed her demand for dates on which she could depose Cecelia Jackson. Hillstrom demurred with a variety of excuses about his own tight schedule and the fact that

Cecelia was on an extended vacation and unavailable by phone.

"She's not checking in with her lawyer during the height of discovery?" asked Rebecca incredulously.

"I'll get back to you on that, Becky." Hillstrom closed his briefcase, thanked the court reporter, said his goodbyes to Rebecca and Billy, then bolted out the door.

Chapter 13

Late Monday evening, Cecelia pulled into the parking lot of a road-side motel in Rapid City. She had spent the better part of eleven hours crossing the state of Wyoming and musing about her situation. It had been more than a week since she'd left Arkansas, more than a week since she'd spoken with her only child. Her stomach felt a palpable tug toward home, an ache that couldn't be placated by food. She momentarily wondered after the exhausting day of driving whether she should go on to Minneapolis or turn south instead. Was there any point in going farther, in pursuing Corey Flanagan to achieve a vengeful death? She recognized that some of her rage and instinctual need to *do something* had dissipated after shooting Miguel. But he was the wrong man, so why not pursue the right one to the end? After all, it was possible she would end up in prison despite her best efforts to evade capture. Expecting that Corey had already identified her to the police, she was now a wanted woman. Her resolve to go on to Minnesota returned. She wasn't about to be imprisoned for killing a man until she succeeded in killing the one who mattered.

A wanted woman. *Wanted by those who didn't matter but not by the one man who did—Bennett. In fairness, Bennett did want me, but not completely in the way that I needed, the way that I deserved to be wanted. If only he had been honest from the start, things might've turned out differently.* Cecelia knew herself well enough to know that she would never have consented to shacking up with, let alone marrying, someone gay. *I was the Homecom-*

ing Queen Runner-up, for God's sake. She had her pick of the lot yet was seduced by Bennett's charm, good looks and sensitivity. What's more, he was the rebound guy once she and her first true love called off their engagement. Bennett was supposed to be a fling. Cecelia's girlfriends even said so. Yet that is what fed their undoing. In each other, both Bennett and Cecelia had likely been seeking escape—she from heartbreak, he from an unwanted label.

Together, they partied hard, drank too much, and threw caution to the wind in the back of Bennett's pick-up. Eight and a half months later, along came Julia and a small family wedding after that. Still, she loved him and wanted the marriage to work. Bennett showed every sign of feeling the same way, at least until the first incident at the wayside rest stop. After that, Bennett seemingly tried harder to please her, to be present and attentive to her needs. In many ways, he succeeded. Bennett was her husband and a loving father to Julia. He certainly deserved better than how his life ended, no matter what his shortcomings. He deserved justice, but that was denied to him by that farce of a legal proceeding in Minnesota. From that, Cecelia drew strength and a willingness to keep going, motivated by a deep desire to redeem her man.

* * *

She entered a motel room and fell upon the bed. She wasn't used to driving so many miles, and certainly not on back-to-back days. How did Bennett do this all the time as a long-haul trucker? All she did was sit on her rump all day, yet exhaustion overcame her. She rose from the bed before sleep arrived, though, as there were three things she needed to do, starting with a hot shower. Then, once she finished eating, Cecelia reached into her purse to accomplish the last item on her mental list. She pulled out her cell phone and placed a call. She dialed her friend Tricia, who knew what to do upon seeing the unidentified number—ask no questions and immediately connect with Cecelia's mother on a three-way call.

Upon hearing the older woman answer, Tricia followed the memorized instructions, designed to evade any possible screening by the authorities of unidentified calls that might be coming in from Cecelia Jackson herself. She spoke with Julia for roughly five minutes, assuring her that everything was fine and that she would be home within a few days. Julia asked why the police had interrogated her grandmother and why they had asked Julia where her mother might be. Cecelia assured her that everything would be fine and that she was still on her weeklong retreat with friends. After multiple expressions of love, she ended the call. Though she had held herself together upon hearing Julia's voice, she lost it once they said their goodbyes and hung up. She wept for fifteen minutes without ceasing, dampening multiple tissues during her wails of despair.

Cecelia certainly had thought consciously about having to be away from Julia when she imagined this audacious plan, but she never could have imagined the difficulty she would encounter at the mere sound of that soft, sweet voice. Cecelia and Julia were close; they were, after all, almost the only direct family each other had left. Their closeness took her by surprise; Cecelia didn't remember ever feeling about her own mother quite that way. Perhaps it was an only-child thing; Cecelia's mother had four other kids to bond with and protect. For Cecelia, there was only one. Her connection with Julia was all she had left.

She willed herself to focus again on the quest at hand—find Corey and exact revenge so that she might return to her daughter. And even though the police were apparently on to her, wouldn't killing Corey also extinguish Cecelia's likelihood of prosecution? After all, Corey was the only witness who could place her on top of the Hermosa Beach Pier. Once Corey was dead, Cecelia figured she could move on and start a brand-new life.

* * *

No one spoke. Corey watched as his mother, Billy, and Rebecca each looked down at their respective dinner plates, intently chewing the tasty pork roast with sauerkraut that Ginny had slow-cooked all day for their dinner on Monday night. The setting reminded Corey of his childhood and all those family dinners where he and his parents ate in silence—with his father Frank too drunk to make sense and Corey and his mom too afraid to say something wrong.

"Tastes great, Mom."

"I was happy to prepare it. And thank you, Rebecca, for letting us stay here while the police sort things out."

"Of course. Stay as long as you'd like."

"Thanks, Rebecca," Corey said. "I called the LA Sheriff's office today, but they had no real update. It's as if Cecelia vanished into thin air. They promised they are working hard to track her down, and I'll get another update tomorrow. I'm hoping they find her so we can go home. We need to get out of your hair so you two can have some privacy."

"No worries. Billy and I get plenty of that, and he'll be here all week, so we've got time."

Billy swallowed and audibly cleared his throat. "Well, that's true. I'm not heading to California until Sunday morning, but I am driving to Pepin on Wednesday and staying overnight at Mom's."

"What? When did you decide this?" Rebecca's tone was direct. Corey once again looked down toward his plate.

"Today."

"I was with you most of the day. But I don't recall you mentioning it."

"Well, I guess I just did."

No one at the table was drunk or close to it, but Corey instantly sensed the same level of tension from those silent family dinners all those years ago.

"Well, please say hello to your mother for me," Ginny said. "I hope she's doing well."

"Thanks, Mrs. Fischer. Mom asks about you and your new life in California. She'd like to get your address so the two of you can keep in touch."

"That would be lovely. I'll write it down for you."

"Say, why don't you come along with me and give it to her yourself? You could stay in the guest bedroom and maybe visit a few old friends."

Ginny looked at Rebecca and Corey as if to obtain their approval. "Well, I guess I could. I've got nothing else to do here unless Corey needs me close by, and Rebecca wants more of my homemade meals?"

"I'd love that," Rebecca said. "But you should go with Billy, keep him company on the drive there and back."

"Or maybe," Corey chimed in, "your sister could meet you in Pepin and take you to Grandma's overnight?"

"Better yet," Billy added, "I could drop you off in Eau Claire along the way. And Corey could come, too."

Corey seized up, with a mouthful of pork and sour cabbage in his mouth. He swallowed and washed it down with a gulp of ice water. "I would, but I think I need to stay here. I promised Carol I'd come back and help her at the studio for the next two days."

* * *

After dinner, Billy and Corey drove to the grocery store. Rebecca had a short list of items on which they were running low. It was Corey who suggested that the boys run the errand while the gals clean up. He wanted to force an interlude between Rebecca and Billy in the hopes that their evening might end more harmoniously than it seemingly began.

"Thanks," Rebecca said. "And, if you don't mind stopping at Falls Liquor, we're almost out of chardonnay."

* * *

Corey waited in the car while Billy ran into the liquor store. There was nothing inside Corey needed. The sight of so much alcohol used to leave him feeling bilious in the first few years after he quit drinking. Now, he simply didn't notice or care. As he waited inside the car, it dawned on him that he had dominated their conversation since leaving the house. He hadn't asked Billy a single question about the deposition or what gnawed at him and made his mood tonight seem so annoyed. He decided to remedy that failing as he watched Billy approach the car and get inside.

"Listen, man, I'm sorry. I've been rambling on about my morning with Nick. Tell me, how did things go at the deposition? No offense, but you seemed a bit perturbed at dinner. Everything okay?"

Billy relaxed his shoulders, slumped in the seat, and let the car keys drop into his lap. "I'll be fine, but yeah, today was intense. It wasn't so much the deposition itself, though. I've been deposed plenty of times in my construction business."

"What's going on, then?"

"I don't know. It's this thing with Rebecca like we talked about the other night. I mean, everything had been fine between us, and then this visit comes along, and nothing seems to be going right."

"Does it have anything to do with Mom and me being in your way? We can totally get a hotel room."

"No, it's not that. I think it's helped having you guys here. Well, at least your mom and her cooking help. You, on the other hand, are a pain in my ass as usual." Billy flashed a mild grin—the first one Corey had seen from Billy all night.

"Thank God. There's the real Billy that I know and love and who pisses me off. Glad to have you back, man."

"Yeah. I think we've inexplicably switched roles. I'm the one bemoaning the woes of relationships and feelings now."

Corey laughed. "You sure know how to thrust a knife deep into a guy's heart yet make him think it hit the funny bone. But while it's nice to have the old Billy back, is there a version of him who can speak with a little softer edge on the truth?"

"Unlikely. That guy's been missing since junior high."

"Don't I know it."

They remained parked in the liquor store lot, though Billy rolled down the windows to let in some fresh air. "Maybe I'm getting soft in middle age," he said. Corey assured him that was not the case and that everything Billy expressed was natural. If anyone knew what was worth worrying about in a relationship, it was Corey. Billy also spoke about the deposition, including attorney Hillstrom's focus in the afternoon upon Corey and the Barron County cabin.

"The guy must have bad information. Mom sold the cabin a year ago. If the lawyer sees her name in the records, then he's looking at stale data."

"That's what I told him."

"It is weird, though—first Cecelia's obsession with my family ties, and now a similar line of questions from her lawyer. Remember what Rebecca's investigator uncovered in Arkansas?"

"Yeah, all those printouts about you, your mom, and even the cabin. I'm surprised he didn't find Samantha's name on that board too."

Samantha. The mention of her name hit Corey like a splash of ocean water. Being here in Minneapolis again was the closest he'd been to her geographically since first meeting her at the Foxtails Lounge last year. He'd made no effort to initiate contact or find out more information despite Miguel's frequent prodding. In Miguel's reasoning, Samantha was Corey's one and only sister. She was Corey's sole living genetic connection to his father and would be his closest living relative when Ginny died.

"Well, that changed your mood considerably."

Corey awakened from his thoughts. "Huh." An imploring look remained on Billy's face, forcing Corey to respond. "Funny that you mention Samantha. Nick brought up her name this morning, too. I think it's a conspiracy."

"Maybe you should give it some thought? Miguel and I were of one mind on this topic, as I recall. We both urged you to make a connection, to let her know that you are each other's only sibling."

"I thought we were done solving my problems today and focusing on yours."

Billy laughed. "I'm tired of talking about my problems. What do you say we don't talk about either and head back to see what our womenfolk are saying about us behind our backs."

"Deal."

"Good." Billy began, then paused briefly before saying more. "Hey, thanks for listening and putting up with me when I get a bit grouchy."

"*Bit* is an understatement, my friend. Add a *ch* to the end of that word, and you'll have a better description of what you've been like tonight."

Billy softly punched Corey's shoulder, then brought their bare arms together as he had done many times over the past twenty years. "*Amigos de por vida,* like the tattoos suggest. You're stuck with this bitch for life, my friend. Deal with it."

* * *

The boys hadn't returned with the chardonnay fast enough, so Ginny and Rebecca sat on the patio in front of a roaring fire in the chiminea and sipped from glasses of single malt whisky that Rebecca had been gifted on becoming a partner at the firm.

"This is really good, thank you."

"Cheers to us." They clinked glasses.

"You know, I never enjoyed drinking when I was married. I guess I was too hesitant to imbibe because one of us had to stay sober and take care of Corey. But I occasionally partook in an effort to drink as much from the bottle as possible so there'd be less for Frank to get crazy on."

"Yikes. Well, then, I need to expand my toast. Cheers to us— women who know how to hold their liquor and tame their men."

Ginny laughed. "I'm not sure about that last part, but yes— cheers to us."

Once again, they clinked glasses and then savored long sips.

"Speaking of men, how are things going with you and Billy?"

Rebecca set down her drink and grinned sheepishly. "I guess you sensed tension at the table tonight?"

"A little. I don't mean to pry, but what's going on?"

"You're not prying. I'm glad you asked." Rebecca launched into an explanation of her history with Billy, the excitement of their unexpected mid-life passion and the subtle strains on their bond that appeared only this week. She described the awkwardness of their unplanned discussion about sexuality and the dance in which they seemed engaged about the future. Would their relationship survive long distance? Would one of them be forced to move across the country? "I love him, Ginny, and I want to make this work. Hell, I'm in my forties, and this might be my last shot."

Ginny poured each of them another splash of scotch. The first round had gone down fast. "I hear you. Love isn't easy, hon. There's no getting around that. But don't look at it as being your last or only shot. I'm in my late sixties, and I think my best shot at love may still lie ahead."

Rebecca rose to place another log on the fire. She knew the Fischer family's history, and she contemplated the hope that Ginny was trying to convey—the idea that life's best romantic moments might be yet to come, notwithstanding a forty-year marriage in the past. Rebecca turned back toward the pair of Adirondack chairs and sat down.

"I appreciate that, Mrs. Fischer. I love how you and I seem to be able to talk so freely on this topic. And it's not the scotch speaking; we've only had one drink! It's your demeanor and openness. I've never even talked with my mother like this."

"You're welcome. And, please, it's Ginny."

"Ginny. No offense to your story about the possibility of love arriving later in life, but I don't want to wait until I'm sixty or seventy. I've got this guy I'm crazy about right now."

"And he's crazy about you. I've known Billy since he was a little kid, and I've never seen him act like he has since you two got together."

"Then why do I feel him slipping away?"

Ginny swirled the scotch in her glass and stared at the amber spiral before looking at Rebecca. "Can I tell you a little story?"

"Of course."

"This memory came back to me as you were talking. I haven't thought about it in thirty years. Huh. I've never told this story to anyone, not even Corey. Funny how the mind works that way, storing things away until the right moment. Anyway, this incident I'm thinking about happened when the boys must've been about nine or ten—in fifth grade, I believe. Billy was at our house for a sleepover, and they were in Corey's room playing with matchbox cars. Frank and I were in the living room. It was after supper. Frank was several beers into his evening and watching sports while I did needlepoint and only paid half attention to the TV.

"I heard the bathroom door close, and moments later, Billy came roaring through the living room, plowing a toy semi-truck through our thick, shag carpet. The game must've been on a commercial break because Frank turned all friendly and began peppering Billy with questions. *What kind of truck are you driving? Will you be playing baseball this spring? How many girlfriends have you got?* Billy was always such a polite boy, and he answered Frank's inquiries as fast as he could to get back to truck driving. *It's a Ford, sir. Yeah, I'm trying out for catcher. Only one—her name is Susan.*

"Frank latched onto that last one, teasing Billy that he had better treat little Susie well or another boy might steal her away from him, perhaps even Corey. *He wouldn't do that,* Billy casually replied. *Corey's my best friend. Besides, he doesn't like girls.* Frank and I exchanged a quick, nervous glance before I refocused on my needlepoint. Frank turned to Billy and probed some more. *Did Corey tell you that?* I remember looking up and seeing how Billy looked at Frank with a curious expression. *No. I just know, that's all.* Frank went quiet, and I stayed that way, too. Billy must've taken our silence as his cue to resume playing. He put his hand atop the semi-truck and pushed it through the rest of the living room towards Corey's room, making revving noises all the way there."

Ginny smiled and uttered a small laugh. "After that, I heard Corey flush the toilet, followed by doors opening and closing, then the muted sound of boys playing through the thin walls of our home until bedtime."

Rebecca listened, yearning to discern the moral of Ginny's story. "What made you think of that long-ago incident?"

"Good question. I guess it reminds me of who Billy Preston is—a perceptive, honest and loyal man. He knew things about Corey before Corey knew them about himself and certainly before Frank or I ever did. He's had these great qualities for as long as I've known him. And I think you see them, too."

"I do."

"But there's more to that story for me. It reminds me that burying your head in the sand is a recipe for failure. I ignored what Billy had to say that day about Corey. I guess I just pretended that he never said it. And look what that mindset did for me and to Corey—years lost to silent suffering that might've been avoided had I gently followed up. That's what I'm trying to tell you now, Rebecca. Don't hide from what you're feeling, and for Heaven's sake, don't ignore it. Find a way to talk to him, to ask him why things this week feel so distant, so tense. Ask him, and you'll get an honest answer. Guaranteed."

Rebecca looked at Ginny and slowly nodded her head. "You're right. Thank you, Mrs. Fisher. I hope to be as wise as you are someday."

"Oh, Rebecca. You already are. We're not so different."

"How's that?"

"You followed your professional aspirations with a passion while pushing personal ones to the back burner. I did the opposite. But look at us now. Each of us is filling in that missing gap and pursuing what we had set aside years ago. Bring your relationship with Billy to the front burner, Rebecca. That's my bottom-line advice. You've accomplished so much as a lawyer. Give that same level of commitment and sacrifice to love."

"So... are you saying I should quit my law practice and move to California to be with Billy?"

"No, not exactly, unless that's what you think is best. I'm only suggesting balance. Pursue them both, neither one at the expense of the other."

"Huh. I guess that's possible. Other women my age seem to have navigated both work and love with success. Facebook is full of their stories."

"Oh, don't you believe all that you see on social media. People are only showing you their best selves, not their actual struggles. Besides, it's not a contest. Make these things happen for you and for Billy. The rest of the world can fuck off."

Rebecca had taken a sip of scotch, then spit it back out. "Mrs. Fisher! I mean, Ginny!"

"What, a woman my age can't swear once in a while?"

"It's the first time I've heard you do it."

"I'm doing a lot of things these days I never did before, like moving to California and pursuing my nursing degree. Who knows? Maybe I'll find true love out there at the beach as well."

"Hmmm, I like the sound of that. You're an inspiration. Is there more to your new chapter, perhaps someone you've already met?"

"No, but that's what Tinder is for, isn't that right?"

Rebecca laughed once more and finished her drink. "Apparently so. I wouldn't know, thankfully. But good luck to you. And Ginny, if I may, here's a piece of sound advice that a wise woman once shared with me."

"Yes?"

"Don't believe everything you see on that Tinder app. People are only showing you their best selves, not their actual fucked-up life."

Chapter 14

"Geez, are you turning the place into a sauna?" Corey felt a wave of heat across his face the moment he walked into Carol's studio on Tuesday morning.

"Very funny. I want it warm in here if I'm stripping down to nothing."

Corey halted mid-stride. "Um, what?"

"We agreed you needed a fresh start, remember? A distraction from your current situation to spark new creativity in your art."

He struggled to make sense of Carol's words.

"What? You can't handle looking at a naked, sexy woman?" A playful grin crossed Carol's face. "You did it before, in college." He caught the double meaning. "Drawing 101, remember? We sat together and sketched nude models with charcoal?"

"I remember, but those were strangers, not one of my best friends."

"Well, nothing you haven't seen before, right?" She tossed him a freshly shaved pencil, then turned and walked toward the utility room while motioning with her hand toward the opposite corner. "You can set up over there. I'll be out in a minute."

Corey walked to the spot Carol directed. A metal stool sat in front of an angled standing desk. On top of it lay a spiral-bound sketch pad and two more graphite pencils, along with an assortment of charcoal. An aging metal heater sat immediately behind the stool, radiating warm air. Behind the heater was a large, single-paned window. Despite the cooler-than-normal summer temperature this morning, the fogged-up glass revealed its tenuous strain as the almost transparent boundary between warm and cool air.

He sat down atop the chair. Directly ahead of him lay the sofa on which he sat yesterday drinking tea, a piece of furniture dating back to his own occupancy of this studio. He shuddered at the memory of a sexual tryst with Nick atop that tufted upholstery years ago before his thoughts segued back to Carol. Was this really happening? Should it? Maybe she was right—he needed a distraction and a reason to throw himself into an all-consuming artistic mindset. But did it have to include a naked woman and his briefly former lover at that?

The creaking door interrupted his thoughts. Carol walked toward him, wearing nothing more than a wide, impish smile. He watched as she approached the sofa, then turned her back toward him and lay down. She struck a traditional first pose, one familiar to any student of art—her body against the fabric, her head resting atop a throw pillow and one hand holding her chin like *The Thinker* while the other rested with her arm draped across her torso. Corey stared for longer than he should have. Carol was in remarkable shape for her age, nearly as tightly curved as he remembered from that night in her sorority house bedroom twenty-some years ago. He also noticed her legs crossed at the ankles, and how a wild tuft of blonde hair erupted from the spot where those long legs met her torso.

"Ok, Da Vinci. Let's get started, shall we?"

Carol's playful command motivated his hands to move. One opened the sketch pad while the other searched for the optimal tool. He began drawing haltingly, as if it were his first day of college. Tension filled his shoulders as the work began, but the eventual rhythm of sketching and casting his eyes back and forth between Carol and the desktop soon slackened his rigid cock. He began with her face and worked his way down her body. He carefully recast upon the page everything observed through his eyes—her moles, folded skin, long blonde hair, and opulent breasts. He paused upon reaching her torso, still enveloped as it was with her limp left arm. She had cast aside all her clothing, but a gold wedding band remained on her left hand. The sight of it halted Corey's drawing motion mid-stroke. He thought back to Friday night and to Miguel offering Corey a cherished family heirloom. What happened to the ring? Ginny had checked with the detectives as she promised, but they reportedly searched and found nothing on the pier. It must have fallen into the ocean. Or worse, it was found by an unscrupulous opportunist who pawned it for a few hundred bucks. Regardless, there was nothing he could do about it now. Corey shook his head and willed his suddenly shaky hand to resume drawing. Carol's ring reminded him of something else, too—the fact that she was married. Yet here she was, modeling nude in front of another man. It was okay, though, he thought to himself. Right? After all, this wasn't sexual. This was a kind gesture by a longtime friend. Plus, everyone knew that Corey was attracted to men. But as his gaze upon Carol's body moved ever lower, he found his eyes lingering on the strands of blonde hair above her pudendum.

The sudden feeling of warmth now running from his chest down to his lap caught Corey off guard. He'd been with a woman before—with *this* woman, in fact. And it was that long-ago failed copulation that had convinced him he was gay. Still, it dawned on him here in the studio that he had never looked at that part of Carol before. Her sorority bedroom had been dark when he found himself in her bed, naked. And when he did have the chance to look upon the tempting space of her back then, his eyes had been closed. Now, Corey's eyes were open. And his growing arousal was both surprising and obvious. Why in the hell was he feeling this way—now, in the wake of Miguel's death and with a woman? Perspiration dropped from his forehead onto the drawing paper. The elevated thermostat setting needed for Carol's warmth made Corey uncomfortably hot. He stopped sketching, then unbuttoned and removed his shirt, leaving only a tank top that stuck to his chest with sweat.

Carol looked up. "You can turn down the heat or crack the window. I'll be fine."

Corey found it increasingly hard to breathe. "Okay."

He rose from the stool and walked toward the wall. He turned the latch on the window and heaved with his shoulders until the window thrust upward, ushering cool air into the room. He turned toward Carol with beads of sweat running down his face and a protruding bulge in his pants. Carol lifted herself onto an elbow, her left arm still draped across her stomach. The two of them locked eyes. Corey froze where he stood—equidistant from Carol on the one hand and the standing desk with sketch pad on the other. Both summoned him. Carol rose from the sofa and walked toward him. Corey felt as though he might faint, so he stumbled toward the stool and sat down. Carol met him there.

"This feels like a good place to stop. I think we've accomplished the goal of inspiring you. I'll get dressed and meet you on the sofa with a joint." She leaned in and planted a soft kiss on his cheek. Before turning to walk back toward the utility room, she whispered into his ear. "And thank you for the *big* compliment. I'm flattered."

* * *

An hour later, both Corey and Carol had a decent buzz. They had talked through what happened during his sketch of her naked body, and laughter replaced Corey's initial awkwardness.

"I love you, Carol. But in a unique way."

"I know. I figured that out years ago, remember?"

He laughed. "Yeah, vividly. Thank you."

"For what?"

"For this. And for being an amazing friend. I'm glad we reconnected after my drama years."

"Me, too. I like to think that I'm still the number one woman in your life."

They both laughed, and Corey said, "You are—you're irreplaceable, obviously."

"Well, there is one woman who could." She paused to take a long draw from the joint. "Have you thought any more about what Nick suggested—going with him to find your sister?"

"Geez, I see everyone's sticking to the script here. In addition to you and Nick, Billy suggested the same thing. So did Miguel on several occasions."

"Maybe that means you should do it?"

"Maybe I'm too buzzed to make good decisions right now."

"That's the best time to make decisions, Corey."

He laughed. But then he considered Nick's proposal again and got lost in thought. Carol was saying something, but he didn't pay attention. His mind was fixed on an image of his half-sister. She had no idea of their true relationship. Didn't she deserve to know the truth? And wasn't Corey the best person to deliver the message?

"Just a minute, Carol." He pulled the phone from his pocket and texted Nick. *Hey, if you're serious about driving to Wisconsin, I'm in. Can we leave tomorrow morning?*

* * *

Late Tuesday afternoon, Cecelia pulled off Interstate 90 in Albert Lea to get fuel and grab some snacks. It had been another long day on the road. In the past week, she had traveled nearly three thousand miles, far more than she had ever driven by herself before. A series of yawns reflected both her physical condition and her state of mind. She was close to her goal and nervous. The drive time from Rapid City to Albert Lea should have been seven hours, but Cecelia did it in nine. She couldn't resist two unplanned stops—at the infamous Wall Drug Store and then to see the Mitchell Corn Palace up close. These were two places on their list—hers and Bennett's—to take Julia on a summer road trip. Stepping inside both tourist sites earlier today sent chills up Cecelia's spine. She could picture their small family together in these places—snapping the same photos that everyone takes, buying the gaudy tourist trinkets and overpaying for lodging and cheap food. That imagined longed-for trip would never happen—nothing on the list would. Bennett was dead. It still felt impossible to comprehend, and now, she realized, her vengeance might prevent her from taking Julia to these places, too.

She took the burner cell out of her handbag and swore when its battery appeared to be dead. Instead, she grabbed for her own phone resting in the cup holder. It slipped from her hands and fell to the floorboard, but she reached down, felt for it, and raised it to her sights. She also lifted Corey's cell phone from her lap and hit the information tab on Ginny Fischer's name in Corey's texts. She located the number and then dialed it from her own phone.

"Hello?"

"Hi! May I speak with Virginia Fischer?"

"This is she."

"Great. My name is Candy Adams, and I'm calling from Santa Monica College on behalf of your professor."

"Oh? My classes haven't started yet, not until the beginning of next month."

"Exactly. That's why I'm calling. We've been trying to hand-deliver a syllabus to your address in Santa Monica, but no one seems to be answering the door. It's important you receive this ASAP."

"Unfortunately, I'm heading to Wisconsin tomorrow for a couple of days, and the friend I'm staying with will be at her office, so I'm afraid no one would be home."

Damn, Cecelia thought. *If no one would be home, that means Corey isn't there with Ginny.* "Hmmm. I see here that your emergency contact is a Mister Corey Flanagan in Hermosa Beach. Perhaps we could deliver your syllabus to him tomorrow, and then he could give it to you when you're back in town?"

"Gosh, that won't work either. You see, he's here in Minnesota but making his own separate trip to Wisconsin tomorrow, too. I'm afraid I'm not being very helpful."

Cecelia continued after a brief pause. "No worries, Mrs. Fischer. I guess you'll just have to get it once you get back to California. Have a nice day."

She cursed after ending the call. "Shit." She turned to face Bennett's urn, then closed her phone and threw it down on the passenger seat. She pushed herself against the headrest and took a pair of deep breaths. Her scheming brain needed a break. She admonished herself to let go of any more guesswork tonight. Her thoughts returned to her current whereabouts in Albert Lea and the much easier challenge of finding a spot to lay her head for the night. Then, it dawned upon Cecelia exactly where she was— only a few miles from where Bennett drew his last breath. She had listened to the details of the truck stop in a courtroom last year. Back then, she didn't want to visit the scene. There was too much pain in envisioning the spot where he died. Now, though, her pain had morphed into anger, with all of it directed at two men—Corey, who snuffed out her husband's life, and Bennett, for putting himself in a position to get killed. As she sat in the car at the rest stop, her hands gripped the wheel. She had time to kill before the hopefully final leg of this quest tomorrow, and now she had somewhere specific to go.

She drove twenty miles north on I-35 and exited the freeway upon seeing the darkened sign for *Trucker's Haven* alongside a well-lit one for the new *Kwik Stop* nearby. At the bottom of the offramp, she had a choice—left through the underpass to the newer-looking place or right to the now-shuttered truck stop where her husband had been killed. Cecelia turned right. She entered the gravel lot of the abandoned facility. The only light illuminating the property emerged from the Malibu's headlights. The parking lot was empty, and the building was boarded up and looked lonely. She looked at Bennett's urn in the passenger seat and felt pity. Somewhere out here is where he died. She pulled the car up to the former front door of the truck stop, past the now useless gas pumps. She shut off the engine and stepped outside. A strong breeze blew across the surrounding prairie and assaulted her in the face. She walked toward the boarded-up glass window and attempted to peek inside. There was a faint red light shining dimly inside what used to be a cafe. An exit sign, perhaps? "I'm sure that will help guide the ghosts," she said aloud before it dawned on her what she had unwittingly said. She backed away from the window and surveyed the wide parking lot. She pulled her cell phone out and took a panoramic pic.

"This is where it happened, isn't it?" Cecelia realized she was talking to herself, so she walked back to the car and opened the passenger side door. She reached in and unshackled the urn, then lifted the heavy box into her arms and stood up. She felt a large lump forming in her throat. "This is where you died. This is where that bastard took your life." Tears welled up behind her eyes. Four years after hearing the unspeakable news from a policeman at her front door in Pine Bluff, the pain of losing Bennett felt as raw now as it did back then. But it was mixed with bitterness, too. "How did it go down, Bennett? Something happened between you and Corey, didn't it? Something sexual. Were you weak like before? Is that how he lured you into his trap?" For once, Bennett's urn stayed silent. She couldn't hear him utter a single word. "Answer me, goddammit!" She set the box gruffly onto the gravel and unfastened the screw top lid. She pulled back the plastic lining to expose her dead husband's remains so he would hear her loud and clear. "Tell me what happened! I loved you. I changed for you. Why wasn't I ever enough?"

Still, Bennett's voice remained mute.

She squeezed her hand through the opening and pulled out a handful of ash. "Answer me, I said! Were you weak like before?" Other than the sound of her own shrieks and rapid breaths, only a breeze filled the night air. Then she threw the fistful of ash to the ground and screamed before feeling a pain in her gut. In between gasps for air, she vomited but avoided spilling her puke into the urn, though some of it did land in the same spot as the ash.

I was murdered by that pervert.

She froze upon hearing Bennett's voice rise from the ashen ground.

It wasn't my fault. It was Corey's.

She fell to her knees and began frantically sweeping up his remains with her hands and picking out pieces of barf to discard from the pile.

"I'm sorry, Bennett. I'm sorry!" She kept saying the same two words over and over until she had collected all she could. She culled a few pieces of gravel from the clump of ash cupped in her left palm, then gently poured it back into the urn. She sealed the box shut, returned to her car, and then drove north to Minneapolis, where she paid cash for a room at the Midway Motel near the fairgrounds.

Chapter 15

Wednesday morning began with bright sunshine. Corey stood at the edge of the lawn waving goodbye to Billy and Ginny as they drove away in Rebecca's car, turned left at the street corner, and disappeared from sight. Within seconds, Nick pulled up to the curb in a convertible with the passenger side window rolled down.

"Morning. Ready to ride?"

"Hmmm, yeah. I need to grab my backpack from inside. Nice car, by the way. Experiencing your mid-life crisis already?"

Nick laughed. "No, just something fun to drive."

"Sweet, but it doesn't look like there's enough room inside for much more than the two of us, Nick. You'll need to leave your ego here on the lawn until we get back." Corey gestured toward the grass.

"My, my. Someone has a sharp tongue this morning," said Nick, laughing. "You always did gravitate toward bitchiness in times of stress. This ought to be a fun few hours. I'll be sure to drive fast."

Corey laughed as well. With the prospect of confronting his half-sister later in the day, his angst was cresting.

"And besides," Nick added while pointing toward his crotch, "driving a smaller sports car is nice. Not everything in my life needs to be huge." In lieu of laughter or throwing up, Corey shook his head and walked into Rebecca's house. He grabbed the backpack, which held a book, two granola bars, a pen and one of the leather-bound journals Rebecca had given him last year. He hadn't

known how to prepare for the day's journey or whether he needed to bring anything at all. But he wanted to have something to
do, or at least an excuse to look busy, in case Nick's penchant for
annoying banter overwhelmed him on the long drive to Barron
County and back.

* * *

Cecelia woke up in her motel room at nine-thirty Wednesday
morning. It was later than she had planned to start her day, but
she welcomed the hours of solid rest. She once again found herself
in the same city as Corey. She could feel it. But she also knew he
would be heading somewhere today with Nick, at least according
to the text exchange she read on Corey's original cell phone last
night. Cecelia needed a plan to discover where Corey was going
and fast. She reached over to the bedside table and grabbed his
phone. Thankfully, she had remembered to charge it overnight.
After connecting to the motel's Wi-Fi, she scoured Corey's phone
for clues. There was nothing new in his texts or emails, but she
did notice he had installed a new app—Snapchat. She tapped on
the icon to see what information might be inside.

"Huh," she said while looking over to Bennett's urn resting
on the table. "It looks like Corey only has one friend. How sad.
And that friend is Nick. Miguel ain't been dead a week, and Corey
already raced back to his former lover. Disgusting."

She looked through the app, but whatever message Corey
had sent to Nick was marked *Delivered 1d* and had since disappeared. Probably one of those gross nudes, she thought. She left
the Chat page and then viewed the one labeled Stories filled with
generic videos from random strangers. She knew from monitor-
ing Julia's use of Snapchat that these images were pre-filled by
whoever runs the app. Then she tapped the location button, and
up popped a map depicting the wider area surrounding Minneap-
olis/St. Paul. She immediately saw a cartoonish character labeled
"me" located on a freeway at the eastern edge of Minnesota. Minutes later, the character crossed the river and entered Wisconsin.

She reached for her investigatory notes on the nightstand and began to read. She focused on information about Nick Parker and about Corey's ties to Wisconsin. The notes reminded her that Nick worked as a vice president for a bank. He lived in a home with his lover, Evan, in Minneapolis. He drove a 2017 black BMW and graduated from the University of Minnesota. The information in her notes about the Fischer family's ties to Wisconsin was more extensive. Earlier this year in Pepin, Ginny Fischer had sold the home in which Corey grew up. But Ginny's mom—Corey's grand-mother—still lived in nearby Eau Claire with another daughter. There were no other first-degree relatives. The only additional connection between Corey or his mother and the state of Wisconsin was the family cabin in Barron County. The property was still listed on the tax rolls as being owned by Mrs. Fischer, though the first names strangely didn't match. She looked again at Corey's Snapchat. His character was somewhere in western Wisconsin along Interstate 94.

"Holy shit, Bennett. We got him. We know where Corey is, and now we can track him no matter where he goes. Looks to me like he's on his way to the family cabin in Barron County. Come on, let's get dressed and go."

* * *

As Nick sped further into Wisconsin, Corey's stomach rumbled. Nick had dominated the discussion thus far, and it veered toward the banal—regaling Corey with developments at the bank and gossip about who was sleeping with whom among their former friends. But it wasn't Nick's banter that unnerved him. To the contrary, he was content being chauffeured into the Dairy State in lieu of driving there himself. Last year's car accident in Barron County had brought him nothing but trouble. And then, too, there was Sheriff Todd Coles, who had warned him never to drive through *his county* again. Although he would soon be squarely within the confines of the sheriff's jurisdiction, at least this time, Corey wasn't behind the wheel. He glanced at Nick and knew he was better off with this harmless harlot than facing the sheriff's penchant for retributive justice.

Despite that recent history, it wasn't the thought of the sheriff that first stirred disquietude in Corey as they crossed the St. Croix River. Rather, it was the *Welcome to Wisconsin* sign, a towering reminder that he was coming back to the place of so much heartache and unrequited love. Yet, wasn't that partly why he decided to return? To tell Samantha that he was her half-brother? And that the father she never knew was the same man Corey often wished he didn't know either? Despite their common parentage by a man who was as often mean as he was absent, connecting with his half-sister was about more than meeting the only remaining blood relative in his father's line. Instead of sharing stories about what Frank Fischer didn't do for either of his children, Corey secretly desired to capture through Samantha something he never quite did with Frank. He wanted to know that his father had produced something beautiful—someone beautiful—amidst the wreckage of an otherwise self-absorbed, controlling life. He hoped to discover in Samantha a pure and tender heart. He hoped to find in her a person who might give him through his father what he already had in spades via his mom—understanding, acceptance, forgiveness and love.

Nick looked over at Corey sitting in the passenger seat. "I've already pissed you off, haven't I?"

"What? No, of course not."

"I know you, Corey, especially the things you never say. We were together for a long time. I'm sure you know what I'm thinking most of the time, too. No need to reply to that."

Corey uttered a small laugh.

"It's not the same with a second relationship, though, is it?" Nick asked. "I mean, I love Evan and everything. I hope we get through this rough patch and move on together. But it takes time to get to know someone new like you do the first time around."

Corey nodded, uncertain where Nick might take this conversation. There's no way Corey would admit difficulty or regret in his relationship with Miguel; he was everything Nick wasn't. What Corey found in Miguel was exactly what he needed—someone who treated him with love and respect and who made Corey a better person—indeed, the person he was meant to be. Yet, he appreciated Nick's forthrightness in the moment.

"And if I'm being completely honest, Corey, it was easier to leave you than to forget you. Take that for what it's worth."

"I appreciate that, Nick, and good luck with Evan. Maybe you guys should try counseling?"

"We are—had two sessions already, and the next one is Saturday afternoon."

"How's it going, if I may ask?"

"You mean my weekly appointment with failure?"

* * *

Nick's car entered the Foxtails Lounge parking lot at eleven. The neon sign indicated the place was open, and a collection of pickup trucks in the lot meant there were at least half a dozen men inside. He commented sarcastically about the unsavory-looking place being a perfect fit for Frank Fischer. Corey silently agreed, thinking that Nick could just as well have been talking about himself. They entered the bar, and Corey scanned the place for Samantha. He didn't see her and indicated as much to Nick with a shrug and upturned palms.

"Go ask at the bar if or when she'll be in. I'll get us a table."

Corey complied. He spoke with the bartender, then walked over to join Nick, removed his jacket and sat down. "Her shift begins at 11:30. The bartender says she's always early, so should be here soon."

"Great. How about something to eat? I'm starving."

"Suit yourself if you're looking to fulfill your daily requirement of grease."

After ordering food and drinks from the bar, Nick walked back to the table, where he and Corey sipped their drinks in silence. Nick fiddled with his phone, and Corey spun his head toward the front door every time someone entered. Ten minutes later, everything important occurred within the span of a few seconds. Nick's steaming hot pizza emerged from the kitchen, and Samantha walked into the bar. She wasn't alone. Corey's mouth fell agape as several unexpected remembrances erupted in the space between his table and the front door. He recognized the man who had walked into the bar behind Samantha and brought his hand up to cover his mouth. The man's recognition of Corey followed within seconds.

"Corey Flanagan. You're the last person I expected to see here."

"Wait, you know him?" Samantha asked. Hearing the name jogged her memory. "He was in here a year or more ago but left abruptly. I had forgotten his name."

Nick was the last to understand. It was the man's voice that triggered his recollection. Nick had been in the courtroom the day Sheriff Todd Coles testified from the stand. With Corey, Samantha and Todd all wearing varying degrees of confusion and curiosity on their faces, Nick spoke first.

"Well, I see most of us know each other. What a nice surprise."

The others looked at Nick, puzzled.

"And you are?" Todd asked.

"Nick Parker—I'm a friend of Corey's."

"Hold on. We've met before. I interviewed you after you were shot in the woods out on County Road V a few years back." Todd halted, looked at Corey, then grinned and turned toward Samantha. "These two here are lovers, or were until Corey shot him. Have I got that right?" Coles looked back and forth between Corey and Nick.

"In a nutshell," Nick said. "Yes."

"Well, isn't this a happy reunion? What, did you come back here to Barron against my advice, Corey, so you could finish the job?"

Corey summoned the courage to speak. "No, I came here to talk with Samantha and not to cause trouble. I've got something important to say, and it doesn't require police presence."

"First of all, I'm a sheriff, not the police. And secondly, Samantha's with me, so whatever you want to say to her, you can say in front of me."

"Enough," Samantha shouted. "I can decide who I'll talk to and where and when." Her sharp words rendered the sheriff mute. She turned and looked at Corey. "I seem to recall you live in California?" Corey nodded yes. "Fine. If you came all this way to speak to me, then let's sit down and talk. My shift starts in fifteen minutes."

"Hey, Sheriff," Nick said. "How about you and I grab a seat by the bar and let these two talk at the table, huh?" Samantha looked at Todd and gestured toward the bar with her head. He slowly obliged. Nick grabbed his pizza and cocktail from the table and joined the sheriff on adjacent barstools. Corey pulled out a chair for Samantha, and they both sat down. He pulled his cell phone from his pocket and turned it off as Samantha waited for him to begin.

"Thank you for agreeing to talk."

"Of course. You've piqued my interest, seeing as you apparently know Todd and all."

"Yeah. I'll get back to that piece—maybe. He's your boyfriend?"

"Fiancé."

"I see. Congratulations. I remember you saying something about a boyfriend last time I was in here—you know, when we met."

"Yeah, well, Todd proposed on New Year's Eve. We're getting married next spring. But never mind that. What does you coming back here have to do with me? If I remember, your family lives in the Pepin area. You were passing through here on your way from Minneapolis to see them, though it's quite an odd detour."

"That's what I wanted to explain. But first, I need to apologize."

"For what?"

"For leaving so abruptly last time. I didn't eat my food or say goodbye."

"No apology needed. I seem to recall you left a decent tip. Compared to all the cheapskate locals, your generous gratuity was a gift from God."

The smile emerging on Corey's face mirrored the one on Samantha's. Though she was being playful, Corey had recognized a familiar cliché—*a gift from God*. It was a phrase his father uttered often in Corey's presence. How strange to hear it now from her. As far as Corey knew from their prior visit, there had been no contact between Samantha and her father. Could the instinctive utterance be genetic?

"Getting to your question—yes, my visit here last year was the result of an intentional detour. I came to Barron County for one last look at our family's cabin before my mother sold it. It wasn't due to nostalgia, though. I hated the place, to be honest. But I had to see it one more time in some vain effort to find closure with my father."

"Does he live around here? I only remember you mentioning you had a mom."

"He doesn't anymore. Well, he never did, but he spent a lot of time at that cabin and dragged me there kicking and screaming, at least until I was a teenager and found excuses to stay home."

"Cool. So, again, Corey, what does any of this have to do with me?"

He noticed her glancing at the clock on the wall.

"I'm not sure how to say this, and I have no intention of upsetting you."

"Spill it."

Her abruptness made him shudder.

"When I was here last time, you mentioned your mom and an absent father. I remember you saying that one thing your mom confessed to you was that your father had another family."

"Congrats on your stellar memory. I don't mean to be rude, but why are you reciting my own history to me?"

"Because I have a strong suspicion we have the same father."

"What? How could you possibly know that? I don't even know who he was."

"Technically, I don't. But several things you said last time made it clear."

"Such as?"

"Such as your mom's name being Judy, and that she was a waitress. When I was a kid, my father brought me up to the cabin, and he always insisted we eat at Slippery Sam's Cafe."

The expression on Samantha's face confirmed Corey's suspicion that her mom was the same Judy with whom Frank overtly flirted while Corey sat uncomfortably in his booth seat inside the cafe.

"And your eyes. They're exactly like Frank's—blue and deep as if holding secrets few could detect."

She looked away toward Todd. Corey looked there as well, wondering how much of this same story Nick was now explaining to the sheriff. Samantha bit her lip and turned back toward Corey.

"Frank, you say? Well, ain't that something." She exhaled slowly, leaning back in her chair and pulling her long blonde hair into a ponytail. Her hands continued circling her head, behind her ears and then along her jawline until they came to rest in a gesture of prayer, with her fingertips touching the bottom of her nose and her two thumbs gently supporting her chin. She then dropped both hands to the tabletop.

"I completely forgot about something until just now. Shit, it happened so long ago. I think I was only ten. I was rummaging through my mom's bedroom closet, looking for a pair of shoes. My friend and I were playing dress up, and I wanted to wear Mom's fancy black heels. But they were missing, and instead, I came across a shoebox full of cards and letters. Not sure what compelled me, but I read them. I can't remember if Mom was home at the time, but I sat there in the bottom of that closet reading her intimate letters. And every single one of them was signed, *Love Frank*."

Corey took advantage of the pause in her reply to briefly recite his own family history and the random parallels that made him suspect he and Samantha were siblings.

"So, you're telling me my last name should be Flanagan? Not sure how I feel about that. No matter, I'll be a Coles soon enough."

"Technically, no. I changed my name to Flanagan when I moved to California." She cast him a curious look. "That's a long story for a different day. Your last name should technically be what mine used to be for almost forty years—Fischer. Corey Fischer."

"But that's my last name already. Same as my mom's."

They stared at each other. He resisted saying more, hoping that she might offer insight into the strange coincidence of their last names. Instead, she abruptly rose from the table.

"Hold on a sec. I'll be right back."

He watched as she walked over to Todd and whispered into his ear. Then, she walked to the far end of the bar and disappeared through the swinging kitchen door. She emerged two minutes later and headed straight toward the table where Corey sat waiting.

"Sorry about that. I had to talk with Gus in the kitchen and then call another waitress to cover my shift."

"I'm sorry. I didn't mean to upset you or to make you not work your shift."

She held up her palm as if to stop him from saying more. "You didn't—upset me, that is. But you are the reason I won't be working this afternoon. I need to confront the person who is making me upset based on what you've told me—my mother."

"Samantha, maybe you should think it over first. I mean, I don't know you that well. Hell, I don't know you at all. But maybe you should process everything we've been talking about before you talk with your mom."

"Thanks for the free advice, but I'll pass. I'm not one to stew and have never been one who waits for tomorrow's sunrise when there's plenty of daylight left today."

Corey drew his hand to his mouth, unsure whether to express shock or to laugh. How many times had he heard his father say that exact same phrase? Who knows, maybe Samantha learned these adages from Judy, who in turn had learned them from Frank?

"And just so we're clear, Corey, am I correct in understanding that the shooting Todd referenced earlier happened between you and Nick out in the woods next to your family's hunting cabin north of Barron?"

"Yes, my grandfather—well, our grandfather—built that cabin with his own two hands. It stayed in the family until last year. Neither Mom nor I wanted anything to do with it after Dad died."

"Huh. That makes one more thing my mom needs to explain." She looked once again toward Todd before shaking her head as if trying to force the universe to make sense. When Todd returned her stare, she motioned her head toward the door and then looked at Corey.

"Listen, thank you for coming all this way. I don't mean to brush you off, seeing as you may be my brother and all, but I need to talk with my mom. Maybe we can connect by phone sometime after you're back home and figure out what this all means."

"Sure, no problem. But if it's okay with you, I'd like to stick around and talk with you after you confront your mom. I'm more than curious about what she'll have to say."

"Are you sure about that? From what you're telling me, she was your father's mistress. How are her explanations going to help you?"

"I don't know. Maybe they won't. But I've come this far to meet you and to discover the truth. If I've learned anything these past few months, it's that the only way to handle the truth is to take it all in, and not only the parts you like. I want to hear what Judy has to say."

Samantha looked at him, then once more at Todd, and back again to Corey. "Fine, I'll do you one better. How about you come along with me, and we confront Judy together?"

A wide range of emotions crossed fleetingly through Corey's mind. "Sure, I guess."

"Okay, then."

"Wait a sec, though. Does your mom live nearby? I'll need to convince Nick to drive there, and hopefully, it's not too far out of our way."

She laughed for the first time since entering the bar twenty minutes earlier. "Don't worry, Corey. It's not that far. In fact, you should know the precise distance. Both you and Nick have been to her house before."

Chapter 16

Billy steered Rebecca's Volvo east along U.S. Highway 10, traversing the rolling hills of western Wisconsin. Their journey had begun under cloudless skies, but the further east they traveled, increasing wisps of white and gray appeared high above them in the sky. Ginny audibly exhaled as she sank deeper into the seat beside Billy, watching out the window and holding her paper cup of black coffee. After taking a sip, she turned toward Billy. This was their first-ever road trip together. She smiled upon looking more acutely at Billy's familiar face, the face of a boy she had known and fed and watched grow up across the years.

"Well, who'd have thought I'd be in Wisconsin this week, huh?"

"Indeed. What a wild ride." He glanced at Ginny and then toward the road ahead. "Is the temperature okay?"

"I'm good, thank you." She instinctively reached out and lightly touched his shoulder. "How are you doing with all of it?"

"You mean this week? Miguel dying, and you and Corey flying out here?"

"Yes, that, but also everything on your plate in the wake of your father's passing, too."

"I'm fine. It was rough at first—losing him. But we all go through that at some point, right? At least I'm not alone. My mom and siblings are going through the exact same thing."

"Hmmm, that's a good perspective."

"Yeah, we're lucky to have each other."

"And Rebecca, too."

Billy cast her a quick and quizzical look, prompting Ginny to say more.

"You and Rebecca have each other. It's clear you two have formed a deep bond."

He nodded his head while also raising and lowering his thick, blond eyebrows, revealing bewildered eyes. He didn't respond in words.

"No?"

"Yeah, of course. I mean, I guess we've grown close. But who knows where that'll lead?"

"Who knows? Shouldn't *you* know?"

He laughed and looked askance at her once more. "What is it with you mothers and their sons' love lives? Ever since Rebecca and I started seeing each other and traveling back and forth between Minneapolis and LA, Mom asks me a thousand questions every time we speak."

"We've got nothing better to do, I guess." Ginny laughed, too. "In our defense, you boys need a nudge when it comes to relationships, even if you're forty-something years old."

"Fair enough, Mrs. Fischer."

She smiled at Billy. "I'm still waiting for an answer to my question."

He squirmed in his seat like all those fish he caught in the Mississippi River with Corey as a boy, their mouths held captive by a hook no matter how hard they wriggled to break free.

"I do know where I want things with Rebecca to lead. But I have doubts, you know?" Ginny nodded and listened. "I mean, I have a thriving business in California that I've worked hard the past twenty years to build. As for Rebecca, she has her law practice here and recently made partner, for God's sake. How can we be together long term?"

"Hmmm. That's a dilemma for sure."

"Of course, I would never ask her to give up her career to move west. She'd have to start all over—take the California bar, find a new firm, and basically start from scratch. That's not fair."

"But you love her?"

Billy laughed. While keeping one hand on the steering wheel, he ran the fingers of his other hand through his thick blond hair.

"It's a serious question."

"I know. I was thinking about that old saying, *turnabout is fair play*. Usually, I'm the one asking the pointed questions with no semblance of subtlety. I'm not used to having that tactic thrown back at me." He laughed again. Ginny laughed, too. "Geez, of course, I do, and in ways I never felt before. It's different with Rebecca. I feel like I can be myself—the good and the bad—but she sticks with me anyway. It's comfortable and casual yet erotically complex." His voice trailed off. The muscles around his face formed a grimace. "Never mind that last part, sorry. Forgot that I wasn't talking to Corey, but instead to his mom."

"Oh, for goodness sake, Billy. I'm not a nun from the convent, and you're not a teenager anymore. Speak freely. You're like a son to me, and life's too short to hold back. I'm glad to hear how you feel about Rebecca, and I, for one, think you need to take the reins and make a big move."

"You're right."

"About expressing your feelings or making a bold move?"

They exchanged a quick look before Billy turned his attention back to the road. "I'm not getting out of this conversation until I get out of the car, am I?" Ginny nodded with a smirk. "I don't disagree with anything you've said. But I'm scared. And torn. I feel as if I'm at a fork in the road of my life. I'd be happy walking down either path, but sooner or later, I gotta choose one to the exclusion of the other. The question is, how long can I stand at the crossroads before taking the next step?"

"Billy Preston, I've known you since you were a little boy. Good grief, you spent half your childhood within the four walls of my house. I know you, and I know that you know the answer here."

"Oh yeah?"

"Yes. It's clear—deep inside of you—and has been since the day your life and hers entangled once again. You're simply letting irrelevant details like your professional lives and unnecessary fears get in your way."

He drove on silently.

"Not clear yet? Well, let me try this question. What would your father do in this situation, hmmm? Follow his paycheck or follow his heart?"

Her question brought an immediate reply. "He'd follow his heart. I mean, he was a good lawyer and all, but family and friends and helping other people came first. Hell, look at how Dad left this world—choosing to save Corey from going to prison over preserving his own reputation."

"Exactly."

Billy remained quiet in the driver's seat, though clearly pondering all that had been said. They rode along for several miles, watching the passing landscape. The green fields of Wisconsin's summer were giving way to shades of brown and gray as some crops were harvested while others remained standing to be gathered later in the fall. This was the land where Ginny had spent most of her life, and Billy had lived half of his. The woodlands and farm country they passed outside the window were at a tipping point among the seasons. The excitement, warmth and rapid growth of the spring and summer receded. The heavy lifting of farm field work would soon end. People closed seasonal cabins and stored away their boats and outdoor toys. Preparations were made for the onset of winter—windows sealed shut, sensitive shrubs covered in cloth and lawnmowers drained of gas while snow blowers were unsheathed and tuned up. An aroma of seriousness hung in the air during this turning point on the Wisconsin calendar, along with that innate Midwestern feeling that now was the time to move from frivolity into seriousness and from the carefree impulsivity of adolescence into the intentionality of a maturing life.

"I never heard about your deposition, Billy. I'm not sure if you're allowed to talk about it, but I hope everything went okay."

"Yeah, it's been a wild week, like I said. But the depo wasn't too bad. Cecelia's lawyer asked a lot of questions about Dad, his assets and his estate. Rebecca kept him in check whenever he veered too far afield. But the guy is kind of an ass, excuse my French."

"Yes, she told me a little about him last night."

"He's also either a bit daft or on a fruitless fishing expedition."

"How so?"

"Well, for example, he had a line of questioning about your family's cabin and asked if you still owned it."

"What?"

"Exactly. Rebecca objected as irrelevant and suggested it had nothing to do with me, so the guy should move on to something else. But he reminded us that Corey's a defendant too and that the lawyer had a right to ask me about anything I might know related to his assets or entitlements."

"I sold that place before moving to California. I mean, it took a while to sell, but thankfully, a buyer came along."

"That's what I told him. But he was adamant that *Mrs. Fischer* still owned the place according to the tax records."

"Well, let's hope the lawyer's incompetence will serve you well in the end."

"By the way, I haven't asked you much about your big changes yet. Are you ready to start classes once you get back to California?"

"Yes. It's funny you bring that up. I received a call on my cell yesterday when I was at Rebecca's. It was from the teaching assistant from one of my new classes. She needed an address where they could deliver my class syllabus ASAP."

"Sounds routine."

"Well, that's what I thought. I told her about being here in the Midwest and that she shouldn't overnight the papers because no one would be home to accept a package."

"Does something bother you about that? I'm sure Rebecca would be fine with you giving out her address."

"No, it's not that. I had a funny feeling after hanging up the call. The teaching assistant offered to send the documents instead to my emergency contact, Corey. And while I did list him on my registration forms, I only provided his cell phone number. After ending the call, I remember the assistant mentioning that Corey lives in Hermosa Beach. I'm not sure how she'd know that."

Billy's face turned serious as he remembered all Rebecca had learned from Charlie Moore. He looked over at Ginny. "Take out your phone." She did. "Do you see the phone number in your recent calls column?" She tapped different parts of her screen until she found what Billy was seeking.

"Yes."

"Okay, touch that number and see what happens."

Ginny complied, then held the phone to her ear. Billy watched for several moments before Ginny turned back toward him.

"It went to voicemail."

"Did the outgoing message say anything about Santa Monica College?"

"No—just a woman's voice, but she didn't state her name."

"Okay. Type the three-digit area code from her number into your web browser." She did. "What does it say?"

Ginny stared at her screen and its near-instant display of an answer. Her mouth fell agape. Her heart and stomach began to sink. Then, she turned back to face Billy and read from her screen. "The 870 area code covers the southeastern portion of Arkansas, including the city of Pine Bluff."

They exchanged alarmed looks. Billy said, "Call Corey, now."

Ginny hit Cory's autodial. All three attempts went straight to voicemail. Why wasn't he answering? Thinking quickly but clearly, she then typed in the name of the Foxtails Lounge into her browser. She had remembered that is where Samantha worked and the place where Corey and Nick had been headed. A man answered the phone, and Ginny hit the speaker button so Billy could hear, too. After the briefest of explanations, the man told Ginny that Samantha was in the bar a while ago and that she had been

talking with a stranger before her shift. He then said both Samantha and the stranger abruptly left the Foxtails Lounge, but he had
no clue where they went.

"You might try and contact her boyfriend at the Barron County Sheriff's station. He was with her when they all left."

Ginny's stomach could sink no further, but her slumping
shoulders pulled her entire body down toward the floor mat.

"What's her boyfriend's name?"

"Todd Coles, the Sheriff himself."

* * *

Cecelia couldn't believe her luck as she drove into Western Wisconsin. *People can be so damn trusting,* she thought. *That reality
didn't work well for Bennett in the end, but it's what will lead me to
Corey by this afternoon.*

First, she had convinced Ginny that Cecelia was calling from
Santa Monica College. Perhaps all those roles in the Pine Bluff
High School drama productions had paid off. Then, she learned
from the text exchange between Ginny and Corey that he was
headed somewhere with Nick. The last piece of the puzzle fell into
place when she discovered Snapchat on Corey's device and that
his location feature had been turned on.

She pulled off the freeway at a truck stop east of Hudson. She
went inside to buy a soda and to access the free Wi-Fi. She could
only track Corey's whereabouts while his old device was connected
to the internet, and she had been itching for an update on his location for the past thirty miles. There weren't enough bars on her
own phone for the hotspot to work. She pulled up the app on his
phone and spotted Corey sixty miles east, outside the town of Barron. She tapped on the hazy blue dot indicating that others in the
Snapchat world had posted photos or videos from this spot. What
she saw surprised her. *Half-dressed women dancing on poles? A lit
neon sign for the Foxtails Lounge? What in the actual fuck?*

She went back out to the car and followed up on a hunch.
She grabbed photocopies from a banker's box in the back seat

and began scouring the papers in search of one in particular. She found it. In her hand were copies of the research results she had posted on her corkboard back home in Pine Bluff. Cecelia zeroed in on the address of Ginny's only remaining property in the state of Wisconsin—a cabin in Barron County. That must be where Corey was heading. It was in the same county as the Foxtails strip club. As she looked through the documents, Cecelia refreshed her memory. A *Mrs. Fischer* still owned the property on County Road V that was previously held in the name of Frank Fischer alone. That was the same place where the news articles indicated that there had been a shooting in the woods in 2013, an incident involving the owner's son as well as the alleged victim, Nicholas Parker. Cecelia dug through her papers until she found the photocopy of that news item, too. Parker had been rushed to the hospital in Chippewa Falls, where a bullet wound had been treated before he was released. After an initial investigation by Barron County Sheriff Todd Coles, no charges were filed, as Parker declined to pursue the matter.

"That was Corey's first successful evasion from criminal responsibility," she said to Bennett, "but it'll also be his last."

Chapter 17

In the parking lot of the Foxtails Lounge, three different negotiations ensued. Todd Coles was needed back at the Sheriff's office for a meeting in fifteen minutes. For her part, Samantha wanted a ride to the cabin-sized home that her mother had recently purchased north of Barron. Todd and Samantha talked next to his patrol car, discussing how to meet both immediate needs. Nick stood near his own car a few feet away, talking on a cellphone.

Corey stood alone, half listening to those two conversations and having one with himself. The earlier bright sunshine in Minneapolis had given way to cloud-filled skies in Barron County. Corey smelled rain and felt a touch of it on his nose. He watched the others in the parking lot engage in tense discussions while he stood negotiating with himself. Should he really meet Judy, his father's longtime lover and the mother of Frank's only daughter? What Pandora's Box might that unexpectedly open? What truths might Judy reveal, sending Corey on yet another of his trademarked downward spirals? And whatever he might learn, if indeed Judy speaks to him at all, wouldn't Corey then be duty-bound to share everything with his mom?

Minutes later, Todd drove away in his patrol car toward Barron while Corey and Sam rode together with Nick in his car, heading northeast along Redemption Lake Road, heading toward Judy's home. Samantha sat in the front passenger seat while Corey rode in back. Nick told Samantha the highlights of who he was and all that he had accomplished in life to date. Corey tuned out;

he had heard it all before. With each successive turn and curve in the road, Corey's stomach sank. First, they passed the spot where he had pulled the family car onto the shoulder when he was seventeen. It was the night Frank had brought him to the Foxtails Lounge during deer hunting season so that Corey might be, in Frank's blunt vernacular, *initiated into manhood like my father did for me.* When it was time to leave the Lounge, Frank had the stench of booze on his breath, so Corey grabbed the car keys. When Frank announced that he was sick, Corey slowed the car and pulled onto the rocky shoulder of the dark road. The first chunks of vomit hit the passenger side window and ran down along the door. He threw the car into park, then bolted out his own door and raced around to the far side of the vehicle, yanking the door open in time for Frank to finish vomiting onto the gravel, with some of it landing on Corey's new shoes.

He reflexively placed his hand to his mouth as Nick's car sped past and away from that memory. Soon, they reached another, more recent recollection—the spot where Corey ran off the road last year, sparking the horrible cascade of events that led to his arrest. He sat up tall in the back seat, straining to look out the car's front window. He hadn't seen this location in the light of day. The accident, caused when he swerved to avoid hitting a deer, occurred shortly after dusk. By the time he awoke from his blackout after being trapped in the car, everything around him was dark, with the only illumination coming from the flashing red and blue emergency lights atop Sheriff Coles' patrol car.

Now, craning his neck forward in the back seat of Nick's car, Corey spied the blighted tree whose gray bark had been shorn off where his rental car had smashed into it. Half a mile later, Nick slowed the car to a rolling pause before turning onto County Road V, a road that Corey knew all too well. As the car turned directly north, he had an epiphany. Everything suddenly made sense— his mother not knowing the name of the person who bought the Fischer family cabin, the reason the cabin's contents looked exactly as he remembered when he peeked into the window during his last furtive visit and Samantha's puzzling earlier comment that he and Nick had been to Judy's house before. Five minutes later, Nick steered the car into the familiar grassy drive. Before them stood the Fischer family cabin turned Judy Fischer's new home.

"Holy shit," Nick exclaimed.

* * *

The second it stopped, Samantha jumped out of the car and ran toward the house, leaving Corey and Nick to gape at each other as she strode toward the front door. Nick got out, slammed his door and walked around the grass, turning in a complete circle, taking in the scene of the place he had visited five years before and the place he last saw through the back window of an ambulance. At first, Corey sat transfixed. After a few moments and one deep breath, he unbuckled himself from the seat and got out of the car. He then stood in the narrow, protected space created when he opened his backseat door, his hands clinging to the metal edge. He stared at his family's former cabin, a deluge of memories assaulting his brain. He watched as Samantha pushed her way inside, then he waited for something to happen as he stood there, unable to take another step.

From his vantage point in the vast grassy yard, not much, if anything, had changed. There stood the cabin. For sixty years, it had been a seasonal cottage, a place for the Fischer men to hunt, escape from their wives and engage in hidden pleasures. Now, it belonged to someone else—someone whom Corey had met but didn't know and someone now bound to him indirectly by blood. He continued staring at the cabin, then shook his head. This place of such nostalgic importance to his father and grandfather had once again summoned Corey to its doors like an all-powerful magnet, refusing to relinquish its grip on him. *What does this place want from me?* Or perhaps there was something he needed from it? For each of the times he reluctantly passed through the cabin's menacing door, Corey had a conscious choice to flee before stepping across its threshold. He could have escaped from his father

and taken a bus back home to Pepin as a boy. He could have refused his inheritance of the cabin and its sheltered hunting rifles
when Frank died in 2013. He certainly could have avoided this
place one year ago. No one told him to make the detour for that
crazy one last look. And here he was again today. Samantha had
given him an out. She hadn't invited him to tag along. Yet again, he
chose to return to this place of misery. He remained standing on
the lawn, a product of his own inexplicable choosing.

Samantha opened the screen door and yelled to Corey, summoning him into the cabin and jolting him from his thoughts. He
noticed Nick pacing across the yard, a cell phone glued to his ear,
hand gestures flailing and Nick's shrill voice yelling into the device. Should he try to grab Nick's attention and convince him to
drive them both away? Wasn't this the perfect opportunity for a
clean break from the past and to avoid a potentially messy future
once he heard what Judy and Samantha had to say? Instead, Corey gently closed the car door and made his way across the lawn
toward the house.

* * *

The interior no longer looked familiar. The brown shag carpet had
been replaced by laminate hardwood flooring with a few braid-
ed rugs laid out to better define the living area as separate from
the dining room. Atop those gleaming floors rested furniture Corey didn't recognize either. The pieces weren't new, just different.
Perhaps Judy had brought the furnishings here from wherever
she lived before. He sat in a lounge chair. Judy took a seat across
the room on the end of a couch, with Samantha already settled at
the opposite end. No one spoke for a while; rather, each of them
stared around the room after awkward introductions. Corey noted that wood paneling still adorned the walls, though the neon
beer signs and wildlife photos were gone. Instead, Judy had decorated the home with nondescript, framed prints as well as family
pictures of Judy, Samantha and an older couple—presumably Judy's parents. A large, framed photo of Judy and Frank caught his

attention. In it, they stood together under a tree in what appeared to be summertime. The pair held hands with a bouquet of sunflowers gripped in the middle.

Judy must have followed the direction of Corey's gaze from across the room.

"It was taken the day we said our vows."

Corey turned his head away from the wall and looked Judy straight in the eyes.

"Vows?"

"Your father and I exchanged promises—commitments to one another. Our bond was strong, especially after Samantha was born."

"But Frank was married—to my mother."

Judy's eyes dropped. She appeared to be looking down to the floor. "I realize that, Corey. And I'm sorry. I never meant to hurt you or your mom and had no intention of ever making my relationship with Frank known, either to you or anyone for that matter."

He listened. So many questions arose in his mind, but he didn't verbalize any of them. He wasn't certain where to begin, so he decided to let Judy tell her own story.

She looked up once again. "That was one of my commitments to your father—to support the fact that his family in Pepin was his first and only official one and that I wouldn't ever threaten it. I accepted the best role I could hope for and all that I received in return. For his part, Frank promised to support and protect Samantha and me in person whenever possible and from a distance, at the very least. He also honored my request that neither Samantha nor my parents would know his identity. I thought that was best for everyone, including you."

"Me? How so?"

"Because I knew Samantha would grow to be a curious young woman. She does have half my genes, after all. I was concerned that someday she might figure out she has a half-brother and seek you out. That would unravel everything for Frank, for all of us.

Again, I didn't want to hurt you or your mom. I only wanted as much of Frank as I could get. We were in love, whether you want to hear that or not."

Prompted by questions from Samantha, Judy revealed information that brought mysterious elements to light. She had changed her last name to Fischer when Samantha was born, giving her parents a made-up story about needing to make the switch due to a recent identity theft. She also explained how she submitted an anonymous bid to purchase the cabin from Frank's estate through a nondescript LLC. Fortunately, Ginny had not insisted on knowing the buyer's name; the fact that Judy had made a full-price offer in cash and waiving inspection seemingly smoothed the path for her quiet acquisition of the home she had grown to love as much as the man who filled its rooms with laughter and tenderness and joy.

Corey felt his face twitch. Did she say *tenderness and joy*? Conflicting emotions coursed through his gut, with sympathy for Judy surprisingly among them.

She turned and looked at her daughter on the other end of the couch. "And Sam, I need to apologize about one specific thing. I lied to you about who your father was."

"Oh? You told me he was from Pepin and had a family of his own. All of that seems to be true."

"Yes, it is. But I also said that you never met him. In fact, you did—many times."

Judy paused, and Samantha filled the void. "You mean your boyfriend, Don? Huh. I knew it in my gut. But I believed your story about the unknown stranger in Pepin, so I ignored what I felt deep inside. Don was actually Frank, my father?"

"I'm sorry for lying to you, honey. It felt like the right thing to do at the time and the only way for you and Frank to spend time together without making things more complicated than they already were."

Corey ended his silence. "Don. It's short for Donald. That was my father's middle name, the same as my—or I guess *our*—

grandfather's first name." Corey pointed back and forth between himself and Sam. "Thank God my mother doesn't know about this. At least not yet, anyway."

At the mention of the word *mother*, Judy looked away from Corey and toward Samantha. She once again expressed contrition. Samantha and Judy continued talking, almost as if Corey were not in the room. Thus far, the two women spoke from their fixed positions on either end of the sofa. There was no movement toward the middle, no motion that might suggest a forgiving or remorseful hug. Corey found himself staring at Judy, trying to figure her out. He had to admit she was pretty, in a different way from his mother. Judy's hair was a wispy collection of strawberry blonde, most of it in a bob with several strands falling around the back of her neck and over both ears. She had a much lighter skin tone—almost pale—and far fewer wrinkles than did Ginny. There were no tight lines around the edges of Judy's eyes or her mouth. She probably didn't smoke, he figured, and must have spent most of her life shaded from the damaging rays of the sun.

For the past year, since he first suspected that Samantha was his half-sister, he had begun to concoct in his mind the worst possible image of Judy, everything short of horns growing from the sides of her head. In his mind, she was a home-wrecking whore, a seducer of a susceptible man—a woman without redeeming qualities. Now, sitting across from her in the comfortable home that she had fashioned from Frank's cliched man cave, he felt conflicted. Judy didn't emit the same aura of evil that he had imagined. Rather, she seemed welcoming, gratuitous and kind.

A gentle knock at the front door summoned everyone's attention. Corey had forgotten about leaving Nick in the front yard. Judy rose from her seat and welcomed him in, then stepped into the kitchen to address the whistling tea kettle while Nick took her place on the sofa. Corey acknowledged Nick with a nod of his head, then turned his attention to Samantha, who was already looking straight back at him. Their mutual stares remained locked. Corey imagined he could read her mind now—the same probing questions floating through their genetically similar brains. His suspicions had been confirmed.

First, of course, was his more recent guess that he had a half-sister. Then, too, the long-held one—that Frank and Judy's overtly friendly banter and physical touch at Slippery Sam's Café all those years ago vindicated Corey's innate sense as a boy that his father was doing something wrong. And yet, to hear Judy affirm these long-buried truths so matter-of-factly and without any sense of shame startled him. His father had exchanged commitments—vows!—with a woman who was not his wife. *Who does that?* he wondered to himself. A clear answer followed immediately behind—*Frank, my swine of a father, that's who.*

With a devilish smirk, Nick said, "How's the family reunion going?"

Corey and Samantha both glanced at Nick before returning their gaze upon each other.

Samantha pointed at Nick and then directed her words toward Corey. "This is the guy Todd was telling me about? The one you shot in the ass out in the woods? Suddenly, it all makes perfect sense."

Nick laughed louder. "She's got your sense of sarcasm, Corey. Must run in the family. I like her."

Samantha rolled her eyes and looked toward the kitchen. Sounds of teacups being set atop a metal tray could be heard from the other side of the wall.

"So, did you ask about the rifles?" Nick seemed as giddy as a grade-schooler on the first day of summer break.

"Rifles?" Samantha asked.

"For God's sake, Nick. Is that the best topic to discuss right now?"

"What?" Nick threw up his hands in feigned innocence. "Neither of you are saying anything, and I was curious. We did talk about it on the drive over from Minneapolis, Corey. Remember? We both wondered what happened to your dad's hunting rifles that we left here."

Samantha bit her lip and shook her head. "I know exactly where they are. Mom bought this place as is, including all the contents. But while she replaced the furniture and flooring, she did keep those old rifles. Todd and I asked why she didn't sell them. After all, she's never gone hunting in her life. Well, at least not that I know of. Still, Mom insisted on keeping them. Now that she was living alone out here in the country, she said she might need them one day for self-defense against a deranged killer. As if that ever would happen in Barron County."

* * *

Cecelia walked into the public library in the middle of Barron. It was the only place she could find with a sign advertising free Wi-Fi. After pretending to browse for books in between rows of full shelves, she pulled Corey's device from her pocket and checked his location on Snapchat, but it revealed he was no longer online. Damn. Either his phone was off, or he deleted the app. The only two places she could think of to look for him were at the cabin or his last known location—the Foxtails Lounge. She pulled up the local map on her phone and located both spots. The cabin was closer, so she decided to check there first.

Chapter 18

Billy had turned the car around, and they were speeding toward Barron County. Ginny tried calling Corey's cell phone for the fifth time in ten minutes. Each call went directly to voicemail. Her texts went unanswered, too.

"Try calling the sheriff's office," Billy said.

She searched for the information in her browser. But they were in the middle of rural Wisconsin; the cell reception was slow. She finally found the number and dialed.

"Barron County Sher..."

"Hello. I need to speak to Todd Coles immediately. Can you please connect me?"

"I'm sorry, ma'am. Who's this?"

"Virginia Fischer. It's urgent."

"Ma'am, what's your emergency?"

"My son is in danger. A woman is trying to kill him."

"Where? What's the address?"

"I'm not sure. Somewhere in Barron County, I think. Please connect me to the Sheriff. He'll know what to do."

"Sheriff Coles is in a meeting. We have other officers who can respond to your situation, ma'am, but I need you to give me more information."

Ginny explained as quickly as she could her suspicion that Cecelia Jackson had tricked Ginny into revealing that she and her son were in the Midwest and that Cecelia knew about the family's former cabin in Barron County. She also described the connection to Samantha at the Foxtails Lounge. Because Ginny couldn't reach Corey, she said that her only hope was the sheriff. She looked over at Billy, who was listening intently. She waited for the person on the other end of the line to say something and realized how insane she must sound. A madwoman on the loose in Barron County? Hunting down a man who killed the woman's husband? And that same man was meeting with his half-sister to tell her for the first time that they were related? Who in their right mind would believe any of that? Ginny felt the car accelerate and saw the speedometer on the car reach eighty.

"Ma'am, it doesn't sound as if there's an immediate threat. I'll alert the Sheriff as soon as he gets out of his meeting. If it makes you feel better, I can send a patrol car over to Samantha's apartment here in Barron. She lives about a mile away. Maybe she and your son are there."

"Thank you, officer. Please have Sheriff Coles call me as soon as possible."

* * *

Judy walked into the living room carrying a plastic tray and four cups of hot tea. She set it down on the coffee table before stepping back, standing up and dropping her folded hands to her waist.

"I overheard your conversation from the kitchen. Nick, would you like to see the rifles?"

He nodded his head enthusiastically before jumping from the sofa and walking after Judy as she headed down the hall. Corey and Samantha reluctantly followed. They all entered the spare bedroom, crowding into the cramped space between the bed, the chest of drawers and a nightstand. Judy pointed toward a glass case in the corner. Nick said he recognized the rifles inside. Samantha asked why in the world Judy was keeping firearms in an unlocked case.

"For Heaven's sake, no one's going to break in and steal them. Who would even know I own a rifles?"

"But if any kids are in the house, that's a real concern."

"I'll worry about that when you and Todd give me a grand-child."

Corey barely listened to the conversation. He hadn't looked once at the corner case holding the rifles. Instead, he was capti-vated by a painting on the opposite wall. Judy must've noticed his stare.

"Frank loved that painting. He gave it to me as a gift."

Corey looked at her, straining to read her lips because he couldn't quite understand or believe her words. Then he looked again at the painting. He had not seen this artwork in more than twenty years. It was a piece he had created as a junior in college and had entered the annual student fine arts contest. Of all the competitions Corey entered across the years and among the var-ious awards he had won, this was the prize that he had coveted least. And yet, he had won first place. The contest theme that year was "creating something difficult." Corey's fellow art students pro-ceeded to craft challenging works using laborious techniques, for-midable materials, and inspiring new points of view. One classmate entered a charcoal drawing made upon a series of cardboard boxes while another cast her sculpture in a rare variety of white clay.

But Corey's piece interpreted the contest theme in a whol-ly different light and one that no others thought to undertake. He used a standard canvas fabric, typical oil-based paint and the same variety of brushstrokes that he and his fellow students had used multiple times before. Certainly, there was nothing inspiring or difficult about his materials or his approach. Instead, he chose to create a work of art whose *subject matter* was personally diffi-cult, at least to him. And the judges seemed to have appreciated the agony implied in his work. He painted a scene that had eluded him throughout his youth, a scene that at times he had yearned for yet at other moments for which he felt dread. He painted a scene set outside the dwelling in which he now stood. The paint-ing depicted Corey and his father at the center of the canvas, the two of them serving as both visual and emotional focal points of the art.

As he stood before this painting again, Corey was initially self-critical. The brushstrokes weren't his best. The choice of hue could have been more precise. He had attempted a realist impression of the Barron County woods with the browns and greens of its foliage surrounding a modest tan cabin nestled snugly in the forest's embrace. Yet, the piece was the best Corey had created thus far in his young life and clearly better than anyone else's work, at least according to the guest judges from Macalester College in Saint Paul. They must have seen what Corey saw now, as his harsh subjective appraisal gave way to a more equitable appreciation for what he had achieved.

The human figures at the focal point of the painting were lifelike in ways Corey had never painted before. Though he had cast them upon the canvas from memory, most would suspect that the artist had posted a photograph of a father and his son close within sight while the brushstrokes were laid. The father in the painting was a stationary cliché—tall, dark and handsome and wearing a warm smile. Viewed from dead center, the man appeared to gaze dotingly upon the boy beside him with feelings of deep fondness and pride practically dripping from the pearls of paint on the man's face. From that same vantage point, the boy appeared to be looking toward his father with equal admiration. And yet, if the observer moved left or right and examined the painting from an angle, the smile on the man's face, as well as the boy's, disappeared, replaced by something akin to anguish, hesitation or fear.

From any vantage point, the older man's arm in the painting rested gently around the boy's shoulders, their bodies gathered with no speck of daylight between. Their pink faces looked devotedly toward one another, both illuminated by the sunshine in front of them and with pale shadows of their bodies falling behind them off toward the woods. It was those two shadows that drew the eye's attention, for they did not fit logically with the sunlight, the source of their existence. The man's shadow bent sideways in the opposite direction of the younger man, at a preposterous angle from the direction of the sun's warm rays. The boy's shadow was small and cast essentially straight down between his bowed-out legs. His shadow screamed out a message of confusion, as if it didn't know whether to follow that of the father, submit to the sunlight's true direction or strike out in a new direction all its own. Corey remembered the hours spent thinking about those shadows before he lifted his brush.

He had struggled with color, at first wanting to paint the father's silhouette in the darkest shade of black. Yet, Corey innately knew that wouldn't be true, so he summoned self-restraint and chose a moderately lighter hue. For the boy, the battle was reversed. Corey's inclination was to cast the son's umbra in tones of steel gray, yet he ultimately skewed toward a darker shade, unknowingly choosing the exact same color for both figures' shadows with divergent contours to those shadows the only discernible difference.

As Corey looked upon that last aspect of the painting—the shadows—and then down to the script in the lower right corner of the canvas, he felt himself smiling. He had completely forgotten about this painting, including its tortured symbolism and its success, until a few moments ago. Likewise, he had failed to remember all the fawning praise from the three contest judges. *The tension in those two faces dripped deliciously off the canvas. The change in mood of the man and the boy from suffering to contentment, then back to woe when viewed from left to right is genius. The strange desperation and angst of those shadows capture the entire meaning of this work; uncanny; bravo!*

He took a step closer to read the inscription he had left upon the painting all those years ago, in the spot where an artist might normally sign his or her own name. It was a line from Haruki Murakami that felt as if the writer had penned these words intentionally for Corey and for this stunning work of art. *Where there is light, there must be shadow, where there is shadow there must be light.*

"Corey?" The sound of Judy's voice jolted him from his fixation on the painting. He hadn't noticed that Nick and Samantha had left the bedroom. "Are you okay?"

"I, uh, yeah. I'm a bit stunned to see my own painting on your wall—*this* painting."

Judy looked Corey directly in the eye. They both stayed quiet. He heard murmurs of conversation from Nick and Samantha down the hall and grew uncomfortable, sensing that Judy was reading the scattered thoughts inside his head. She broke the silence first.

"How about you and I take a little walk out in the woods and get some air, huh?"

* * *

Judy pulled the poncho tight against her neck. Corey held the red umbrella above his head and slightly to one side. Rain fell steadily, pelting them from an angle and driven by a gentle wind. They walked across the wide lawn toward the woods. It was the same direction Corey had walked many times before. He could likely follow this path blindfolded, even after all these years he'd been away. Good and bad memories flooded his brain. He passed the shed where he and Nick held target practice in 2013, and he saw the boulder where Frank had buried Corey's childhood dog. Within minutes, Judy and Corey had reached the entrance to the vast hardwood forest that Corey had often explored as a boy and where he had hunted countless times. After exiting the lawn and entering the woods, the raindrops falling on them diminished under the protective canopy of the trees. Judy pulled the poncho's hood toward the back of her neck. Corey retracted his umbrella, folded and fastened it, then used it as a walking stick.

"Well, that's better, right?"

"Hmmm," was the best Corey could muster. While the umbrella had shielded him from the drizzle and the initial absence of conversation spared him from whatever it was Judy wanted to say, both protections vanished, leaving Corey exposed. He shook his head as if to cast the thoughts from his mind and flung them to the damp, leafy ground. How did he arrive at this strange and familiar place with this familiar stranger, a woman he first met as a boy almost thirty years ago and who gave birth to his father's child?

"That painting was your father's favorite, by the way."

"You could tell I was shocked to see it hanging on your wall?"

"Well, you did seem surprised."

"I haven't seen that painting since college. It went up for auction like all the other student artwork in the contest. The proceeds went to charity, but I never did learn who submitted the winning bid. How did he get it?"

"Well, your father gave me a blank check and told me there was no limit."

"Told you? What do you mean?"

"Frank asked me to drive to Minneapolis and buy that painting. He said he couldn't be seen at the auction. And he didn't want your mother to know he'd bought it either."

"Well, that part I do believe—him keeping secrets from Mom. But I don't understand the mystery. Why not simply buy the painting himself?"

"I think you know why."

He did, but Corey wanted to hear her say it, to affirm what he had suspected for years, but never heard Frank confess before he died. He disingenuously shook his head no.

"Frank was proud of your talents, Corey. But after fighting you about going to art school in Minnesota rather than his alma mater in Eau Claire, he was too proud to admit it."

"He told you this?"

"Yes. Your father and I had an honest bond."

"You sure about that? My father's long trail of lies and half-truths stretch from here all the way to Pepin."

He sensed her looking over at him as they continued walking. He caught a glimpse of a smile on her face from the corner of his eye.

"You're a lot like him, you know? Not the lying part, I mean. I'm sure you're as honest as the day is long. I only meant that you're handsome, like him, and quick with a sarcastic retort."

Every bone in Corey's body wanted to dislike Judy Fischer, to find her as detestable as he'd felt about Frank nearly all his life. But he couldn't disagree with anything she said so far. She had nailed the similarities between father and son far sharper than she could have known. He needed to change the subject.

"So, you bought the cabin. Was it nostalgia?"

"Something like that. Frank wanted me to live here. He loved this place, but he knew you didn't want anything to do with it, and neither did your mother. So, he established a trust years ago for me to access when he died, with more than enough funds to buy the place. I honored his request. And, for what it's worth, I do love it, especially the quiet beauty of the woods. So yes, I suppose part of me feels nostalgic. I can feel Frank's presence in this place."

Corey shuddered. The cool, damp air permeated his skin.

"And I'll give this place to Samantha one day, if she wants it, or to her future kids. That way, Frank will get his wish."

They approached a memorable landmark—the incomparable deer stand built by Corey's grandfather, maintained by his father and then ignored these past five years since Frank died. Corey knew exactly where he and Judy stood in the greater scheme of the Fischer property. Once they had passed a large elm, he saw it. The perch standing high above the ground looked from a distance as though she were sturdy enough yet to hold at least one hunter. But the custom-made wooden ladder ascending upward toward the stand was missing two rungs. As they walked closer, Corey saw boards rotting from underneath, and a piece of the protective railing now lay on the ground several feet away and covered in moss. He stopped for a moment and looked up, pondering how the deer stand's fate followed lockstep with the hunting legacy of the Fischer family men.

Judy kept walking, and Corey ran to catch up. She followed the deer path that had been worn through these woods for as long as Corey could remember. Despite all the animals slayed by a bullet shot from the tree stand now fading in the distance behind them, the deer kept using this same goddamn path. Corey shook his head in wonder at the simultaneous innocence and stupidity of these creatures, drawn to the woods and following this trail heading toward the approaching creek for water as the animals' parents did and their parents' ancestors long before that. Despite the lurking, they all kept walking the same worn path, just as Corey and Judy kept on walking, too. They soon crossed the sleepy stream, then turned immediately left and continued following the path along the banks of the mostly clear water as it flowed toward the farm field that lay a few hundred yards ahead.

Judy resumed the conversation. She spoke of how she and Frank became friendly and fell in love despite her knowing he was a married man. She accepted that fact and her own contribution toward his adultery. They had spoken only once about the prospect of Frank leaving Ginny, but Frank rejected it in the same breath. Judy explained what Corey already knew—that Frank's deep Catholic faith prevented him from ever pursuing a divorce. He would honor at least one of his sacred vows and stay with his wife until death did they part.

"I'm not saying that makes sense. But it's how Frank rationalized the situation. I had my own justifications, too, but I have no intention of defending them to you. It's too late for me to judge what we had and what we did as right or wrong. It simply is and was. But I can offer you an apology, hon. I'm sorry for any hurt I've caused you."

Judy continued her one-sided conversation as they approached the farmer's field. She spoke of Frank's kindness, his good humor and of his love for his son. She spoke of Frank's stubborn self-awareness that he didn't know how to show that love for a boy who Frank knew was gay from an early age. He wanted to but couldn't and didn't. Judy spoke of Frank's feelings—regret and remorse and ineptitude as a father. It wasn't an excuse, in her telling, but Frank had a terrible role model in his own father, and he simply never learned how to be a good and loving man for his child. She spoke of that horrible night in 2012 when Frank banished Corey from the family home for good. Corey could hardly believe Judy knew about that awful night.

"Yes. He drove here to Barron the next morning and asked me to come over right away. I'd never seen him so upset in all the years I'd known him. He explained what happened the night before and the hurtful things he had said. He was seemingly unable to fix it or to make amends. *What's done is done*, I remember him saying. Despite my plea that he drive straight back to Pepin and beg your forgiveness, he simply couldn't muster the decency and strength to do it. I know this sounds lame, and you certainly don't have to accept it, but I don't think Frank was capable of being the father you deserved him to be."

After listening to such intense information, Corey was finally triggered into a reply. "And yet, you knowingly had a child with this man. How could you ever explain that to Samantha?"

"It's why I agreed to Frank's demand that he be distant in Sam's life and that she not fully know who he was. Listen, I fully understand Frank's failures as a father, but he was a loving, honest and thoughtful partner to me. And as for deciding to have a child with him, I didn't. Samantha was, as they say, an accident. But she was the best surprise of my entire life."

They reached the edge of the woods, and the stark emergence of a field rising before them. The stream continued through the meadow. It was no longer being used as farmland to grow corn, as Corey remembered, but now appeared as a fallow sward filled with tall grass, wildflowers and random young trees that had crept their way into the pasture, breaking away from their parentage.

"Wow, this sure looks different. I remember it being a cornfield to feed the deer."

"Yes, that's one thing your mother changed before I took ownership. The realtor told me that your mom ended the farmer's land lease. Apparently, she didn't need the money and wanted to sell the land unencumbered to a new owner. I'm grateful she did. I love walking out here among the wildflowers. On occasion, I'll bring a blanket and read a book in the sunshine."

"Sounds peaceful. I doubt Frank would've approved, but I certainly do."

Judy smiled, and he realized it was the first kind thing he had said to her. A shiver of disloyalty rose up his spine. What had compelled him to say something nice to his father's mistress, the mother of Frank's bastard child and the betrayer of Ginny's marriage? Despite those heavy moral judgments, he found it difficult to dislike Judy. In the past hour of being in her presence, they had talked about the most difficult and emotional topics imaginable with no preparation. Yet, she handled herself with notable calm and compassion—a compassion that also extended to Frank. When pressed with the most pointed questions by both Corey and Samantha, Judy had yet to offer any defensiveness or lame excuse. Instead, she exuded forthrightness and an acknowledgment of her own moral failings.

He pointed across the expansive meadow to its farthest edge. "Over there is where it happened—where I killed my first and only deer. I shot him, and then he ran off. Nick and I followed, passing under a barbed wire fence and eventually found the wounded deer lying next to this stream a ways beyond."

"That means you were on state land. Everything past the fence is government property."

"Oh yeah? I didn't know that. Dad never took me that far."

"Yes, it's quite beautiful. If you follow the stream to its mouth about another half mile or so, it empties into Redemption Lake. Frank and I walked that route more than a few times. There's an old hunting shack at the confluence of the stream and the lake. Frank said it was someone's homestead a hundred years ago, a family by the name of Smith. But they abandoned it once the state took over the land on back taxes."

They surveyed the scene quietly until Corey said, "This is nice, Judy. Thank you."

"For what?"

"For this walk and the stories. And for honoring my family's legacy here in ways that I never could or wanted to. It's probably a cliche to say that my relationships with Frank and even my grandfather, for that matter, were complicated. It's strange to say, but after seeing all the changes to the cabin and the land, I no longer feel guilty about abandoning it. So, thank you."

"You're welcome, Corey. Again, I'm sorry for everything your father and I did wrong. I have a feeling that it's going to take time to mend fences with my daughter, but I know her. She'll come around. And I hope you'll be okay too. We haven't had time for you to say much about your own life since Frank died. I have no idea what's been going on with you, but I'd like to."

Corey shook his head and thought about Miguel. Those thoughts hit him like a punch to the gut. He resisted the impulse to cry and instead felt a sudden freedom to spill his guts, to tell Judy about the man whom he loved and had lost.

"You have no idea, Judy. Come on, let's walk back to the cabin—I mean, your house. I'll catch you up on my life."

Chapter 19

Billy sped down Highway 53, closing in on the town of Barron. The drizzle and curvy roads forced him to drive slower than before. He barely slowed the car as he exited onto U.S. Highway 8 east of Barron, almost swiping a blue Chevy Malibu going the opposite direction. After another fifteen minutes of driving, they arrived in Barron. They found the sheriff's station on the north end of town after crossing a bridge over the winding Barron Flowage. Billy parked the vehicle askew across the painted lines, and together, he and Ginny ran inside. Billy stopped at the reception desk, asking where he might find Todd Coles. Ginny walked past him and directly toward the man standing next to the snack machine in between the men's and women's restrooms. She could never forget that face, especially the face of the man who had stood so smugly in her driveway back in Pepin a year ago and arrested her son on a charge of murder. He turned around as she approached.

"Mrs. Fischer! May I help you?"

"Yes," Ginny replied before breaking down into long-held tears. Billy joined them and explained the situation. A deputy sheriff walked up to them as well, informing Todd about the earlier call from Virginia Fischer and that he had sent a patrol car over to Samantha's apartment but found no one at home.

"That's because she's at her mother's new place out on County Road V. Everyone, hold on." Todd reached for the cell phone in his pocket and dialed Samantha's number. Ginny heard half the conversation.

"So, you're there with Nick in the house, but Judy and Corey went for a walk?"

"Is anyone else there?"

"Take a look outside the window, just to be sure."

"Are you sure it's a blue car that just pulled into the drive?"

"Lock the door, Sam, and try calling your mother."

"Damn. Put Nick on the phone and go get your mother's rifles."

* * *

The clouds unleashed their contents. Rain lashed down heavily across Barron County. Judy pulled the poncho's hood over her head, and Corey unfurled his umbrella, holding it above them as they emerged from the woods. In the distance, across the lawn, stood the cabin. Off to the west, Corey noticed a car pull into the drive, though the now pouring rain occluded his view. Judy said she didn't recognize the car. No one she knew owned a blue Chevy Malibu. They continued walking across the lawn. The car came to a stop one hundred yards away, and the driver jumped out. Now, they were close enough for Corey to recognize who she was.

"Judy, run toward the house. Now." He gave her a not-so-gentle nudge in the direction of the cabin. Then, he yelled at Cecelia. "Hey! I'm the one you're after. But you'll have to catch me first."

Judy stood where Corey left her as he ran back toward the entrance to the deer path in the woods from which they had just emerged. "Corey," she yelled as he ran away. Only five minutes earlier, he had finished telling her the story about Miguel's death at the hands of Cecelia Jackson. "Run to the Smith Shack! You know the way!"

Corey looked back to see Cecelia turn toward her car and reach inside. He also saw Judy run toward the house and burst inside the front door.

* * *

Cecelia distinctly heard what the woman had yelled to Corey—*run to the Smith Shack*. She reached over to the front passenger seat of the car, grabbed her handgun and cell phone, kissed Bennett's urn goodbye, and then ran in the direction that she had seen Corey flee. She entered the woods at the only obvious opening, a well-worn path beginning at the base of two towering white pines, the muddy trail now smeared by unmistakable boot prints, spaced apart and alternating with left and right imprints, as if made by someone running to save his life. She ran for almost five minutes before stopping at the base of a large oak. She leaned against the immovable hardwood, its trunk providing her a supportive place to rest and its canopy protecting her from the falling rain. She breathed deep and rapid—in and out, out and in. She looked ahead on the deer path, boot prints still marking the dirt, though less pronounced than before as less rain fell here in the depths of the forest, the fulsome leaves of summer catching and keeping the lighter drops and delaying the descent of heftier ones. She had thrust her phone into the left pocket of her windbreaker, the handgun into her right. She silently thanked the universe for leading her to choose a light jacket earlier this morning. Its minimal weight didn't drag her down, and the sheen fabric was impervious to water.

Cecelia caught her breath. With her back still pressed against the tree, she surveyed the bosky surroundings. She stood amid a vast and varied forest. Though she had never stepped foot on this land before today, it felt familiar—like the Arkansas Timberlands near Pine Bluff. The Timberlands consisted of a dense pine and cypress forest covering hilly terrain and lining myriad tributaries. It was a place where she had gone deer hunting and bass fishing as a young girl with her father and then as a wife with Bennett. The Wisconsin woods in which she now stood held strangely familiar reminders of that land, including an aging salt lick she passed moments before and a decrepit deer stand high atop a hardwood tree.

She walked farther up the path toward a gurgling stream as she continued to catch her breath. The scene reminded her of Poison Springs back home. It was one of Bennett's favorite places to

hunt. Cecelia fondly remembered tagging along with him as support. She remembered how Bennett waxed nostalgic about the
history of Poison Springs, the pyrrhic victory of the Confederate
Army during the last stages of the Civil War. There, the Confeder-
ates routed the Union army, gathered stolen corn and four canons,
and then slaughtered every captured Union soldier. A key aspect
of their victory was poisoning the nearby spring water, leaving
the northern fighters no source of fresh water to drink. Cecelia
drew strength from that story whenever she heard Bennett tell
it because he spoke so passionately about the heroic ingenuity
of the South by focusing upon the water and upon God's will that
justice be done. *Water is the source of all life*, he said. *After all,
water makes up ninety percent of our bodies, right? And the Bible
teaches us that man was created in God's own image, so it must be
that God is in the water and that God is the water.*

Recalling Bennett's words gave her strength now, too, as
she remembered even more. *In the Bible, God also says that vengeance is his alone and that if anyone is thirsty, let him come to God
and drink. Let the thirsty come to God for vengeance. That is what
brought us justice against our enemy in these woods*, Bennett said
while gesturing with his hand toward the thick pine forest. *They
channeled God's own words and focused upon the water, poisoning
the stream and then killing all those thieving invaders and bringing
back to the good people of Arkansas exactly what God ordained—
vengeance.*

Cecelia felt invigorated by these memories with Bennett.
Yet, perhaps they weren't memories at all but instead prescient
thoughts about once again finding justice and vengeance against
someone who had done her wrong and stolen life from the people of Arkansas. She resumed running down the path, heading
straight toward the rippling stream.

* * *

Corey reached the spot where the creek left the forest and entered a wide meadow, the same spot where he had stood with

Judy not more than thirty minutes ago. He had been jogging at a steady pace, neither fast nor slow. He figured that he had a few minutes' head start on Cecelia if, indeed, she had followed him as he implored her to do. He stopped to listen for evidence of her behind him but only heard the expected sounds of the landscape—a breeze blowing through the wet canopy of the forest and the light splash of water rolling over smooth rocks in the stream nearby.

He decided it was safe to take a break. Though he hadn't run at a full sprint, the jog had tired him, especially with his still sore and bruised ribs. He wasn't a runner now like in the old days. Surfing and biking created a different kind of endurance not amenable to sustaining him on this unexpected dash. Also, when combined with the elevated anxiety and adrenaline coursing through his veins, the cross-country run through the forest quickly sapped him of strength. He saw a fallen elm tree on the ground a few feet off the path and headed toward it, then sat down to rest. He still had the red umbrella. He did not recall fastening it but laid it beside him against the elm.

It felt good to sit for a moment. As he stared in the direction from which he had run, and presumably the direction from which Cecelia would soon come, he could see the rippling stream, and it generated inside of him a powerful thirst. He'd had nothing to drink since the Foxtails Lounge, where he sipped a glass of ice water while waiting to talk with Samantha. And although Judy had brewed and offered tea back at the house, it had not cooled in time for him to swallow a drop before he and Judy set off for their walk in the woods.

He had only been this parched once before in his life—a long time ago, but in these same woods. It was when he and Nick pursued the wounded deer, the eighteen-point buck Corey had shot. That day, he had been forced to run on his recently lacerated knee, the injury he sustained while running and daydreaming along the bike path near the condo he shared with Nick in Minneapolis. So much had changed since that time, but at least one thing tied those events together—Corey had a fear-driven thirst while running across treacherous uneven terrain on both occasions, both five years ago and now again today.

He considered the stream running several yards away. Would he dare lower himself to the ground and scoop water into his mouth? He knew this was a spring-fed stream whose headwaters emerged from a rocky hill on the neighboring property to the west. Frank had taken him there only once, saying that it was called Destiny Springs. Corey remembered how each of them had scooped a cold swig with their bare hands, swallowing gulp after gulp of the amazingly fresh liquid, which Frank playfully referred to as *Adam's Ale, the purest water on God's green Earth*. But that was at the tributary's source, he warned. Downstream, others shared from this same water—deer, birds and other creatures of the north woods. The chance of being poisoned by parasites was high. Despite that grotesque warning, that first hike to Destiny Springs was the only time Corey could remember seeing his father express something close to spirituality.

Frank's piety abounded for sure—especially inside the sanctuary at St. Bridget's—but Corey remembered only seeing a sliver of his father's love for something sacred that one time. *This is a true circle of the godly life,* Frank had explained. *Look here. Water pure enough to drink flows out of the hillside and stays that way for only a short time. Soon, it's defiled by temptation and treachery as the stream meanders through the forest on its long journey to Redemption Lake. There, the water from Destiny Springs becomes one with all the others flowing in from other sources, including the sky, and it has reached its furthermost point. Redemption Lake doesn't flow into any river or other lake. It's a dead end, the culmination of an innocent life that has run its course. Eventually, though, the water seeps down into the land, replenishes the aquifer and returns here to Destiny Springs to begin its journey anew.*

He reflected on that story but with more insight than when he was a boy. He wished he could walk back to Destiny Springs now and drink from her unspoiled waters. But danger lurked in that direction, so he had no choice but to press on. He looked away from the stream, knowing he would have to defer quenching his thirst a bit longer. Instead, he stared off toward the meadow that lay beyond the edge of the woods.

Despite the falling rain, it echoed scenes from *The Four Seasons*, a series of four paintings by Frenchman Nicolas Poussin that Corey had seen hanging in the Louvre. The four paintings depicted scenes labeled *Spring, Summer, Autumn* and *Winter* and were heavily laden with mythological and religious symbolism. He looked out through the trees into the meadow and was reminded of *Spring*, which depicted the Garden of Eden before the serpent slithered onto Adam and Eve's path. The surrounding verdant forest hemmed in a fulsome pasture with the forbidden fruit hanging deliciously from the tree nearby. Above it all sat God atop a dark gray cloud, observing his creation and awaiting the inevitable fate of mankind.

Corey could also see the other four Poussin paintings in these misty Wisconsin Northwoods as he sat atop the fallen elm. *Summer* depicted a vast field of crops eerily like what the field before him looked like on his last journey here with Nick—a vast sward of tan-colored crops. *Autumn* sparked a thought of strange coincidence now that the previous farmland had been returned to wildflowers and tall grass. It looked like the painting's scene of a meadow in fading daylight, with spies bringing fruits from the promised land. The last painting, *Winter*, was gloomy and much darker than the others. It depicted a land flooded with water reminiscent of the great flood and the end of the world, with floating bodies strewn across the canvas and a boat in the distance their only salvation. Corey felt the mood of *Winter* as he scoured the panorama before him—dark and foreboding and wet.

The snap of a tree branch jolted him from the heavy recollections. He turned his head like an owl, quickly moving his gaze from the field on his left toward the woodland path on his right, the same path from which he had emerged several minutes earlier. He saw movement and a violent shaking of shrubbery near the ground. Something or someone was on the move several yards away. He jumped to his feet and ran behind a nearby oak to gain a hidden vantage point from which he might see what had caused the stir. But before reaching the tree, he tripped on a loose vine made taut by the weight of his own body as his foot caught the vine, sending him with a thud to the ground.

The sounds behind him grew frantic but also moved quickly away. Now lying in the damp dirt of the forest floor, Corey saw through the thicket a rafter of wild turkeys foraging for acorns beneath another large oak. They moved in near unison away from him and the heavy noise created by his fall. As the turkeys moved out of sight, his left ankle throbbed. He tried getting up but felt an instant, searing pain when he placed too much weight on that same foot, and the umbrella busted in half as he leaned on it, trying to get up.

"Shit!"

He considered his options. He could find a nearby place to hide, perhaps covering up with leaves to camouflage himself by the time Cecelia eventually came down the path. But there were those boot tracks he'd left in the mud. If she had any tactical sense, she'd notice the point where Corey's imprints ceased their forward motion and moved off the path into the woods. Like the wounded deer he pursued with Nick years ago, Corey would be captive to fate by sitting down in the forest, waiting for the hunter to locate and kill her prey. He cast those thoughts from his mind. Instead, he would keep going and take charge of his destiny. The pain endured, yet Corey rose and staggered away from the elm along the edge of the stream to better hide his footprints. He rejoined the path after several yards and endeavored to channel his agony into a motivation to run. Thoughts of his current and past pains propelled him forward. Corey once again reached the point where the stream entered the meadow. He took a deep breath and exhaled before setting off across the damp grass, and he didn't look back.

Chapter 20

Todd Coles steered his squad car into the driveway and approached the Chevy Malibu. Billy tapped his shoulder. "That's the same make and model of car Rebecca's detective said that Cecelia drives."

Todd stopped abruptly and threw his car into park. "Wait here." He jumped out of the vehicle, unholstered his gun and walked toward the blue car. No one was inside—at least, no one alive was inside. A camo-colored ossuary was buckled into the passenger seat, and the photo of a man was taped to the dash. He motioned for Billy and Ginny to exit the sheriff's car, and then all three of them walked quickly toward the house. Judy pushed the door open before they reached the threshold and promptly locked it up once the three newcomers were inside.

"Everybody all right in here?" Todd asked.

"Couldn't be better, Sheriff," Nick said. "Didn't think I'd see you again so soon."

Todd ignored him. "Judy and Sam, this is Virginia Fischer. Sam, where's Cecelia Jackson? Tell me what happened since we spoke."

"After her car crawled up the driveway, Nick and I saw Mom and Corey walk out of the woods. Then, Mom ran toward us while Corey raced back into the forest, and the woman ran after him."

"Judy, are you okay?"

"Yes, but that woman has a gun. I saw it in her hand when I looked back after reaching the doorstep. As far as I know, Corey's unarmed."

"Which way did they go?" Todd asked.

Everyone moved toward the front window as Judy, Samantha and Nick all pointed toward the deer path between the giant pine trees off to the southwest.

"I think I know where Corey is headed, or at least I hope I do," Judy said.

"Where?" Ginny asked with a shaking voice.

"He and I were on a walk before this happened. I told him about the Smith Shack over on the state land by Redemption Lake. He had no idea it was there all these years. And I remember telling him—*it's easy to find if you follow the stream.* As soon as we separated out in the yard, and after I heard him yell for Cecelia to follow him, I shouted that he should head for the Smith Shack. I figured it was a place he could aim for and where you'd be able to intercept him by car."

"Good thinking, Judy." Todd rubbed his chin while pausing to think. "The problem is—the quickest way to get there is County V, and the bridge over the Vermillion River is under repair. The detour through Cumberland would take at least half an hour from here. I can reach the shack on foot in less time than that."

Samantha spoke up in a stern voice directed at Todd. "Did you hear what Mom said? That woman has a gun. I don't want you getting ambushed or shot. She already killed Corey's partner, Miguel."

"I'm aware. And I won't get hurt." He reached for Samantha and pulled her into an embrace. He kissed the top of her head before releasing his grip and turning back to Judy. "You say both Corey and Cecelia ran toward that path over there?" He pointed out the window.

"Yes, we saw them both go in," Judy affirmed. "The woman entered a minute or so after Corey."

Billy yelled. "Enough of this chit-chat! We've gotta do something—now!"

"Listen up," Todd said calmly. "I'll take a more direct route to the Smith Shack on foot, starting out past the shed. The path that Corey is on follows the long, winding stream from Destiny Springs toward the lake. I can cover that distance in half the time by going straight through the woods, to the north of the meadow that lies between." He turned to look at Samantha. "And yes, I'll be careful. Cecelia Jackson can't possibly know these woods as well as I do, or as well as Corey, for that matter. Here, look." He pulled out his cell phone and tapped his maps app. "We're here, and the stream runs that way around Manning Point, across the old farm field and then in a roundabout way to Redemption Lake." He then showed the screen to Ginny and Judy. Nick and Billy strained to look over Todd's shoulder. "I'll go along this route," he said while hovering his finger over the phone. "Then, I'll meet one or both of them at the lake. I'll call for a backup to meet me."

Todd pulled Samantha aside and whispered into her ear as her face wore a serious look. She remained stoic and said nothing in reply. He then turned to the others. "I need all of you to stay inside the house with the door locked until one of my deputies arrives, understand?"

"We can't sit here on our asses while Corey's in danger," Billy said. "I'm coming with you."

"You most certainly are not. That is an order, and you'll obey it."

Billy stared at Todd with his steely blue eyes. "Fine."

* * *

As soon as Todd ran past the shed and out of sight, Billy turned to Nick and said, "Let's go."

"What?"

"We've got to help Corey. You've been in these woods before, and I haven't. I need you to show me the way and keep us from getting lost."

"But you heard the sheriff. We're supposed to wait here for a deputy to arrive."

"Fine, stay and wait with the other women, Nick. But I'm going to protect my friend."

Nick looked down at his phone as if it held a secret message or an answer to the unfolding drama. Billy continued to stare at Nick as if taunting him to step up and be a man. After Nick's silence passed the fifteen-second mark, Billy turned and walked toward the door.

"Wait." Nick ran to the picture window below which he and Samantha had placed the two rifles that once belonged to Frank Fischer. "We're going to need these."

Judy ran into the spare bedroom and returned within seconds, handing Nick and Billy a small box. "You'll also need some ammo."

Billy and Nick each cocked open a rifle and carefully loaded them with a cartridge while standing in the living room with the three women watching them. Then, they slammed the rifles shut, pulled the straps over their shoulders, and hurried out the front door. Nick motioned for Billy to follow him toward the trail at the entrance to the woods. "Todd went that way," pointing off to his far left, "but we'll track Corey by taking the same route he did. And Cecelia, too. We'll catch her from behind."

Billy followed Nick as they hustled into the forest.

* * *

Judy and Ginny stood at the picture window, watching as Nick and Billy disappeared into the woods. Samantha approached them at the window after locking and bolting the front door. The three women turned to face each other. Samantha spoke first after initially looking at her mother and then turning toward Ginny.

"Mrs. Fischer, I am, uh, not quite sure what to say. This has certainly been an unexpected day."

Ginny paused as if considering where to begin. All she could think about was that a mad woman was hunting Corey, and she felt helpless to stop him from being killed. Judy took advantage of Ginny's hesitation.

"Ginny, each of us clearly has a lot to say. But our first concern now should be your son." Ginny nodded her head in agreement.

"Come on, let's get in my car and head toward Redemption Lake."

Ginny and Samantha showed looks of confusion and uttered no verbal reply. But soon, they walked out the door following Judy's lead.

"Mom, aren't you going to lock up?" Sam yelled ahead toward Judy.

"No," Judy yelled over her shoulder, as she walked briskly across the lawn. "Leave it open in case Corey returns and needs a safe place to hide out."

Ginny kept pace two steps behind Judy. Sam soon caught up. The three women stepped into the vehicle, buckled up and Judy locked their doors. She started the engine and backed the car up violently before braking and switching into drive. She lurched the car onto County Road V, turned north toward Cumberland and sped down the highway.

* * *

Having regained a reservoir of energy after a brief rest, Cecelia moved quickly to follow the slowly disappearing bootprints. This deep in the forest, the diverted raindrops no longer muddied the path, and traces of Corey's flight were increasingly difficult to follow. But there was enough of a boot-shaped depression in the dirt to give her confidence that she was still hot on his tail. Bennett had taught her well.

All those cool autumn days and nights, following him through the woods in pursuit of deer, coon and grouse had served her well now that she was hunting alone. She remembered how he had told her that one of the best clues for determining if a track was fresh was to look for clearly defined edges. *Wind, rain, and time all conspire to wash away tracks. They become less visible as more time passes. That's why looking for animal tracks after heavy rain or fresh snow is a sure way to know that the tracks you see are fresh.*

It surprised Cecelia that she remembered those details now. Bennett had been gone for five years, and she had not hunted again until today. But she didn't think of her pursuit of Corey as a hunt. In her mind, hunting involved innocent prey, a creature blameless and oblivious as to why it was being pursued. Corey knew damn well why Cecelia was here and why she showed up on the Hermosa Beach Pier last week. Corey had struck first, felling her husband in the back of his semi-truck and leaving him to meet a horrible end—bleeding to death and never again to see or love his wife and daughter. Yes, Cecelia had struck and killed Miguel by mistake. Perhaps that meant they were even? No. In Cecelia's mind, Corey had committed two wrongdoings, and she only one. He had killed Bennett and then lied to avoid justice in the court-room. Soon, he would pay the price for that grievous falsehood, a wholly separate sin for which she intended to deliver a final ver-dict on Corey's murderous life.

She walked deliberately along the path, trying her best to jog lightly and avoid stepping on branches or making a noise. She needed the element of surprise once she spied Corey ahead of her in the woods. For all she knew, Corey had a gun. He certainly knew how to use one and probably carried a firearm on him since fleeing California and knowing he was being pursued. In fact, he probably had the same gun on him now that he used to kill Ben-nett. Cecelia didn't believe one word of that false confession by Larry Preston at the criminal hearing back in Minnesota. And she didn't for a minute believe that Larry had indeed turned over the actual gun used on that fateful Thanksgiving night. Rather, she was convinced Corey, the conniving liar, still held that Colt Woods-man close to his chest.

She glanced to her left and stopped abruptly. From the cor-ner of her eye, she saw something bright red lying next to a fallen log a few feet to the left of the path as she approached an open-ing in the trees. She took a few steps closer and found a broken red umbrella pulled loosely into itself. There were drops of water scattered across the fabric, but no sign of mud or mold or any-thing that might have dropped from a tree if it had been lying here for days or weeks on end. She leaned down and picked up the umbrella by its wooden handle. Corey. She was gaining ground.

But why had he left the umbrella behind and in such an obvious spot? Was it a ruse?

She rose quickly to the tips of her toes and scanned the horizon in every direction. Nothing moved in the trees. She looked down at the discarded umbrella. She noticed more boot prints leading away from the fallen log and onto the path in the direction in which she had been moving. Corey left it here by mistake. She was sure of it. From everything she had learned about him in her investigation, he tended toward carelessness. After all, once she set her mind to tracking him, it hadn't taken all that long to find him, so he wasn't good at covering his tracks.

Now, standing deep in the woods of Barron County, she reflected with satisfaction on her effort to locate Corey in a nation of three hundred and thirty million people and four million square miles of land. She still held the red umbrella in her hand and had an idea. She threw the umbrella to the ground and reached into her pocket, pulling out her phone. She tapped the GPS app, put it into satellite mode, and quickly saw where she was—standing in a vast sea of green forest, intermittently dotted with blue lakes and random open spaces colored light brown. She pinched her fingers on the screen, capturing a close-up view of what lay nearby. She saw that an open space was ahead of her, bisected by a small rivulet of water whose ripples she could now hear immediately to her right. Beyond that field, alongside the stream, ran a narrow opening in the forest, likely a continuation of the same path on which she and Corey had tread. She drew her index finger downward, pulling the end of that path into view. The trail ran directly into a wide lake. A small building sat at the mouth of the stream, where it emptied into Redemption Lake. It had to be the shack Cecelia heard that woman yell about back on the lawn, the one she told Corey to run toward.

Cecelia lifted her head and looked ahead toward the field. That is where Corey was headed. Surely, he knew of that shack's existence from his years of exploring these woods as a kid. Corey was predictable—she knew that from her year-long pursuit and profiling, and he proved it again today by returning to Barron County. She knew it like she knew her own self. Cecelia stuffed the cell phone into her pocket and felt the other pocket for the hard outline of the gun through the fabric of her coat. She took a deep breath, preparing to run toward the edge of the forest and alongside the stream through the broad meadow that lay ahead.

Chapter 21

Corey reached the far edge of the meadow, having run as fast as possible given his injuries. He bent over and rested his palms on his knees. It hurt having to breathe so deeply. As he looked up, Corey saw the same barbed wire fence that used to be the boundary of the corn field and, before that, a pasture for beef cows, the sharp fence the only means of keeping the animals from wandering into the woods and getting lost. He remembered standing at this exact same spot with Nick all those years ago when they pursued the wounded buck. As he looked straight ahead into the woods beyond, Corey couldn't see far. The thick pine forest filtered what little sunlight broke through the still-dense clouds. Rain no longer fell, but a dampness hung heavy in the air. He continued breathing more heavily than he expected.

He wondered, too, whether his sudden sense of foreboding had less to do with Cecelia being behind him rather than what lay straight ahead. Within that thick pine forest was the spot where he and Nick tracked down that wounded buck in 2013 as it lay gasping for breath and lapping water from the stream, the effects from Corey's bullet piercing the beast's abdomen. And, of course, the path ahead is where Corey and Nick also had their penultimate confrontation that same night when Corey shot Nick in the ass. That spot, where the first two victims of Corey's Thanksgiving rampage fell to the ground, was the farthest point that Corey had ever ventured from the cabin into these woods. He had never traveled as far as the Smith Shack before. He only hoped he might

find his way in the unfamiliar forest and not be overcome by Cecelia along the way. He strained to recall Judy's directions now.
Follow the stream until it enters Redemption Lake. You'll see the
shack off to the right as you emerge from the trees.

There was one significant difference between that day in
2013 and today, Corey thought—the difference between being the pursuer versus the prey. Back then, there were scores of
hunters scouring the northern Wisconsin woods on the prowl for
thousands of deer. Today, there was but one hunter in these vast
woods, and her only target was him. He turned to look once more
in the direction from which he had just run. He couldn't quite see
all the way across the meadow. The spot where he had emerged
from the forest, where the stream entered the grassy field, was
now occluded by a light fog as the air temperature cooled more
quickly than the heat rising from the ground. Somewhere within
that light fog, though, Corey swore he saw movement—someone
or something at the edge of the forest. He hoped that it was only
a deer and not Cecelia. Then, he suddenly remembered leaving
his umbrella behind. While he no longer needed it once the rain
stopped falling, it was nevertheless a stupid mistake—a careless
clue left behind for Cecelia, confirming that she was on the right
path.

He turned toward the barbed wire fence and ran. In doing so,
he made a calculated but foolish error. Corey thought he would
leap over the sagging fence, for it was lower than those hurdles
over which he had run all those years ago in school. He didn't.
Corey's back leg scraped the top of the wire fence, and a rusted
barb grabbed hold of his knee. The metal hook dug deep enough
into his flesh to break his forward momentum, causing him to
fall to the ground, arms first on the other side of the fence, a tear
ripped through his jeans, and blood now dripped from his knee.
Corey bit down on his lip, refusing to emit a location-revealing
scream. He rolled through the tall grass until he butted against a
medium-sized tree. He looked down to see the ruins of his pants
and the wound on his knee, the same knee he injured so violently

when falling on that run near St. Anthony Falls the same day he learned that his father had died. Yet here he was again, running from his regrettable past and wounded. He could no longer keep his emotions inside. He emitted a helpless whimper, the culmination of all his pains and grief from this terrible, unbelievable week. "Miguel," he cried with intense restraint, "I need you. Help me, love. Please, I need you."

* * *

Cecelia was about to run toward the meadow but stopped upon hearing a human voice. It was the voice of a man from not too far away, but from which direction she couldn't be certain. She stood as still as a statue, hoping to hear the man speak again. He did. The voice came from behind her, from the route she had traversed along the stream since leaving her car. She thought Corey was somewhere not too far ahead, but had he somehow circled back? Is that why he left the umbrella, to throw her off his trail? Or had she unwittingly run past him in her chase through the woods? She heard the male voice once more, and it was getting closer. Cecelia could neither discern the man's words nor identify him. She knew Corey's voice from hearing it on the street in Hermosa Beach, but out here, the noises of the forest blocked recognition. She took several quiet steps off the deer path, pulled the handgun from her coat pocket and fixed herself behind a wide oak. There, she waited.

A flurry of footsteps and heavy breathing approached. The brush beneath the tree was thick with climbing, blooming vines. She peeked left around the trunk of the oak, waiting with restrained, rapid breath for Corey to emerge into sight. She saw the sandy brown hair atop the man as he ran past. She pointed her gun and then moved it horizontally and precisely in line and time with the runner. She pulled the trigger and fell back against the tree. The bullet hit him in the side of his chest.

"Aaahhh," Nick yelled as he fell forward and off the path into the brush.

Then, Cecelia heard another man's voice approaching.

"Nick? Did you shoot at something? Nick!"

The second man stopped several yards short of where Cecelia stood behind the tree. She could see him—bent over with blonde hair and breathing as though he had just finished a race. Billy. She recognized him from the courthouse and then again when she followed him several days ago on the way to LAX. What was he doing in Barron County? She thought Corey had traveled here with his former lover, Nick, and not with his lifelong best friend.

Nick. That was the name Billy had clearly shouted. Cecelia looked over at the man writhing and moaning in the dirt. He was looking toward the stream, so she couldn't see his face. He had a similar build than Corey. She had been certain it was him. But it wasn't.

"Nick, was that you who fired your gun? What's going on?"

A faint voice from the man on the ground said, "No. I've been shot."

Cecelia peeked around the tree at Billy, still bent over and breathing hard in the distance. She also saw the rifle that had been strapped to his shoulder fall purposefully to the ground, so she took off and ran toward the field.

Billy glanced up in time to see Cecelia run away, his rifle on the ground and his hand fumbling in his pockets for the bullets Judy had given him. Then, he remembered that he had already loaded it.

"Shit!"

"Help," Nick uttered once Cecelia ran past him.

Billy threw the bullets to the ground and picked up the rifle. Cecelia had disappeared through the trees, and he heard snapping branches in the distance ahead of him. He moved carefully to where Nick lay injured. Upon reaching him, Billy saw blood flowing from the side of Nick's jacket and pooling in the dirt.

Cecelia ran across the meadow, scanning the horizon for Corey while frequently glancing back to ensure that Billy hadn't followed her.

* * *

The gunshot caught Todd's attention, and he stopped his all-out run. He was already halfway to the Smith Shack along the northern border of the Fischer land. The sharp crack in the air came from behind him and off to the right, in the direction of Destiny Springs. He looked swiftly to his left and then to his right. Had Cecelia caught up with Corey before reaching the abandoned shack? The gunshot had to have come from Cecelia's gun because Corey likely wasn't carrying, and it wasn't yet deer hunting season in Wisconsin.

Todd stopped, changed course, and trekked through thick brush southward in the direction the shot had been fired. Branches whacked him in the face, and he avoided near-certain injury after jumping over a perfectly camouflaged hole in the limestone ground rather than stepping into it while on the run. He stopped to catch his breath at the edge of the meadow, leaning against a rusted old hay cutter left here years ago. Todd listened for more sounds, perhaps some evidence that Corey was alive and that Barron County's first murder in five years had not occurred on Todd's watch. Something moved near the crest of the field, but the meadow's bowed shape blocked his view of whoever was traversing the downslope where the stream bisected the grassy expanse. A faint male voice bellowed somewhere in the distance. Todd took another pair of deep breaths, then headed out across the grassy plain toward the human sound.

* * *

Billy pulled out his phone and dialed 911. Then, he comforted Nick. The accumulated years of loathing Nick for how he had treated Corey evaporated. Cecelia had shot Nick in the torso, and blood poured out of him. Billy removed his jacket and rolled it into a ball, then kneeled and held it tight against Nick's rib cage. Nick seemed to be alert but breathing with a wheeze. Given the location of the blood emerging from the hole in Nick's jacket, the bullet had torn a path below the rib cage and was likely embedded somewhere in his gut.

Nick writhed in pain.

"Hold on, man. Help is on the way." Billy couldn't possibly know whether the words he used to comfort Nick were closer to the truth or a lie. The 911 operator had a difficult time discerning Billy's and Nick's location at first. Thankfully, he had enough bars of cell service to text her a photo of his coordinates. The operator's only assurance was that EMTs and a sheriff's deputy would arrive by truck to Judy's cabin within fifteen minutes and then travel via ATVs after that.

"She told us to listen for the roar of the four-wheelers' engines. Can you do that, Nick? Can you help me listen for the EMTs?"

Nick nodded his head yes, with his eyes closed tight. His lips were slightly parted. "Thirsty."

Billy looked around. "I'll find you some water and be right back."

Nick nodded once more. Billy stood up and searched the area around him for something he could take down to the stream that might hold more than a sip. Nothing on the forest floor looked viable for carrying water long enough for him to walk from the stream back to Nick without spilling it all over the ground. Then, something red caught his eye, and he ran toward it—a broken umbrella lying on the edge of the path. He leaped toward the umbrella, picked it up and ran a few yards through tree branches toward the stream. He scooped water with the red fabric of the umbrella, held it upside down while gripping the skeletal sides tight and walked as fast as he could back to where Nick was lying on the ground. Billy knelt beside him, holding the open end of the umbrella upright to keep the water from spilling out.

"Here." He deftly held the umbrella with one hand while gently lifting Nick's head with the other. "Let's get you a sip."

Nick grimaced as Billy lifted Nick's head and upper back, but he opened his mouth and let a small stream of cool water flow in.

Plenty spilled onto Nick's jacket and onto the ground to his right. After barely a sip, Nick began to gag.

At that moment, Todd burst through the brush, causing Billy to flinch and almost drop Nick's head to the ground. Nick coughed while struggling to regain his breath. Billy set the umbrella aside and wiped the excess water from Nick's face before looking back up at Todd.

"Jesus, man, you scared me. But damn, you're a sight for sore eyes."

"What happened? And what are you guys doing out here?!" Todd was out of breath.

Billy succinctly explained. Todd cursed at him for leaving the cabin and then knelt close to Nick.

"Listen, Nick. EMTs are on their way. I'll check with them to gauge their location, but I need you to help us listen for the four-wheelers. Can you do that?"

"Yeah," Nick uttered.

"Good. Now I'm going to call my deputy and see where they're at, all right?" Nick nodded his head but didn't speak. Todd turned his attention toward Billy and summoned him several steps away, then spoke in a whisper. "Keep the pressure on that wound, and do not give him any more water. I'm going to call the station and get a status."

"Got it."

"And for God's sake, keep him calm and slow down his breathing. Nick can make it, Billy, but he's going need your help."

Billy nodded.

"Did you see which way she went?"

Billy pointed toward the meadow beyond the tree line.

"Shit, she's headed toward the Smith Shack, goddamn it."

"You better get going."

Todd looked into Billy's eyes without responding. He seemed to be deep in thought. "Let me make this call first, then I'll decide."

* * *

Judy sped down County Road V at sixty miles per hour. Samantha sat in the passenger seat with Ginny immediately behind her in the back. The only noise inside the vehicle consisted of the wind whirring past the windows and an occasional thud when the tire hit uneven pavement. All three women stared straight ahead out the front window. At best, they'd be on the road for the next twenty minutes before reaching the shack. Ginny glanced at Judy through the rear-view mirror, then returned her stare outside the back seat window and spoke.

"I noticed that you have a cat."

Ginny's voice jolted Judy from concentrating on the road. "Yeah, Eddie. He's almost ten."

Ginny nodded her head, seemingly deep in thought about something other than this conversation. "He's a handsome Tom. I noticed him through the window in your house, stalking something in the backyard."

"That's Eddie, all right."

"Is he an outside cat only?"

"No, both in and out. Mostly outside during the day, then back in where it's warm, at night." Judy offered a weak smile through the mirror. "Fat Eddie never misses a meal."

"I'm guessing he's not declawed then, being an outside cat here in the forest?"

"No." Judy started to say more, then stopped.

"We had a cat named Swiffer when Corey was younger. He and Billy found the poor thing abandoned in a shed at the Pepin athletic field. The boys brought it home and caught Frank in a weak moment. He relented to Corey's pleas to keep the kitten, but only if it got declawed. We had quite a row over that the next day when Corey was at school. I thought declawing the poor thing was cruel, but Frank insisted. He even made Corey pay for it out of his own savings account."

"I'm with you on the declawing, Ginny. It's cruel indeed. Can you imagine having your fingernails ripped out of your hands? And how can a cat defend itself outside without claws?"

"That's exactly what I told Frank, but he made it clear that Swiffer was getting declawed. Period. If it meant he was too weak to defend himself outdoors, well, then Swiffer would be an inside cat—forever trapped in the house, never to enjoy the freedom of roaming outdoors. *He's a kitten. He'll never know the difference,* I remember Frank saying. And that was that."

Finally, Samantha chimed in. "I like cats. I don't have one now, but someday we will—Todd and I."

"You should," Ginny replied. "Cats are great entertainment."

All three women smiled.

"So, you must've had Eddie for a few years while Frank was still around?"

Judy glanced at Ginny in the mirror before returning her stare toward the road ahead. "Yeah. He helped pick Eddie out of the litter from a farmhouse outside Spooner."

"And he didn't insist that Eddie get declawed?"

"Oh, he did all right. But I stood firm. I told him that if he didn't like Eddie the way God made him, then Frank could hit the road and not come back." Judy looked at Sam, who returned her brief stare and then glanced into the back seat with a sudden look of regret. "Ginny, I'm sorry. I've said too much."

"No, no, not at all. Good for you—sticking to your guns and sticking up for Eddie. Yes, good on you."

Chapter 22

At the confluence of Destiny Creek and the edge of Redemption Lake, Corey could see the decrepit shack standing with a slight lean across the broad lawn at the water's edge, exactly as Judy described it. The wooden walls of the building appeared gray and worn, though Corey assumed that they had once stood brown and strong. Time and neglect had surely diminished the shack's appearance, though it still retained its general shape and purpose—a place of shelter and escape from the elements. The unmistakable echo of a gunshot jolted him from contemplation. He turned back toward the woods, but the sound came from far away, so he saw nothing, as expected. Still out of breath after the hurried run along the stream and through the woods, and despite the throbbing pain in his leg, Corey summoned his remaining energy, turned back toward Redemption Lake and ran like Hell toward the shack.

Random thoughts and questions raced through his mind. Was the gunshot fired from Cecelia's weapon? What could she possibly be shooting at, and why? What were Nick, Judy and Samantha doing back at the cabin? Did they call for help? And wasn't it Nick who had suggested years ago on that fateful hunting trip that he and Corey follow Destiny Creek here to its end and then, when Corey refused, asked for a blow job on the spot? Corey blurted out a laugh, either at the thought or out of panic and strained nerves. Indeed, how could he laugh when he was running away from a woman who wanted to kill him? Maybe he wanted to be murdered. Maybe it was time to be dead and join Miguel. Let Cecelia have her revenge, pay the ultimate price for his sins, and go out clean.

He reached the shack and collapsed onto the exposed front porch. He turned his head to stare back at the woods, at the opening in the trees alongside Destiny Creek from which he had emerged minutes earlier. That is most likely where Cecelia would exit the forest as well if, indeed, she were still on his trail. He could only hope that she took a different turn, perhaps thinking Corey had circled back toward the cabin. If she did, though, his hopes turned to prayer—*please God, don't let her hurt Judy, Sam or Nick.*

After watching the woods for several minutes and catching his breath, Corey stood up and surveyed the modest shack. It had an old, unlocked door and a window visible on its front side. Most of the glass on that front window had been busted out long ago, the wind flowing freely into the structure. He figured that the abandoned shack was a place now where teenage lovers snuck away to have sex and perhaps a destination for daytime poets to steal away for a quiet moment of repose. The positioning of the shack on the land provided Corey some comfort. He would be able to see someone approaching on the gravel road from the north or via the woods to the south. In between lay the edge of Redemption Lake—a broad blue sheet of fresh water constantly replenished by the trickling Destiny Creek that provided a nonstop supply of spring-fed water as well as other nutrients gathered during her two-mile journey.

He paused at the threshold of the shack, feeling as though he were trespassing into someone else's home despite the clear sense that no one had lived here for the past fifty or more years. He pushed the front door open, took a few steps inside the shack and shuddered. It was unexpectedly cooler inside than out, a product of the wind sweeping in through the uncovered windows and the absence of direct sunlight into the musty interior. There was nothing inside on which to sit or rest other than a rectangular piece of rusted iron with holes every few inches. He realized that it was once part of a bed frame that held springs to support a mattress but had clearly not been used as an actual bed in decades. Beyond that, the lone countertop was bare. No food and nothing to drink. He was again reminded of his deep thirst. Altogether, the empty shack offered him no comfort and no reason to stay, other than this is where Judy had yelled for him to go. But why? The shack offered him no real protection, no answer to his needs—for safety, a drink of water or an escape from the madwoman hellbent on killing him.

He moved further into the shack and beyond the larger front room, peeking into the two areas in the back, which he figured to be modest bedrooms long ago. Each had a single window frame with dirty, near-opaque glass. He rubbed a circle in the first window with the sleeve of his jacket and looked through the clouded glass to see Redemption Lake. He did the same in the second bedroom, this time noting the gravel road leading away from the shack and a small parking area adjacent to the lake. Beyond that lay a concrete boat launch and a tall wooden post holding signs too distant to read. He returned to the main room. There was no indication of an interior bathroom inside this cabin—no plumbing or holes in the gray wooden floorboards through which water might have at one time been pumped in and sewage flowed out. He figured that there must've been an outhouse on the property—somewhere not too far from the shack—but he couldn't see it outside the window. That much smaller structure must have disappeared long, long ago.

He continued surveying the property through the broken front window. He could see the trail upon which he had emerged from the pine forest as well as the stream that had accompanied him along the way as he ran from the safety of his family's former cabin toward this unfamiliar and unsecured shack. The scene outside the window sparked an unexpected memory, one he had long ago forgotten—or, more likely, had long ago suppressed. It was from the summer when Nick dragged him on that arduous, all-day hiking adventure along Minnesota's North Shore. They had trekked through hilly, wooded terrain—for five excruciating hours. The weather was damp and cool like today, and Corey felt the echo of his wounded knee back then almost as keenly as he felt that same re-wounded knee and twisted ankle today. On that day, too, Corey and Nick had for a time followed a trail that hugged a freshwater stream, one whose trickle became a steadier flow once it merged with another, then dumped its wet contents into Lake Superior, akin to how the stream running outside the window of this shack rambled toward its end at Redemption Lake. Nick. Why couldn't Corey shake the thought of him right now? Of course, he had spent part of this day with Nick being chauffeured all the way from Minneapolis. Part of him looked ahead to getting away from this mess and riding back to Minneapolis with him, the former lovers sharing stories about this unexpectedly dramatic turn of events.

How strange indeed to think of Nick now and more so to recall that day of hiking along the northern Minnesota trail. That was the day when Nick shockingly proposed to Corey atop the rocky outpost after acting like an ass for most of the morning. Why did Corey say *yes* at that moment? Hadn't he known Nick's penchant for infidelity and selfish, ego-driven desires? Wasn't Corey aware that Nick was unlikely to change? Yes, and yes. But there had been good times, too, and Corey was a person whose devotion and loyalty often lingered far longer than they should—not only with Nick but also with Frank. Thinking of that memory now as he stood looking out from the Smith Shack, Corey no longer felt regret or shame at his decision to accept Nick's marriage proposal when almost every instinct back then suggested that he say *no*, leave Nick and begin a brand-new life. He couldn't change the past, and he accepted that now without regret. What's done was done. Besides, Nick had good qualities, right? Weren't there at least a few?

That thought progression brought a brief smile to Corey's face. He knew he had crossed a new barrier. He had already out-grown his hatred for Nick's hurtful acts and had been living for years now with an attitude of indifference. For the most part, he thought little of Nick and could have cared less whether the man was alive or dead. But now, as he looked upon the memory-inducing scenery outside the shack, appreciation replaced indifference. There was a reason for the years he had spent in a relationship with Nick, and there was a sense of value and purpose, too. The hurtful times faded in importance, and he could honor the good memories while also wishing Nick well in his future with Evan. Though he felt no need to re-connect with Nick's life—other than getting a free ride back to Minneapolis—Corey felt as if a spell had been broken and that he could fully and finally release Nick from all the past pain and send him on his way to whatever future he desired, a future free from interactions with Corey because their time and purpose together had been fulfilled.

Corey's thoughts turned once more to the present. He moved through the shack, peering out each of the three windows, trying to observe his surroundings and, of course, look for either a savior or executioner. Judy obviously had a purpose in telling him to run here and not anywhere else. Perhaps she had called 911 and told them to meet him here? He could only hope that help arrived before Cecelia did. Absent walking down the gravel road to who knows where, staying hidden here in this shack seemed to be his best option. His leg and rib cage still throbbed. Running farther through the woods or down the gravel road would only further weaken him and make him more visible to Cecelia if she were still in hot pursuit. He decided to trust Judy's instruction and await his fate in this old cabin.

* * *

Sheriff Coles ended the phone call and walked over to Billy and Nick. He had only been away for mere minutes. But by the time he returned, Nick's condition had taken a drastic turn.

"Nick's getting delirious. He's talking gibberish."

Todd knelt beside Nick. He looked at Nick's torso and then at the pool of blood in the dirt.

"Hold him here, tighter." Todd pointed toward Nick's side. "We've got to stem the blood loss until the EMT's arrive. They're at the cabin and making their way up the trail right now."

"Corey, help me, Corey." Nick's eyes were wide open, but his stare was that of a blind man—loosely focused yet searching for what they could not see. "Please." His hand slid away from his body, and he gripped Billy's arm. He uttered a few indecipherable words and then said, "We're fine. Love you. Help. Please."

His arm still gripped by Nick's hand, Billy looked at Todd with an imploring stare.

"Talk to him. Comfort him." Todd's voice was in a whisper, but his tone was intense. "Role play, for God's sake."

Billy turned to look at Nick. "You'll be okay. Hold on, Nick."

"Corey, I'm sorry. Forgive me?"

"Of course, Nick. There's nothing to forgive."

"I'm cold. Hold me, Corey. Please."

Billy again looked at Todd as if seeking permission. Todd gruffly tilted his head toward Nick. Billy moved down from his knees into a prone position, lying next to Nick in the dirt alongside the path and deep in the Barron County woods. He wrapped his free arm across Nick's body, barely touching Nick's coat so as not to add any pressure to his chest.

"Thank you. Better."

"Good. I got you. Everything will be fine. You need to hold on until the paramedics arrive."

"Corey?"

Billy kept a light grip on Nick's chest. His rapid breath blew across Billy's face. Nick's hair and exposed skin were both drenched in sweat.

"Yeah?"

"You still love me, right?"

Billy paused before uttering a weak reply to the last words of a dying man. "Of course, Nick. I always loved you."

Nick's blank stare into the treetops ended when he closed his eyelids and smiled. "I knew it."

For the next few moments, Nick simply lay there and breathed, with Billy beside him and Todd mopping Nick's sweat-filled brow with his shirt sleeve. For his part, Billy kept his eyes focused on Nick, ignoring the sheriff kneeling above their heads.

"Where are they?" Todd's deep voice echoed against the trees.

Nick began to say more, but his words were unclear. He also began to shake, a thousand shivers coursing through his body as he lay on the hard, cold trail, bleeding to death in the damp afternoon air.

* * *

The sound of the ATVs rose from the forest in the distance. But Nick didn't move, and he didn't hear the far-off engines racing toward him. Instead, he heard the babbling stream that lay a few feet from his body and the gentle breeze of cool autumn air rippling through the treetops. He heard the distant sound of a turkey gobbling in the forest a mile away as it sought food and a potential mate. He heard the clanging of a church bell in the nearest town twenty miles over. The number of chimes was unclear; the hour of the day unimportant. Then he heard the rushing waterfall on Willow River as it cascaded across layers of limestone an hour's drive from where his bullet-torn body lay, deep in an unfamiliar wood with the person he thought to be the one true love of his life holding him tight. And, finally, he heard the creaking screen door—the sound he had heard and made a thousand different times as he entered and exited his parents' home in Minnesota nearly two hundred miles away. Nick then heard that door slam shut.

* * *

The EMTs arrived minutes later atop their all-terrain vehicles. Both Billy and Todd moved away from Nick's body so that life-saving measures could begin. But it was too late. Nick was gone. The lead paramedic declared Nick dead at 3:02 in the afternoon. Billy's body shuddered. He had, of course, never liked Nick. Yet, he was affected by Nick's dying declarations of remorse and love for Corey, a partner to whom Nick had just as often been cruel as kind. These were the final thoughts that apparently consumed Nick at the end of his life—an apology, a plea for forgiveness and a declaration that Corey was the true love of his life. Had Corey heard this, he might well sense that wrongs had been made right, that Nick had owned up to all the shit Corey unnecessarily endured, a redeeming closure to Corey and Nick's relationship, which came better late than never.

Todd broke the silence. "Listen up. I'm heading down the trail toward the Smith Shack. Billy, you stay here with the paramedics, and then you can all make your way back to Judy's place." Todd cut off the beginning of Billy's protest with an exposed palm in his face. "Please do as I say this time. We don't need anyone else dying today."

Billy relented, looking down at his bloody hands.

Todd removed the buzzing phone from his pocket and read the short text from Samantha. *Mom, Ginny, and I are in the car headed to the Smith Shack thru Cumberland. Meet you there?* He responded *yes* then hit send. He waited a few seconds, then wrote more. *Nick's dead. Billy's with EMTs. I'm headed toward Redemption Lake. If you arrive before me, STAY IN THE CAR.* He took one last look at Nick's limp body as the paramedics prepared a large plastic bag in which to encase Nick's body before securing him onto the flatbed platform on the back of an ATV. Todd could have commandeered one of those two ATVs in order to move faster than on foot, but the path from here to the Smith Shack traversed through a pine grove too narrow for the four-wheeler. He nodded his head at Billy, then took off running east along the path.

* * *

Billy sat atop a granite boulder and stared down into the stream flowing past. The lead EMT had told him they needed to wait for the deputy who would photograph Nick's body and gather evidence before the EMT's could remove Nick's body. So, he stepped away and waited for them to finish their work. He pulled the phone from his jacket pocket and saw the four bars of cell service. He tapped Rebecca's name and waited for her to answer. When she did, her warm and bubbly voice greeted him, and he answered her first question with, "I'm fine." He then proceeded to let Rebecca speak about her morning at the law firm and what lay ahead for her in the afternoon. When she returned the favor and asked him how things were in Pepin, he gave it to her straight. He delivered the story monotone, sticking as close as he could to the facts. There would be time for adding details later. Rebecca expressed shock about Nick and concern for Corey. Then, she focused like a laser on Billy, peppering him with questions, frustrated that there was nothing she could do at the moment to help.

"I'm safe. The EMTs are here, and I'm certain at least one of them is carrying a gun." He decided not to mention that he was carrying one as well. "Rebecca, I love you."

"I love you too, Billy."

"No, I don't think you understand. I love you. I really love you. This past week hasn't exactly gone the way I had planned. Things between us have been a bit tense. Our vibe is off."

"I know. I sensed it, too. But not every minute of our time together will be perfect. We're still okay, right?"

"That's just it, Rebecca. We're more than okay. But I let my crazy insecurities get in the way. The whole thing about your past encounter with a woman and then the dynamic about our physical distance and respective lives in Cali and Minnesota. I let it all get into my head and cloud what truly matters."

"What's that, Billy?"

"You. Us. That's what's important. The rest are details—most of them insignificant at that."

Rebecca listened. She suppressed her inner litigator while the love of her life spoke his truth, the words emerging from his heart.

"I mean, my dad hasn't been dead a full year, and I've already forgotten the central message of his life—love those you love with everything you've got and do right by them; the result will be a happy life." His voice began to crack, but he pressed on. "It took seeing another man die beside me to bring Dad's core life lesson to the front of my mind. Hell, I hated Nick since the day I first met him. You know that. And while the man certainly was an ass more often than he was good, I only focused on the bad parts. I judged Nick's entire life based upon his worst self and gave no mind to what might be honorable or what might have caused him to act out toward Corey in shitty ways. As I lay there beside him, holding Nick in his final moments and hearing what was at the center of his thoughts as he was about to die, it struck me. All that shit in our lives—who did what to whom and why—it doesn't ultimately matter. The kind of person we want to be, the love we feel inside and the need for forgiveness; that's what matters, not our failure to achieve it."

Rebecca stayed silent while listening to Billy's unusually deep words, then too when he said nothing more. She soon heard his muffled cry through the phone. In the past year since they had been reunited, Rebecca had seen a wide range of emotions cascade across Billy's face and emerge from his silence or his voice. But today was the first time she had truly heard him cry. There had, of course, been tears at Larry's funeral, but today was different. Today, she couldn't see him. Instead, she could only hear his distant sounds, and they were the sounds of someone mourning a profound life moment, where a single traumatic event triggers the release of all the tears and feelings and grief that a person dams up over time, a break in the levee resulting in an unstoppable flow.

* * *

Judy rolled through the stop sign, then turned onto the highway headed toward Cumberland and in the direction of the Smith Shack. She didn't worry about a traffic stop or earning a driving violation today. If caught, she was certain the county sheriff would understand.

"So, are we only going to talk about cats or about the larger elephant in the room?" Samantha directed her words toward her mother but gave an inclusive glance at Ginny in the back seat. Judy and Ginny locked eyes for a moment in the rearview mirror. "Fine, I'll start then." Tension and sharpness filled Samantha's throat. She directed her aim at Judy first. "Why on Earth did you buy the Fischer's cabin?"

Judy stared straight ahead, both to navigate the curvy road at the car's elevated speed and to avoid looking at either Samantha or Ginny. "I loved Frank Fischer, and he loved that piece of land. It was important to him, so it was important to me. I'm not saying that was a good decision on my part, but it felt like the right thing to do."

"And you didn't think anyone would put two and two together?"

"Again, Sam, I won't defend my actions as being smart or well thought-out. But when I heard it was for sale, I knew that no one in his family must've wanted it. And I submitted a cash bid through a made-up LLC so that Ginny and Corey wouldn't ask questions about whether Judy Fischer was a relative."

"Seriously?" Sam sounded indignant. "Like they couldn't simply look up the county records at a later date to see who owned the LLC?"

"All I can say is this. We can debate whether buying Frank's cabin—I mean, the Fischer's cabin—and how I went about it was a good idea. But by then the dye was cast. The bad decision I made was more than twenty years ago when I let myself get involved with him knowing he was a married man. I have no excuse for that and can't change the past. But I regret to this day the hurt I caused to you, Ginny, and to your family." The two women locked brief stares once more, then Judy returned to watching the oncoming road. "I can also say that I have no regrets about getting pregnant and having you, Sam. You are the best part of my life and have been since the day you were born. Once you came along, things changed. I was torn between doing right by you and doing what was right period in terms of the affair. I was damned either way, so I chose to do what was best for you. I kept Frank in my life, and in yours to some extent. I brought that dilemma upon myself and accept the consequences. I don't blame either of you, or anyone else, for judging me on that. But believe me—no one will ever be a harsher judge than myself."

Ginny spoke next. "Thank you for that, Judy. For the record, I'm not overly interested in doling out judgments anymore. I would have years ago, but now it feels like wasted energy. I am curious, though. Did Frank ever express the kind of remorse that you just did? Was there ever a time when he told you that he felt bad about what he was doing to his family?"

Judy bit her lip for an awkwardly long time before speaking. "Regrettably, no. Or at least he never said such things to me." She glanced at Ginny through the mirror, but Ginny's gaze was fixed on the rapidly passing landscape. "You know, it's funny and sad at the same time. Here I was—head over heels about a man who I knew was treating his family so callously—lying to his wife and avoiding his only son. How in the hell could I fall for a man like that? I mean, if he was already cheating on you, maybe he was cheating on me too?"

Ginny smirked, shook her head, and suppressed a knowing laugh. She instead stared out the side window so as not to make eye contact with Judy. It was such a beautiful opportunity to inflict the kind of delayed pain on Judy that had been thrust upon Ginny last year when Corey first uncovered Samantha's existence and confirmed the harsh truth of Frank and Judy's affair, but such a gesture would be pointlessly cruel.

"For what it's worth, Frank did tell me one thing that might be of comfort to you, Ginny. He and I were talking about the cabin's future at one point, not too long before he died. I don't think he knew he was about to die. It was simply one of those pondering life kind of talks. Anyway, he expressed how neither you nor Corey seemingly had any interest in the place. And he was concerned that one day after he's gone, the property that had been in his family for two generations—a place that his father had built—would be sold to someone else who lacked appreciation for its history like he did. He mused about finding a way for me or Samantha to inherit it without raising eyebrows back home. He never did figure that out before he died."

"He actually mentioned me? About having me inherit the property?" Samantha's voice suddenly softened, though a vein of incredulity remained.

"Yes. And, right or wrong, he did put away money for you, Sam. It helped raise you and take care of your needs growing up." Judy looked at Samantha, hoping to elicit a smile, but she looked back without expression. "Anyway, my point here, Ginny, is that during that same conversation, I suggested to Frank that he have his ashes scattered here in Barron County, somewhere deep in the woods on the Fischer land. He looked as though he were considering it for a moment, but then he said something like this—*No, my place of eternal rest should be in Pepin alongside Ginny. It's the proper Catholic thing to do. Besides, I haven't always given her my best self in life. I owe her the peace of mind that I'll do the right thing when I die.*

Ginny's eyes opened wide as the pine groves sped past outside the window. So, Frank did have a conscience after all? Certainly not a big one, but at least something was there. And his plan for showing loyalty or respect—or maybe even love in his own distorted way—was to lie side by side with her, six feet underground outside of Pepin, for all of eternity? Yeah, that wasn't going to happen. Her decision had been made last year when she signed the papers with Larry and conveyed her after-death wishes to her son. Had she known this information then, it wouldn't have changed a thing, though it may have made her question whether the choice to abandon Frank in the cemetery and instead be cremated and spread upon the sea was one made from spite. At least now, she was assured that she made that decision for herself and not because of anyone else. Ginny was doing what she wanted to do; everyone else be damned. It probably wasn't the Catholic or right thing to do, but so what? Her motivating impulse now was to do what made her happy. And at this stage in her life, that was reason enough.

Chapter 23

Cecelia followed the stream. Guided by the digital map on her phone, she continued along the creekside path upon entering the thick coniferous forest. Not far inside the pine grove, she crossed over a barbed wire fence and noticed a small patch of cloth caught on the wire, as well as several spots of blood on the ground. She knelt to touch them and determined they were fresh. She stood up and resumed a torrid pace, racing down the trail and following boot tracks through a long stretch of mud. The imprints were the exact same footwear she had been tracking before, but now they were closer together, and the left print was less deep than the right. Why was Corey favoring one leg? Had he been injured on the fence and forced to slow his pace? The thought of him wounded and limping away to save his life invigorated her. She quickened her steps and kept looking forward, hoping to see the Smith Shack and corner him there once Corey had nowhere else to run.

It was now half-past three in the afternoon and more than four hours away from dusk. She figured that she could locate Corey in the waning light of day, then navigate her way toward the highway that, according to her map, lay beyond Redemption Lake. From there, she would hitchhike toward Eau Claire or perhaps Green Bay and catch a Greyhound Bus heading south. It meant leaving Bennett's ashes behind, but she couldn't do anything about that now. Instead, she focused on the thought of reuniting with her daughter in Arkansas and making a new plan to be on the run. Cecelia knew she couldn't return to the family home in Pine Bluff.

She had shot two men, killing at least one, and she was about to shoot and kill one more. Her car in Judy's driveway proved Cecelia was there. The life she knew was over, but a new one would begin with her and Julia in a new place with a new life story and, of course, a brand-new last name. Hell, if Corey Fischer-Flanagan could do it, so could she. And Cecelia would be smarter than him; she knew how not to get caught. But first things first—she needed to reach Redemption Lake, where she suspected Corey was waiting to receive his fate.

Yet, must the immediate future unfold as she imagined? Did she truly need to kill Corey to achieve justice? To exact her revenge? She felt the weight of two souls resting upon her body, an angel on her left shoulder and a devil on the right. The angel whispered memories of Bennett and Julia, reminding Cecelia that she was a good person who had done her best to live a good life. The devil screamed about fairness and retribution. Cecelia and her family had been wronged, and it was her duty to make things right. The angel endeavored to calm her, urging Cecelia to stop, throw away the gun and head toward home. But the devil fueled her rage and coaxed her into doing the only thing that could relieve her suffering—kill the man who killed her husband and exorcize the homosexual demons who triggered everything bad, starting long before that fateful Thanksgiving night.

She followed a wide curve in the stream and soon noticed an opening in the woods. She could see the dark waters of Redemption Lake in the distance and a shack sitting on its shores. She had arrived at the spot where she expected to find Corey hiding. She had him cornered, but she also worried about him having a gun. Cecelia emerged from the grove of trees at a jogging pace, making a beeline for the Smith Shack at the edge of the lake. She checked her coat pocket to confirm that the gun hadn't fallen out. It was still there. She thrust her hand inside and tightly gripped the handle. Whatever happened next, she would be ready. The devil on her shoulder had won.

* * *

Corey stood in the back room of the shack, gazing through the window toward the lake and daydreaming about a recent outing with Miguel. They had stolen away for the weekend—the weekend prior to their one-year anniversary and the last weekend of Miguel's life. They had rented a condo with a view of Big Bear Lake and spent the weekend hiking, cooking and breathing fresh mountain air. Corey had awakened from a nap that Saturday afternoon, left Miguel asleep beside him and walked over to the large picture window. He stood for a long time watching the rippling waters of the alpine lake being caressed by a steady wind and imagining how he might paint that scene. Now, two weeks later, he was standing in a similar place—someone else's dwelling, looking out across a remote lake amid a vast forest and contemplating the natural beauty before him.

"Corey! Get out here. I know you're inside that shack."

The sound of Cecelia's voice jolted him. He rushed to the front room and looked out the window across the expansive grassy yard. There she was, moving toward him—her hands stuck in her coat pockets and one of them surely grasping a gun. He stayed quiet, hoping that she'd conclude he wasn't there.

"You're cornered. I've tracked you through dirt trails and mud. And I also know you're injured. You can't outrun me even if you try. Now, come out here and face me like a man."

"Cecelia," he yelled back through the window. "You're right. I'm here. I won't run. But can we talk this through? We've each lost someone at the hands of the other. Isn't enough, enough?"

He saw her stop walking and lean against a large oak tree. She appeared to be fiddling with her gun.

"Enough? You think what's happened is enough? Not even close. All you lost were sexual conquests. I lost everything!"

"Conquests? Is that what you think?"

"You're a predator, Corey. You seduce other people's men and get them killed. An easy fuck with no feelings, then you throw them aside, right? That's what you do, without regard for who gets hurt. Yeah, that's what I think. All of this is on you."

Was she nuts? he wondered. What a skewed version of reality Cecelia spewed from behind that tree. Or was she right? If he hadn't followed Bennett into that truck, if he had not gone out on the first date with Miguel, each of them would be alive today, and neither Corey nor Cecelia would be standing here deep in the Barron County woods.

"Nothing to say? I guess that means I'm right."

Beads of sweat formed atop Corey's brow. He couldn't decide if Cecelia was right or wrong. And what if she were right? Was Corey indeed responsible for both men's deaths? Should he surrender, walk out of the shack and let her render the judgment he deserved? Was this his opportunity to finally pay his debts? It wasn't far away from this spot where Corey had killed an innocent eighteen-point buck and almost killed Nick. He had never truly paid a price for either of those assaults. And then there was Bennett. For that crime, Corey had paid no price at all. It was Larry Preston who took the blame and Miguel who took the fall, each of them paying for Corey's sins. To give up now would waste Larry's sacrifice, but guilt consumed Corey's mind.

The sound of an approaching car summoned Corey's attention and seemingly stopped Cecelia from dashing toward the shack. The car raced down the gravel road, coming to a stop at the edge of the grass and three women jumped out. Corey, of course, knew them all but was only surprised by one. He yelled out the window and toward the car.

"Mom? What are you doing here?"

Cecelia stepped out from behind the oak tree with her hands thrust inside her jacket pockets.

"Get back in your car, Mrs. Fischer, both you and your friends. This is between me and Corey."

Ginny yelled across the grassy lawn. "Cecelia, please. Let's talk about this."

"No. This is none of your concern."

"Corey is my concern. And you are, too. I'm sorry for what happened to Bennett, truly. I understand."

"You understand? What, because you're a widow, too?"

"No, because I was also married to a complicated man. None of what happened to Bennett was your fault. He had needs no woman could fulfill."

Cecelia removed the gun from her pocket and pointed it at Ginny. Samantha and Judy stepped closer together.

"Bennett wasn't gay! I know that's what you're saying. But you're wrong. He loved me and would be alive now if it weren't for your homo-killer son!"

"Then think about your daughter," Ginny implored. "She needs her mom. She wouldn't want you to hurt anyone. Please, let's sit down and call her—make sure she's doing all right."

"Don't bring Julia into this. You have no right! What do you know about having a daughter anyway? All you have is a faggot, killer son." Cecelia turned her head toward the shack. Corey remained standing inside at the window.

"I have a daughter," Judy yelled as she stepped away from Samantha and walked a few feet closer to Cecelia. "That's her." Judy pointed behind her. "I named her Sam. I can relate to the bond you must have with your daughter, too."

"Who's she?" Cecelia gestured toward Judy with the gun.

"This is Judy Fischer," Ginny explained. "Frank's second wife. And this is Samantha, her daughter. Our daughter."

Corey listened and watched in shock at the exchange from his hiding post inside the shack. His feet felt as if they were encased in cement. His mind wanted to rush outside and save the women from being Cecelia's next victims and from being his next victims, too. But his legs wouldn't move.

"Wait," Cecelia yelled. "Second wife?" She didn't recall that from her research.

"Samantha and Corey are brother and sister. They're family. So, Judy and I are as well. And we're all here for Corey, to help make some peace."

Cecelia pointed her gun at the three women to her left and stared at them with squinting eyes. Ginny and Samantha had now stepped up to join Judy in unison on the lawn. Corey still peeked out from the window, cowering yet again as others stood up in his place and took responsibility for the things he had done.

"No. There's nothing for us to talk about. I have no beef with you, Mrs. Fischer—neither one of you nor your daughter. It's Corey I want. He killed my husband."

"Please..." Ginny pleaded.

"Stop talking. I'm here for Corey and him only. Get back in your car and let him man up for a change." Cecelia turned and began walking toward the shack. Judy grabbed Ginny's arm so she couldn't move.

Cecelia stopped walking once Corey emerged through the shack's front door. He stepped onto the lawn, his arms raised in surrender above his head.

"Cecelia's right, Mom. This isn't your concern. It's mine."

"Corey, get back inside!" Samantha's voice rang out across the grassy space and echoed off the trees in the distant woods.

He ignored her plea and spoke directly to Cecelia. "Most of what you said is true, Cecelia. I am responsible for Bennett's death and Miguel's, too. I never meant for any of it to happen, but it did. And I'd give anything in the world to bring them back."

"It's too late for that."

"I know. And I'm sorry. I truly am."

"Sorry isn't enough, Corey. You took a life. You killed a man."

He felt a sharp pain in his gut. She was telling the blunt, awful truth.

"And now you'll pay for what you've done."

He looked at the three women huddled together, unable to save him from their position across the lawn. Then, he turned and spoke to Cecelia, only loud enough for her to hear. "You're right. I should. Do what you need to do."

She resumed walking. Corey stood tensely still as Cecelia narrowed the distance between them. Back at the Hermosa Beach

Pier, she had taken her shots from too far away. Today, she moved in closer. The two stared at each other as they did one week ago on that pier, but this time, Corey didn't cower behind anyone else, and he didn't make a run for his life. He surrendered. He felt at peace.

"No!" Ginny screamed in concert with both Judy and Sam. Cecelia was twenty yards from reaching Corey.

"It's okay," he yelled back at them. "She's right. I've run as far as I can from my troubles. It's time to take responsibility. I never meant to hurt Bennett, but it's still my fault. If only I had walked away when he came on to me in that restroom, none of this would've happened."

Cecelia had closed the gap in yards to ten, then abruptly stopped walking.

"What?" She dropped the gun to her side and cocked her head toward Corey.

"Bennett approached me. He drew his finger across my back as I stood at the urinal and told me to meet him in his truck."

"You're lying, Bennett! You were supposed to love only me."

Corey looked at Cecelia with confusion. Judy, Samantha and Ginny did the same. Each of them likely saw the same person—a woman with eyes darting back and forth between everything in front of her as if searching for something or someone or perhaps even the truth. Corey sensed an opening, a possible break in Cecelia's psyche that might allow her to back down.

"Shoot me if you must, but I hope we can just agree we're even. We've each lost someone, but maybe we can move on and make it up to those we love who are still here."

His words backfired, seemingly drawing Cecelia out of her momentary stupor and reconnecting her to a rage inside. She resumed walking faster and once again raised her arm and aimed the gun at Corey's head.

"Even? We're not even. But soon we will be."

The sharp crack of gunfire filled the air of the county park. The bullet hit its intended victim in the chest. Judy, Samantha and Ginny all gasped. Corey fell to the ground, instinctively clutching his chest and trying to calm his rapidly beating heart as it pounded so loud that he couldn't hear anything going on around him. Each of the three women ran in a different direction. Ginny raced to her son's side, who lay confused on the ground a few yards from the shack's front door. Samantha ran toward Todd as he emerged from behind a pine tree, jumping into his arms and refusing to let him go. Judy ran over to the body of Cecelia Jackson, now lying in the grass on the same spot where she had stood, from where she had aimed her gun at Corey and failed to pull the trigger before being felled by the bullet from the Barron County Sheriff's gun. The weapon in her hand had flown into the air and landed several feet away at the same moment Todd's bullet entered her body. By the time Judy reached Cecelia's body, all movement had ceased. She had been shot dead by Todd's perfect aim, the bullet piercing her chest and exploding inside her heart. Judy kneeled beside the body, brushed a few strands of hair away from Cecelia's eyes, and then reached over to hold Cecelia's hand with hers as Judy closed her own eyes and began to pray.

Ginny reached Corey and immediately turned him over and examined his body. Where was the gunshot that hit her son? He didn't appear to be hurt, but the expression on his face reflected fear. He looked straight into the sky without blinking, as if he were either catatonic or dead.

"Corey, it's Mom. I'm here. You're all right." Her voice was calm, opposite from the adrenaline-fueled anxiety now coursing through his veins. She caressed his sweat-filled hair. "Corey, say something. Please."

He looked toward his mother, the first person on whom he had fixed his eyes forty-five years ago and the same person who he thought would be his last. "Mom?"

"I'm here. You're going to be fine."

"What happened? Where's Cecelia?"

Ginny pointed across the grass toward Judy, who was kneeling over a body and genuflecting the sign of the cross. "She's gone, Corey. The Sheriff showed up just in time."

"He apprehended her?"

"No, honey. I think she's dead."

Corey abruptly turned his head to see Judy, Todd and Samantha hovering over Cecelia's body. He then saw Todd pick up a handgun from the grass and walk alongside Samantha toward him.

Todd knelt to Corey's side as Ginny backed away to make room. "Are you all right?" He checked Corey's vitals and examined his body in the same manner Ginny had done only moments before.

"He wasn't shot," she said. "I checked."

"Good. I'm sorry it was a bit closer than I'd hoped. I only saw Cecelia walking across the lawn as I came out of the woods. I raised my gun as soon as I saw Cecelia raise hers."

"Sorry? You have nothing to be sorry for," Ginny said. "You saved Corey's life."

Corey pushed himself up and braced his body against the ground with an elbow. He no longer wanted Ginny, Samantha or Todd looking down on him as if he were a victim. He wasn't a victim, at least not anymore. Judy appeared at Corey's side, along with the others, in time to hear Todd continue the conversation.

"Well, maybe I am sorry for other things, like treating you less respectfully in the past than you deserved. Sorry about that, man."

"There's nothing to forgive. We're fine. We're family." Corey looked at Samantha, then again toward Todd. "I can't believe you saved my life."

"I'd say that saving people is simply my job. But I'm glad I got here when I did. It's not every day you get to save your girlfriend's brother from being shot."

Corey shook his head. "To be honest... I can't believe it's finally over. I'll be glad to get back to Minnesota and then home to Hermosa Beach." He exhaled a long breath. "I remember once you discouraged me from coming back to this county, Sheriff. Maybe I should've listened."

"Corey, what I said last year was inappropriate. I'm sorry."

"No, you were right. No offense to you or Judy or Samantha, but I think I'm done with these woods for one lifetime. I simply want to go home and stay there."

Everyone continued their audible sighs of relief. Peace eluded Corey and likely the others as well, given that Cecelia lay dead a few yards away. Yet Corey endeavored to lighten the mood.

"I suppose the only insufferable part left for me is the ride back to Minneapolis with Nick. But hey, he's got to have sympathy for me now, right?" No one around him laughed.

"Here, Corey." Todd reached out a hand, which Corey accepted. With additional help from Samantha and Ginny, Corey stood and brushed dirt off his clothes. "Come over here to the bench, and we'll sit. There's something I need to tell you."

Part 3: California

Chapter 24

Corey sat in the living room of his Hermosa Beach apartment, removed the lid from a large box and smiled. He once again took inventory of what lay inside—a Nikon D850 DSLR, the digital version of the analog single lens reflex and the *creme de la creme* of cameras for professional photographers. The box also contained three different lenses and various starter accessories whose purposes he vowed to master. It had been a perfectly timed gift. He thought back to the night three weeks earlier when he tore through the wrapping paper and first laid eyes upon the contents of this box. It was his last night in Minnesota before flying home to California. They had gone out to dinner, the two of them, meeting up at an old favorite—Jax Cafe in Northeast. The conversation had flowed with ease—just like old times. Corey recalled the conversation that followed the opening of his gift.

Carol, it's too generous. But I love it, I really do.

I'm glad. I hope this brings you inspiration and perhaps a brand-new start.

It definitely will. Thank you.

He remembered leaning across the table to place a soft kiss on Carol's cheek. They looked at each other with warm smiles and deep admiration. Now, back in his apartment, he sank into the sofa and thought. He envisioned all the places in LA County he might go on his days off from work at the frame shop, places that he could photograph—especially with a telephoto lens—and see new perspectives. As a teenager, Corey painted realistic images of people but from the point of view of an artist who could see past his subject's physical traits and portray onto the canvas the emotions and angst he sensed deep inside. The painting of Ginny with a riven face at the school art fair was a symbolic piece from that stage in his artistic development. Now, he would borrow from that same phase but with a pair of new twists.

The paintings would be based upon what Corey could see through the camera lens that others with mere twenty-twenty vision could not. Then, he would add one specific detail to each painting—something in the artwork that even Corey could not see but what he imagined or hoped might be there beyond the power of his scope. The ideas came quickly. He pictured himself focusing on the kelp bed floating in Malaga Cove, a sea of green weeds that, to this point, he only observed from a distance at the top of a hillside overlooking the sea. The hidden detail in that painting might be the elusive tip of a dolphin's fin. He often spied them in pairs or groups of three swimming a few hundred yards offshore along the beaches in Redondo and Hermosa, but they popped up at unpredictable intervals, always too brief to catch in a photo.

Or he could stand atop the cliffs at Palos Verdes below the Wayfarers Chapel, looking across the channel to Catalina Island. With the high-powered lens, he would likely see the actual landscape of those towering brown and green cliffs that appeared as hazy gray from twenty miles away. It was unlikely that his lens could capture one of the famous wild buffalo roaming carefree on the island, descendants of a small herd brought over from the mainland for the filming of a movie in the 1930s and abandoned when the film crew returned to LA. But Corey would paint them into the artwork anyway.

He wore a broad smile as he contemplated the future of his art. Then, he looked at the clock. It was time to get ready for work. He thought about how grateful he was for the frame shop. It wasn't the best paying job he could land, but he adored the owner and the clientele, and it gave him a platform on which he could speak all day long about art and do something creative with his hands. He lived frugally enough that making a ton of money wasn't important. His expenses were light—food, rent and gas— and through the frame shop, he was able to order art supplies at cost without having to pay a dime in sales tax.

He showered, dressed, downed a yogurt parfait, then hopped on his bike heading south. He rode along the oceanfront path toward Riviera Village. He had traversed this route hundreds of times by now, but it never got old. The first landmark he passed was, of course, the pier at Hermosa and the broad plaza at 14th Street. Shops were starting to open for the day as he rode past at nine o'clock. A street performer sang covers through a small amp to a crowd holding their morning coffees. Corey pedaled past rows of volleyball nets and then through the arcade of fishing shops and seafood vendors in the Marina at King Harbor. He alighted from his bike and pushed it while he walked across the Redondo Beach Pier as the posted signs required. He resumed riding along what was perhaps his favorite stretch of the trail, from below Veteran's Park all the way to its southern end and then up the long, steep concrete ramp at Dolphin Cove. From there, he stopped briefly at the Yellow Vase to grab a black coffee and orange cranberry scone before locking his bike on the rack outside Framed By The Beach and walking inside.

The shop opened at ten, but there was plenty to accomplish before that—deliveries to unwrap, shelves to stock and an unfinished framing job for his favorite client, Mrs. Graner. He was still putting some finishing touches on her project when he heard a light knock on the front door. He left the back room and entered the front of the shop, then smiled wide upon seeing the old lady standing outside in the sun wearing a blue patterned dress with heels and holding her Goyard handbag. She wore a wide-brimmed sun hat. Mrs. Graner looked as if she were about to step into Café Citron on the Champs-Elysées in her native Paris. He unlocked the door, let her inside the store and said, *"Bon jour, Madame."*

"Merci, mon cher. Comment ça va?"

"Je vais bien, merci. You are early today, no?" Corey knew a few words in French but certainly wasn't fluent. He did endeavor

to adopt the old lady's manner of speech, however, often adding her inquisitive "no" at the end of an otherwise obvious remark.

"*Oui, j'ai beaucoup de courses à accomplir aujourd'hui.*"

Corey squinted and smiled.

"Ah, my dear Corey. It saddens me that you do not understand more French after all this time. I said that I have much to accomplish today. That is why I've made an early start."

"Of course. I'm happy to see you." Though he had not learned sufficient French to meet her desire, Corey had absorbed Mrs. Graner's mannerisms and customs during the nearly four years she had been coming into the shop. He reached out and placed his hands in a light grip upon each of her arms and leaned in for the barest brush of a kiss on each cheek.

"My painting is ready, no?"

"Almost." He uttered a nervous laugh. "Come in and sit down. I'll brew you a cup of tea while you wait."

"*D'accord.*"

He went into the back room and put a kettle on the hot plate. He then gathered the owner's tea set and brought it out front. He was certain that no one used these special ceramic cups other than when Mrs. Graner came into the store. He then retrieved her framed artwork and brought it out front to wrap. The old lady certainly had an eye for art and excellent taste as well. Her latest acquisition had been a piece by Patrick Angus, the so-called painting chronicler of gay life in the late 1970s and 80s. Though Angus died young from AIDS, his work wasn't a political statement on that era of despair, but rather a depiction of basic human needs, desires and fears, as well as a visualized focus on the eroticism between gay men. Corey was surprised Mrs. Graner had purchased an Angus piece, and yet he wasn't.

Despite the air of personal conservatism that accompanied her impeccable appearance and tightly constrained words, she seemingly had friends and acquaintances of every stripe and always made Corey feel as though he were nearly the status of being her only son. Besides, he mused, the woman was a ruthless and savvy art buyer. She could spot a bargain and went out of her way to support emerging artists, something she explained to Corey as being *mutuellement bénéfique*—benefiting both the artists' future and her own net worth.

As he worked to carefully encase her newly framed artwork in bubble wrap, he listened to Mrs. Graner tell him all the village gossip during the weeks he'd been away. It was surprising how much transpired in so short a span of time and more stunning how the old lady kept a tight finger on the pulse of Riviera Village. Mrs. Graner might be the heir apparent to her predecessors and fellow Californians Hedda Hopper and Rona Barrett, he thought. She then brought Corey up to speed on the recent auction. It was held at the Long Beach Museum of Art. While the museum normally was a place where art was on display and not for sale, this event was different. This was an opportunity for the art-buying public to get their hands on something new—pieces created by California's most promising, emerging artists. And Corey was one of them. All the pieces submitted to the 2019 Emerging Artists Showcase were required to be auctioned off. The artists were to receive half of the money bid and collected for their work, with the other half going to fund an endowment for young artists in lower-income communities, enabling them to attend college and pursue their creative life dreams.

"It was spectacular, Corey. I'm so sorry you couldn't attend."

"Me too. Both Miguel and I were supposed to be there, given that I had won first place."

Mrs. Graner smiled.

"But I was still in Minnesota. As you know, I stayed for another week after that awful day in Wisconsin. I felt I needed to pay my respects at Nick's funeral. I couldn't get back here in time."

"Of course. But you would have loved it, Corey, and likely been embarrassed as well."

"Oh?"

"*Oui.* Patrons could not stop talking about your triptych, that fantastic autobiographical painting." He pictured the piece in his mind as a melancholy smile overcame his face. He had received a text from the museum director saying that Corey's artwork had garnered the highest bid—from an anonymous buyer—and that it had been spirited away that night, so he would likely never see his most successful creation again. He interrupted the old lady's almost nonstop monologue to fetch the steaming kettle and pour them each a cup of jasmine tea. When he returned, she summoned him to sit on the chair beside her. He had finished with her project, and there was something important she wanted to say.

"Corey, I am so sorry about *monsieur* Miguel."

"Thank you, *Madame* Graner. I truly appreciated your call when I was in Minnesota."

"*Bien sur.* It was such a shock, and I felt helpless after hearing what happened and then that you had to flee."

"It has definitely been a surreal few weeks."

"You will recover, I promise you. *Mon* Thomas has been gone for ten years now. And while the wound is still fresh, I can tell you that hope lies ahead. We all go on, Corey. We must go on, no?"

"*Oui*," was the best Corey could reply before choking up and declining to say more.

"And when you are ready, there will be love again. For you, I am sure of it."

"Oh? Has there been new love for you since Thomas passed?"

"But of course, *mon cher.* I am widowed, not dead."

Corey laughed. He appreciated Mrs. Graner's unique skill at rescuing a seemingly sad conversation with her inimitable charm and wit.

"That's good. I'm glad. Perhaps I could meet him sometime?"

"Him?"

"Yes, whoever your new love is. I didn't catch his name."

"Oh, *mon joli garcon*, I did not say that there was only one." She winked and took a long sip of her tea. Corey did the same. "But you are still young, far younger than me. I think there will be someone—just one—for you someday when the timing is right."

Corey set down his cup and sat back in the chair to consider her words. He couldn't imagine loving someone again like he loved Miguel. That dream seemed foreclosed to him now. And deep down inside, that was okay. Despite being together for only one year, Miguel was nearly everything Corey could have wanted in a mate. For now, at least, that experience and those memories were to be treasured and might be enough to sustain him for the rest of his life.

"I see that you doubt me. That is okay. Give it time, *mon cher*, but mark my words—you will love again. And possibly sooner than you think." She paused, sipped her tea, then spoke on. "My nephew from San Francisco is visiting me in the coming months. I will bring him to the shop to say hello."

Corey shook his head at his not-so-subtle friend, then drained the last of his tea. They both rose from their chairs and prepared to move on with their respective days.

"Would you help me out to my car, Corey, *si vous plait?*"

He happily agreed. Mrs. Graner led the way out of the shop and then to the trunk of her Bentley parked alongside the curb in front of the store.

"Oh, I almost forgot. Before you place my newly framed work into the trunk, I'll need you first to take something else out. It's my latest acquisition, and I need you to frame it at once."

Corey held the bubble-wrapped Angus artwork carefully with both hands as he waited for Mrs. Graner to engage the Bentley's automatic opener. He wondered for a moment what it must be like to be as rich as her, to be able to buy whatever her heart desires and sometimes on merely a whim. She fumbled with her car keys before finding and pressing the button she sought.

"Ahh, there. You shall see it in a moment."

Corey watched the trunk slowly rise. He then saw the image of familiar lions coming quickly into view, wrapped behind a translucent layer of sheer plastic. Soon, he saw all three panels clearly, the entirety of his award-winning work.

"*You* placed the winning bid? I can't... uh." The words Corey sought eluded him as his throat seized up. Mrs. Graner looked at

him with a broad smile. "Huh," Corey continued, with tears building behind his eyes. "I guess I should have known." He wasn't certain whether to laugh or cry, but soon he was doing both.

"But of course, I did, *mon cher*. Why not? It will look *tres bien*
alongside the piece by Hopper hanging in my study. Also, I have
great faith in this artist; he is destined for more fantastic work
in the years ahead." She then winked and flashed a wide smile
toward Corey. "Besides, at two hundred thousand dollars, it was
a bargain, *no*?"

* * *

That evening, after making himself a light supper at the apartment, Corey thought again about the triptych, about how it had
been Miguel who urged Corey to enter the piece in the Emerging
Artists Showcase contest and about how Miguel sat with Corey at
the awards dinner only six months ago applauding louder than
anyone else in the room when they announced that Corey had
won first prize. The memories made him smile and tear up at the
same time.

He then thought about the day last week when he met Maria at Miguel's apartment so together they could clean it out.
Though he had only met Maria one time before—at her mother's
funeral last December in Houston—they enjoyed a quick bond,
one forged in tragedy and expressed in a balance of laughter and
tears. According to Miguel's wishes, there would be a small, family ceremony in Houston in another month's time. In the notes he
had left behind, Miguel asked that he be cremated and scattered
in the sea at a place of Corey's choosing. Miguel left most of his
possessions and savings to Maria, but the instructions noted that
Corey was also to receive a modest amount of the money and that
he should choose three items from Miguel's apartment that he
desired to keep. As he walked through the apartment with Maria that day, Corey at first considered choosing the painting he'd
created of Miguel's mother. But then he saw Maria's tearful reaction to the artwork and instead told her that Miguel had loved it

and that Maria should take it home. After perusing the apartment a bit more, he made his first choice. He asked to keep Miguel's beach cruiser bicycle, the same one atop which Miguel had ridden on that beautiful day-date last October when he treated Corey to breakfast at Mango Cafe before pedaling on to Wayfarers Chapel. Next, he asked to keep a plaid, tri-colored shirt. It was the button-up Miguel had worn on their date to see Urban Lights at the Los Angeles County Museum of Art and the same shirt Corey had nearly torn off Miguel's wanting body before they made love for the first time on the beach at dusk later that same night.

For his third item, at first, Corey was stumped. Plenty of things caught his eye—Miguel had impeccable yet modest tastes—but Corey was searching for meaning. He only wanted to select something of deep personal value to him, something to remind him of the person Miguel was and the person Miguel helped Corey to become. The answer dawned on him without even seeing it. He had remembered their final date—the anniversary dinner Miguel had prepared in the apartment. Corey walked over to the kitchen sink and opened the cupboard below. There stood the garbage pail still unemptied from that fateful night a few weeks ago. He ignored the rotting food smell and dropped his hand gently into the trash. He pulled out the four broken pieces of Miguel's mother's antique serving dish. Her carefully wrapped the shards inside a dish towel and placed them into his pack, envisioning how he would later glue the pieces back together. He finished cleaning out the apartment with Maria, then strapped on his backpack and pedaled Miguel's beach cruiser all the way home to Hermosa Beach.

* * *

On the morning after his tea with Mrs. Graner, Corey awakened early and set out once again on Miguel's bike. He returned three hours later after a breathtaking ride out to the tip of Palos Verdes and back, only stopping once—to take photos at the Wayfarers Chapel, which was open to the public for self-guided tours until the next service at noon. Back at home, he gathered his art supplies—an easel, a new canvas, and various paints—then scoured through the digital work produced from his morning and sat atop his stool as he began to paint. He worked all afternoon, only taking a break to refill his tumbler of water and then later to relieve himself from all that he'd consumed. In addition to photos snapped today inside the chapel, Corey wove in a few earlier ones from his phone—pictures of Corey and Miguel taken at random moments over the first six months of the year, from the time they reunited in January until the end of Miguel's life in July. He painted what he saw in vivid detail by replicating the church, Miguel's facial features and the details of Corey's own hands. When it was finally complete, he took several steps away from the canvas and stared for a long time at what he had made. He looked upon his creation and muttered to himself, "It's good." Corey didn't smile, and he didn't cry. Instead, he kept a steady stare. This was the first attempt at what he now called *paintography*, his own unique new brand of art.

The painting showed the interior of the Wayfarers Chapel, its glass walls adorned with hundreds of climbing or hanging green plants, birds of paradise and other flowers framed by dark oak beams and wooden pews placed orderly throughout the relatively small space. He depicted the details of the tiled floor, the sunlight streaming through the glass and a pair of handsome men standing at the altar holding hands. The men were, of course, Corey and Miguel, each dressed in rented tuxedos—Corey in white with a black bow tie and Miguel the exact same in reverse. Those images were taken from a photo at the Emerging Artists Showcase in June, a black-tie affair at which Corey won the award for his triptych and where several people they had met declared them unofficial winners of "best dressed couple." Those details in the painting were all taken from what Corey could see in the photos, either on his phone or in the new digital camera. True to his newly minted method, Corey added one detail that neither the camera nor the phone had caught, but something that he imagined would be there if only the events in their lives had been altered. At the center of the canvas where the two men held hands, something unique stood out and sparkled on Corey's finger as his hands and fingers intertwined with Miguel's. It was a diamond ring with as much of the detail as Corey could remember from his brief encounter with it atop the Hermosa Beach Pier before the ring tumbled over the edge, fell into the water and disappeared from his sight for good.

Chapter 25

Three weeks later, Corey arrived at Ginny's apartment on a Saturday night. This would be the first time he'd been to her apartment since the night they had fled almost two months ago. He surprised her at the door with a dozen sunflowers. She ushered him in and went to find a vase while Corey plopped down on the sofa and exhaled, welcoming the chance to rest after his busy morning navigating the surf at Manhattan Beach. He looked up to see the four framed pieces of his own art still hanging on the wall. He was surprised afresh to see them in this arrangement. Something about their chronological appearance made him uneasy. Though one could clearly see the progression in his skills, Corey felt self-conscious about what the first one glaringly lacked in comparison to the last. Perhaps no one else noticed. He had mounted the pieces in overly gaudy frames, hoping that any onlookers might be distracted by the gilded edges and overlook the flaws that only Corey could see.

"Here you go." Ginny entered the living room and handed him a glass of iced tea. She set her own drink on a coaster, returned to the kitchen and came back with the sunflowers standing tall in the vase. She set them atop the mahogany buffet.

"Thanks, Mom." He pointed toward the wall. "Any luck figuring out the meaning behind those paintings?"

"Yes. It took me a while, but I think I finally did observe some hidden message within each work."

"Hmmm," he said with a hint of coyness. "What did you observe?"

"Do you remember how I pointed out the dark circles in each painting? And how three are similar, but one is different?"

"Yes. And?" He grinned.

"And I think I might know why."

"Oh really? Do tell."

"Well, if you don't know, then my guess is pointless. The meaning of any artwork rests in the eye of the beholder, you know. The artist's message only becomes clear once the piece is studied long enough. Or at least, that's what I've been told."

Corey's grin widened into a smile. "When did my mother become such a smart ass?"

"When I started college at age sixty-four and began hanging out with eighteen-to-twenty-year-olds, apparently."

"Oh, that'll do it for sure. College kids these days are smart mouths and think they know everything because they can Google it at the tip of their fingers. They're insufferable, really." Both of them laughed. "And another thing to watch out for, Mom—kids these days are into dating older people, like sometimes a person twenty or more years older. I read an article about it in the LA Times. It's an actual trend."

"Not to worry, dear. There's no cougar in this old gal."

"Well, you never know. Some young buck may try his luck when you least suspect it."

"Seriously, Corey, that's not going to happen. In fact," she continued after a long draught of her iced tea, "I have a date with someone next Friday, and he's around my same age."

This was not the reply he expected when the teasing began. "Wow. That's, um, great. Where'd you meet?"

"Oh, we connected online like all the kids do these days." She smiled at him and winked. "I met him on Tinder."

Corey had taken a swallow of his tea and then almost gagged as the liquid flowed down against a gasp of air fighting its way up. "What?"

"Oh, don't tell me you were never on those apps before you met Miguel. I know it's all the rage. Would you feel better if I had said we met on Christian Mingle?"

He coughed several times until his throat returned to its natural equilibrium. He looked across the end table at his mother sitting in the upholstered chair mere feet away from his spot on the couch. Who was this woman who looked so much like the one with whom he had grown up but who, of late, acted nothing like that mother from his youth? This woman sitting here in Santa Monica had enrolled in college as a senior citizen, absorbed a ton of shocking news about her late husband and gleefully abandoned her life in Wisconsin for a new and promising one out west. Who in the hell was she? They locked eyes for several moments as Corey continued to catch his breath. When he eventually did and completed his rapid succession of introspective thoughts, he reached for his tea and held it in the air.

"To you, Mom. Cheers. And Godspeed with your date Friday."

Their glasses clinked, and Ginny replied to Corey's toast with a simple "Cheers." They proceeded to talk about Jim, the man she had met online, as well as her classes and immersion into Santa Monica, both the college and surrounding community. He welcomed the excitement in his mother's voice. He had never before heard her talk so much in one sitting, barely pausing long enough for him to say anything at all. The changes in his mother's life over the past five years looked good on her, and he repeatedly said how proud he was of her and how he couldn't wait to see what she eventually did with her degree.

"I've applied for an externship next summer. Did I tell you?"

"No," he replied. "But after all you've said so far, I'm not the least bit surprised."

"Yes. It's in southern Mexico—the state of Oaxaca. There's only room for ten students, but my advisor thinks I've got a good shot. It's unpaid, so the kids who need summer income won't apply. The program takes us high into the mountains—to the village of Jayacatlan—where we'll live for three months to staff a local clinic, help build houses, teach kids to speak English and whatever else the community needs."

He marveled at the palpable excitement in his mother's voice. "I know you'll get it, Mom. I have a good feeling about this."

She talked about the externship for another ten minutes. "And I'm sorry, but the program doesn't allow visitors. If I get it, I'll be down there all summer with only the other students and the villagers. You'll have to do our every other Saturday night dinners with someone else. I don't mean to abandon you, honey, but life is short and only getting shorter at my age."

She eventually turned the conversation toward Corey, asking how things were going now that he had settled into his routines. He gave her a bland update—work, painting and exercise for the most part. He considered telling her about Mrs. Graner's unbelievably overpriced auction bid for his artwork but opted to save that for another time. This felt like Ginny's night and a time to focus on her. It also felt too soon to be bragging about his own good news, still so fresh off losing Miguel.

He sniffed the air and detected a burnt scent. "Mom, is something in the oven?"

"Oh, my heavens, the enchiladas!" She bolted from her chair and yelled over her shoulder as she ran to the kitchen. "I was so deep in conversation that I completely forgot about dinner!"

He stood up and followed her into the kitchen, arriving as she opened the oven to a cloud of gray smoke, removed a pan full of blackened tortillas and set it down on the stove. That's when the smoke detector began blaring and causing them to laugh.

He yelled above the droning alarm. "All those things I said about how you've changed? Well, maybe some things about you haven't changed at all."

She covered her face with the oven mitts and shook her head back and forth.

"Here, let me have those." Corey reached for the mitts. "Open all the windows you can. I'm taking this directly downstairs to the trash."

"But what about dinner? I'm still hungry and you must be too."

"I'm taking you out, Mom—my treat." He pulled on the mitts, grabbed the still-smoking pan and walked toward her. Ginny opened the door upon seeing that Corey's hands were full. "And Mom, please do those Mexican villagers a favor. When you get to Oaxaca and crave a pan of enchiladas, please leave the cooking to the locals."

* * *

Samantha made her first trip to Los Angeles later that same month. It was Sam who had first reached out to Corey only a week after they parted ways in Barron County. Following an exchange of emails and calls in the ensuing weeks, they both expressed a desire to spend time together—to get acquainted without the distractions of mothers or boyfriends and to see what kind of relationship they might forge in the years ahead. The decision to meet in California rather than Wisconsin came easy. Samantha was eager to visit the Golden State and explore the famous places she'd heard about or seen on TV. Corey had looked forward to her visit with a mixture of curiosity, trepidation and hope.

The first day went smoother than he'd expected, and Samantha's easy-going style vibed well with his own. She was once again the person he first met at the Foxtails Lounge last year—bubbly, extroverted and wearing a constant smile. The days passed swiftly. Other than those times when he was at work, he and Samantha explored as much of Southern California as time and their budgets allowed. He showed her Griffith Park and hiked the surrounding hills. They sat on the beach in Malibu and traversed the Hollywood Walk of Fame. An entire afternoon was spent touring the Getty Art Museum atop the Santa Monica Mountains, followed by Chinese food and a movie night in the heart of Westwood Village.

During these adventures, Corey and Samantha talked—a lot. Each spoke of their respective childhoods, both the good and the not-so-good. There, they found a common theme—the absence of a consistent, supportive and healthy father figure while growing up. They shared something else in common from their childhood years—mothers who loved them unconditionally with kindness and encouragement, but also women who didn't always model the way of standing up for oneself and standing up to a bullying man. Yet both Sam and Corey acknowledged their mothers' respective growth in the years since. Both Judy and Ginny eventually found their way toward self-care and self-fulfillment, even if those things only came to them after the man they shared had died.

On the second to last day of her trip, Corey had the day off from work. The weather forecast promised an unseasonably warm late September day across the Southland, a perfect day for morning yoga, brunch at a seaside cafe, a long afternoon bike ride and perhaps a barefoot walk on the beach. Samantha said she loved the plan and followed him as they headed toward Manhattan Beach for his weekly sun salutations with a group of surfing pals. He pointed out the group gathering below the pier as Corey and Sam stood atop the hillside looking down toward the sand.

"All of these guys and gals are surfers?" she asked with her mouth agape.

"Yes. We meet here on Friday mornings to do our downward-facing dogs. Yoga, meditation and stretching are all fundamental disciplines for surfing."

"Cool. I can't imagine what the folks back home would say if I organized a yoga in the park every week. They'd probably freak out."

"How about Todd?" Corey laughed. "Not sure I can see him rocking the warrior pose by your side."

Samantha smiled. "It's funny. I would've laughed at your comment in the past. The idea of Todd doing anything different or sensitive, like yoga, was laughable. Don't get me wrong—he's romantic in a reserved, straight guy sort of way. But ever since that day out in the woods when he watched Nick die, and then after he shot and killed Cecelia, something has been different. He's changed."

"How so?"

"I don't know—more aware and attentive, maybe? He used to be someone who jumped to conclusions and stuck to his guns, figuratively speaking. Since that day, he's more of a thinker and a listener. It's as if he became more empathetic toward others. I can't explain it."

Corey nodded as they continued walking toward the beach, closing in on the yoga class. What Samantha had described was eerily like changes Corey had noticed in Billy since that day as well. In addition to beating himself up for convincing Nick to fatefully leave the cabin, Billy had, of course, recounted to Corey word for word what Nick said as he lay dying and delirious on the cold, damp trail. Billy's version closely echoed what Todd had explained a bit more briefly to Corey as they sat on the bench overlooking Redemption Lake. This is what Samantha confirmed now as well—something happened on that dreary, deadly afternoon that changed both Todd and Billy in unforeseen yet noticeable ways.

* * *

They finished the yoga class and then walked in the direction of Corey's apartment. They stopped for brunch at Martha's Cafe, eating at a patio table overlooking the Pacific. Though they had skimmed the edges of relationships in earlier conversations, today Corey sensed urgency, knowing that Samantha would soon be returning home and that conversations might be less personal by phone. She raised the topic first, asking him to speak about Miguel. She wanted to know everything about him and why he was so special in Corey's life. He obliged and spoke for twenty minutes nonstop. It felt good to recap the history of his and Miguel's relationship with someone who didn't witness it first-hand. He spoke with energy and joy and only occasionally teared up. By the end of his story, he saw the entirety of that beautiful year-long dance with Miguel for what it truly was—the most passionate relationship of Corey's life.

For her part, Sam talked about her *party years* between ages sixteen and twenty-two and the revolving door of boyfriends she fell in love with fast—all of them to Judy's dismay. "Looking back, I doubt that I loved any one of them. I drank a lot in those days and did things I regret. Not sure if you can relate to that or not."

He smirked. "I think you proved yet again that we're related. Like you, I inherited my unquenchable thirst for alcohol from Frank."

"Well, I gave it up the day after my twenty-second birthday when I awoke in the Barron County jail after a spectacular display of public drunkenness at the County Park by Redemption Lake."

Corey raised his inquisitive eyebrows while sipping his coffee.

"Trust me, you don't want to know."

He nodded his head while forming a knowing smile.

"Anyway, that was also the morning I met Todd. Decked out to the nines in his Sheriff's uniform, he gave me *the speech*. At first, I was annoyed. I mean, he wasn't saying anything I didn't know. But then I realized that he wasn't judging or lecturing me like my unknown father might do. Instead, I could tell it was coming from a good place—his heart. He didn't give that talk to either of my friends who spent the night in jail, though. Instead, his words were directed solely at me. After Mom came to get me—and, by the way, her words that morning *did* have plenty of judgment—I didn't see Todd again for quite some time. But I thought about him and about what he said and how he made me feel. For some reason, it was his calm words, not my mother's yelling, that motivated me to get help and quit drinking. Best decision I ever made."

"I know exactly what you mean, and I've been in your shoes. Congrats on pulling yourself out of that hell. It's not an easy thing to do."

The server brought their food, and Samantha spoke about running into Todd six months later at a summer picnic in Barron and how he asked her out on a date. They've been together ever since.

"He grounds me, Corey, like no one else ever did before. And he supports my dreams."

"Dreams? Tell me more."

"It'll probably sound silly, but I want to open my own fitness center, either in Barron or more likely Eau Claire where there's more potential clients."

"That's not silly at all. But are you sure you want to give up your lucrative career at the Foxtails Lounge?"

"Now I know that we're related, too, Corey."

"Because I'm a smartass?"

"Exactly—very slapable."

* * *

After brunch, they walked to the apartment, put towels and a few personal items into a backpack and headed out on their bikes. He lowered the seat on Miguel's beach cruiser so that Samantha could ride comfortably and reach the pedals safely. First, they rode north all the way to Playa del Rey. Then, they pedaled south to the opposite end in Redondo. Corey offered to stop and turn around at least three times, but she wouldn't hear of it.

"In two days, I'll be back in Wisconsin. I intend to soak up every minute of sunshine and mile of beachfront I can until the time my plane takes off."

Upon their return to Hermosa, Corey steered his way off the bike path and onto the sand several yards north of the pier. Samantha followed and asked why he had stopped.

"Come on. We've both burned enough calories for one day. It's time to relax."

He locked their bikes to a lamppost, then led her to a spot a few yards from the water. He opened the backpack, pulled out two towels and laid them side by side. She eagerly shed her shoes, socks and shirt, revealing the swimsuit she had been wearing underneath. Then, she looked impatiently at him. "Well, aren't you coming in with me?"

"The water hasn't gotten any warmer than when we were in it yesterday, you know. Ideally, we'd have on our wetsuits."

"It felt fine to me, and I'm going in again—wetsuit or no wetsuit. You're not going to let your little sister show that she's tougher than you, are you?"

Corey laughed and shook his head. "You're tough as nails." He removed everything but his T-shirt and swim trunks. "But that toughness suits you, Sam. Now, let's see who can get to the water first." He threw his bundled socks onto the towel and took off running toward the sea.

* * *

They only stayed in the water long enough to dive into two oncoming waves. After that, Samantha's teeth began to chatter, so they went ashore, toweled off and got dressed. Corey suggested a walk under the pier and on toward King Harbor. She agreed, and together they traversed the sand just above where the waves reached their apex on shore. She noted the frequent, tiny holes in the sand where the water turned and receded toward the sea. Corey stopped, leaned over and immediately began digging with his hands. He implored her to do the same.

"Yeah, like that—right above any of those holes. There, you've got it. Now, cup your hands together with all the sand and let it sift slowly through your fingers."

She did. Then, she screamed. "What *are* those?"

They both watched as three tiny white creatures burrowed deeper into the remaining sand cupped in her hand and closer to her skin until Samantha threw all of it onto the beach.

"Sand crabs. They're everywhere. I don't know exactly why, but they tend to show themselves where the water hits its highest point on shore, and these air holes suddenly appear in droves. I'm guessing it's how they breathe?"

"Awesome and disgusting." She rubbed her hands on her shirt, washing away any remnant of the wretched crustaceans.

Then she stopped and pointed skyward. "Hey, this is where it happened, isn't it?"

He assumed she was referencing the pier above their heads where Miguel had proposed marriage and upon which Miguel was shot.

"It is," he said quietly.

"Is this where the ring fell in the ocean? We should look for it. Maybe it washed ashore."

Corey was touched that she had remembered that detail. Frankly, he had told the entire story of Miguel so quickly that he didn't remember what he had shared or not.

"I've done that a few times but come up empty-handed. I even went out on my surfboard to the point where I estimated it fell in and tried looking down into the water, hoping I might see it sparkling on the bottom of the sea. I realize how stupid that sounds. As if a person could see twenty feet down into the water and spot a tiny ring."

"It's not stupid, Corey. It sounds damn normal to me."

"Thanks."

They came together in an embrace that she initiated. They had already hugged several times so far this week, starting at the airport when Samantha arrived. Despite being virtual strangers, Corey sensed an invisible connection, and he knew that they shared the same blood. Today's hug felt different—a bit more intense and lasting longer than the rest. Eventually, they both let go, yet Samantha still held onto Corey's arms.

"Thank you for everything this week. You've gone out of your way to make me feel welcome and show me this incredible city. I appreciate it."

"You're welcome. I'm glad you came, and I hope you'll be back again soon. Who knows, maybe next time you'll bring Todd too?"

"Maybe. I think he'd like that." They walked further along the sand, emerging from the shadow of the pier and into the waning sunlight. "So, what's on tap for tomorrow? You know we can totally chill. We don't have to do anything extravagant. I mean, we've done so much this week already."

"Oh, I've got a special plan for you in mind." The smile on Corey's face widened, and he looked somewhat far away in thought.

"And that is?" She returned his warm smile.

"Tomorrow's your final day in LA, so I saved the best for last. We're coming back here after sunrise, which happens to coincide with high tide. Ready or not, Sam, tomorrow is going to blow your mind. I'm going to teach you how to surf."

Chapter 26

The following weekend, Corey awoke early and heard the cawing of seagulls. Waves crashed ashore on the beach at Cardiff by the Sea, hundreds of feet below the bluff where he now lay. He felt snug nestled inside the sleeping bag, though his back ached after a long night with only a thin pad separating his body from the hard ground. He turned over to see a huge lump buried inside the other sleeping bag within the four-person tent. Billy seemingly had himself zip-locked into his sack. How in the hell could the man even breathe, Corey wondered. He pulled on his jeans and a sweatshirt, then quietly exited the tent to greet a late September sunrise and the cool, early autumn air. A few others were stirring about at their nearby sites in the campground at San Elijo State Beach. He gathered wood from the pile in the back of Billy's truck and, within minutes, had a decent flame going in the fire pit. Corey laughed at himself with pride. He hadn't successfully started a campfire in nearly thirty years. It felt good to be out in nature like this, and he was grateful Billy had invited him along for the trip. In contrast to Corey, Billy had never relinquished his love for sleeping in the great outdoors. At least once a month since moving to California, he set out in various directions from LA to find solitude and unspoiled natural beauty that eluded him inside America's second-largest metropolis.

Corey grabbed the beat-up metal pot, filled it with water from the jug, scooped coffee grounds into the filter and then set it atop the fire grate. He eschewed Billy's generic brand in favor of the hazelnut-flavored gourmet beans he purchased at the Yellow Vase before the trip. He sat down in a camp chair and stared into the fire, keeping one eye on the coffee pot and willing it to percolate fast. He heard rumblings from inside the tent a few minutes later and turned to see Billy emerge, looking not yet fully awake and stumbling toward the fire before plopping himself into a chair.

"Is my breakfast ready?"

"No, but the coffee almost is."

"What in the hell kind of room service is this? I brought you along so I could relax and not have to do a thing."

Corey laughed, then rose to pull the percolating coffee away from the fire. He poured them each a cup, making sure to deliver Billy's in his favorite mug, a formerly white ceramic cup now stained brown inside with a St. Thomas University logo almost completely worn off the exterior.

"Here you go, buttercup."

"Ah, that's more like it." Billy took a sip from the steaming cup and exhaled. "You ain't the prettiest thing I've ever slept next to in that tent, but your coffee certainly rocks."

"Thanks, glad you like it. And thanks for bringing me along this weekend."

"Of course. San Elijo is one of my favorite spots. I think we both needed to get away from everything and everyone. We needed time to chill. It's been an insane few months."

"Make that an insane entire year." Both men nodded their heads and sipped their coffee. "I can see why you escape like this, Billy—to get away from the city, enjoy the fresh air and have space to think."

"That's the secret formula right there. Always has been since I was a kid."

"Yeah, you guys camped a lot. I was envious."

Billy laughed. "Isn't that how it goes? You wanted to go camping with my family, and here I was, jealous that yours had a cabin where you could fish and hunt. The grass is always greener, huh?"

Corey sipped his coffee and smiled. "Yeah, that's true. Say, speaking of the cabin and our crazy recent months, what's the latest with the lawsuit?"

"A lot. Rebecca called yesterday with an update. There was a hearing last Thursday, and she won her motion to limit damages in the event plaintiffs win their case. Well, I should say *plaintiff* rather than *plaintiffs*. That was the whole point of the hearing. Now that Cecelia is gone, her daughter is the only one left with a viable claim and potential damages. Rebecca got the judge to agree to cap any eventual award."

"But there still could be a judgment?"

"Yes, but Rebecca says there's an opening for possible settlement. The grandmother is Julia's guardian now, and she gets to make decisions about the lawsuit. Their lawyer indicated that the old lady isn't overly keen on pressing forward. She's not as invested in revenge over her son-in-law's death as Cecelia was. Besides, Cecelia would've been the main witness. And because she didn't sit for a deposition before she died, their side essentially has no evidence to support her claims of emotional distress and loss of companionship. Also, the daughter got a life insurance payout for both parents. Rebecca thinks all those factors combined mean that the grandmother is looking for a quick settlement and probably at a steep discount from the original million-dollar demand."

"Sounds like good news?"

"It is, though we still have to come up with the money, and Mom doesn't want to sell the house."

Corey stared into the fire and avoided looking at Billy. His suppressed feelings of guilt over Larry's false confession and Corey's responsibility for Bennett's death returned.

"We'll figure it out. I have a call scheduled with my siblings on Tuesday after I get back. But enough about all that. This weekend is about getting away from serious things and enjoying the beautiful view." Billy pointed toward the ocean in the distance beyond the edge of the bluff. "And it's about adventure and trying new things."

"New things? What happened to the Billy I knew and loved? The guy who drives a shitty ten-year-old truck, drinks nothing but Red Stripe and has had the same best friend since 1979?"

"*Touche, mon ami.*"

"For fuck's sake, now you're learning French, too? Who are you, and what have you done with Billy Preston?"

"I don't know, man. I feel different now, like I want different things. You're one hundred percent correct—I'm a creature of habit and hardly ever take chances. But something inside is pushing me. Could be a mid-life crisis or the impact of my dad dying or maybe meeting Rebecca. I don't know. What I do know is that my life has changed, especially after that day in the woods."

Corey knew exactly which day Billy meant.

"Seeing Nick die so unexpectedly and hearing what he had to say, it affected me, Corey. I'm sure that sounds weird. I mean, I never liked the guy. I still hate how he treated you all those years. But in those moments when I held him and listened to his heartfelt thoughts come bubbling to the surface—they had an impact. I can't explain it any more than that."

"You don't need to, Billy. I get it."

"And it's more than what happened in the woods. I was feeling some of these things before that. I mean, I've been happily single since my divorce. Then, I randomly reconnect with Rebecca, and this happens."

Corey knew exactly what Billy meant by *this*.

"Who am I? Who is this guy contemplating plans that would shake up my otherwise happy life? Did I tell you that Rebecca is considering giving up her law firm partnership and moving here?"

"No, you didn't. Wow, that would be, um, a huge step for both of you."

"I know, right? And it honestly excites me because I can't imagine my life without her. I love her, man."

Corey knew exactly how Billy felt.

"But if I truly love her, how can I let her walk away from her dream job? Sure, she could take the bar out here and find a decent job, but she worked her ass off for years to get where she's at. And I don't want her to resent me later."

"That's valid, Billy. There is another option, you know."

He looked over at Corey as he drained the bottom of his coffee mug. "Yeah, but remember who you're talking to? I'm the guy who hates change and loves California." Billy said no more. Neither of them did for quite some time. Finally, Corey breached the silence.

"So, what's on tap for the day? You said you had an adventure planned?"

Billy checked his watch. "Yep. We better get showered and dressed. Our reservation's at ten."

"Reservation?"

"Yes. It's about a fifteen-minute drive to Torrey Pines. I signed us both up for lessons."

"Golfing?" Corey knew of the famous course in north LaJolla and masked his disappointment at the prospect of a day spent in frustration learning a sport in which he had zero interest. He bit his tongue, though. If Billy was open to trying new things, Corey could do that, too.

"Nah, bro. I know golf wouldn't be your thing. I decided it's time we both put on a pair of wings and learned how to fly."

Corey looked at him with a furrowed brow. He had no clue what Billy had planned.

"I purchased a tandem experience at the Torrey Pines Gliderport. We'll each be strapped to a hang glider and an instructor. Get ready to step off the cliff at Black's Beach, my friend. We're about to soar with the birds three hundred feet above the sea."

* * *

Rebecca flew to California the following week. On the day before she was to return to Minnesota, she joined Billy and Corey for their standing Sunday morning brunch at the Long Beach Museum of Art. Corey was already seated at an oceanfront table when the happy couple arrived. He rose to greet them, embracing them each in turn.

"It's great to see you, Corey. Thanks for letting me crash your boys' brunch."

He smiled. "Of course. How's your week been? Seen any new sights, or have you two been shacked up in Billy's condo the entire time?"

"That information is attorney-boyfriend privileged, sorry." She offered a playful shrug with upturned palms. They both looked at Billy for an honest reply, but he lifted the menu to hide his blushing face. "No, it's been a chill week. Billy had to work a few of the days, so I used the time to catch up on emails and do some shopping at South Coast Plaza." She displayed her latest Louis Vuitton purchase. "Do you like?"

Corey nodded with approval. "Nice."

A server stopped to take drink orders—two breakfast margaritas and a passion fruit iced tea. Then, Corey and Rebecca exchanged updates while Billy listened patiently to news he'd probably already heard. Corey explained how he continued to learn the ins and outs of using a professional-grade camera and how he employed it to create his own unique paintography. He then showed them a series of pictures on his phone, the first one a snapshot of his painting at the Wayfarer's Chapel, followed by the actual photos upon which the artwork was based.

"How beautiful," Rebecca fawned. "It's incredible how you've recreated what's in those photos and then made everything more detailed and lifelike."

"Yeah, super cool, man. I've always said you've got more talent than the rest of us put together."

Corey soaked in the praise and somehow inherited the facial blush that moments before had belonged to Billy. His former self would have demurred or rejected the compliments, part of a lifelong pattern of denying his true self—both the good and the bad. Today, however, he simply said *thank you*, then paused before turning the conversation toward Rebecca. In response, she told him the latest from her law practice and showed a few photos of the emerging fall colors in Minnesota. She also gave him an update on the Jackson's lawsuit. She confirmed what Billy had conveyed a week earlier—that the case was ripe for settlement and the Prestons were considering how best to raise the funds.

They paused as the waitress returned with drinks and took their food orders.

"Billy said you also have breaking news to share with me this morning. I can't imagine what it is." Corey enjoyed his playful tease, expecting that Rebecca was about to reveal her plans to move west.

"I do. But Billy told me that you might have news today as well?"

"True. But please, ladies first."

"All right. Here goes. I'll be getting a roommate soon. What do you think about that?"

"You're going to love California—that's what I think. I'm sure passing the bar won't be a picnic, but you're the smartest person I know, so you'll be fine. It's living in that tacky bachelor pad he calls a condo that I'm worried about. The place needs a woman's touch, and I can't wait to see what you do with it."

Rebecca looked nervously at Billy, who simply laughed and shook his head in reply.

"You're right about one thing," Rebecca said as she turned back to look at Corey. "That condo is in need of TLC and a severe makeover."

"Hey, it's a genuine man cave. An original!" Billy protested.

Corey and Rebecca each laughed and nodded in agreement.

"But you've misunderstood the other part, Corey, the part about me getting a roommate. I'm not moving to LA. Billy's moving in with me."

The look on Corey's face revealed the words churning inside his brain—*what the fuck?*

"It's true, man. I've decided to sell my business to a competitor who's been bugging me for years to join him. Then, I'm going to pack up that tacky bachelor pad, as you called it, and sell it for a tidy sum."

Corey was momentarily stunned before finding a few coherent words. "When did you decide this?"

"It's been running through my mind for a while now. I guess I didn't mention it out loud because I wasn't convinced of it myself. But after our hang-gliding experience, I figured, *what the hell*? If I can jump off a cliff while tethered to a total stranger, why not this as well? I can't believe I'm saying this, Corey, but I'm moving to fucking Minnesota."

Thoughts raced through Corey's mind, starting with shock but soon moving toward acceptance. He had never seen Billy look so happy as he was right now.

"So let me get this straight. For years—decades—you tried convincing me to move west, to join you in California. Then, when I finally do, you up and leave me for some girl?"

"Damn straight, bro. Sorry."

Corey laughed. "Don't be. The happiness on your face—on both of your faces—tells me this is the right thing to do."

"So," Rebecca said, "it's your turn. What's your news? Are you moving back to Minnesota, too?"

Corey had taken a sip of iced tea and proceeded to spit part of it out. "Uh, that's a *hell no*."

"Then tell us," Billy said. "Honest to God, I have no idea what you're about to say."

Corey wiped tea droplets from his lips with a napkin. "Well, do you remember that Emerging Artist Contest I participated in last spring, the one Miguel had encouraged me to enter?"

"That was the painting with the lions, right? The one where you won first place?"

"Yes." He pointed to Billy. "I see you do listen to me occasionally. Anyway, they held an auction for all the winning artwork while I was in Minnesota. Apparently, someone bought my painting—a person I know, in fact. And she bid a hefty price. I'll net around one hundred thousand dollars."

"Oh my God, Corey, that's fantastic!" Rebecca reached across and squeezed his arm.

Billy softly punched Corey's other arm. "Awesome, my friend. You deserve it. Way to go."

"Thanks. I might've deserved to win first place, but I don't deserve the money. I've decided to give it away. I'm giving it to you and your family, Billy. I want you to use it to settle the lawsuit."

Billy said nothing. His eyes filled with tears.

Corey turned toward Rebecca. "Do you think the Jacksons would accept that amount?"

"Could be. There's a decent chance. If you're sure about this, I'll call their lawyer and ask."

"Do it, please."

She looked at Billy, who gave a slow, approving nod of his head.

"Okay." Rebecca pushed back from her chair and walked toward a spot closer to the museum and away from the buzzing crowd.

Billy composed himself and began to speak, but Corey interrupted.

"I'm doing this, Billy, and you know there's a million reasons why. If you have anything to say other than *thank you*, I simply won't listen."

"Thank you, Corey. Thank you."

"You're welcome. And I have a question for you before Rebecca returns. Are you selling your business and your condo to fund the settlement? Because if so, you don't need to. I got you covered, and if the proceeds from the art auction aren't enough, I'll find a way to make up the difference. Please, only sell those things if it's what you want to do."

Billy folded his hands as if in prayer and tucked them under his chin with his elbows on the placemat. "Honestly, it did factor into my decision—that it would be win-win to move in with Rebecca and have cash for the settlement." Corey began to interrupt but was shushed. "But your generous gesture doesn't change the true reason I'm selling everything and leaving LA. I don't need my old life anymore, now that I'm going to be with my love."

"Then you're making the right decision, Billy. Congrats."

"Thanks, man. And don't think you're getting rid of me that easy. I'll be out here often to check on you. Since I'll no longer have the condo, looks like I'll be staying with you when I visit. Can't wait to rearrange your neat-freak apartment into a shitty bachelor pad more to my liking."

Chapter 27

Today would be the day. It was the anniversary of perhaps the best twenty-four hours of Corey Flanagan's life—one year since Miguel had treated him to breakfast at the Mango Cafe and biked together to the Wayfarers Chapel, where Miguel first hinted at the possibility of marriage. Corey awoke with a melancholy spirit but with purpose in his heart. He didn't remember dreaming during the night, but a singular thought welcomed him into the morning. Today was the day he was meant to release Miguel's ashes, and he knew the exact location where he would set the love of his life free.

He made a quick mental plan. His short shift at Framed By The Beach would be the perfect interlude to an expectedly meaningful day. He would paint and work with photography all morning, then head toward the ocean later in the afternoon when his work at the shop was complete. For now, though, he set up his easel in the living room and queued the necessary photos on his digital camera and phone, as well as an old album of collected pictures. Then he sat for a moment with eyes closed, preparing for what he was about to paint. The photos at which he had glanced were mostly taken by Ginny a few weeks earlier when she visited him in the South Bay, and they did a photo shoot of each other atop the Palos Verdes cliffs. Corey smiled at the memory and at Ginny's uncanny, untrained knack for capturing vivid, focused photos of her son. He also retrieved pictures taken recently with Billy and Rebecca, then conjured in his mind remembered favorite images of Nick, Frank, Carol, Larry and, of course, Miguel.

With all of them in mind, Corey opened his eyes and took a long look at each of the selected photos—the most influential people in his life. He asked himself what he saw in each of their faces and what he imagined that he could see if he stared at their photos forever. When he finished gazing at them, he set the photos aside, reached for a brush and eagerly began to paint. He started with the shape of a head—Frank's head, to be precise. Corey always saw his father as intelligent, occasionally for the better, like in running his own business, but too smart for his own good when it came to matters of the heart. Corey acknowledged that he inherited the shape of his own head from Frank, perhaps an explanation for why Corey was an over-thinker, too.

Next, he painted the contours of the face, both a uniquely shaped nose and protruding cheekbones. In his mind's eye, these were Ginny's features, which epitomized her stoicism and sharp sensibilities hewing toward logic, caution, and patience. Admittedly, those facial features could have been Corey's as well, for he and his mother shared those genetic shapes. He wasn't as certain that he shared the traits they represented, but if pressed, he could see versions of himself in Ginny's strengths, and he longed to be more like her someday. Above his mother's nose, Corey next painted a pair of eyes that sparkled in a hue of aquamarine. They were more round than oval but opened wide as if straining to see things that couldn't be seen and looking for all that could be hoped for. They were Billy's eyes, and they fit nicely into the emerging portrait of a man standing tall in front of scenery that was yet to be created.

For now, Corey kept painting the man. He added a wild shock of hair, a shade somewhere between auburn and sandy brown. It was unkempt yet in a purposeful and stylish way as if the person from whose head the hair emerged had the confidence to wear it how he chose—the naysayers and fashion critics be damned. What Corey painted was the hair from a photo of Nick, taken in the year before their relationship went to shit, but at a time when Nick still possessed a handsome full head of hair, somewhat darker in tone than Corey's but similar in texture, the direction of a cowlick and thickness.

Beneath that hair, on either side of the person's head, Corey painted the lower half of two matching ears. The tops were to be imagined hidden from sight behind the flowing locks. The ears that Corey painted belonged to Carol, minus her usual dangly earrings. He recalled focusing on those ears during his recent visit, the first thing he looked at as he sketched an image of his lifelong friend fully nude before letting his eyes roam toward more sensitive parts. And while her ears were supple and unblemished, they also represented, for Corey, his friend's best quality. Carol was an excellent listener, someone who used her God-given sense of hearing to take in what was being said and oftentimes what wasn't. Whenever he was in Carol's presence, and especially those times of great emotion, he knew she heard him, which made him feel as though whatever he had to say was important, whether it truly was or not.

With the face on the canvas nearly complete, he moved on to fill in the scenery behind. Like the photos taken above Malaga Cove with Ginny only weeks earlier, Corey painted a blufftop scene behind the image of the man in the middle of the canvas and a distant blue ocean toward the top. He included white on the tips of the rolling waves as they neared the shore and green on the tops of the bluff, turning into brown dust as they dropped into the sea. While painting this majestic landscape, Corey thought of Rebecca and Larry, two lawyers who had saved him from a lifetime in prison and two unshakeable friends who left the taste of freedom on his lips and gratitude in his heart.

He painted a sun straining to shine through the hazy marine layer floating in from the ocean on toward land. As the sun sat above the left shoulder of the artwork's central image, Corey painted a faint lemon-hued ring that circumnavigated the blurry yellow sun, almost forming the shape of a halo around the person's head. He smiled at this addition, something that he could see inside his mind as he remembered the photos of Rebecca and

Larry. It was fitting, he thought, to remember them that way—two people who, despite their flaws, set perhaps the best examples that he had yet encountered of lives well and intentionally lived.

By now, only one detail remained to be painted. Corey stepped away from his easel and once again stared into his phone, gazing at the face of the man he loved more than any other and the person who had brought such unexpected joy to Corey's life. Emotion overwhelmed him as he continued looking at the photo of Miguel, especially on a day that held so much meaning, both for what the two of them had experienced together one year ago and for what Corey planned to do only a few hours from now. He resumed his place at the easel and painted a broad and playful smile, the same one worn by Miguel in the photo and the same one spread across Corey's tear-filled face right now.

He set down his brush and wiped his hands on a cloth and his tears on the sleeve of his shirt. He walked across the room and fell into the living room chair. From here, he could see the painting clearly—every detail and every flaw. He resisted the impulse to fix the imperfections. They were meant to be part of the painting, a piece not intended for public viewing. Corey painted this work for himself because, in the end, he realized that the painting was of himself. No one else would recognize the image in the center of the canvas as Corey Flanagan, but he saw himself there as clear as a California sky. He had painted parts of those who'd exerted great influence over his life, but when put together in one painting, Corey understood that he was looking at the person he had slowly become and the person he might yet be.

He checked his watch and knew it was time for work. He grabbed the new painting off the easel and carried it into the bedroom. He set it on the floor and then turned to the wall opposite his bed. There, he looked upon Frida Kahlo's *Wounded Deer*, the framed print that Nick had given Corey as a birthday gift all those years ago, and the same piece that Corey had shipped home from Minneapolis when Nick sold the condo last November. Corey had hung it here on the bedroom wall after it arrived. It had been his most favorite painting for nearly twenty years, but now its appeal had waned. He gently removed it from the wall and hung his self-portrait in its place.

* * *

He finished his shift at Framed By The Beach, grabbed his backpack from the store room and headed out on his bike. The urn, his camera and a bottle of water were tucked snugly inside his pack. He felt a solemn quietude as he rode south from Riviera Village and into the rolling hills of Palos Verdes. He pedaled to a remote spot above Malaga Cove. Here, on a late Friday afternoon, Corey had the vista completely to himself. He set his bike against a tree and walked with his backpack to the edge of the cliff. From here, he could see the entirety of Santa Monica Bay, from the steep cliffs of Malibu in the distance all the way around to where he stood now, gazing hundreds of feet down into the ocean. He could see sailboats plying the waves outside King Harbor and airplanes taking off from LAX. He could also see the spot on the beach where he and Miguel had first made love after their date at Urban Lights, a night that now seemed an eternity ago. He removed the urn from his pack and walked to the edge of the cliff. After looking back to confirm no one was nearby, he twisted the top off the silver metal ossuary. Then, he spoke out loud.

"Miguel, I don't know if you can hear me, but I hope that you feel the emotions inside my heart. Although it's painful, I've accepted that you're gone. To be honest, I doubt the pain will ever pass. And that's okay. I want to feel this loss forever because it reminds me that you were real, that our relationship was meaningful and that our love will go on. What I want to say most of all as I set your ashes free is *thank you*. For over half my life, I thought I needed other people to fulfill my needs and make me happy. You taught me that I didn't, that instead, I must find happiness within. I remember you saying once that a person should imagine all the most important people in their lives disappearing and that if a person can picture being fine—alone—only then are we capable of giving and receiving deep love. Now, those closest to me are either gone or taking paths leading away—you, Larry, Billy and, in a way, my mom, too. But I'm not sad, Miguel, because you taught me I'll be okay. The love from all of you will stay with me no matter where I go or how long I live.

"I also want you to know how proud I am of you. Your mama raised a wonderful son—brave, smart, selfless, funny and kind. You left this world a better place than you found it and never took love for granted, whether it was love given or love received. This is how you'll be remembered, Miguel—by me, by Maria and by everyone who loved you so very, very much."

Corey paused, took a deep breath, and cast one more long look across the bay in front of him.

"I guess that's all I have to say. Don't be surprised if I still talk to you at random. I feel better knowing you're near, at least in spirit. And I'll keep looking for signs of you, too. I love you beyond measure, Miguel. You lived a tremendous life. I'm honored to have known you and grateful for the person you helped me to become."

Corey's throat was tight and dry as he knew the time for casting Miguel's remains into the ocean was near. He choked back tears, then looked into the urn and finished what he wanted to say.

"I'll see you again, Miguel. Count on it. *Adiós, mi amante de por vida. Te quiero.*"

Corey reluctantly pushed the urn away from his chest and turned it on its side. He thrust the ossuary forward while holding on tight, releasing the ashes from inside. He watched as the wind carried Miguel's remains over the cliff and down toward the ocean, eventually splashing ash by ash into the swirling, life-sustaining sea.

* * *

Corey rode toward home more slowly than normal, as if on autopilot. He reached the Hermosa Beach Pier and didn't quite remember the route he had covered in between. The sun was a half-hour away from its daily drop into the ocean and Corey decided to park and lock his bike and walk out onto the pier. This was still one of his favorite spots in the world, even if it also was the backdrop of his life's worst night. Yet, he no longer thought of the night of Miguel's death that way; instead, Corey was at peace as he approached the spot where Miguel drew some of his final breaths and said his last words, all while being held tight in Corey's arms.

He stopped mere yards after walking onto the pier. He didn't feel compelled to walk all the way to its end; rather, he felt drawn to a spot along the railing where he could see the ocean at low tide. He scanned the shore in either direction, surprised at the number of beachgoers enjoying one of the last best days of the extended California summer. He pulled the camera out of his pack and looked north from the pier once more. He wanted to get a closer look at the faces of these random souls—families, couples and a few people walking the beach alone. What were they seeking? Why were they here? Was there anything unique in them that Corey might capture on film and later paint to memorialize this spectacularly important day?

He focused first on a lone woman sitting atop a beach towel and reading. Most likely, she came here after a long week at the office, searching for a moment of Zen in a place of such immense beauty. He empathized with her imagined need for privacy. Not wanting to intrude upon her solitude, he moved on. He panned the camera to his left and spied two men boogie-boarding together in the water and laughing. They were young and clearly oblivious to the cooler ocean temps of early October. Perhaps they were a pair of friends—a bit like Corey and Billy as kids—seeking a joyful release at the end of a long week at school.

He then looked away from the camera lens and spotted four people on the beach a hundred yards from where he stood atop the pier. He focused the camera on them as they walked toward him along the sand—two women, a teenage girl, and a younger boy. He wasn't sure why, but something inside urged him to keep focused on this foursome. The two women appeared to be deep in conversation as they walked. The girl trailed behind, looking down into a device. As for the boy, he seemed to be examining various items along the beach. Corey wondered about this foursome. Perhaps the two women were lovers or sisters, and the young ones their kids? From their movement toward him, it wasn't clear. And the girl, consumed with her phone, gave him not a single clue.

So, he focused more intently on the boy. Corey turned his lens to its most powerful magnification and watched as the boy inspected empty crab shells, random washed-up trash and the enticing though pungent piles of seaweed pushed ashore by receding waves. He saw the boy linger over one of those piles, composed of a unique-looking seaweed that Corey, too, found intriguing on his beachcombing strolls. The thick green mass included random, round translucent balls that made a sharp popping sound and squirted water when pressed tightly between two fingers.

Through the camera lens, Corey saw the boy suddenly summon the two women, motioning with his hands for them to turn around and observe what he had found. The boy then dropped to his knees and sifted through the seaweed while the women answered his call, spun around and walked toward him. The girl with the phone briefly looked up and then returned her attention to the device. She stopped walking and stood halfway between the women and the boy.

Corey wished that he could hear what the boy was saying and read what thoughts filled the women's minds. Instead, he stayed focused on what he could see through his lens. The boy suddenly stood up and began jumping in place, holding clasped hands close to his chest. Corey imagined their conversation while maintaining a clean sight line through the lens, watching the moment unfold.

"Walk faster!" the boy likely yelled.

The women surely implored him to be patient. "What is it, honey?"

"Come see what I found."

"Is it something that's going to gross us out?"

"No. Better!"

The women appeared to laugh. "Then show us."

The boy ran eagerly toward the women, still clutching his arms to his chest. As the three of them converged upon the spot where the teenage girl was standing, she looked up from her phone, seemingly also now intrigued by what had fascinated the boy. He reached them all within a few seconds, staring at his three companions with an exuberant face bursting with news. After a dramatic pause, the boy thrust his hand triumphantly into the air.

"Look, a ring!"

Acknowledgments

There are many people to thank for encouraging, enlightening and educating me on this unexpected literary journey. First and foremost, my loyal and supportive readers. Without your excitement and enthusiasm for Corey's tale, this trilogy would not have been written or published. I'm humbled and grateful for each and every one of you.

Immense gratitude also goes out to the incredibly talented writing community to which I belong. I have learned so much from so many. They include teachers and mentors Sandra Scofield, Peter Geye, Ian Graham Leask, and Robert Russell; independent bookstore owners Sue Zumberg and Scott VanKoughnett; Paul Willis and the lovely Louisianans at the Saints and Sinners Literary Festival; and fellow writers and creative artists Gary Lindberg, Ron Nelson, Nicole Sobchack, Lisa Orts, Lorie Hope, Rosanna Staffa, Drew Miller, Amit Bhati, Susan Schaeffer, Catherine Dehdashti, Brian Duren, Terry Newby, Ken Flies, Emilio DeGrazia, and the late Jon Hassler.

Readers have asked whether this is truly the end of Corey Fischer-Flanagan's story. The answer for now is yes. These characters and their travails have been a constant presence in my mind for the better part of nine years. It's time for them—and for me—to move on. It will be strange not to think and write about these imaginary people to whom I've become so attached, though. And I'm not sure whether it says more about them or me that after writing the final words of the final chapter in this final book, I set down my pen and wept.

It has been suggested that the characters and emotions in *Panic River*, *Reckoning Waves*, and now *Destiny Springs* are an allegory of my own life during those nine years. I'm too close to these stories and too far away from self-awareness to tell you whether there's any truth in that. What I can tell you is that I've grown as a writer and hopefully as a person during that time thanks to all the people mentioned above, as well as my closest family and friends and, in particular, Marco, to whom this book is dedicated. He dropped into my life unexpectedly four years into writing these stories and taught me a valuable, overdue lesson about the importance of self-love, *coincidentally* the same lesson that Corey finally learns by the end of this book. Marco, it's as if you found me resting alongside a long and arduous trail deep in the woods and stopped to give me a fresh new pair of hiking boots. Thank you. Come now, love, let's go climb some mountains.

About the Author

Elliott Foster is the author of *Whispering Pines* (Wise Ink), a 2016 Indie Next Finalist for Best Fiction. His latest novels comprise a trilogy: *Panic River* (2019), *Reckoning Waves* (2022), and *Destiny Springs* (2023). *Reckoning Waves* debuted at the Saints & Sinners Literary Festival in New Orleans and won the award for Best Gay Fiction at the 2022 San Francisco Book Festival. Elliott also co-authored the memoir *Retrieving Isaac & Jason* with his father. His poems, essays and short stories have been published in journals worldwide.

Made in the USA
Monee, IL
28 April 2024

57644283R00184